I0819214

When the Wolves Are Silent

TITLES BY C. S. HARRIS

What Angels Fear

When Gods Die

Why Mermaids Sing

Where Serpents Sleep

What Remains of Heaven

Where Shadows Dance

When Maidens Mourn

What Darkness Brings

Why Kings Confess

Who Buries the Dead

When Falcons Fall

Where the Dead Lie

Why Kill the Innocent

Who Slays the Wicked

Who Speaks for the Damned

What the Devil Knows

When Blood Lies

Who Cries for the Lost

What Cannot Be Said

Who Will Remember

When the Wolves Are Silent

When the Wolves Are Silent

A Sebastian St. Cyr Mystery

C. S. Harris

BERKLEY MYSTERY
New York

BERKLEY MYSTERY
Published by Berkley
An imprint of Penguin Random House LLC
1745 Broadway, New York, NY 10019
penguinrandomhouse.com

Library of Congress Cataloging-in-Publication Data

Names: Harris, C. S. author
Title: When the wolves are silent / C.S. Harris.
Description: New York : Berkley, 2026. | Series: A Sebastian St. Cyr mystery
Identifiers: LCCN 2025030034 (print) | LCCN 2025030035 (ebook) |
ISBN 9780593953891 hardcover | ISBN 9780593953907 ebook
Subjects: LCGFT: Detective and mystery fiction | Fiction | Novels
Classification: LCC PS3566.R5877 W4753 2026 (print) | LCC PS3566.R5877 (ebook)
LC record available at https://lccn.loc.gov/2025030034
LC ebook record available at https://lccn.loc.gov/2025030035

Printed in the United States of America
1st Printing

The authorized representative in the EU for product safety and compliance is Penguin Random House Ireland, Morrison Chambers, 32 Nassau Street, Dublin D02 YH68, Ireland, https://eu-contact.penguin.ie.

For Zydeco,

2007-*ish to* 2024.

Farewell, my old friend.

You will be forever loved and forever missed.

There are nights when the wolves are silent, and only the moon howls.

—George Carlin

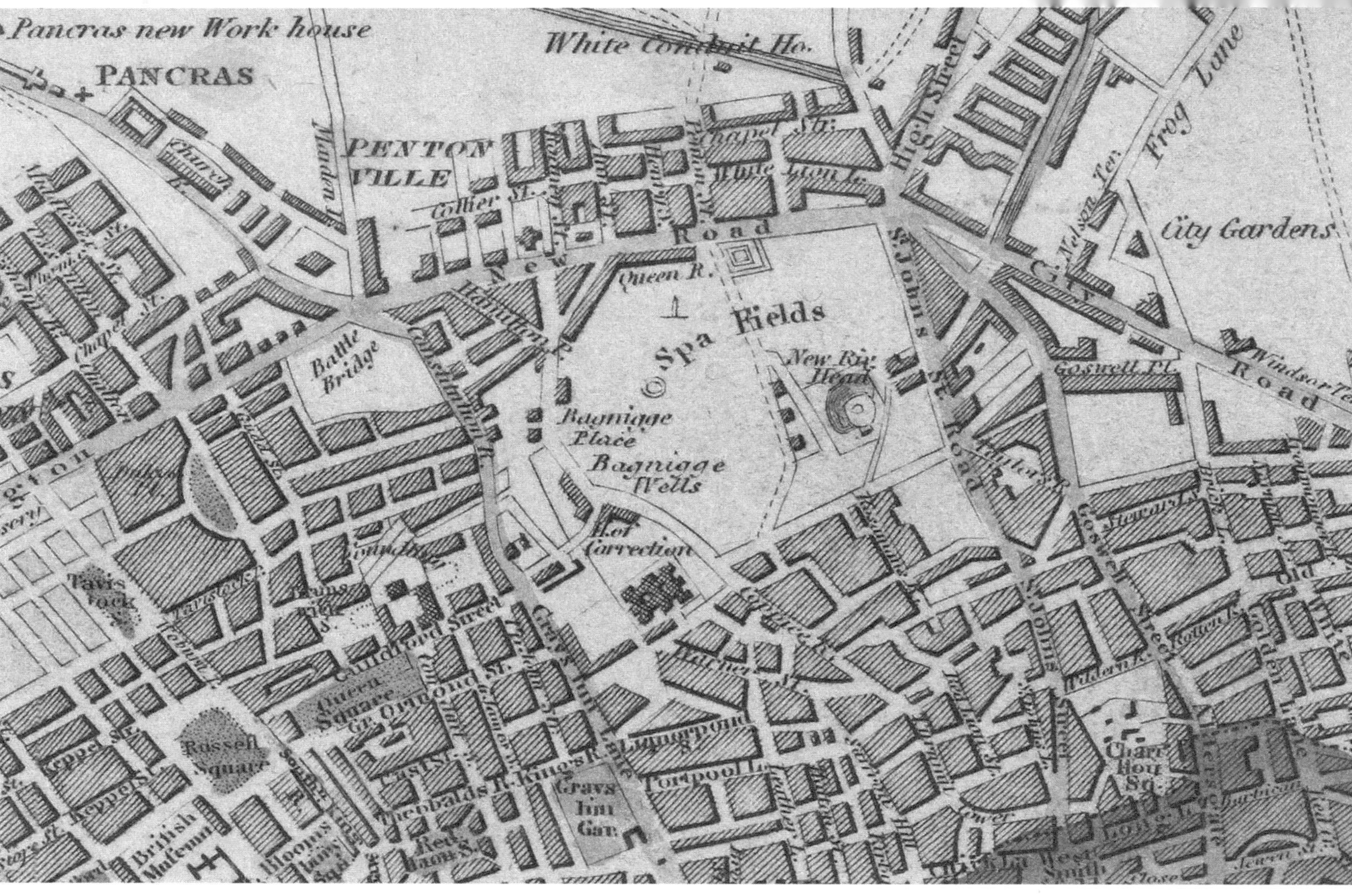

Pancras new Work house
PANCRAS
White Conduit Ho.
PENTON VILLE
Church R.
Maiden L.
Collier St.
Chapel St.
White Lion L.
High Street
Frog Lane
Nelson Ter.
City Gardens
City Road
Windsor Ter.
Gaswell Pl.
New Road
Queen R.
Spa Fields
New Riv. Head
St. Johns St. Road
Battle Bridge
Bagnigge Place
Bagnigge Wells
Ho. of Correction
Guildford Street
Queen Square
Gr. Ormond St.
Russell Square
Keppel St.
British Museum
Grays Inn Lane
Grays Inn Gar.
Theobalds R.
Kings R.
Portpool L.
Goswell Street
Old Street
Golden Lane
Chart. Hou. Sq.
Long L.

When the Wolves Are Silent

Chapter 1

Primrose Hill: Saturday, 23 November 1816

Where the bloody hell am I?

The Right Honorable Bayard Wilcox, Thirteenth Lord Wilcox, blinked up at the storm-churned night sky, its full moon little more than a ghostly aura obscured by roiling clouds. Then his stomach gave a sick lurch and he squeezed his eyes shut again with a groan.

Swiping one gloved fist across his runny nose, Bayard sucked in a deep breath and realized he was lying flat on his back on the bloody ground with the dried stalks of some bloody plant tickling his bloody ear. He was so cold his teeth were chattering, and he smelled of blue ruin, woodsmoke, and piss.

Bloody Marcus Toole and his bloody cork-brained ideas.

Cautiously opening first one eye, then the other, Bayard rolled onto his side and stumbled to his feet. He stood swaying for a moment, aware that his flap was undone and the front of his pantaloons was soaked with urine. He had a vague memory of leaving the fire to take a piss and Toole laughing at him, telling him to look for some more scraps of wood while he was at it.

Bloody Marcus Toole.

Clumsily buttoning his flap, Bayard staggered back toward the golden, crackling glow of the fire, now blazing up hot and bright. Toole must've found his own bloody firewood, Bayard thought as he caught the scent of roasting meat hanging heavily in the frosty country air. But where the hell was Toole?

"Toole?" Bayard roared. "Are you cooking a bloody rabbit or something? And where the devil did you find that tree trunk?"

The sight of the long black log engulfed by the fire struck Bayard as ridiculously funny, and he doubled over in a gale of laughter that brought tears to his eyes. Except that when he straightened, wiping away his tears, he realized the thick, charred mass feeding those leaping flames was no log, and the pungent scent of roasting meat had nothing to do with a rabbit.

"Marcus?" whispered Bayard. Then he staggered back with a scream as the spreading flames ignited the smoking soles of his friend's fire-scorched boots.

Chapter 2

Grosvenor Square, London

Sebastian St. Cyr, Viscount Devlin, repositioned his black knight and said, "Check."

His opponent, Alistair St. Cyr, the Fifth Earl of Hendon and for some years Chancellor of the Exchequer, frowned as he leaned back in his overstuffed leather chair, one hand coming up to cup the smooth wooden bowl of his pipe. The two men faced each other across a well-used chessboard set up between them and illuminated by the soft golden pool of light cast by a nearby brace of candles. A half-empty glass of brandy rested at each man's elbow; the fire dancing on the library hearth nearby filled the book-lined room with a cheerful crackle.

The sprawling Grosvenor Square town house was the Earl's London residence and had been for many years. A big, barrel-chested man in his early seventies, he had a thinning shock of white hair, a heavy-featured face, and the deep, vibrantly blue eyes that had been the hallmark of the St. Cyrs for centuries. Sebastian was younger, in his mid-thirties, tall and lean, with dark hair and strange yellow eyes that most men found disconcerting. He was known to the world as Hendon's only surviving son and heir, although he was not in fact Hendon's biological child. There had been a time when that painful truth—and the manner of its revelation—had driven a seemingly irreparable breach between the two men. But those days were now in the past.

"Not checkmate?" said Hendon, his teeth biting down on his pipe's stem as he studied the board.

"Not yet," said Sebastian, reaching for his brandy and taking a slow swallow. "There is a way."

"For all the good it will do me," grumbled Hendon.

Sebastian smiled. "You used to tell me—" he began, then paused, his head turning at the rattle of a curricle and team drawing up in the street outside. "Expecting someone?"

"No. Why?" said the Earl, just as the sound of a heavy fist beating a frantic tattoo on the front door reverberated through the house.

A man's familiar shrill voice came to them as Hendon's butler opened the door. "He is here, isn't he? My uncle—Devlin, I mean. With Grandfather? *Oh, God;* please tell me he's here!"

Hendon frowned. "Bayard?"

"Bayard," said Sebastian, his voice flat. Now nearly twenty-seven, Bayard was Hendon's grandson by the Earl's firstborn child and only daughter, Amanda, the Dowager Lady Wilcox. He had come into his title some five years before, on the death of his father, the previous Baron Wilcox. And while Sebastian couldn't help feeling sorry for the younger man in some ways, he'd always suspected Bayard took after his late father too much for comfort.

"My lord," they heard Hendon's butler, Hervey, say, his voice kept deliberately low and soothing. "If you'll just—"

"Where are they?" demanded Bayard, his bootheels clattering as he quickly crossed the entry's marble floor. "The library?"

Hendon pushed to his feet as the door to the library flew open and his disheveled grandson burst into the room. "Bayard? What the devil?"

Bayard's hat was gone, his cravat askew, his brown hair wildly disordered, his soft, plump face pasty white. His greatcoat hung open, and what looked like charcoal and unidentifiable muck smeared his extravagantly tailored navy blue coat, white-and-navy-striped silk waistcoat, and pale yellow pantaloons. He brought with him the pungent odors of woodsmoke, cheap gin, and urine.

"Sir," he said, bowing jerkily to his grandfather. But it was to Sebastian that he turned. *"Devlin!* Thank God you're here. You must help me! I—" He broke off, his breath coming in shallow pants as he brought up trembling hands to rake his limp straight hair back from his forehead. *"Oh, God;* I don't know what to do! He's dead, and I don't even understand what happened. I went to take a piss, you see, and I guess I must have stumbled and passed out, because when I came to, the fire was blazing and he was in it!"

"Who? Who the devil are you taking about?" said Hendon.

"Toole! Marcus Toole."

"Sir Samuel Toole's son?"

"Yes, yes!"

"Where?" said Sebastian. "Where did this happen?"

"At the top of Primrose Hill."

"What the hell were you doing there?"

Lying just to the north of London, beyond what was now being called Regent's Park, Primrose Hill was an unusual two-hundred-foot-high hill that rose somewhat like a massive ancient burial mound. Perhaps because of that it had lately become popular with those seeking to resurrect the culture and religion of Britain's legendary pre-Roman inhabitants, the Celts, and the mysterious Druid priesthood for which they were famous.

"It was Toole's idea. We were drinking at Chalk Farm Tavern, and Toole—" Bayard's voice faltered as his grandfather let out a startled oath, for as popular as the tavern's tea gardens were during the day, the place's proximity to the road from Hampstead Heath gave it an unsavory reputation after dark.

Bayard sucked in a deep breath and began again. "Toole, he got this idea in his head that he wanted to climb to the top of Primrose Hill—on account of the Druid ceremonies they're always having up there, you see."

"God help us," said Hendon. "Please tell me you haven't taken to dressing up in white robes to mumble a bunch of heathen nonsense under the full moon."

"What? Good God, no. We were laughing about how batty the lot of them are. It was just a lark."

"So you climbed to the top of the hill," said Sebastian. "And then what happened?"

"We built a fire." Bayard's voice shook, and he had to swallow hard. "There are all sorts of old firepits put there, you know, I suppose on account of whatever it is those Druid fellows do there. Someone'd even left a bundle of unburnt wood, so Toole, he starts this big, roaring fire. And then, like I said, I went to take a piss, and the next thing I know, when I open my eyes, the fire is blazing up like it's Guy Fawkes Day and *Toole is in it!* Dead!"

Sebastian and Hendon exchanged silent glances.

"What? You don't believe me?" said Bayard, his face taut as he looked from one man to the other. "Don't you understand? Someone must be *targeting* us! First Gil, and now Toole!"

"Gil?" said Sebastian.

"Gilbert Keebles. You must have heard what happened to him."

"Ah, yes," said Hendon.

"No," said Sebastian, who had only recently returned to London with his family after a several months' stay at his Hampshire estate.

Bayard looked incredulous. "It's only been a couple of weeks since he was killed!"

"How?" said Sebastian.

"Somebody stabbed him and threw him in the Thames. There's six of us who've been friends since we were in short coats, and now two of us are dead—murdered! It can't be a coincidence. It's like someone is deliberately killing us one by one! What if they mean to kill *me* next?"

Sebastian found that unlikely, but he simply drained his brandy and set the glass aside. "I take it you have your carriage waiting outside?"

Bayard shook his head. "I've got Toole's curricle—that is, if his stupid team haven't wandered off by now. But they're blown—I drove them hard coming back into town."

Hendon stared at his grandson. "Are you telling me you left the man's horses in the street unattended? Where is Toole's groom?"

"That bloody bastard? He was supposed to be waiting for us at the base of the hill, but I had to walk all the way back to Chalk Farm to find him. And then the worthless idiot was dead drunk, so I left him there and took the curricle."

"Good God," said Hendon, starting for the door. "I'll get someone to tend to the horses right away. And if you're planning to go back out there, Devlin, I might as well go ahead and have the stables get my carriage ready while I'm at it. It'll be quicker than sending to Brook Street for yours."

"You are going to help me, aren't you, Uncle?" said Bayard. "I mean, you've dealt with this sort of thing before. You'll know what to do."

"I'll go have a look, yes."

Bayard's features took on a pinched, sickly look. "There's no need for me to go out there with you, is there?"

"Actually, there is," said Sebastian. "Tell me this: How did you know where to find me?"

"I went by Brook Street first, and Lady Devlin said you were here."

"You told her why you wanted me?"

"Sort of."

"I'll send one of the footmen with a note to Hero, explaining where you've gone," said Hendon, coming back into the room. He glanced at his grandson. "And to your new bride as well, Bayard?"

"What? Oh, no need to bother. Fanny knows better than to be expecting me anytime soon."

"Indeed," said Hendon. He waited until Bayard had taken himself off, mumbling something about finding a pisspot, then said to Sebastian, "Will you notify Bow Street?"

"Not until I'm certain this isn't some prank or drunken muddle. Knowing Bayard, I wouldn't be surprised if we find Marcus Toole passed out beside his fire. Unless of course he's managed to make his way back to Chalk Farm Tavern, in which case he is no doubt as we speak shouting down the house because he thinks someone's pinched his curricle."

"It does sound like a farrago of nonsense."

"It does. But . . ." Sebastian paused.

Hendon looked over at him. "But?"

"What if it's not?"

Chapter 3

The smell of burnt meat hung like a dirty presence in the cold night air. It was a stench that no man who'd ever smelled charred human flesh could forget.

Sebastian found the odor clinging to his nostrils as he climbed the narrow footpath that wound up Primrose Hill, the frost-tipped, winter-killed grass of the gentle slope glowing silver in the fitful moonlight, the white fog of his exhalations billowing around him in a ghostly nimbus. And he felt himself hurtled back in time, to the days when his life had been filled with the roar of cannons and the reek of gunpowder and the screams of dying horses and wounded, sobbing men.

He pushed the memories away.

The old bullet wound in his right leg was beginning to ache, and he paused for a moment, glancing back at the base of the hill to where he had left Bayard snoring in Hendon's carriage. Still more than half-drunk, the younger man had fallen asleep and been impossible to rouse. And the truth was, Sebastian no longer needed him. The pungent smell carried by the wind told its own story.

He walked on. He was close enough now to the top of the hill to see the faintly glowing embers of the dying fire. He tried to recall whether he'd ever met Marcus Toole, and resurrected a memory of a young man of average height, medium brown hair, and unremarkable features; a man unapologetically proud of his ancient pedigree, of his ringing baritone and firm seat in the saddle, and of the wealth, title, and Norfolk estate that would someday be his.

Except now he was just a charred lump of black, burnt flesh on a cold, windswept hill.

"Bloody hell," whispered Sebastian as he drew up beside the dead man's scorched boots.

What was once a roaring bonfire had been reduced by now to a crumbling pile of blackened, half-incinerated lengths of wood resting on a bed of white ash, with only the faint glow of a few hot coals visible here and there. The hideous remnants of Marcus Toole lay sprawled on top like a late addition or an afterthought. Had he already been dead when his clothes went up in flames and the fire began to lick at his flesh? Sebastian hoped so. The man had fallen—or been thrown—onto the fire on his stomach, with one leg bent at an angle and his arms flung out at his sides.

If a man passed out and fell into a fire, would he wake up? Sebastian wondered. Maybe it depended on how drunk he was. What about an apoplexy or heart seizure? They might be rare in young men still in their twenties, but not unknown. There could be an innocent explanation for what he was looking at.

But he doubted it.

He began to walk in an ever-widening circle around the firepit and its reeking, mutilated horror, studying the ground, looking for something—anything—that might explain what had happened here. But the ground was hard, and the dead vegetation in the area well trampled by many feet, for even without the neo-Druid movement, Primrose Hill was near enough to London to be a popular spot.

Frustrated, Sebastian was turning back toward the carriage when for a brief moment the clouds that had obscured the moon shifted and he caught the gleam of something smooth lying half hidden in the rank dead grass at his feet. Reaching for it, he found himself holding a small piece of wood carved in the shape of a wolf. Seated on its haunches, its head thrown back in a howl, the wolf was perhaps five or six inches tall. It was a beautiful piece, haunting and powerfully evocative.

And high on the wolf's flanks, on both sides, the artist had carved an intricately intertwined Celtic knot.

The early hours of Sunday, 24 November

"Merciful heavens," said Sir Henry Lovejoy, one splayed hand pressed against the small of his back as he leaned over to study the stiff, hideously burnt corpse in the flickering light of a horn lantern held aloft by one of his constables. More constables were fanning out around them in a search of the area, the feeble glow of their lanterns wavering pinpoints in the blackness. The wind had come up shortly after midnight, cold and damp and heavy with the scent of promised rain. "What a frightful sight."

"That it is," said Sebastian, standing beside him.

He watched as Lovejoy tilted his head first one way, then the other, his gaze solemn as he studied what was left of the dead man's black, ravaged face. Barely five feet tall, the magistrate was slightly built, with a bald head, an almost comically high voice, and a fierce dedication to truth that sometimes brought him into conflict with both his fellow magistrates and the powerful men around the Prince Regent. He was the least senior of Bow Street's three stipendiary magistrates and had at one time been a successful merchant. But the brutal, senseless murder of his wife and child and the profound spiritual crisis that followed had altered the course of his life forever.

It was now nearly six years since the time when Sebastian had been a fugitive accused of a murder he didn't commit and Lovejoy the man charged with the task of bringing him in. In the years since, the magistrate and the aristocratic former cavalry captain had forged an unusual but strong friendship, based on mutual respect and a shared determination to find a measure of justice for the victims of murder.

"Hopefully the poor man was dead before this happened." Lovejoy straightened with a quickly concealed grimace, his hand dropping back to his side. "You say he's Sir Samuel Toole's son, Marcus?"

"Probably."

Lovejoy glanced over at him. "Only probably?"

Sebastian nodded to the charred figure before them. "Who could recognize him like this?"

"True." His features set in thoughtful lines, Lovejoy turned to stare out over the rolling plain to the south, where the dim glow of the lights of London showed in the distance. "I suppose it is theoretically possible that Marcus Toole—or someone else—could have killed another young man and dumped his body on the fire in the hopes it would be burned beyond recognition. Improbable, perhaps, but certainly possible."

Sebastian could think of another possibility, but he was careful to keep that one to himself. "Tell me about Gilbert Keebles. How did he die?"

"It was rather strange. A couple of mud larks found his body washed up on the riverbank down by Rotherhithe. He was last seen in what I gather was an advanced state of intoxication when he left his friends at the cockpit on Birdcage Walk, so initially it was assumed he'd fallen into the river drunk and drowned. Then the surgeon who performed the autopsy discovered a knife wound in his side. The curious thing, though, is that he hadn't been robbed."

"I'm surprised the mud larks who found him didn't strip him."

"I've no doubt they would have if a constable hadn't chanced to come along at just the right moment."

"Fortuitous."

"Indeed. The generally accepted explanation is that he must have been stabbed by footpads, then tumbled in the river and drowned while trying to escape them. But there's no proof of it, obviously."

Sebastian watched as a couple of the men from one of London's deadhouses unloaded a shell from the cart they'd left at the base of the hill and began to trudge up the footpath toward them. "The murders of two friends occurring so close together is rather . . . odd."

"It does lend a certain amount of credence to your nephew's fear that someone is deliberately targeting his friends." Lovejoy's face took on a flat, pained look. "Marcus Toole's father, Sir Samuel, is both a substantial Norfolk landowner and a member of Parliament, while Keebles's father, General Sir Peyton Keebles, was a hero of the American War. I fear the city's newspapers are going to whip their readers into a frenzy over this."

"Which means the Palace will want someone arrested and hanged. Quickly."

Lovejoy met Sebastian's gaze, nodded, then looked away. "It's unfortunate Lord Wilcox was too"—he hesitated as if searching for the right word—"*distraught* to be of any further use tonight."

"Hopefully when he sobers up later today, he'll be able to recall more clearly what happened," said Sebastian. He had insisted Bayard take Hendon's coach and personally explain the situation to Sir Henry, while Sebastian himself stayed to keep watch on the murdered man's body. But in the end Lovejoy had given up trying to get much sense out of the younger man and simply dropped Lord Wilcox off at his doorstep in St. James's Square before heading out to Primrose Hill with his constables.

"What precisely were Toole and your nephew doing here, anyway?"

"From the sound of things, they were drinking at Chalk Farm Tavern and one or the other of them—Bayard says it was Toole, but who knows?—came up with the brilliant idea of climbing the hill and lighting a bonfire."

"Don't tell me they're part of this new movement to resurrect the culture and religion of the Druids."

"Bayard says no. They were just drunk and kicking up a lark."

Lovejoy frowned, for he took as dim a view of the excessive consumption of alcohol as of the neo-Druid movement. "I doubt that will stop Fleet Street from publishing endless speculations linking what happened here tonight to the ancients' propensity for burning human sacrifices." He paused, then added, "You don't think that's what's at work here, do you?"

"No."

Lovejoy nodded. "Let's see that carving you found again."

The magistrate's frown deepened as he took the piece and turned it over and over in his hands. "Where precisely was it?"

Sebastian jerked his head toward where the men with the shell had almost reached the crest of the hill. "About there, just off the footpath."

Lovejoy studied the geometric design incised on the wolf's flank. "It does look as if it might be a reproduction—or perhaps a re-creation—of something Celtic, does it not?" He handed the carving back to Sebastian. "Lost no doubt by one of the participants in the heathen ritual held here a few weeks ago on All Hallows' Eve—or 'Samhain,' as these 'Druids' have taken it calling it."

"Probably," said Sebastian, tucking the carving back into his pocket.

Hopefully.

The two men fell silent as they watched the workers from the deadhouse rest their shell beside the remnants of the bonfire and gingerly set about lifting the stiff, blackened corpse onto it.

"Your nephew is fortunate not to have also fallen victim to this killer."

"Yes," said Sebastian, and left it at that.

Dawn came late that morning, the rising sun wreathed in a mist that gradually dissolved into a steady rain.

Sebastian stood at the windows of his library in Brook Street, his gaze on the wet, windswept pavement outside, a glass of brandy cupped in one hand. He had stripped off his greatcoat, coat, waistcoat, boots, and cravat, but the scent of the fire and its gruesome contents seemed to linger about him still.

He had not yet made it to his bed.

He took a sip of his brandy and listened to the sound of light footsteps descending the stairs, then turned as his wife, Hero, appeared in the doorway. A brilliant, dark-haired, handsome woman, she wore a soft blue wool morning dress with a colorful paisley shawl draped around her shoulders. At close to six feet, she was nearly as tall as Sebastian and built on generous lines. They had been married for four years, had two children of their own and a third child they were raising, and he loved her with a desperation that sometimes scared him.

"How bad was it?" she said.

"Bad."

She came to stand beside him, her gaze, like his, on the falling rain. "I've been hoping Bayard either made the whole thing up or was in some way exaggerating. But it's true? Marcus Toole was murdered? Set on fire?"

"It's impossible to say for certain at this point, but it certainly looks that way—assuming the body in the fire was actually Toole, which is still only an assumption. He was burned beyond recognition."

"Dear God."

She slid her arms around his waist, and he held her close against him. He sometimes wondered if he'd be able to continue doing what he did without this woman, without her strength, her calm courage, and her love. He said, "Bayard tells me another of his friends, Gilbert Keebles, was murdered just a couple of weeks ago, while we were in Hampshire."

She leaned back so she could meet Sebastian's gaze. "He thinks the two deaths could be related?"

"He's convinced they are—that someone is deliberately targeting his friends. And him, of course."

"It sounds ridiculous, but at the same time it would be a rather strange coincidence for two friends to be murdered within weeks of each other simply by chance."

"It would be. Which I suppose means one of the first things I need to do is find out more about the death of this Gil Keebles."

Hero looked thoughtful. "His mother, Lady Keebles, was a lifelong friend of my mother, so I've known her as long as I can remember. I can try calling on her this afternoon, if you'd like."

"You don't have an interview scheduled?" For some years now, Hero had been writing a series of articles for the *Morning Chronicle* profiling the lives of London's poor. It was a project that never failed to provoke the ire of her powerful father, Lord Jarvis. But Hero was one of the few people in the kingdom undaunted by the thought of incurring Jarvis's wrath.

She shook her head. "Only this morning."

"Did you know him? Gilbert Keebles, I mean."

"I did, but not well. He was an only son, born late in his father's life when his parents had given up hope of ever producing a male heir, and quite spoiled and full of himself as a result. He was a general, you know—the father, I mean. Knighted for some feat of brilliance or valor in the American War, although I don't know that I ever heard exactly what it was."

She fell silent, and for a time they simply stood side by side, watching a costermonger make his way up the street, his head bowed against the cold rain. And then she put into words the fear that had been eating at Sebastian all night, although he had never voiced it. "Is it possible . . . I mean, do you think the tale Bayard told could be a lie? That *he* killed his friend?"

Sebastian turned to meet her gaze and hold it. "I wouldn't put it past him; would you? And given how drunk he was, I can see him killing his friend in an argument, then passing out and utterly forgetting what he'd done when he came to."

She chose her words carefully. "It would devastate Hendon if he were to discover his own grandson is a murderer. And if he were then forced to watch Bayard hang—" She broke off and shook her head, unwilling to put the thought into words. When she spoke again, her voice was a whisper. "If the killer is Bayard, what will you do?"

"I can't let him get away with murder. Not even for Hendon's sake."

"No. But . . . would Hendon forgive you, do you think? If you were responsible for his grandson being convicted and hanged?"

In the silence that followed, Sebastian was aware of the painful pounding of his own heart. Then he said, "I know it would grieve him profoundly. But would he hold it against me? I honestly don't know." He cupped a hand behind her neck, drawing her close enough to bury his face in her hair. "I just hope to God we don't need to find out."

Chapter 4

Charles, Lord Jarvis, opened the pearl-studded lid of his gold snuffbox with the flick of a finger, raised a delicate pinch to one nostril, and sniffed. The other two men in the room—one a former prime minister who now served as Home Secretary, the other Chief Magistrate of the powerful Bow Street Public Office—watched him anxiously.

They were assembled in the chambers reserved exclusively for Jarvis's use at Carlton House by his cousin George Augustus Frederick, Prince of Wales and—thanks to the madness of the Prince's father, King George III—Regent of the United Kingdom of Great Britain and Ireland. A large, fleshy man in his early sixties, Lord Jarvis held no government portfolio and never would, for he'd learned long ago that ministers come and go, while those who exercise power quietly and competently from the shadows endure. He was both brilliant and cunning, with a reputation for uncanny omnipotence and utter ruthlessness. But no one was more dedicated than he to preserving and expanding the power of Great Britain and its beleaguered monarchy. Without Jarvis, the British royal family could easily have gone the way of the French, and they knew it.

He took another pinch of snuff, then snapped the box closed and fixed his cold, intense gaze on the Home Secretary. "I was expecting Liverpool to join us this morning."

A slender, loose-limbed man in his fifties with a long nose and wispy, receding hair, Henry Addington, First Viscount Sidmouth, gave a tight smile and adopted an airy tone. "The Prime Minister believes it would be better if he were to keep his distance from these discussions. For appearances' sake, you understand."

"Indeed," said Jarvis in a way that caused the color to drain from Sidmouth's face.

"I mean— That is to say—"

Jarvis held up a hand, cutting off the man's stammering. "This public meeting is scheduled to take place in a little over a week. I trust all necessary preparations have been made?"

This remark was addressed to the third person in the room, a stout older man with thick, dark gray hair and an obsequious manner. As Bow Street's Chief Magistrate, Sir Nathaniel Conant was the metropolis's most senior stipendiary magistrate; his public office's activities in fighting crime throughout the kingdom had been famous for decades. But Bow Street's most important role was considerably less well-known, for it was Conant—through his chief clerk—who controlled the legion of domestic spies, informants, and agents provocateurs used by the government against reformers, republicans, Radicals, Spenceans, and anyone else who dared criticize the monarchy or Parliament, or even suggest that

Britain's current political and social systems might in some way be improved. Nominally the Chief Magistrate reported to Lord Sidmouth, the Home Secretary. But he was Jarvis's creature and always had been.

"Never fear, my lord; we're ready," said Sir Nathaniel Conant with a precise bow. "Our agents are all in place and understand their assignments." He allowed himself a tight smile. "These Radicals are about to discover that crowds might be easy to stir up, but they're not so easy to control once they get the bit between their teeth. With any luck, we should be able to lop the heads off a good half dozen of the treasonous rascals and transport another twenty or thirty more. Enough to squash this nonsense for a generation."

"Hopefully for rather longer than that," said Jarvis, tapping one forefinger on his snuffbox's lid. "Now tell me, what's this I'm hearing about the son of a member of Parliament being burned alive at the top of Primrose Hill like some sort of heathen sacrifice?"

The two men's quick exchange of glances was not lost on Jarvis.

Conant gave another of his obsequious smiles. "Unfortunately, Fleet Street's editors do have a habit of allowing their imaginations to run away with their sense."

"You're saying the man wasn't set on fire?"

"Oh, he was definitely set alight. Burnt to a crisp, actually. It's just that we don't know if he was alive at the time. As for this nonsense about human sacrifice, well, there's no evidence we're dealing with anything of the sort."

"Except for the man's crispy corpse, one assumes," said Jarvis dryly. "Frankly, gentlemen, I don't care if this Marcus Toole was alive or dead at the time he was turned into a human torch, or what his killer's religious motivations may have been. All I know is, the last thing we need at the moment is to have something like this causing mass hysteria. I want whoever is responsible identified and behind bars—preferably by next Monday, if not sooner."

"A week from tomorrow, my lord?" said Conant. He was no longer smiling. "But we have no idea who—"

"Good God, man. If you can't find the person responsible, then find someone else. One of these bloody Spenceans you're watching should do just fine. Pick the most annoying one and charge him."

The two men exchanged another quick glance, then bowed in unison. "Yes, my lord."

Chapter 5

Sebastian cleaned up, then tried to grab a few hours of sleep. But thoughts of Hendon and Bayard, and the prospect of the choice Sebastian might ultimately be forced to make, haunted him until he finally gave up.

Walking downstairs, he found Hero seated at the small round table near the drawing room windows, her head bowed as she looked over the questions she was planning to ask in her interview. On the carpet at her feet sprawled their year-old daughter, Miss Guinevere St. Cyr, playing with a stuffed rag doll; on the far side of the room, the two dark-haired little boys, Simon and Patrick, were laughing as they trailed a length of yarn for the big, long-haired black cat that lay curled up on the hearth, ignoring them. The boys were close in age and so similar in looks they might have been twins, although they were not. Only the younger boy, Simon, was Sebastian's son. Patrick was an orphan, the son of a mysterious tavern keeper who'd looked enough like Sebastian to be his brother—and died because of it.

"I thought you'd be gone by now," Sebastian said to Hero as he sank to his haunches beside his daughter.

"I'm just waiting for Claire to get back from the apothecary's. And I've been hoping the rain would stop soon. But it doesn't look like it, does it?

"No." To Guinevere, he said, "Good morning, young lady. Is that a new doll? I don't believe I've met her before. She's quite lovely."

"Claire made it," said Hero as Guinevere, solemn-faced, held the doll out to her father.

"Why, thank you," he said, taking it. "You're very generous. And look: She has lovely blond hair and bright blue eyes, just like you. Except of course hers are made of yarn. And she has no fingers."

"I suspect someone would try to eat them if she did," said Hero, closing her notebook.

He looked up, laughing, just as a polite knock sounded on the front door below.

"Any idea who that might be?" she said.

"No. None."

A moment later, Morey appeared at the entrance to the drawing room. "A young gentleman to see you, my lord; a Mr. Phineas Upcott." The majordomo hesitated, then added, "He says it's about last night. I've put him in the library."

Sebastian exchanged silent glances with Hero. "I'll be right down," he said, then added, "And you'd best bring us some tea. I've had all the brandy I want at this point."

"Do you know him?" said Hero quietly after the majordomo had bowed himself out.

Sebastian handed the doll back to his daughter and pushed to his feet. "I've met him once or twice. He's a friend of Bayard."

Sebastian found Phineas Upcott standing before the fire in the library, his gaze on the crackling flames, his hands clasped behind his back. A fair-haired, slightly built man of less than average height, he wore a coat with a nipped-in waist and buckram-wadded shoulders, which combined with his shirt's absurdly high starched collar to suggest a tendency toward dandyism. At Sebastian's entrance, he jerked around, showing a pale, fine-boned face and wide, frightened blue eyes.

"Mr. Upcott," said Sebastian. "How may I help you?"

The younger man took a step toward him, then drew up abruptly. "I heard—that is to say, I understand that—well, you are planning to investigate what happened on Primrose Hill, aren't you? To Toole, I mean. You do that sort of thing, don't you? Chase down murderers? M'father always says it's a queer hobby for an earl's son to take up, but—" He broke off, flushed, then pushed on. "What I mean to say is, I understand you're quite good at it, and—"

He broke off again as Morey appeared with the tea tray, settled it on the table near the front windows, and then withdrew.

"Have a seat, please," said Sebastian, walking over to the tray. "Tea?"

Upcott sank into one of the chairs beside the fire, his hands clasped between his spread knees. "Yes, please."

Sebastian reached for the first cup and began to pour. "Marcus Toole was a friend of yours?"

Upcott nodded solemnly. "Since our first days at Eton. He was the best of fellows!"

"You do realize this entire conversation could be premature? We don't yet know for certain that the body recovered from Primrose Hill is actually Toole's."

"But we do! You haven't heard? Theo says Sir Samuel—Marcus's father—identified him this morning. Marcus had a chipped tooth, you see, from getting hit in the mouth with a flying cricket bat when we were at Eton." Upcott tapped the tip of one forefinger to his upper left incisor. "It was quite distinctive. I think Sir Samuel recognized Marcus's signet ring, too, but what really sealed it was that tooth; there could be no mistaking it. Theo was just telling me about it."

Sebastian handed the younger man his cup. "Theo?"

"Thank you," Upcott said automatically, taking the cup with hands that were noticeably shaking. "Theo Bridgewood, Lord Bridgewood's heir."

"Ah, yes," said Sebastian, pouring his own tea. He was only vaguely familiar with the younger Bridgewood, but Lord Bridgewood himself was a well-known, outspoken crony of the reactionary Home Secretary, Henry Addington, First Viscount Sidmouth. "I take it Theo Bridgewood was also a friend of Marcus Toole?"

"Yes, of course. We've all been great friends forever."

"Do you have any idea what my nephew and Marcus Toole were doing up on Primrose Hill last night?" asked Sebastian, raising his own cup to his lips.

"Me? No, no idea at all. Last I heard they were heading out to Chalk Farm Tavern. Bridgewood and I were supposed to go with them, you know, but, well, we must've eaten something at that pub we went to the night before that disagreed with us because . . ." He broke off in embarrassment. "Let's just say neither of us was in any shape to go anywhere, if you know what I mean?"

"Wilcox and Toole weren't with you at this pub?"

"Oh, they were. But they've both got the strongest stomachs you ever did see."

"And what pub was this?"

"The White Horse, in Piccadilly." Upcott paused. "To tell the truth, I was thinking how lucky Toole and Wilcox were—to have not got sick, I mean. But in the end I reckon it would have been better if we'd all been hit, wouldn't it?"

"So it would seem," said Sebastian, taking another sip of tea. "Did you ever hear Toole express any interest in the Druids?"

"Druids?" Upcott's eyes widened. "I shouldn't think so. Whatever gave you that idea?"

"Primrose Hill."

"Oh," said Upcott faintly, frowning in a way that suggested he was unaware of the neo-Druid fascination with the place.

Sebastian drew the wooden wolf from his pocket. "Ever see this before?"

Upcott glanced at it, then shook his head. "Don't think so, no. What's it got to do with anything?"

"Perhaps nothing," said Sebastian, slipping the carving back into his pocket. "Have you spoken to Bayard this morning?"

"Bayard?" Upcott was surprised into a ragged laugh. "No one ever sees Bayard till after one, even under the best of circumstances. Never an early riser, Bayard. Ever."

"True," said Sebastian. "So tell me this: Who do you think killed Toole? Did he have any enemies that you know of?"

"Enemies? Toole? God, no. He was an easygoing, bang-up fellow, always laughing, and up to every rig and row in town."

"Is there perhaps someone he quarreled with recently?"

Upcott was silent for a moment, as if considering this. "Well . . . I suppose there was that fellow out at Chalk Farm Tavern."

Sebastian took another sip of his tea. "What fellow out at Chalk Farm Tavern?"

"He was quite the rum character—on the 'bridle lay,' as they say."

Sebastian stared at him. "Are you telling me Marcus Toole tangled with a *highwayman*?"

Upcott nodded. "Stupid thing to have done, if you ask me. Aggravated the hell out of the fellow."

"When did this happen?"

"Couldn't say exactly. A month or two ago? Something like that."

"Was Gilbert Keebles also there that night?"

"He was, yes." Upcott licked his dry lips. "You heard he was murdered, too? Keebles, I mean. Just a couple of weeks ago."

Sebastian watched the other man's face. "Do you know why?"

"No. It doesn't make any more sense than what happened to Toole." Upcott's voice broke. "You are going to try to figure out who's doing this and stop them, aren't you?"

"You think both of your friends were killed by the same man?"

"They must have been, surely. I mean, it's the only thing that makes sense, isn't it?"

"Bayard said something last night about Keebles and Toole being part of a group of six friends. Keebles, Toole, Bayard, and you make four, and I assume Theo Bridgewood is the fifth. So who is the sixth?"

"Well, I suppose he must've been including Emmanuel—Emmanuel Royston-Jones, that is. Although the truth is, we don't see much of him anymore."

"Is there anyone else?"

"Not really. It was always just the six of us—until recently, like I said, when Emmanuel started going his own way."

"When was this? That Royston-Jones 'started going his own way,' I mean."

Upcott shrugged. "I dunno. Some months back."

"Any particular reason?"

"That he stopped doing things with us? Not that I know of." But the younger man's eyes slid sideways when he said it, and Sebastian knew it for a lie. "To tell the truth, he never quite fit in with the rest of us, you know? I mean, his grandfather was a lumper, and his mother's Irish!" Upcott's lip curled in derision. "And while I know her father was an earl—the Earl of Glenraven, of course—he was dead broke, and it's only an Irish peerage, besides."

"In other words, almost worse than nothing," said Sebastian dryly.

"Very nearly," agreed Upcott, completely missing his tone.

Sebastian set aside his cup. "This highwayman you were telling me about—do you remember what he looked like?"

Upcott screwed up his face with the effort of thought. "I think maybe he was a bit on the tall side, but frankly, I don't remember him all that well."

"Do you recall his name?"

The younger man shook his head. "It may've been something like Sid, but I could have that wrong."

"Dark haired? Fair?"

Upcott kept shaking his head. "Sorry. I've never been one for remembering names or faces." He tightened his grip on his cup. "But if it is that highwayman who's doing this, you will catch him, won't you? Catch him and see that they hang him before he can kill anyone else?"

"If it is him."

"But who else could it be?"

Sebastian watched the younger man carefully. "What exactly was the quarrel with this highwayman about?"

"Some trifle." Upcott pursed his lips and looked away. "Can't say as I recall exactly."

"Seems an odd thing for someone to do—kill not one but two men over a 'trifle.' Even if he is a highwayman."

A faint flush crept into the younger man's cheeks. "I hear this one used to be in the Army—the cavalry. They say he came back from the wars not quite right."

"Interesting."

As if becoming aware of the fact that he was holding an empty teacup, Upcott quickly set it aside as he rose to his feet. "I've taken up far too much of your time. Thank you for agreeing to see me. And you will remember what I said—about the fellow out at Chalk Farm? You will look into him, won't you?"

"Have you told Bow Street about him?"

"Bow Street?" That quick rush of color drained from the younger man's face. "I haven't, no. I thought . . . Well, it seemed best to let you handle it. It's all a bit awkward, you know. That is to say, it wouldn't be good if word of any of this were to get back to my father. So you will keep it to yourself, won't you?"

Sebastian studied the younger man's tense, anxious face. "If I can. For now."

"Why did he want to see you?" said Hero, coming to stand in the doorway after Phineas Upcott had taken himself off.

"I could be wrong," said Sebastian, pouring himself a second cup of tea as he watched Upcott stride away toward Bond Street, "but I think his main purpose was to set me after a highwayman named Sid who frequents Chalk Farm Tavern."

"A highwayman? You can't be serious."

Sebastian set aside the teapot with a soft *thump*. "I wish I weren't."

Chapter 6

The rain had eased up by the time Sebastian left for the Tower Hill surgery of the anatomist Paul Gibson.

"Best walk 'em," he told his tiger, Tom, as they pulled up before the surgeon's medieval stone house. "That wind is bloody cold, and I don't know how long I'll be."

"Aye, gov'nor," said the lad, scrambling forward to take the reins. Small and sharp-faced, with lanky brown hair and a jaunty, gap-toothed smile, Tom had been with Sebastian since the dark days when Sebastian was a hunted fugitive and Tom an orphaned pickpocket living in the shadow of the gallows. "As cold as it is, I'm thinkin' we'll be lucky if it don't snow soon."

"God help us," said Sebastian, turning away to cut down the narrow passage that ran along one side of Gibson's house. Pushing open the warped wooden gate set in the high old stone wall, he entered a long, sloped garden, cold-nipped now but still peaceful despite the dark secrets buried there. At the base of the garden stood the high-windowed stone outbuilding Gibson used for his postmortems. It was also where, less openly, the surgeon practiced new techniques and expanded his knowledge of anatomy on cadavers filched from the area's churchyards by body snatchers.

As he followed the stone-lined path that wound through the wet, dripping shrubs and shriveled perennials, Sebastian could hear his friend whistling "Seán Ó Duibhir A' Ghleanna" as he bent over the charred corpse that lay on the elevated stone slab in the center of the old building's single room.

"One of these days," said Sebastian, pausing in the open doorway with one hand on the frame beside him, "you're going to get yourself transported for singing that bloody song."

Gibson looked up with a grin and wildly exaggerated his brogue. "Sure then, but I wasna singing it, now, was I?"

Sebastian laughed. The friendship between the two men dated back more than a decade, to the days when Sebastian had been a captain in the 25th Hussars and Paul Gibson the regimental surgeon. Irish by birth, he was only two years Sebastian's senior but looked older, his dark hair heavily laced with gray, the grooves beside his mouth dug deep by years of phantom pains from his missing limb, and his frame gaunt as a result of the opium dependence he'd developed trying to control them. Thanks to the efforts of his brilliant, enigmatic French lover, Alexi Sauvage, the pains were gone now. But so far her efforts to help him overcome his love affair with poppies had been less successful.

"I was expecting to see you bright and early this morning," said Gibson, his peg leg tapping on the flagged floor as he reached for a rag to wipe his gore-smeared hands.

"Bright and early this morning, I still hadn't made it to my bed."

Sebastian took one look at what Gibson had been doing to the body before him, then glanced pointedly away. "I hear Sir Samuel Toole has already positively identified this as his son. Is that true?"

"It is," said Gibson. "Recognized his son's chipped tooth, then flew into a towering rage when I told him he couldn't take the body away with him. Not only is the very idea of an autopsy an affront to the nature of being, but if the Lord God had wanted dirty Irish surgeons cutting up and gawking at the bodies of well-born, God-fearing Englishmen, he wouldn't have sent bonny William of Orange to put so many of us in our graves."

"He said that?"

"He did. I don't think our Sir Samuel—the Sixth Baronet, mind you, not some mere puffed-up knight, as he was at pains to tell me—is accustomed to being told no. He stormed off threatening to call the constables on me."

"Did he? Call the constables on you, I mean."

"He may have tried. All I know is, I haven't heard from him again. One must make allowances for a father's grief, but . . ." He hurled the rag he'd been holding onto a nearby shelf and blew out a long, hard breath. "Does he have other sons?"

"No."

"Ah, the poor man. 'Tis a terrible thing, to be sure, to lose a son so young. And then to have to see him looking like this . . ."

"I can't imagine it," said Sebastian. He didn't want to even try to imagine it. He had to force himself to take another look at what was left of Marcus Toole. "Please tell me the man was dead before he fell—or was thrown—onto that fire."

"Probably not."

Sebastian glanced over at his friend. "God help us."

"He was shot first. But the bullet only tore the aorta; it didn't directly hit his heart. I could be wrong, but I think he was still alive when he went in that fire."

"He was shot in the back?"

"He was not; from the front. Given the way he was found, it's possible the impact spun him around so that he then pitched forward into the fire. Although it's also possible that whoever shot him then picked him up and deliberately threw him on the fire. Either way, odds are he was still alive at that point, although it wouldn't have been for more than a moment or two."

"Even a few seconds in that fire would have made his last moments on earth a screaming nightmare," said Sebastian, his gaze on the dead man's charred skull. Most of the flesh of his face had been burned away, leaving only bone and hideously exposed teeth. "And there truly is no doubt about the identification?"

"I don't see how there can be, given the chipped tooth. Otherwise, I suppose someone could have dressed the body of a different man of about Toole's age and size in his clothes and slipped his ring on the man's finger and Toole's watch into the fellow's pocket before tossing him in the fire. But I don't see how they could have replicated that tooth. There's enough wear on the broken edge to indicate that it happened years ago."

Sebastian went to stand in the dank building's open doorway, his hands on his hips, his gaze on the rain-soaked, haunted garden.

Gibson watched him for a moment, then said, "I understand your nephew was there, passed out drunk."

"So he claims."

"You don't believe him?"

"Frankly? I don't know." He turned to face his friend again. "Two weeks ago, another young gentleman named Gilbert Keebles was murdered. Did you by chance do that autopsy?"

"I did not; that was Robert Fink, over in Rotherhithe. From what I've heard, it sounds as if Keebles was stabbed in the side before being thrown or falling in the river. Fink is an idiot, but he did have the sense to check to see if there was water in the man's lungs, and there was."

"So he drowned?"

"It's likely. Although according to Fink, the knife wound would have killed him soon enough."

"Any idea what kind of knife we're talking about?"

Gibson shook his head. "That sort of analysis is beyond Robert Fink." He paused. "Were both young men friends of your nephew?"

"They were. And now Bayard is convinced that whoever murdered his friends is going to try to kill him next."

"I can understand that fear."

Sebastian found himself staring again at the charred, gruesomely grinning face of Marcus Toole. "So can I."

Gibson hesitated a moment, then said, "Primrose Hill is where they've been holding all those Celtic ceremonies, isn't it?"

"Yes."

"My Latin was never the best, but from what I remember from my days of slogging through *De Bello Gallico*, the Celts used to burn sacrifices to their gods—human sacrifices, sometimes shut up in a big wicker cage shaped like a man."

"Or so Julius Caesar claimed."

"You think that could be what's going on here?"

Sebastian met his friend's worried gaze. "I sincerely hope not."

Chapter 7

Hero found her interview that morning unexpectedly disturbing.

"You're writing an article on the economic impact of the ending of the war on tradesmen?" said the first man, a leather staymaker, crossing his arms at his chest as he leaned one shoulder against the doorframe of his shop. A tall, flaxen-haired native Londoner named Caleb Jackson, he was surprisingly well-spoken. But it was obvious from his shabby corduroy breeches, worn worsted stockings, and thin, pinched face that he was not prospering. His small shop on Apostle Lane, off Cheapside, was little more than a stall hung with samples of his wares and smelling pungently of recently tanned hides.

Hero opened her clothbound notebook, settled on the high wooden stool he'd offered her, and picked up her pencil. "Tradesmen, shopkeepers, and artisans, yes."

"Why?"

"Because people need to know."

He nodded to the row of shops that lined that side of the old, narrow lane; many were shuttered and obviously had been for some time. "You think they can't see? I could give you the names of a dozen tradesmen and shopkeepers who've already gone out of business, but I reckon all anybody needs to do is take a look around. Not many women in this part of London can afford to be buying new stays—or anything else, for that matter. They make do with what they have until it falls apart, and if they can't fix it, they go without."

He fell silent for a moment, his eyes narrowing as he stared blankly at the chalk-defaced expanse of brown brick wall across the street. "It's hard to credit it now, but time was I made a good living, bringing home more than a pound a week, sometimes two. These days I'm lucky if I earn ten to twelve shillings, and some of that comes from work I do on the side." He gave a faint, disbelieving shake of his head. "My Julia and me, there was a time we had three rooms, furnished. At first, when business started getting bad, we sold some furniture, thinking it would turn around soon enough. But things just kept going from bad to worse, so we moved into two rooms. Only it wasn't long before we had to move again—all six of us in one room. Though I know I shouldn't complain. I've seen worse—ten and twelve in a room not much bigger than my shop here."

"You have children?"

He nodded. "Had four, all little girls. But the baby died last month, just a couple of weeks after her mama."

"I'm sorry," said Hero.

He nodded again, his lips pressing into a painfully tight line.

"To tell the truth, I don't know how I'm gonna keep going, without Julia. The girls are too little to send out into the street selling nuts or apples or whatnot. Julia has a brother, a blacksmith, lives up in Clerkenwell, and I'm hoping maybe he and his wife'll agree to take the girls till I can get back on my feet. But the problem is, they're struggling, too. And the thought of sending my girls away . . ." He paused, his throat working as he swallowed. "Tears at something inside me, it does."

It was a moment before he could keep going. "My Julia, she used to laugh at me when I'd say it's not right that a man can work hard all day and still not make enough to keep his family. She'd say, 'The world just *is*, Caleb. If you go around expecting it to be *right*, all you're gonna do is let yourself in for nothing but grief.'"

Hero fell silent, her gaze on the long stretch of dilapidated brick wall that formed the western side of the crooked lane. It was covered with what the Italians called graffiti but Londoners traditionally referred to as chalkings. The rain had washed away much of the writing, but she could still make out some of the slogans: SPENCE'S PLAN AND FULL BELLIES and, nearby, EQUAL JUSTICE FOR ALL. More worrisome was the boldly scrawled BREAD OR BLOOD.

"It's not God-given, you know," he said, his gaze following hers. "The way things are now. Things can change; the French showed us that, didn't they? Liverpool keeps saying they can't do anything to relieve the suffering of the poor because the government is so far in debt on account of the war. Only, they always somehow managed to find enough money for their war, didn't they? And who benefited from that? Not staymakers like me. If they're so worried about all that debt, why'd they repeal the income tax as soon as the war was over? You know why? Because it was a tax on the likes of Liverpool and Sidmouth, that's why. But all the taxes that crush people like me are still there. I pay taxes on soap, candles, salt, and just about everything else a poor man's gotta buy. Those taxes hurt us; they hurt us real bad. But you know who they don't hurt? They don't hurt the comfortable people. That's why you're here, talking to the likes of me, rather than some grand shopkeeper over on St. James's or Bond Street. Because their businesses are booming."

Hero closed her notebook. She had long since quit taking notes; if she put any of this in the article she was writing for the *Chronicle*, they would never, ever publish it. If they did, they'd open themselves up to a prison sentence for libel. A lot of people thought "libel" meant printing lies, but it didn't. Basically it covered anything the Regent or his government didn't like. "You said you work at another job besides this one. What do you do?"

He looked vaguely uncomfortable, almost shy. "I write articles for some of the Radical journals. I won't deny I'm not as eloquent as others; my father died when I was ten, so I was only able to go to school for a few years. But I belong to a couple of reading societies and I read as much as I can, educating myself. Always have. I've even been working on teaching myself a bit of Latin."

"Did you attend the big public meeting up in Spa Fields a few weeks ago?"

"Aye. Signed the petition, too—along with twenty-five thousand other people. But that fat booby over in Pall Mall refused even to accept it. You know, the old King might be mad, but when all is said and done, I think he was a good man."

"Yes," said Hero.

Caleb Jackson raked his hands through his overlong hair, then laced his fingers together behind his neck and arched his back in a stretch. "They're having another meeting, you know, in a week or so. Think the Regent is gonna accept their new petition?"

Hero met his gaze and sadly shook her head.

Chapter 8

"Why we jist sittin' here?" asked Tom when Sebastian returned to the curricle, gathered his reins, and then sat staring silently at the worn cobbles of the lane before them.

"I'm trying to recall if I number amongst my acquaintances any antiquarians with a particular interest in Celtic history."

"Any whats?"

"Celtic historians. Alas, I fear the answer is no. But," said Sebastian with a smile as he gave his horses the office to start, "hopefully Lady Devlin has finished her interviews by now, because I have confidence she knows at least one, if not more."

The antiquarian of Hero's acquaintance was a solidly built man of perhaps fifty named Mr. Erasmus Inkberry. He had a balding head shaped like a cannonball, an outthrust heavy jaw, and a thick neck that made him look more like a bricklayer or lumper than the scholar he was. The son of a Yorkshire vicar, he had at one time reluctantly taken orders himself. But a fortuitous bequest from a benevolent uncle had allowed him to leave the church and devote himself entirely to study. Hero had known Inkberry for nearly ten years and had tremendous respect for both his knowledge and his reasoning abilities.

"Thank you for agreeing to see us on such short notice," she said when the scholar's pleasant, middle-aged housekeeper showed her and Sebastian into the jumbled, overstuffed room that served as the antiquarian's combination parlor and study. "And our apologies for intruding upon you on a Sunday."

Inkberry waved one big, strong hand through the air in a dismissive gesture. "It's always a pleasure to see you at any time, my dear Miss Jar—I mean, Lady Devlin. And you as well, my lord. Unfortunately," he added as they settled in the worn chairs drawn up to the room's small fire, "after reading this morning's papers, I can guess only too well why you're here. The editors have outdone themselves with a stream of ridiculous nonsense linking this tragic death on Primrose Hill to the ancient Druids." He sighed. "Julius Caesar has a great deal to answer for."

"But he wasn't the only one who wrote about the Celts burning human sacrifices, was he?" said Sebastian.

"No." Inkberry cast a quick, significant glance at Hero, then tweaked the tip of his nose between his thumb and forefinger before saying, "Of course, there is growing evidence that those we know who wrote about the subject—from Strabo and Diodorus Siculus to Caesar himself—used Posidonius as their source. And one should never place too much faith in anything *he* said, wouldn't you agree?" Inkberry leaned forward in his chair. "The unfortunate truth is, we don't actually know all that much about the Celts in general or the Druids in particular. It seems likely they believed in an 'otherworld' to which I suppose what we would call their 'souls' traveled after death and from which they were reborn again and again. But beyond that, most of their beliefs or even the nature of the Druids' role in their society has been lost in the mists of time. They didn't write anything down, you see."

"They were illiterate?"

"Oh, no; we have Celtic inscriptions on memorial stones and such. But they had a religious prohibition against committing their knowledge to writing; everything had to be passed down orally. It was said to have taken twenty years for a young man or woman to become a Druid—truly a most astonishing feat of memory, wouldn't you say? But as a result, virtually everything we know about them comes from the accounts left by their enemies—mainly the Romans who fought against them or the Christian monks who came later and were nearly as dedicated as the Romans to wiping out the old Celtic beliefs and traditions."

"So what do we know for certain?" said Hero.

"Basically only what can be gleaned from a careful reading of the surviving Celtic legends and myths, and by analysis of the few ancient traditions that have somehow managed to persist on down through the ages, particularly in places like Ireland, Scotland, Wales, and Brittany. Those were the only outposts of the Celts to survive the Roman Empire largely intact, and even they were eventually overwhelmed in the Dark Ages by Rome's Christianity."

"But we do know that the Druids were their priests?"

Inkberry cleared his throat. "Actually, as far as we can tell, the Druids were more like what we might call the intellectual class of the ancient Celts. Have you been to India?"

"Unfortunately, no," said Hero.

"Dreadfully unhealthy place, I'm afraid. But fascinating, nonetheless, particularly for those interested in the Celts. It appears to me that the Celts and the people who settled in northern India might have had a common origin; recent linguistic analysis in particular seems to support that theory, you know. And from what I can tell, the Druids played essentially the same role in ancient Celtic society as the Brahmins do in today's Hindu culture. They were the poets, the historians, musicians, physicians, and astronomers of their day—and advisers to the kings, of course."

"But they were also the priests?" said Sebastian.

Inkberry shifted uncomfortably in his seat and threw another significant glance toward Hero. "Well, yes; so it would seem."

"And what role did Primrose Hill play in all this?" said Hero.

"Absolutely nothing, as far as I can tell. The current fascination with the place can be traced directly to Iolo Morganwg."

"Who?" said Sebastian.

Inkberry gave a rude snort. "That's what he calls himself—Iolo of Glamorgan. He's a Welsh antiquarian who was born as plain Mr. Edward Williams, but he uses Morganwg as a pseudonym, and he's managed to make himself the generally acknowledged authority on ancient Welsh literature. The problem is, he's lately taken to publishing collections of previously unknown poems and manuscripts he claims to have discovered. Except he refuses to let anyone see the originals. And frankly, after studying the texts he's produced, I've come to the conclusion the 'originals' don't exist; they're forgeries, more likely than not fabricated by Mr. Williams himself. Unfortunately, I am virtually alone in that opinion. And it is based on those supposed new 'discoveries' that he has come up with, which he claims are 'authentic' ancient Druidic rituals."

"Those are the rituals his followers now enact on Primrose Hill on Midsummer's Eve and Samhain?" said Hero.

Inkberry nodded. "There and other places. If you ask me, these 'rituals' are nothing more than a fantasy mishmash of Christian traditions blended with Arthurian legend and a dash of some rather strange dreams I suspect have their origins in hefty doses of laudanum. Yet he's managed to convince a startling number of people of their authenticity."

"He's based here in London?"

"Not exactly. He is here off and on, although he's currently spending the winter in Wales." Inkberry pulled a face. "If only he would stay there."

"I assume he doesn't write much about human sacrifices or the wicker man, does he?" said Sebastian.

"Good heavens, no. I doubt many people would find that appealing. Or at least, I hope not." Inkberry gave a forced laugh but sobered quickly. "I was not myself acquainted with the young man who was killed on Primrose Hill, although I did once have an unfortunate encounter with him up in Clerkenwell when I chanced to stop at a small coffeehouse just as he and some of his friends were arguing with the owner about something. The owner is a former militiaman, I'm told, and when he refused to take their abuse, they vented their anger by wrecking the poor fellow's place. It was a truly shocking display of wanton destruction, and yet, because of their exalted birth, I'm told none of them were ever held to account. Not to say," he added hastily, "that anyone deserved the dreadful fate that befell that young man on Primrose Hill."

Sebastian drew the wooden carving from his pocket and held it out. "Have you ever seen anything like this before?"

"Interesting," said Inkberry, his heavy gray brows drawing together in a frown as he took the wolf from Sebastian's hand. "Wherever did it come from?"

"It was found on Primrose Hill. Last night."

Inkberry looked up, his frown deepening. "You think it might have something to do with that young man's death?"

"It might. Or it could simply have been dropped by one of the participants in the Samhain celebration held there a few weeks ago."

Inkberry ran his thumb over the knotted design inscribed on the wolf's flank. "It reminds me of an ancient relief carving found some years ago at the Hill of Tara, in Ireland. Obviously, this itself is not an historic piece; most likely something inspired by that carving—or one like it—and recently produced." Features pinched, he handed the wolf back to Sebastian. "Surely you don't think the papers are correct, do you? That what happened to that young man has something to do with the neo-Celtic ceremonies held on the hill?"

But all Sebastian could do was tell him basically the same thing he'd said to Gibson. "I hope not."

"I think," said Hero a short time later as Sebastian settled beside her in their waiting carriage, "that it might be worthwhile for you to return, alone, for a more open, frank discussion with Mr. Inkberry on the subject of human sacrifice. I had the distinct impression he was deliberately avoiding the topic in a misplaced chivalrous attempt to spare what he imagines must be my delicate female sensibilities."

"One would think he'd know better," said Sebastian, signaling their coachman.

She rearranged the skirts of her moss green gown as the carriage started forward with a gentle jerk. "It never ceases to amaze me how otherwise intelligent, reasonable men can have such faulty, antiquated notions about the true nature of fully one half the human race."

"Well, Inkberry never has been married, has he?"

Hero looked over at him in surprise, then drew a quick breath and went off in a peal of laughter.

Chapter 9

Hero waited until later that afternoon, when the hour for paying formal social calls had finally arrived, before ordering her carriage brought round again and setting out for the Half Moon Street home of Gil Keebles's widowed mother.

As the carriage rolled through the gloomy wet streets, Hero found her thoughts, inevitably, drifting to her own mother. She could remember one time, when Hero was perhaps ten years old, that her mother had taken Hero along on one of Lady Jarvis's regular visits to her childhood friend. Afterward, as they sat side by side in the carriage on the way home, Hero said to her mother, "If you don't like Lady Keebles, why do you visit her?"

For a moment, Lady Jarvis looked startled. Then she choked on a bubble of laughter she tried—but failed—to suppress. "Oh, Hero, I never said I don't like her. She was my dearest friend growing up."

"But you don't really like her much anymore, do you?"

Lady Jarvis's laughter died. She'd always tried very hard to be honest with her daughter, and she now said, "I'll admit I liked her better when we were younger. She was . . . different then—adventuresome, strong, and fun; not bitter and, well, *waspish* the way she is now."

"So what changed her?"

Lady Jarvis thought about it. "Her marriage, I suppose."

It took Hero a moment to digest this. "Does marriage always change a woman?"

"Not always, but it can. Which is why a wise woman chooses her husband very, very carefully."

Hero could remember thinking at the time that her mother had not chosen her husband carefully. As much as Hero loved her father, she knew her mother was deeply unhappy in her marriage and had been for as long as Hero could remember. She'd never become bitter or waspish, but that was obviously a danger. "I don't think I want to marry at all," she'd said.

"Oh, Hero." Lady Jarvis had glanced over at her and smiled. "I suspect you'll change your mind someday."

Lady Jarvis had been dead now for three years, but Hero still found her breath catching at the memory. Still felt the heavy inner ache of yearning for her mother that she'd realized long ago was never going to go away.

Lady Keebles had been in her late thirties when her only son, Gilbert, was born, which Hero figured meant she was now somewhere in her sixties. In Hero's memories she had always been a wispy type of woman, never exactly ill but also somehow not quite well. For years she had worn her fine, silver-threaded fair hair coiled around her head like a faded halo.

Hero found the General's widow dressed in deep mourning and half sitting, half lying on a cream silk–covered sofa before the fire in her drawing room. The room was small but tastefully furnished, with a white marble fireplace above which hung an enormous portrait of the late General Sir Peyton Keebles. At the sight of Hero, the widow let the newspaper she'd been reading fall onto the pile of other papers at her feet and made as if to rise.

"Oh, please don't disturb yourself, Lady Keebles," said Hero, going quickly to take the older woman's outstretched hands in hers. "Just sit there and be comfortable. And please accept my apologies for intruding on you like this on a Sunday."

"Dearest Hero." The widow squeezed Hero's hands and compromised by sitting up straighter. "Do have a seat. I think I can guess why you've come. If I remember correctly, Bayard Wilcox is Devlin's nephew, is he not?"

"He is, yes; his sister Amanda's son."

"I remember their mother, Lady Hendon. She was so very beautiful. Beautiful and vibrant and—" She broke off, as if reluctant to put whatever she was about to say into words.

Hero suspected the word she'd been on the verge of using was "scandalous." But she smiled and said, "Yes, she was very beautiful."

"And she died so young."

She hadn't, of course; after staging her own death when Sebastian was a child of eleven, Lady Hendon had run off to Venice with a lover. But once again Hero simply nodded and said, "Yes."

Lady Keebles heaved a sad sigh. "What a horror this all is. Marcus dead now, too, and Bayard lucky to have escaped with his life." She fluttered one hand toward the papers at her feet. "I can't believe the rubbish I've been reading, all this nonsense about Druids and human sacrifice and goodness only knows what else. But hopefully Bow Street will now quit treating me like a foolish old woman and admit I was right in insisting that Gilbert was not the victim of common thieves."

"You don't think Gil was attacked by footpads?"

"No, I do not. It's what they always do when there's a strange, troublesome murder; have you noticed? Blame it on footpads! Much easier to accuse some common thief and hang him in front of the roaring crowds at Newgate than to actually set about unmasking the true killer."

Much easier, thought Hero.

"Not that I would object to them clearing the city of those detestable reprobates," Lady Keebles was saying. "But it should have been obvious to everyone from the very beginning that my son was deliberately murdered, and why. And yet, for reasons I'll never understand, Bow Street has refused even to consider holding the man responsible accountable."

"Who do you think was responsible?"

"That German!"

Hero gave a faint shake of her head. "What German?"

"Accum, of course."

Hero stared at her. "You can't mean Herr Friedrich Accum?"

"Of course I mean Friedrich Accum!"

Hero sat back abruptly in her chair. Friedrich Accum was a German chemist who'd made England his home for over twenty years. It was thanks largely to Accum that more and more of London's streets were now being lit by gas. But Accum was more than a simple inventor; the chemist had made it one of his missions in life to bring the knowledge of science to the general public, writing his books in a way that made them accessible to more people and delivering public lectures on chemistry, minerology, and pharmaceuticals. He also manufactured and sold a range of portable and affordable scientific instruments and laboratory equipment. Devlin regularly used Accum's kits for the analysis of the soils and stones of his fields in Hampshire.

"Why in the world would Herr Accum have wanted to kill Gil?"

"He tried to sue them, you know," said Lady Keebles, her mouth prissing with scornful contempt. "Can you image? He actually tried to sue Gil and the others!"

"'The others' being Gil's friends?"

"Yes. He didn't get anywhere, of course. So he killed Gil, and now he's killed young Toole as well."

"But . . . why would Accum want to sue Gil and his friends?"

"Because of the explosion."

"What explosion?"

Lady Keebles sank back against her sofa's cushions. "He gives lessons, you know—Accum, I mean—in his house in Compton Street. Chemistry lessons or some such thing, where he shows people how to conduct experiments. Gil and Marcus and the others thought it would be great fun, except there was an explosion, and Accum tried to hold them accountable." She pushed out her breath between her front teeth in a derisive, contemptuous sound that wasn't a laugh. "What on earth did he expect?"

"Obviously not that," said Hero. "When did this happen?"

"Last October."

"I can understand Accum feeling . . . aggrieved that he lost his suit," said Hero, choosing her words carefully. "But what makes you think he would then feel moved to commit murder?"

"He's a nasty, choleric man. Have you met him?"

"I have, actually."

Lady Keebles nodded, as if that settled everything.

Hero studied the older woman's pinched, grief-ravaged face and felt a wave of empathy mixed with what she knew was quiet horror, for she did not want to even try to imagine what it would be like to be in this woman's place, to have lost her only son. "Can you think of anyone else who might have wanted to kill Gil?"

"No. He was the sweetest boy. Your mother always used to say so; you remember? She was always saying to me, 'Harriet, that little boy is the sweetest child I've ever seen.'"

Hero could remember her mother calling Gilbert Keebles an overindulged, sulky, entitled brat, but never "sweet." She was still trying to think of a tactful reply when Lady Keebles sighed again and said, "I can only be grateful that Sir Peyton didn't live to see this day. When I think of all the years we tried so hard to have a son. Eight girls the good Lord sent to us before he finally blessed us with Gilbert. And now he's taken our sweet boy away again."

"I'm so sorry," said Hero.

"Of course," Lady Keebles was saying, "your mother went through the same thing with her only son."

"Yes," said Hero, her throat suddenly, painfully tight. Her brother David's death was still raw and always would be.

"But now your father's new wife has given him another son. Such a blessing, isn't it?"

"Yes," said Hero.

"And you have children of your own now, I believe?"

"I do, yes. A son, Simon, and a little girl, Guinevere."

"Only the one son? I thought I saw you the other day with two little boys."

"Patrick is an orphan Devlin and I are raising."

"Oh? He looks very much like your own son, doesn't he?" She paused, then added archly, "And so like Devlin."

Hero realized her fingers were curling into claws and had to force herself to relax them. The inescapable resemblance between Patrick and Simon—and between Devlin and Patrick—had given rise to much speculation and tittering amongst the ton. But Lady Keebles was the first person to have teased Hero about it openly.

"Patrick's father and Devlin were distantly related," said Hero, keeping her voice even.

"Ah. Only distantly? And yet you raise him as your own. How magnanimous." Lady Keebles leaned forward and reached out to rest her thin, bony hand briefly on Hero's knee. "But you must get busy giving your lord a second son. It's so important, especially for a woman in your situation." She sat back. "Fortunately, Sir Peyton's estate was not entailed, so while Gil's sisters and I are left bereft of Gil's protection, we have not found ourselves cast out into the world, homeless and virtually penniless. The author of *Pride and Prejudice* showed only too well what a calamity *that* can be, didn't she?" The widow paused, her head falling back as she gazed in silence at the giant canvas above the mantelpiece. "The General engaged Reynolds to paint that immediately after his return from the colonies, you know."

Hero shifted around so she could look up at the massive portrait. Reynolds had painted his subject in the uniform of the British Legion, wearing a dark blue coat with black cuffs and collar, white breeches, and a plumed Tarleton helmet. The composition was striking, with Keebles portrayed in the act of dismounting from his rearing horse against the swirling, smoky chaos of the battlefield behind him.

"All together he spent nearly six years in the colonies," the widow was saying. "Mainly in New York and the Carolinas. It was in the Carolinas that he was wounded, twice: first at the Battle of Waxhaw Creek, and then again at Yorktown."

Hero looked over at her hostess in surprise. "He was at Waxhaw Creek?"

"Yes, with Tarleton."

Hero found herself looking again at the harsh-faced, powerfully built man in the painting. What the British called the Battle of Waxhaw Creek was known in America as Buford's Massacre. In May of 1780, a cavalry force under Banastre Tarleton overcame a detachment of colonials, who raised the white flag of surrender. But the British simply mowed them down, ignoring the white flag. Not only was the incident a dark stain on Britain's honor, but it had ugly repercussions, for shortly afterward, at the Battle of Kings Mountain, the Continental Army slaughtered the surrendering British forces in revenge.

Hero found herself searching for something to say and finally settled on "You must have been very glad to have him come home."

"Yes," said the widow. "He always hoped his son would follow in his footsteps, but Gilbert never had any interest in the Army. Sir Peyton was naturally disappointed, but frankly, I was relieved. I wanted to keep Gilbert safe in England, away from the wars." Her voice wavered, and she brought up one hand to press her fingertips against her trembling lips. "Except he wasn't safe, was he?"

Hero reached out to take the free hand of her mother's old friend in hers. "I'm so sorry I had to ask you to talk about this. I know how hard it must be for you to think about."

Her eyes swimming with unshed tears, Lady Keebles squeezed

Hero's hand in thanks. "Dear Hero. So sweet. But I think about it all the time, you know—every moment of every day. How can I not?"

It was shortly afterward, as Hero was leaving Lady Keebles's house, that she ran into one of the widow's five surviving daughters on the front steps. A tall, vigorous, practical-minded woman with honey-colored hair and even features, Hannah—now Mrs. Allen Stevens—was about Hero's age, and Hero had always liked her.

"Hero!" said Hannah, her face brightening. "Have you been to see Mother? How very kind of you. Amy tells me she's in a tizzy over what happened to Marcus Toole."

"Yes, and I'm afraid it's churned up the worst of her grief over your brother's death all over again. I'm so sorry."

Hannah was silent for a moment, her lower lip caught thoughtfully between her front teeth, before saying, "She's not nearly as upset as she likes to put on, you know. I mean, I won't deny that Gil's death has shocked and saddened her, but the truth is, she never really liked him much. She always resented the way my father favored Gil so blatantly over the rest of us, spoiling him absolutely rotten. *'My only son,'* he was always saying. As far as the General was concerned, we girls might as well not even have existed. And Gil, well, I think he always sort of knew how Mama felt. He let her continue living with him after he came of age because it suited him to have her running the house for him as an unpaid housekeeper. But he wasn't very nice to her, and she was terrified he was going to marry soon and make her move out. Her portion isn't large, so she would either have had to take some dreadful small cottage in the middle of nowhere or else come live with one of us—which, frankly, *no one* wanted." She grimaced, then added, "But with Gil dead, the house will now be hers until she dies."

Hero studied her friend's open, frank face. "Has she told you she thinks Friedrich Accum killed Gil?"

"Oh, yes; she's been saying that for weeks to anyone who'll listen."

"Do you think she could be right?"

"I doubt it, although I won't deny that what they did to that poor man's house was awful, and they didn't care. They thought it was funny."

"Who do you think killed Gil?"

Hannah shook her head. "I have no idea. I mean, you knew him. He simply wasn't a nice person, was he? And neither was Marcus Toole. They've been doing horrible things to people and getting away with it for years."

"Horrible things like—what?"

"I don't know too many details," she admitted. "The truth is, I'm only reading between the lines of some things Allen has said—you know what husbands can be like. A month or so ago he was going on and on about a piece published in one of the Radical journals attacking Gil and his friends. By initials, of course, rather than by name, but it was perfectly obvious who they were talking about."

"Do you know which journal?"

Hannah shook her head again. "No. Allen didn't tell me. I gather some of what the writer was complaining about was the sort of thing many young bucks get up to when they're first on the town, but not all of it. And Gil was twenty-seven, not eighteen or nineteen. For some time now—before he was killed—I'd had the sense he was getting worse instead of better, and it worried me—even before I heard about the article."

"Did your mother know? About the things he was doing, I mean."

Hannah met her gaze. "I honestly don't know. She might have. But you know Mother: Even if she did, she would never admit it."

Chapter 10

"You need to talk to Sir Nathaniel Conant about these reports I'm seeing from his informants," Lord Jarvis told Sidmouth as he and the Home Secretary walked briskly across Margaret Street toward Westminster. "They need to focus less on complaints about the price of bread and falling wages, and more on the Radicals' calls for heads on pikes and blood running in the streets."

Sidmouth reached up to tighten the red wool scarf around his neck. The day was miserably cold, with thick dark clouds pressing low on the city and a bitter wind that howled through the eaves of the ancient palace before them. "Conant says that, from what he's hearing, things like the price of bread and lack of political representation are what the Radicals talk about."

"And what, pray tell, has reality to do with anything?" said Jarvis, his voice dripping contempt. "Does the Chief Magistrate seriously imagine we are ignorant of the sources of popular discontent?

These reports will be presented in court as evidence at the treason trials. And you can't convict a man of treason and cut off his head for complaining about the price of bread. Conant needs to see this problem rectified. Immediately."

"Yes, my lord. If you'd like—" He broke off, a shadow of concern crossing his features as he became aware of a familiar stout man with a florid complexion and a blobby nose descending on them.

Now in his late fifties or early sixties, Sir Samuel Toole was a steadfast High Tory who'd known Sidmouth for more than thirty years, since the days when both men had been newly elected members of the House of Commons. Normally a neat, fashionable dresser, the man now had a disheveled, dazed look about him, his eyes red and puffy from what must have been hours of private weeping. But for the moment all that soul-destroying grief had been tucked away somewhere out of sight, with the unbearable feelings of loss and pain channeled into a determined outpouring of raw rage.

"My lord," said the dead man's father with a quick, bobbing bow toward Jarvis. "My apologies for the interruption, but something must be done." He turned toward Sidmouth. "Do you know, Henry? Do you know what Bow Street has done with my son? Turned him over to some dirty, lowborn Irishman, that's what they've done!"

"Samuel," said Sidmouth in a low, soothing voice. "I know it's difficult to bear, but Bow Street tells us there is no finer anatomist in all of London than Paul Gibson. If anyone can determine what happened to Marcus, it's Gibson."

"What happened to him? We already know what happened to Marcus! He's been murdered, that's what happened to him. What do they think my son is going to do? Sit up and tell this anatomist who killed him? That Irish piece of filth is cutting Marcus up! *Cutting* on him." Toole's voice broke, his jaw trembling for one unguarded moment before he clenched his teeth. "Have you seen him? Have you seen what some villain has done to my boy? He doesn't even look human anymore, Henry. He doesn't look human!"

Jarvis cleared his throat. "My sincere condolences on the loss of your son, Sir Samuel. Please rest assured that we intend to see whoever is responsible caught and punished to the full extent of the law." He threw the Home Secretary a meaningful look. "When you're free, Sidmouth."

He was walking away when he heard the dead man's father say, "Why would someone do something like that, Henry? Why?"

Chapter 11

Sebastian met up with Sir Henry Lovejoy again midway through the afternoon.

"You've heard the results of the autopsy?" said the magistrate as they walked along the terrace of Somerset House.

Sebastian nodded. "I have, yes. It seems there's no doubt that the dead man is indeed Marcus Toole."

"No, no doubt." Lovejoy paused at the terrace's stone balustrade to look out over the choppy gray waters of the Thames. "Unfortunately, Sir Samuel is refusing to violate his son's privacy by allowing us to search the man's bachelor quarters near St. James's Street."

"That is unfortunate," said Sebastian.

Lovejoy nodded. "We've spoken to Toole's valet, but the man is virtually insensible with shock and apparently fiercely loyal to his late employer. He can't think of any reason anyone would want to kill young Toole, who—to hear the valet talk—should be a candidate for sainthood."

"I suspect he's in need of a character reference from Sir Samuel and knows he won't get one if he does anything except sing the young man's praises."

"So it would seem." Lovejoy sighed and turned to walk on. "Lady Keebles likewise denied our request to search her son's library and bedroom after his murder; the very idea outraged her. I don't think either parent grasps the concept that important evidence as to the identity of their sons' killer might be found amongst their effects."

"Or they know their sons had something to hide."

Lovejoy glanced over at him. "I suppose that's possible as well, yes."

Sebastian kept his gaze on the magistrate's face. "Have you managed to speak to my nephew today?"

"We did, yes, although I can't say he added anything to what he'd already told us. He is still laboring under a great deal of distress." Lovejoy cleared his throat. "Have you seen him?"

"Not yet. I wanted to hear what some of his friends have to say first. Phineas Upcott tells me he and Theo Bridgewood were planning to join Bayard and Toole out at Chalk Farm, but ate something at the White Horse on Piccadilly the night before that disagreed with them. It could simply be a coincidence, but it might be worth checking out."

"Indeed," said Lovejoy, his frown deepening. "I'll have one of the lads look into it." He paused, then added awkwardly, "We also spoke to young Lady Wilcox, but she had nothing to add to our understanding of last night's events, either. I gather they've only been married—what? Three months?"

"Not even that," said Sebastian. The marriage had been arranged and pushed through with almost unseemly haste by Sebastian's half sister, Amanda, for reasons he could only speculate about. The new Lady Wilcox was quite young, barely seventeen years old, a quiet, rather colorless woman who was apparently more than content to be abandoned by her new husband on a Saturday night, when most young brides were eager to be seen at the theater or one of the balls that were starting up again with the return of the ton to London.

Sir Henry was silent for a moment, watching a passing barge. Then he said, "I assume you've seen the papers? Because of the murder's location on Primrose Hill, Fleet Street has seized upon the notion of Toole's death as a reenactment of some barbaric form of ancient human sacrifice and run with it. Needless to say, Sir Nathaniel Conant is doing everything he can to squash the speculation."

"I've no doubt," said Sebastian. Bow Street's new Chief Magistrate was very much the creature of the Prince Regent and Jarvis. When the Regent had sought to push a divorce from his wife, Princess Caroline, through Parliament, it was Conant who'd found and helped bribe witnesses to falsely testify that the Princess had given birth to one of the orphaned children she fostered. His knighthood and the office of Chief Magistrate of London's most prestigious public office had been his reward, and Lovejoy had been chafing under the man's less-than-honorable leadership ever since. "Do I take it the Palace is not pleased?"

"To put it mildly. They want someone tried, convicted, and hanged, and the sooner, the better."

"That's not good."

"No." Lovejoy kept his gaze on the barge. "Do you think your nephew is right? That the murders of Toole and Keebles are somehow linked?"

"It seems likely, doesn't it? The problem is, no one is being at all cooperative about any of this. And that makes me wonder why."

After that, Sebastian spent the better part of the next hour trolling the haunts typically frequented by Bayard and his friends. His nephew proved elusive, but he came upon Theo Bridgewood in the reading room of White's, his head bowed over the *Morning Chronicle*; a scattering of other newspapers and a brandy rested on the small round table at his elbow.

Sebastian ordered a glass of Bordeaux, then went to settle in the red leather chair on the far side of the younger man's table. "Mind if I join you?"

Theo looked up. He was an extraordinarily attractive man of twenty-six or -seven, tall and well-formed, with even, striking features and thick, dark brown hair styled à la Brutus. Unlike Upcott and Bayard, he had at some point abandoned the tendency toward dandyism he'd affected when younger and now wore the sort of somber, dark blue coat, buckskin breeches, and Hessians typical of a Corinthian.

"Not at all," he said, folding his paper and tossing it aside. "I was just reading the press's lurid speculation about Toole's death. Druids and ancient rites of human sacrifice, of all things."

"Do you believe any of it?"

"Good God, no. Don't tell me you do?"

Sebastian shook his head. "So who do you think killed him?"

"Me? I've no idea. How could I?"

"Did he have any enemies that you know of?"

"Toole? No."

"None?"

"None that I was aware of."

"Can you think of anyone he quarreled with recently?"

"No."

"What about the man he tangled with a month or two ago out at Chalk Farm Tavern? A man who may or may not have been a highwayman."

Theo's brows drew together in a frown. "Where did you hear about that?"

"From one of Toole's friends."

"Ah. You've been talking to Upcott, have you? He was in here not long ago, bleating on about Chalk Farm like Mary's little lamb—or do I mean a scared version of little Mary herself? At any rate, I'd no idea the fellow was so lily-livered; it's embarrassing."

"Would you happen to know this highwayman's name?"

Theo pursed his lips as if thoughtfully considering the question, then shook his head. "Sorry, no. Don't think I ever heard it."

"Do you remember what he looked like?"

"Not really. He wasn't exactly what you'd call memorable."

"Tall, or short?"

"Neither, probably."

"Old, or young?"

Theo laughed. "They don't usually live to be old, do they?"

"Not usually, no. Was he fair-haired? Dark?"

"I have no idea. It's not as if I paid a great deal of attention to the fellow, and I can't think why you—and Upcott—imagine he has anything to do with what happened to Toole."

"Proximity, perhaps?"

"Well, I suppose there is that."

"What was the quarrel about, anyway?"

"I don't know if I'd describe it as a *quarrel*, exactly. The fellow took exception to something Toole did, that's all."

"What did he do?"

Theo laughed again, less convincingly this time. "You think I remember? It was months ago, and I was more than half foxed at the time."

"Did you and Toole and the others go out to Chalk Farm often?"

"Not often, no. But sometimes."

"Why?"

"Why not?" Theo cast an expressive glance around the sedate, well-appointed room with its rich velvet curtains, sparkling chandeliers, and thick Turkey carpets. "It's considerably livelier and more interesting than anything to be found around here, wouldn't you say?"

"No doubt." Shifting in his chair, Sebastian drew the carved wooden wolf from his pocket and held it out. "Have you ever seen this before?"

Theo glanced at it, then shook his head. "No."

"You're certain?"

The younger man took the piece for a moment, turned it over, then handed it back. "No; sorry. Are you suggesting it could have something to do with what happened to Toole?"

"It might. Do you know if Toole had an interest in Celtic history or the Druids?"

"Toole?" The younger man gave a sharp laugh. "Good lord, no. What a ridiculous thought."

"What was he interested in?"

A hint of a sad smile tugged at the other man's lips, then was gone. And it occurred to Sebastian, watching him, that it was the first sign of any emotion—other than scorn and amusement—that Theo had displayed. "Horses. The Fancy. The cut of his coat. One of the pretty new dancers at the opera." He grimaced. "Definitely not Druids."

"Could he have quarreled with someone who does have an interest in the Druids?"

"Not to my knowledge."

"What about Gilbert Keebles? Did he ever express an interest in the Celts or Druidism?"

"No. I don't know anyone who's interested in Druids. Do you? My knowledge of them begins and ends with the tales my old Welsh nurse used to tell me when I was a child."

Sebastian took a slow sip of his wine. "What do you think happened to him? Keebles, I mean."

"Gil was a fool. He was drunk as a wheelbarrow when he left us that night, only instead of going home, he decided to take a walk along the river."

"He told you that when he left you? That he was going for a walk along the Thames?"

"Not exactly. What he said was that he was randy as hell and was going to find some threepenny whore and take her standing up against one of the gas lamps on Westminster Bridge. Unfortunately, he picked the wrong bit of muslin, didn't he? So rather than getting fucked, he ended up with a knife stuck in his ribs."

"Except that he wasn't robbed."

Theo reached for his brandy and took a deep drink. "I figure he tried to get away from the whore and her bully boy, fell in the river, and drowned."

Sebastian had to admit the scenario made a certain amount of sense. "So you don't think Keebles's death has anything to do with what happened to Marcus Toole up on Primrose Hill?" he said.

"No, I don't."

"Did Gil Keebles have any enemies?"

"Not to my knowledge."

"Quarrel with anyone—besides this highwayman—recently?"

"No."

"And you can't think of any reason anyone would want to kill either man?"

Theo blew out an exasperated breath. "I keep telling you, no."

"What about a former militiaman with a coffeehouse near Spa Fields?"

Theo stared at Sebastian a moment, then threw back his head and laughed. "*Him?* You can't be serious."

"You, Toole, and Keebles did have some sort of a run-in with him recently, didn't you?"

"I suppose you could call it that. The man's an impertinent, bloody Radical." Theo's eyes danced with silent laughter. "We decided to teach him the wisdom of displaying a proper degree of deference to his betters."

"Were Bayard and Upcott there, too?"

"They were."

"What about Emmanuel Royston-Jones?"

"No."

"Do you recall the name of the coffeehouse?"

"No; sorry. You surely can't think that impudent arse had anything to do with what happened to either Keebles or Toole?"

"Probably not." Sebastian pushed to his feet. "Thank you for your time. If you should happen to think of anything that might be at all relevant, you will let me know, won't you?"

"Yes, of course."

Sebastian started to turn away, then paused to look back at the younger man. "You're not afraid that whoever killed your two friends might try to kill you, too?"

Theo laughed. "You're thinking of Upcott. He's so terrified at the thought he might be next that I'm surprised he's managed to leave his house. But to answer your question, no; I'm not afraid. I find it doubtful that Gil and Marcus were killed by the same man, and even if they were, I'm perfectly capable of defending myself if someone should decide to come after me."

"If you see them coming."

"I'm a very careful man."

"What a pity your friends weren't," said Sebastian, and saw the other man's eyes narrow with a surge of raw anger he made no attempt to conceal.

Sebastian was in White's oak-paneled vestibule, shrugging on his greatcoat, when the door from St. James's Street opened and Lord Sidmouth walked in with Lionel, Fourth Baron Bridgewood.

They drew up just inside the door, with Lord Bridgewood leaning over to say something in an undervoice to his companion. The Home Secretary cast a quick, frowning glance at Sebastian, then continued on without his friend.

"Do you have a moment, Devlin?" said Theo's father, walking over to him. A tall, fleshy man in his late fifties, the Baron had a full, pleasant face, pale blue eyes, and fading fair hair he generally wore powdered and pulled back into a queue, as he had in his youth. Sebastian knew him through Hendon as a typical High Tory who took his responsibilities in the House of Lords seriously.

"It's a miserable day out, I know," Bridgewood was saying. "But I thought perhaps we could go for a walk. That is, if you don't mind?"

"Of course," said Sebastian, reaching for his hat.

The older man waited until they'd walked down the club's front steps and turned toward Piccadilly before saying bluntly, "I'm told Bayard Wilcox came to you last night after he found Marcus Toole in that fire. And then you then went out to Primrose Hill with him and saw the scene yourself. Is that true?"

"It is, yes."

Bridgewood kept his gaze on the traffic at the top of the hill. "You've made something of a study of this sort of thing, haven't you? Murder, I mean. So tell me: What do you make of it all? Two young friends murdered within weeks of each other? One stabbed and drowned, one set on fire like a bizarre reenactment of some ancient human sacrifice? I've just been talking to Sidmouth, and I was at Bow Street before that, and, well, let's just say I have a feeling they're not telling me everything."

"At this point, I'm afraid there really isn't much to tell," said Sebastian.

Bridgewood was silent for a moment, his normally cheerful face taking on a haggard look as he digested this. "Do you think my son is in danger?"

"Theo doesn't seem to think so."

"He's young. The young never believe they're going to die, do they? If they did, that would be the end of wars, wouldn't it? It's always the old men like me who get to stay safe at home while we send the young ones off to fight and die. If they knew what they were getting themselves into, how many do you think would go? If they had a choice?"

"Probably not many."

Lord Bridgewood's lips parted, then closed again before saying, "You didn't exactly answer my question, you know. Do you think my son is in danger?"

Sebastian chose his words carefully. "I suppose that depends on why Toole and Keebles were killed. Do you know if Theo has any enemies?"

"Not to my knowledge, no," said Bridgewood. "The thing is, when it comes right down to it, how much does any father actually know about his son's activities?"

"True," said Sebastian. "Have you seen Sir Samuel Toole today?"

Bridgewood sighed. "I have, yes. And to be frank, I'm worried about the man; I swear he's aged ten years in the last ten hours. Marcus was his only son, you know. As Theo is mine."

"And Sir Samuel has no idea why anyone would have wanted to kill Marcus?"

"No, none—let alone kill the lad in such a brutal way. I mean, how much do you need to hate a man to set him on fire? It's . . . savage."

"Did you know Marcus Toole and Gilbert Keebles?"

"I did, yes—known them since they were lads. Fine young men, both of them. Not saying they were saints, mind you. But then, who wants a saint for a son, eh? Not me. It's not like I was a saint when I was younger, if you know what I mean?" He cocked his head and winked. "Were you?"

"No."

Bridgewood nodded, his gaze following a dark-haired Cyprian in a fur-trimmed red velvet pelisse who'd paused to admire her reflection in a shop window before giving a little twirl and moving on. "Theo has been wanting to take rooms here in St. James's Street, same as Toole and Upcott. But every time he brings it up, m' wife cries and carries on so that he drops the idea. He's a good son, not wanting to distress his mother; there's no getting around that. Truth is, I've been more than a bit annoyed with her over it. I mean, a young man needs to spread his wings and fly, you know? But now . . . well, I must admit it's something of a comfort knowing he's where I can keep an eye on him. At least part of the time. Not that I would ever say anything like that to him, of course."

They'd reached the corner of Piccadilly with its heavy traffic of carts, carriages, wagons, and horses. The Baron drew up and turned to face Sebastian, one hand coming up to catch the brim of his hat as the cold wind threatened to carry it away. "Thank you for your honesty, Devlin. It's reassuring to know you're working on this, too. I've always heard good things about Lovejoy, but this new Chief Magistrate . . ." He pulled a face as he let his voice trail off. "I've called Sidmouth friend for more than thirty years, so let's just say I know exactly why Bow Street was handed to a man of Conant's character. He'll do whatever the Palace tells him to do and, usually, that's a good thing. But not always."

"I'm told the Palace is very interested in having these murders solved, as quickly as possible."

"Yes, Sidmouth says the same. Hopefully all my fears will prove to be misplaced. How is your nephew, by the way? After last night, I mean."

"Frightened."

"Hmm. Perhaps he has more sense than my son."

"Or the sight of his friend engulfed in flames was an inescapably sobering experience."

Bridgewood's face tightened with the effort of controlling his emotions. "Do you think they're in danger? Honestly. My son. Your nephew."

"Honestly?" Sebastian met the older man's stricken, desperate gaze. "Yes."

"One can't help but feel sorry for Lady Keebles, Lord Bridgewood, and Sir Samuel Toole," Hero said that evening as she leaned against the doorframe of Sebastian's dressing room and watched him rub wood ash into his hair. "But their sons don't sound like very nice young men, do they?"

"No." Sebastian turned away from his mirror to pull over his head a worn, yellowed shirt culled from the secondhand stalls of Rosemary Lane. "But then, what else could one expect of friends of Bayard?"

"So far," said Hero, "we know they quarreled with a highwayman—a highwayman!—out at Chalk Farm, wrecked some coffeehouse up near Spa Fields, set fire to a German chemist's house, and generally wreaked enough havoc that a Radical journal felt compelled to publish an article denouncing them."

He looked over at her. "Do you have any idea which journal?"

"No, but I should be able to find out tomorrow. Have you managed to talk to Bayard since he sobered up?"

"Not yet. I sent a message to St. James's Square suggesting he pay me a visit when convenient." Sebastian reached for the folded response that lay nearby, its seal broken, and handed it to her. "This was his answer."

"'Devlin,'" she read. "'Are you reluctant to call at St. James's Square because my mother once instructed Crowley to refuse you admittance? If you will recall, I am now married and this is my house, not my mother's. Crowley is my butler, and he will admit whomever I tell him to. Yours, etc. Wilcox.'" Hero looked up. "Well, it's incredibly rude and juvenile, but also very interesting. Is the worm finally turning?"

"It does sound like it, doesn't it?"

"I suspect Amanda is not pleased."

Sebastian looped a black cravat around his neck and tied it in a casual knot. "No, indeed."

Hero folded the message again, then stared down at it thoughtfully. "What if the two killings—Keebles's and Toole's—aren't linked? What if the two men were killed simply because they were so despicable they'd managed to annoy two completely different people sufficiently to inspire them to murder?"

"That's certainly a distinct possibility," said Sebastian, reaching for a worn brown corduroy coat.

"But you don't think so?"

"I don't like coincidences."

"Yet they do sometimes occur."

"They do."

She watched him shrug into the coat and frowned. "You will be careful, won't you? This Chalk Farm Tavern sounds like a thoroughly disreputable place."

"Oh, it is," said Sebastian, slipping a knife into the hidden sheath in his boot.

Chapter 12

Rather than give the game away by taking his curricle or his own well-bred Arabian mare, Sebastian rode out to Chalk Farm on a suitably nondescript job horse hired from an Oxford Street livery stable. The night was cold but clear, the sky above a panoply of stars that glittered at him from out of the deep black velvet of eternity.

Once upon a time, in the days of the Druids, this area had been woodland, home to deer, wild boar, and wolves. A millennium later, it served as one of Henry VIII's favorite hunting grounds. But then came Henry's break with Rome, the Stuarts, regicide, and civil war, and the Puritans sold off the land to their friends. The trees were cut down, and what had once been the forested hunting grounds of wolves and kings became grassland and neatly tended fields.

The tavern stood on an ancient winding lane just off Hampstead Road. Originally an old white-painted farmhouse, it had two stories, with a central door flanked on each side by a window and a wide veranda that ran across the entire front. As Sebastian reined in, he could hear the laughter and raised voices of drinking men spilling out into the night. The taverns on the outskirts of London were always crowded on Sunday nights, when armies of drovers herding everything from cattle and sheep to ducks and geese converged on the city for the Monday morning markets.

Leaving his horse in the care of an ostler, Sebastian crossed the stable yard to push open the door to the taproom. After the crisp, calm fresh air of the countryside, walking into the noisy, smoky, dimly lit tavern was like entering another world, its atmosphere thick with the smells of sawdust, hot tallow, spilled beer, tobacco, and pungent male sweat. Pushing his way through the boisterous, laughing crowd, Sebastian went to lean against the bar and signal the woman behind the counter.

She looked up from filling a clutch of tankards and frowned.

"Haven't seen you around here before," she said, coming to set a foaming tankard on the bar before him with a soft thump. She was an attractive woman somewhere in her thirties with thick dark hair, creamy white skin, and pale eyes that narrowed speculatively.

Sebastian raised the tankard to his lips and took a slow swallow. "I'm looking for a man named Sid."

"Oh? Sid what?"

"All I know is 'Sid.'"

"I take it he ain't exactly a friend of yours?"

"No," Sebastian admitted. "But I'd still like to talk to him. Is he here?"

She shook her head. "Sorry, don't know nobody named Sid."

"You don't?"

"No." She reached for a wet rag and wiped at an imaginary spot on the scarred countertop. "What you want with him, anyway?"

"I hear he once tangled with the young gentleman who got himself killed last night up on Primrose Hill."

She stiffened. "You a Bow Street Runner?"

"No."

"Didn't think so," she said with a sniff. "We already had 'em out here once today, you know—pokin' around, askin' all sorts of questions. It ain't good for business."

"I wouldn't think it would be."

She rested her forearms on the bar and leaned into them. "So if you ain't a Runner, then what's that dead nob to you, anyway?"

"It's complicated."

"Meanin' what?"

He simply smiled and shook his head. "They were here last night, weren't they? Both young men—the one who was killed and his friend."

He thought for a moment she didn't mean to answer. Then she shrugged and said, "They were here."

"They came in together?"

"They came in together, they drank too much, and then they left together. Lord knows I was glad enough to see the back of 'em. Them kind are always trouble."

"Did they quarrel with anyone while they were here?"

"Not this time."

"But they've quarreled with people here in the past?"

"You mean, besides your nonfriend Sid?" she said archly.

"Yeah."

She straightened. "They're a quarrelsome lot, those young bucks."

Sebastian swiped his thumb at a line of foam running down the side of the tankard. "Did the two men by any chance quarrel with each other while they were here last night?"

She stood very still. "Funny, the Runners who was here today didn't ask that question."

"So did they? Quarrel with each other last night, I mean."

"As it happens, they did."

Sebastian felt a yawning pit of worry open up in the depths of his gut. "Do you know what about?"

She shook her head. "I try to stay as far away from that kind as I can."

Raising his tankard again, he let his gaze drift around the roomful of drovers, farmhands, and tradesmen. He didn't see anyone who looked like he was on the high toby, but then, what exactly did a knight of the road look like when not engaged in his favorite occupation?

"You get many Druids in here?" he asked.

At that, the woman laughed out loud, then rolled her eyes. "Certain times of the year, they're so thick you can't hardly turn around without tripping over one of 'em."

"Were any here last night?"

"Now, how would I know, if'n they wasn't wearing their robes an' all?"

"I suppose it would be rather difficult."

She fixed him with a long, thoughtful stare. "You thinkin' it's true, what they're sayin'? That somebody used that nob as part of a heathen sacrifice, like they did in olden times? Burned him to their gods?"

"Do you?"

She made a scoffing sound deep in her throat. "Reckon them's just old stories folks use to scare children."

"So who do you think killed him?"

"Somebody who knew him, I reckon. We get lots of rough characters in here, and some of 'em can turn real mean when they get the drink in 'em. But those bucks—the ones who was here last night, and their friends, too—they're somethin' else again. Think they own the world, they do; that they can do whatever they want and never have to pay for it. But somebody showed at least one of 'em that sometimes that ain't so, didn't they? And if I was to say I'm sorry, I'd be lyin'."

Then she tossed her rag on the counter with a sodden plop and walked away.

On a clear, moonlit night like tonight, the huddled buildings, church towers, and docklands of London were plainly visible from the summit of Primrose Hill.

Sebastian stood with the reins of his hired horse held loosely in one hand, his gaze on the distant city. A breeze had kicked up, bringing with it the scent of damp earth, dead grass, and, from nearer, the charred stench of last night's fire. He couldn't have said exactly why he'd come here, as if this haunted place could somehow whisper to him the secret truths that he wasn't sure he was ready to hear.

Drawing a deep breath, he listened to the distant lowing of a cow and the quiet footfalls of a man who'd left his own horse down below and was now creeping stealthily toward the top of the hill.

"My hearing and night vision are both quite good, you know," said Sebastian, shifting the reins to his left hand to leave the right one free. "So if you think you're sneaking up on me, you're in for a rude surprise."

Chapter 13

The footsteps stopped. Then Sebastian heard a man's throaty laugh, and a dark shadow straightened slowly, his hands held where Sebastian could see them as he continued walking the last several hundred feet to the top of the hill. "Don't mean you no harm. Just want to talk."

"I take it you're Sid?"

"I am," said the man, touching one hand to his hat as he executed a flourishing bow. "Sid Diamond, at your service." He looked to be around Sebastian's age, of average height and build, his features rugged, his dress that of an ex-soldier or country squire down on his luck.

Or a highwayman.

He straightened slowly. "Now it's your turn; who the hell are you?"

"The name's Devlin."

The man's eyes narrowed. "As in Viscount Devlin? The Earl of Hendon's son and heir?"

Sebastian nodded.

The other man laughed out loud.

"That's funny, is it?" said Sebastian.

Diamond pushed his hat back on his head. "You don't think so?" He went to stand beside the remnants of the fire, his head bowed. When he turned around again, he was no longer laughing. "This where somebody tried to use that bloody nob for firewood?"

"Yes."

"Now, that would have been a sight to see."

"It's a pity you missed it, then. If you did."

Diamond stared at him for a long moment. "You're thinkin' I killed him, are you?"

"You did have a quarrel with him. Him and his friends."

"Don't know if I'd call it a quarrel, exactly. They thought they could treat other folks like they're of no more account than the dung on the soles of their boots, and I showed 'em they were wrong."

"And how precisely did you do that?"

He shrugged. "They were botherin' Alison. I made 'em stop."

"Alison?"

Diamond jerked his head in the general direction of Chalk Farm. "Alison Cross, the tavern keeper."

"Ah. Alison struck me as the type of woman who is more than capable of taking care of herself."

"She is. But there was five of them. And that kind ain't used to being told no."

"So what happened after you told them to stop?"

"They tried pushin' me around, from one t' the other, laughin' and whoopin' like the jackasses they are. So I collared one, put my knife to his throat, and told the rest of 'em I'd give 'em five seconds to get out before I started cuttin' off bits of their friend."

"Which one did you grab?"

The highwayman smiled. "As it happens, it was your nephew."

"What did his friends do?"

"They sloughed off as fast as they could. Then I let your nevvy go—although I may've taken a wee chunk out of his ear first to remind him to mind his manners in the future."

"They simply left?"

"Nah. I'll be damned if they didn't steal Jesse. Took her out on the heath, ripped up my saddle and dumped it in the mud, and probably would've slit her throat, too, if she hadn't reared up and got away from them. She had a knife slash on her neck, and the reins were snapped."

"Jesse is your mare?"

"She is."

"How do you know Toole and his friends are the ones who took her?"

"One of the tavern's ostlers saw them. It's not like they were trying to hide what they were doin'."

"When exactly was this?"

Diamond shrugged. "A month or two ago."

Sebastian studied the other man's roughhewn features and found himself remembering what Upcott had said about him. There was no mistaking the man's way of holding himself, of moving—his manner of speech, even. All told their own story to anyone who'd spent six years as a cavalry officer.

Sebastian said, "Which regiment were you in?"

A flare of surprise flickered in the other man's eyes. "The Eleventh Light Dragoons."

"And now you're on the high toby?"

Diamond's jaw hardened. "You think I'm the only one fallen on hard times?"

"No. But you don't strike me as the type to take what those men tried to do to your mare and walk away."

Diamond's lips curled in a slow, nasty smile. "Maybe. Maybe I'd even come up with a plan to get my own back at them." His gaze drifted again to the cold firepit at his feet. "But it looks like somebody beat me to this one."

Perhaps, thought Sebastian. *Or perhaps not.* Aloud, he said, "Where were you last night?"

This time the man's grin was something less nasty, more rollicking, his dark brown eyes dancing with amusement. "Workin'."

"Alone?"

"I like t' work alone."

"That's unfortunate. If Bow Street gets wind of this, you might find you could use an alibi."

"Huh. You still thinkin' I did that?" Diamond jerked his chin toward the cold ashes at their feet. "Why the bloody hell would I go through all the trouble of settin' the bastard on fire?"

"Presumably for the same reason those men stole your horse and ripped up your saddle."

Diamond shook his head. "That ain't my way." He fell silent for a moment, then said, "That night—the night those coves were goin' after Alison—they started off pickin' on a couple of greenheads who'd come into the tavern. Little more'n boys, they were—not much above eighteen or nineteen from the looks of 'em, and still wet behind the ears. One of 'em especially was a real kinchin cove, and he's the one those bucks focused on. Men like that can smell weakness and fear the same way a horse or a dog knows who's afraid of 'em. Cut the buttons off the poor lad's trousers and pulled 'em down, saying they was gonna whip his bare arse. That's when Alison went over and told 'em to leave the young cub alone. So they turned on her."

"Do you know who this young cub was?"

"Nah. Never seen him before or since. But they knew him, and he knew them. Struck me as a bit of a nan-boy, if you know what I mean?"

"And all five of them were picking on him?"

Diamond nodded. "One of 'em started it—Toole, as a matter of fact. But then the others joined in. Or at least, four of 'em did. There was six of 'em to begin with, you see. But the sixth cove, he hung back; even told 'em to cut it out at one point. Of course, all they did was laugh. Told him if he didn't want to have fun, he could just watch."

"So what did he do?"

"He left."

"Do you know who he was?"

"No; I've no interest in him."

"But you know who the other five were."

"You could say I've made it my business to find out, which is how I come to know one of 'em's your nephew. That's why you're out here, isn't it? Askin' questions and pokin' around."

"Partially."

"He's a rotter, you know. Your nevvy, I mean."

"I know," Sebastian said honestly.

The highwayman tilted his head, as if trying to understand

something he found incomprehensible. "So why you care if somebody's taken to killin' the buggers?"

"Because he is my father's grandson."

"Ah. I see. You're thinkin' his death would grieve the Earl, is that it? Seems to me it'd be better for the old man to wake up one morning to the news that somebody'd quietly garroted the little bastard than to have to watch him piss when he can't whistle."

It was a harsh but aptly descriptive euphemism for hanging, "to piss when you can't whistle." Sebastian said, "What precisely are you implying?"

"You mean you don't know?"

"No."

"Then maybe that's what you ought to be tryin' to find out," said Sid Diamond, turning away. "Rather than worrying about what happened up here."

"You think he did it?" Hero asked later that night. She was standing behind his chair, her hands resting loosely on his shoulders as he sat before the library fire, a glass of brandy cradled in one palm. "This highwayman, I mean. You think he killed Toole and Keebles?"

Sebastian tipped back his head to look up at her. "He's certainly capable of it. Although a simple bullet in the chest or six inches of cold steel in the gut strike me as more the man's style than a crude reenactment of some ancient rite of human sacrifice."

"Gil Keebles got six inches of cold steel before he went in the river. And Marcus Toole was shot before he ended up in that fire. Perhaps they both simply . . . fell. One in the water, the other in the fire. No ghostly echo of ancient sacrifices necessary. Just . . . gravity."

"It's certainly possible," said Sebastian, taking a sip of his brandy.

"Who do you think this 'greenhead' Sid Diamond was talking about could be?"

"I have no idea. But I intend to ask Bayard tomorrow."

Hero walked over to stand with one hand resting on the mantel, her gaze on the fire. "The sixth man—the one who left—could have been Emmanuel Royston-Jones."

"Probably. I plan to talk to him tomorrow, too. If Bayard—"

He broke off at the sound of a hackney carriage pulling up outside. Quick footsteps thumped up the front steps, followed by a heavy hand beating an urgent tattoo with the knocker as Morey moved to open the door. Sebastian felt his heart sink as he listened to the low murmur of voices. "Bloody hell," he whispered.

Hero looked up at him. "What is it?"

"My lord," said Morey, appearing at the entrance to the library with a big, slouch-hatted man Sebastian recognized as one of Lovejoy's constables at his heels. "Someone from Bow Street."

"Lord Devlin," said the man with a bow to Sebastian. Then he glanced over at Hero and bowed again. "My apologies, my lady, for the intrusion. But Sir Henry thought your lordship would like to know that another young gentleman has been found murdered. This one's hanging from a bricklayer's scaffolding by one of those grand new houses they're building up in Marylebone."

Sebastian felt his stomach lurch. *Please not Bayard* was his first, inevitable thought. He cleared his throat and said, "Who? Who is the dead man?"

The constable bowed again. "A Mr. Phineas Upcott, my lord."

Chapter 14

Sebastian found Sir Henry Lovejoy standing beside the north wall of a half-built brown brick villa, his hands thrust deep into the pockets of his greatcoat as he studied the limp body of Phineas Upcott hanging before him. The length of rope tying Phineas's neck to one of the crosspieces of the bricklayers' wooden scaffold was long enough that the dead man's feet dangled only a foot or so above the ground. Lovejoy had set a horn lantern nearby, for the night was dark here, darker than in the city, with its stretches of new gaslights and old-fashioned oil lamps. This was a part of Marylebone that had been laid out in a grid of proposed streets and squares in preparation for a building boom that was expected to accompany the construction of the Regent's New Street and nearby Regent's Park. But a combination of the postwar economic slump and the miserably cold weather Britain had been enduring now for more than a year had dampened enthusiasm for the project. The lights of only a few scattered houses showed here and there in the black emptiness of the surrounding wind-whipped, frost-nipped fields.

"Who found him?" said Sebastian, pausing beside the magistrate.

"A hackney driver coming back from taking a fare up to Alpha Road. He stopped and ducked around here to relieve himself, only to realize he was standing virtually face-to-face with a dead man."

Sebastian was silent, his gaze on the slight, gently swaying corpse, his thoughts on the vital young man he'd seen just that morning. Phineas Upcott's face was so engorged and discolored as to be virtually unrecognizable, his eyes wide and staring, his tongue protruding hideously.

Lovejoy said, "It could be a suicide."

"It could be, but I doubt it. He actually came to see me this morning. He was afraid that whoever murdered Keebles and Toole was going to kill him next. And it looks as if they did."

Lovejoy glanced over at him. "How well did you know the young man?"

"Not well. His father is a baronet—Sir Lawrence Upcott—who owns a prosperous estate in Berkshire and tends to stay there. Phineas is—was—his heir, but preferred life in London. I believe he kept lodgings in St. James's Street."

"Ah. Perhaps this time we'll have the opportunity to actually search the victim's rooms."

"It might be a good idea to move quickly. I suspect Sir Lawrence will be leaving for London as soon as he hears what has happened."

"We'll do it at first light," said Lovejoy, his gaze drifting over the surrounding empty fields. "I wonder what Upcott was doing all the way out here. It's difficult to believe his killer brought him here, but I suppose it is possible."

"Maybe." Sebastian turned to look back toward the street as a cart with a couple of men from the deadhouse drew up behind his waiting curricle. "You'll be sending the body to Gibson?"

"Yes." Lovejoy watched in silence as the men unloaded their shell from the back of the cart. Then he said, "Three wellborn young gentlemen murdered within weeks of each other. It's . . . horrifying."

Sebastian had to force himself to look again at the dead man's ghastly, bloated face. "I think we can now safely assume we're not dealing with a coincidence."

Lovejoy met his gaze and nodded solemnly.

"Ever hear of a knight of the road named Sid Diamond?" Sebastian asked his valet later that night.

Jules Calhoun looked up from brushing Sebastian's coat. A small, lithe man in his thirties with fair hair, a high forehead, and blue eyes, he'd been with Sebastian for years and was invariably both unflappable and affable. "I don't believe so, my lord. Are you interested in him?"

"I'd like to know more about him, if possible."

Most gentlemen's gentlemen would be insulted by the suggestion that they might be familiar with a highwayman. But Calhoun had grown up in a succession of notorious flash houses famous for the unsavory nature of their clientele. His eyes crinkled in a smile. "That should be possible."

Monday, 25 November

Sebastian lay awake for much of what was left of that night. He could hear the wind shifting the bare branches of the distant trees in Grosvenor Square and, from someplace nearer, the howl of a dog that sounded almost like a wolf.

"You need to sleep," said Hero at some point before dawn, shifting her head on her pillow so she could look over at him.

"I am trying." He rolled onto his side to face her. "I keep remembering how frightened Phineas was when he came to see me. He was afraid, he came to me for help, and I let him down."

She rested her hand, gently, against his chest. "He must have known more about what happened to Toole and Keebles than he let on."

"I don't think he knew precisely why they were killed, but he obviously knew far more about the various nasty things they'd done than he was willing to tell me. Hell, he took part in them." Reaching out, he drew her into his arms and held her close. "I need to talk to Royston-Jones. From the sound of things, he left Chalk Farm Tavern the night they tangled with Sid Diamond because he was disgusted by what his friends were doing. If nothing else, I should be able to get the name of the 'greenhead' from him."

Hero rested her cheek on his chest. "Have you learned anything about that Clerkenwell coffeehouse?"

"Not yet." He ran his fingers through her hair. "Sometimes when a man is murdered, it's difficult to imagine why anyone would want to kill him. But with this lot, we've already uncovered nearly half a dozen people with a reasonable motive for murder, and I suspect we've barely scratched the surface."

"I keep thinking about what Sid Diamond told you—that Hendon would be better off mourning a murdered grandson than having to watch him hang. The things we know Bayard and his friends did—to Accum, to the young man up at Chalk Farm, and all the rest of it . . . they might be disgusting, but none of them are anywhere near a hanging offense." She paused. "Well, I suppose stealing Diamond's horse was, but I can't see a highwayman pressing charges."

"No; you're right. Other than the horse, it's all been about intimidation, humiliation, and cruelty as a form of entertainment, of sport." He met her troubled gaze. "Which begs the question: What the hell is it that we don't know?"

Emmanuel Royston-Jones's famous father, Zacharia Royston-Jones, was known as one of the wealthiest men in all the kingdom. Zacharia owed the foundations of his business empire to his own father, Joshua Jones, who'd gone from unloading ships on the docks of Newcastle to building them. But Zacharia had extended the family's holdings far beyond his father's ambitious beginnings, expanding into both wartime shipping and sugar plantations. By marrying the daughter of an earl—albeit an impoverished, relatively recent Irish one—and hyphenating his common last name with hers, he had successfully joined his plebeian blood to the aristocracy. But his crowning achievement had been the betrothal of his only son, Emmanuel, to Lady Anne Crawford, the daughter of a duke.

And then she had died, just weeks before the wedding.

As he mounted the front steps of Emmanuel Royston-Jones's

handsome town house overlooking Berkeley Square, Sebastian was aware of the black mourning wreath on the door, the black crepe festooning the windows. How many months had passed since Lady Anne's death? Four? More? But this was not four-month-old crepe, he realized. Which meant the bereaved groom hadn't been able to bear letting it be taken down and had instead ordered it renewed.

Emmanuel received Sebastian in an icy, half-empty drawing room overlooking the square, standing before a fire that had been newly kindled on the hearth, his hands clasped behind his back. The shipping magnate's heir was slightly above average in height, with curly black hair cropped short, a strong nose and chin, and blue-gray eyes visibly shadowed by a powerful, abiding grief.

"Please, have a seat, my lord," he said, extending a hand toward the two pale blue silk–covered chairs that stood beside the fire. "May I offer you some tea?"

"No, thank you," said Sebastian, adjusting the tails of his coat as he sat.

There was a table between the chairs and a new floral carpet on the floor, but that was the extent of the room's furnishings. "My apologies for the condition of the room," said Royston-Jones, coming to sink into the other chair. "But the truth is, the entire house looks like this. My father bought it for Annie and me, you know, when we were first betrothed. She was the one coordinating the furnishing, but then . . ." He fell silent, his expression vaguely baffled, as if he couldn't quite understand how the half-empty room could still be here when the woman who'd taken such delight in decorating it was gone. "I've been thinking about selling the place, but somehow I can't bring myself to do it. She loved it so much. I can still see her standing at the windows there, smiling at the way the evening sun soaked the grass and trees in the square with a rich golden light." His voice caught. "It's funny, isn't it, how memories can be both painful and dear?"

"Yes."

The younger man brought his gaze back to Sebastian's face and swallowed. "I heard about Phineas Upcott. That's why you're here, is it? Because of what's happened to the three of them—Marcus, Gil, and Phineas?"

Sebastian nodded. "I'm told you used to be friends with all three men."

Something that was not a smile flexed the corners of the other man's mouth, then was gone. "'Used to be' is the operative part of that sentence." He paused. "I have to admit, Phineas's death has hit me harder than the other two. He wasn't like the rest of them, you know, and it wasn't only because he was quieter, more serious. They might have laughed a lot, but it wasn't a nice kind of laughter. They liked to laugh *at* people, not with them."

Sebastian found himself remembering the way Phineas Upcott had sneered at Royston-Jones's "lumper" grandfather and his maternal grandfather's Irish peerage. But all he said was, "Phineas wasn't like that?"

"He went along with them, but I think it was mainly because he liked being part of their pack. Not because he liked what they did, but because they made him feel stronger, less vulnerable. Basically, he was a very weak man." Emmanuel hesitated, then looked away and said more quietly, "Like me, I suppose."

Sebastian studied the younger man's half-averted face. "Tell me about what happened out at Chalk Farm Tavern a month or two ago."

"Heard about that, did you?"

"Some of it."

Emmanuel was silent for a moment. Then he swiped one hand across his lower face. "I was only there for the first part. There were two young Cambridge lads having a drink in the tavern. I had the impression they'd just been sent down for something, but whatever it was, it couldn't have been particularly grievous because they looked and sounded like the makings of a couple of future dons. I mean, there they were, sitting in a notoriously rough tavern that's essentially a bloody thieves' den, and they were talking about Lucan and Pythagoras, of all things."

"Who started it?"

"That was Toole. He and Bridgewood are like that, you know. They can sense weakness in another man the way a spider knows when a juicy new meal has fallen into its web."

Sid Diamond had said something similar, Sebastian remembered. Except that at some point Toole's predator instincts must have failed him badly.

"He's the one who went over first and started picking on them," Emmanuel was saying. "But Bridgewood was right behind him, and then Keebles and Wilcox joined in."

"And Upcott?"

"He was there, but he wasn't really taking part. He rarely did. He'd just stand to one side and snicker. At first they were picking on both lads, but it didn't take long for them to focus on just the one—I think he might be Captain Fenton's youngest brother, Dudley, although I could be wrong about that."

"Do you know who the other lad was?"

"No. Sorry."

"Did he make any attempt to stand up for his friend?"

"No. I think he was just grateful that Fenton was their main target and not him. I told them to stop, but they just laughed at me and said if I didn't like it, I could leave. So I did."

He fell silent again, his gaze on the bare branches of the trees in the square, his face pale except for the stain of color riding high on his cheekbones. "Not one of my finer moments, I'm afraid. When Upcott came to see me afterward and told me what they'd done to the lad and to that innkeeper who tried to step in, it made me feel physically sick. At that point I'd already been staying away from them, and I haven't deliberately seen any of them since. Not even Phineas."

"Who do you think killed them?" said Sebastian.

Emmanuel stared down at the hands he now held clasped between his knees. "I don't know. I've been thinking and thinking, but I can't make sense of it. They obviously tangled with someone who's meaner than they are, but I don't know who it is or what they did to provoke him."

Sebastian drew the small carved wolf from his pocket and held it out. "Have you ever seen this before?"

Emmanuel looked up and frowned. "No. Why? What is it?"

Sebastian tucked the carving back into his pocket. "I don't know exactly what it is. I found it not far from where Marcus Toole was killed. Do you know if he—or any of the others—ever had anything to do with Druidism?"

Emmanuel gave a short, surprised bark of a laugh. "Druidism? Those men? Not hardly."

"You're certain?"

He nodded. "I have a cousin who considers herself a Druid. She's very serious about it. For her it's something intensely spiritual; it's about cherishing the earth and everything living on it, plants and animals alike. She essentially sees nature as divine. I don't think Marcus Toole could even understand what that means." His jaw hardened. "I remember one time I ran into them when she was with me. Somehow or another the subject came up, and she was trying to explain how the ancient ways help her feel a connection with nature, and they acted like they found the entire idea uproariously funny."

"Can you think of someone in the neo-Druid movement they might have angered? Humiliated, perhaps?"

"No. Like I said, except for that night I went with them to Chalk Farm—and when Phineas came here afterward—I haven't seen much of them in the last six months or so. I don't know why I decided to go with them that night, but all it did was serve to remind me of why I'd been avoiding them."

"And why was that, exactly? Why had you started avoiding them?"

Emmanuel hesitated again, as if searching for a way to put what he wanted to say into words. "I was thirteen when my father sent me to Eton. I didn't want to go—I knew I wouldn't fit in. But he said it was important I *learn* how to fit in." He drew a painful, ragged breath. "My first few months were . . . not pleasant. Children—especially privileged boys on the cusp on manhood—can be extraordinarily cruel, can't they? But then for reasons I could never understand, Marcus Toole and Theo Bridgewood decided to become my friends, and everything changed."

Sebastian suspected he could understand quite well. Emmanuel's paternal grandfather might have been a lumper and his maternal grandfather "only" an indebted Irish peer, but Emmanuel's father's wealth made the holdings of men like Sir Samuel Toole and Lord Bridgewood pale into insignificance. Such extravagant wealth typically produced insufferably arrogant sons, but it obviously hadn't in Emmanuel's case. And Sebastian found himself wondering whether Emmanuel's newfound "friends" had somehow found a way to make him feel protected while simultaneously perpetuating his sense of inferiority.

"The other boys were all afraid of them, you know," Emmanuel was saying. "Toole, Keebles, and Bridgewood, especially. They could be nasty in a hundred different ways. But they were also clever and daring and fun. I enjoyed kicking up larks with them almost as much as I enjoyed having them on my side. And yet, even from the beginning, I knew there was a dark edge to them. I just ignored it." He shook his head. "I can find excuses for the lonely, confused boy I was then, but not for the man I became who still stayed their friend. I can't believe it took me so long to end it."

"Was there something in particular they did last summer?"

"No," he said quickly. *Too quickly?* Sebastian wondered. "I think it was because of Annie, to tell the truth. She never said anything to me about them, but I could tell some of the things they did troubled her. And when I looked at them through her eyes, I was ashamed of myself for being their friend."

"What about the coffeehouse out near Spa Fields? Were you there when they wrecked it?"

"You mean the Rising Sun? I wasn't there, but I heard about it."

"Do you know why they did it?"

"Not exactly. I think basically the owner made the mistake of talking back to them—refused to treat them like the superior beings they thought they were." He unclasped his hands and let them fall to his sides. "I wish I could help you more, but I don't understand it myself."

"You've helped me see things more clearly," said Sebastian, pushing to his feet. "Thank you for your time."

Emmanuel walked with him to the entrance hall, the big, empty house echoing around them. They'd almost reached the front door when the younger man said, "Do you think I have reason to be afraid? Of this killer, I mean?"

"I suppose that depends on if these murders are an act of revenge, and if the killer blames you for whatever it was your friends did that has made him want to strike back. If you know anything—anything at all that might explain—"

"But I've already told you, I don't."

Sebastian met the younger man's stricken, haunted gaze. "Even if you don't, it might be a good idea to be careful. Some people can carry a grudge for a long time before they get up the courage to strike back."

Chapter 15

It took Hero the better part of Monday morning to identify the Radical journal that had once printed a cryptic article attacking Marcus Toole and his friends.

The *Poor Man's Weekly* had been begun by a man named Barnabas Price, an advocate of such revolutionary reforms as freedom of the press, universal suffrage, and the need to end child labor. When Price was convicted of libel and sedition for publishing material that might, in the words of the prosecution, "cause the people to hate their government," his young wife, Beth, continued printing the paper while he was in prison. Then Beth, in turn, was sent to Newgate, and Price's sister Kate took over. Even after Beth died in prison and Barnabas—a shattered, disheartened shadow of the fiery man he'd once been—was finally released, Kate continued printing the *Poor Man's Weekly* from the ground floor of a dilapidated, late seventeenth-century brick building on an ancient narrow lane that wound away from Fleet Street toward the river. The paper still advocated many Radical reforms, but Kate Price had learned to be more cautious and crafty than her brother.

Dressed in a simple navy wool carriage gown with a black velvet collar and a short-veiled black velvet hat, Hero left her carriage near St. Bride's churchyard and walked down a decrepit rainswept passage to push open the shop's warped old door.

She found herself in a small workspace crowded with stacks of crates, an old wooden-framed press, a small coal-fired stove, and rows of freshly printed pages that dangled from the clotheslines crisscrossing the room. The musty air was thick with the smell of linseed oil, lampblack, and cheap paper; a slim woman with a stained leather apron tied over a simple long-sleeved, rusty-black gown was bent over the press. She had her back to the door, but at Hero's entrance she looked around and stiffened.

Still somewhere in her early thirties, with dark blond hair, brown eyes, and a square chin, the woman did not smile. "Why are you here?"

The bell on the old door jangled as Hero pushed it closed behind her. "You're Kate Price?"

Rather than answer, the woman turned away again to yank the "devil's tail" on the old-fashioned press, then said, "I know who you are."

Hero studied that half-averted profile. "We've met?"

"No. But I watched your father send first my brother, then his wife, to prison."

"I'm not my father."

A hard smile curled the other woman's lips. "Did you know Beth died in Newgate? Of gaol fever. She was just twenty-three years old. By the time my brother was released, he was so devastated by what his government had done to them that he couldn't bear living in England anymore and immigrated to America."

"I know. I'm sorry."

"Are you?"

"I wouldn't have said it if I weren't."

At that, Kate Price twisted around to stare at Hero again over one shoulder. "No, I don't believe you would," she said after a moment, then turned to peel the wet page off the press. "So why are you here?"

"I understand you wrote an article about Marcus Toole and his friends."

For a moment the woman froze. Then she lifted the wet page and hung it on the line beside the others to dry. "That was some time ago."

"What prompted you to write it?"

"Have you read it?"

"No. I haven't been able to find a copy."

"Good." Kate reached for a rag to wipe her ink-stained hands. "You'd think I'd have learned from what happened to my brother and Beth, but sometimes when I'm enraged, I'm not as cautious as I should be."

"And that article was one of those instances?"

"Obviously." Her fist tightened around the rag. "I take it Lord Devlin has decided to involve himself in the investigation of Toole's murder?"

"His and the others'. Who do you think is killing them?"

Kate stared at her with tight, unreadable features. "How would I know?"

"Because you were paying attention to the things those men were doing, even when no one else was."

"And you think that means I know who's killing them?" Kate Price huffed a sound that wasn't quite a laugh. "Funny how poor people are killed in this city all the time; good people, people with mothers, fathers, husbands, wives, sons, and daughters who loved them and mourn them. But you don't see the *Morning Chronicle* or the *Times* or any of the other 'respectable' papers spilling buckets of ink to bewail the horror of their deaths, do you? Yet let someone go after the wastrel son of one of the country's 'fine old families,' and Fleet Street has a collective apoplectic fit."

Hero studied the other woman's hard, angry face. "What did Toole and his friends do to you?"

Something flared in Kate's eyes, something that might have been fear. "What makes you think they did anything to me?"

"Then why did you write the article?"

"Why?" She hurled the rag away from her as if she'd suddenly realized she was still holding it. "I'll tell you why. Because I was tired of watching them get away with everything from assault to the wanton destruction of property simply because of who their fathers are."

"Who do you know that they hurt?"

"You seriously think I would give you their names? So Bow Street can have someone to hang?"

"I told you—I'm not my father."

"No? So why do you even care? Is one of them related to you?"

"Not to me."

"Ah, I remember now. Lord Wilcox is Devlin's nephew, isn't he?"

"He is. But that's not why I'm here." Hero paused. "It doesn't bother you? Knowing that you're sharing your city with a cold-blooded killer who burns, drowns, and hangs his victims?"

Kate shrugged. "If I were one of Marcus Toole's friends, I

might be worried. But I can't see whoever's doing this coming after me."

"A man who can coldly take three people's lives is a danger to everyone."

"I suppose that depends on what drives him to it, wouldn't you say?"

"If you change your mind," said Hero, reaching for the door handle. "You know where to find me."

But the woman simply tightened her jaw and watched Hero walk away.

Chapter 16

Sebastian spent the next several hours looking into a young Cambridge student named Dudley Fenton, who turned out to be the fourth son and youngest child of a Berkshire earl. The Earl's third son, Captain James Fenton, had distinguished himself in the Napoleonic Wars and was now part of the Army of Occupation in France, while the Earl's second son, Matthew, was the rector of the parish of St. Margaret's, in Westminster. For the past two months Dudley had been living with his brother Matthew, and it didn't take much digging for Sebastian to discover that the lad was in London because he'd been rusticated, although no one seemed to know the exact nature of his sin.

Sebastian found the young, recently expelled scholar in the Reading Room of the British Museum, his head bent over an ancient leather-bound tome. Tall and rail-thin, with lifeless, badly cut sandy hair, a long neck, and a long, narrow face, he looked fifteen but was, Sebastian knew, eighteen.

"Excuse me," said Sebastian quietly, walking up to him. "You're Dudley Fenton, aren't you? I'm Devlin."

Fenton looked up, his mouth falling open and his silver-framed spectacles sliding down on his nose. "I am, but . . ." He swallowed. "How may I help you, my lord?"

"Your brother Matthew told me I might find you here. I have some questions I need to ask, but hopefully it won't take too much of your time. Perhaps we could go for a walk in the gardens?"

"Yes, of course," said the younger man, quickly closing his book and pushing to his feet.

"It's about Upcott and the others, isn't it?" said Fenton as they strolled the central path of the museum's sad, cold-nipped gardens. "You've noticed it, too?"

Sebastian looked over at him. "Noticed what?"

"The pattern I was telling Matthew about."

"What pattern?"

"I thought . . . That is to say . . ." Fenton looked puzzled. "Then what was it you wished to speak to me about?"

"I'm told you had an argument out at Chalk Farm Tavern with Upcott, Toole, and their friends a month or two ago."

The younger man's normally pale cheeks blazed with embarrassment. He swallowed hard and looked away. "Heard about that, did you?"

"Yes."

"You're generous to call it an argument." His voice cracked, and when he spoke again, it was in a whisper. "It was the most mortifying experience of my life."

"Why were you out there?"

"At Chalk Farm? We'd been watching the sunset from the top of Primrose Hill and decided to stop for a drink at the tavern before heading back to London."

"You and who else?"

"George Babcock. He was sent down from Cambridge with me, you know."

"Is he still in London?"

Fenton shook his head. "His father, Lord Babcock, kept insisting he return to Derbyshire, so he finally gave in and went."

"When?"

"When did he leave London? It must be three weeks ago now. Why?"

"Just wondering," said Sebastian. "I'm told the tavern keeper, Alison Cross, stepped in to try to stop what they were doing. Is that true?"

Fenton nodded. "She did, yes. So then they turned on her. They were like a pack of wild dogs sensing a new prey. I'd never seen anything like it."

"Did you know the man who intervened and made them let her go?"

"Did someone?" Fenton flushed again. "I didn't know someone did. As soon as she distracted them, Babcock and I left." He swallowed. "It's not something I'm proud of."

"Was there a particular reason those men picked on you that night?"

"A reason? Not that I know of. They've always been like that. I can remember my brother James talking about them when he was up at Eton."

"They were there at the same time as your brother?"

Fenton nodded. "He used to call them the Fomorians."

It struck Sebastian as a telling nickname. The Fomorians were a supernatural race of monsters from Irish mythology who were said to be the personifications of chaos, darkness, and death. He drew the wooden wolf from his pocket and held it out. "Have you ever seen this before?"

Fenton paused to take the carving in his hands and turn it over thoughtfully. "No. Why?"

"It was found near where Toole was killed."

"On Primrose Hill?"

"Yes."

"It's a beautiful piece, isn't it?" He ran his fingertips over the pattern incised in the wolf's flank. "That's a Dara knot, you know."

"A what?"

Fenton looked up. "A Dara knot; it's a kind of Celtic knot. You see how all the lines are interwoven so that they have no beginning or end? It's a symbol of eternity and inner strength. The word 'Dara' is said to come from the same root as the Irish word 'doirc,' for oak. Some people think 'Druid' comes from the same root."

"You're interested in the Celts?" said Sebastian.

"I'm interested in their myths—all myths, actually. It's a fascinating subject, don't you think? The way virtually the same stories reappear over and over again with only slight variations in civilizations thousands of miles—and thousands of years—apart. It's why Babcock and I were rusticated. We wrote this essay comparing the Egyptian, Greek, and Celtic myths about resurrected gods with, well, you know." He cleared his throat uncomfortably. "I thought it was fascinating. The dons thought it was blasphemous."

"It's only been five years since Percy Shelley was sent down from Oxford for much the same thing, so you're in good company."

Fenton gave him a grateful smile, then said, "But you do see the pattern I was talking about, don't you?"

Sebastian shook his head. "What pattern?"

"How the three of them were killed. Keebles was drowned, Toole was burned, and now Upcott has been hanged!"

"That's significant?"

"Yes! It's the threefold death."

"The what?"

His voice rising with excitement, Fenton handed the wolf carving back to Sebastian. "There are actually two kinds of threefold deaths. The first tends to involve kings, heroes, or gods, and it's where one person dies simultaneously in three different ways. You know—like the fellow who got shot with an arrow, then hit on the head by a boulder that knocked him into a lake so that he drowned. But there's another kind of threefold death that refers to the methods of killing that Lucan says the Celts used for their human sacrifices."

Sebastian remembered Emmanuel Royston-Jones saying that Fenton and Babcock had been talking about the first-century AD Roman author Lucan the night Toole and his friends picked on them. "And what does Lucan say?"

"In his poem *De Bello Civili*, Lucan says that Celtic human sacrifices to the god Taranis were burnt, those to Teutates were drowned, and the ones to Esus were hanged from trees. Of course, Upcott wasn't exactly hanged from a tree, but he was hanged from a wooden scaffold, which is basically the same thing, when you think about it. And Keebles was drowned, while Toole was burnt!"

Sebastian felt a chill crawl up his spine.

"We think Taranis was a sky god, while Teutates was a water god and Esus a vegetation god." Fenton looked at him expectantly, his eyes gleaming with a scholar's excitement behind his spectacles. "So it fits, don't you think?"

"Yes," said Sebastian. "It fits."

Chapter 17

His thoughts in a dark place, Sebastian left the British Museum and went looking for Erasmus Inkberry. But according to his housekeeper, the Celtic scholar had traveled down to Kent to study an ancient hill fort and wasn't expected home until sometime Tuesday. Frustrated, Sebastian went back to his curricle, leapt up into the high seat, and gathered the reins.

"Yer doin' it again," said Tom.

Sebastian glanced back at his tiger. "Doing what?"

"Jist sittin' there, staring at the street."

Sebastian laughed and gave his horses the office to start.

He drove next to Tower Hill, where he found the door to the stone outbuilding at the base of the garden standing open and

Paul Gibson bent over the naked, eviscerated corpse of Phineas Upcott.

"Can you tell me anything yet?" said Sebastian, pausing in the open doorway, his hands braced against the frame.

Gibson set aside his scalpel with a clatter and reached for a rag to wipe his hands. "Not a lot. Probably the only thing of interest is that he was strangled first, and then someone tied that rope around his neck and dangled him off the scaffolding where he was found."

"He was already dead when he was hanged?"

"Either dead or close to it."

"So the hanging was staged?"

"Essentially, yes."

Sebastian let his hands drop to his sides. "They were all staged. Keebles was stabbed before being thrown in the Thames, Toole was shot before being burned, and now Upcott was strangled before he was hanged."

"I hadn't thought about it that way, but you're right."

Sebastian swore under his breath and turned to look out over the dreary, wet garden.

Gibson came to stand beside him. After a moment, he said, "Do you have any idea what's going on?"

Sebastian watched a couple of small fieldfares peck at the windfall apples that Gibson's lover, Alexi, had left for the birds. "A rather earnest eighteen-year-old scholar recently sent down from Cambridge thinks it's a reenactment of the human sacrifices described by Lucan."

Gibson pulled at one earlobe. "Remind me who he was again?"

"Marcus Annaeus Lucanus, a first-century poet. He was born

in Córdoba, Spain, but his mother was the sister of Seneca the Younger, Nero's tutor, so Lucan went off to what everyone expected would be a brilliant career in Rome. His only surviving poem was on the civil war between Julius Caesar and the Roman Senate. He was very young when he wrote it, and then he fell afoul of Nero and was ordered to commit suicide or suffer hideous consequences. So he opened his veins and died reciting his own poetry. He was twenty-five."

"Lovely," said Gibson.

Sebastian nodded. "Ever hear the expression 'History has a cruel sense of humor; it repeats itself'? That was Lucan. He also said, 'Truth is the first casualty of war,' and 'Absolute power corrupts absolutely.' "

"A wise man. Pity he died so young." Gibson was silent for a moment. Then he said, "You think your nephew is in danger?"

"Of his group of six friends, three are now dead."

"It's interesting that if someone is intent on going after all six of them, he didn't kill your nephew the same night he killed Toole. Bayard was there, wasn't he?"

Sebastian looked over at his friend. "He was. And you're right, it is puzzling."

"So why spare Bayard while murdering his friend?"

Sebastian shook his head. He could think of at least one very good explanation, but it was troubling enough that he kept it to himself.

The town house Bayard had inherited from his father, the previous Lord Wilcox, stood in St. James's Square, off Piccadilly. It was the same house to which Sebastian's half sister, Amanda, had come as an eighteen-year-old bride decades earlier, and she had continued as its mistress in the years since her husband's death. But with Bayard's recent marriage, that situation was surely changing. And as Sebastian climbed the front steps to the house's neoclassical portico, he found himself wondering how his sister could possibly adjust to her new situation.

"My lord," intoned Amanda's butler with a bow, opening the front door.

No, not Amanda's, Sebastian reminded himself. *Bayard's butler.* "Crowley," he said evenly.

"Lord Wilcox is in the library," said Crowley in the same carefully colorless voice. "I've been instructed to show you in right away."

"Expecting me, is he?" said Sebastian, following the butler across the marble-tiled entry hall.

"Anxiously, my lord."

He found Bayard standing at the library windows, his gaze on the wet square outside. He was in his shirtsleeves, his cravat gone, his collar askew, his silk waistcoat hanging unbuttoned. He held a half-empty brandy glass in one hand; a day's growth of beard shadowed his plump, pale cheeks, and Sebastian suspected he'd never made it to his bed last night.

"There you are," said Bayard, turning abruptly to face him as Crowley bowed himself out. "You've seen this morning's papers?"

"About Phineas Upcott, you mean?" said Sebastian. "Yes."

Bayard sucked in a quick breath that shuddered his chest. "Do you believe me now? That someone is killing us? One by one?"

"Do you know why?"

"I keep telling you, no!" He drained his brandy, then raised the empty glass toward Sebastian. "Want some?"

"Thank you, but no," said Sebastian. "You might consider going a little easy on it yourself."

Bayard snorted and turned away to slosh more brandy into his glass. "You sound like my mother. She's out with Fanny shopping for baby things. My lovely new bride is increasing, you know."

"No, I didn't know. Congratulations."

Bayard waved his glass through the air in a mockingly magnanimous gesture and bowed. "Thank you, thank you. I've done my duty; the succession is secured—assuming it's a boy, of course. So now I can die and no one would need even pretend to care."

Bayard's tendency toward self-pity had always been one of his more unattractive characteristics. Sebastian ignored it. "I need you to tell me again—honestly—what you were doing on Primrose Hill the night Toole was killed."

"I told you! We were drinking at Chalk Farm Tavern, and Toole took it into his head that he wanted to climb the damned hill. I told him it was a cork-brained idea, but there was no dissuading him."

"Did you try to dissuade him?"

"Of course I tried. I was ape drunk! You think I wanted to go tramping around the countryside in the middle of the night? It was cold as a witch's kiss out there."

"Is that what you were arguing about in the tavern?"

Bayard took a deep swallow and nodded. "Didn't do any good, though. He said if I didn't want to go, he'd go by himself. So I said, 'Hang on; I'm coming.'"

Sebastian drew the wolf carving from his pocket and held it out. "Have you ever seen this before?"

Bayard glanced at it, then looked away, his features quivering. "No."

"You're quite certain?"

"Course I'm certain." Bayard took another quick gulp of his brandy. "Where'd you get it?"

"I found it on Primrose Hill, near where Toole died," said Sebastian, tucking the carving away. "Are you interested in the Druids or Celtic history?"

Bayard laughed. "Me? Are you roasting me?" He laughed again. "No."

"What about Marcus Toole? Was he?"

"No. I told you, he thought it was funny."

"Do you know anyone who is interested in the Celts?"

"No. What the bloody hell kind of milksop do you take me for?"

"Ever wonder why whoever killed Toole didn't kill you that night, too?"

Bayard took another deep drink. "Of course I've wondered! The only thing I can figure is they didn't see me. I walked off a ways when I went to take a piss, and then I was lying down."

"Did you see or hear anything unusual that night before you passed out?"

"Who said I passed out?"

"You did. You said you went to take a piss, tripped and fell, then passed out."

Bayard shook his head. "Don't know if I'd say that I passed out, exactly. I sat down, closed my eyes for a bit, and fell asleep."

"All right; did you see or hear anything unusual before you 'fell asleep'?"

"No."

"Are you certain you remember everything that happened from the time you left the tavern until you 'fell asleep'?"

"Yes!"

"Is it possible that someone followed you from the tavern?"

"Who would follow us?"

"Someone you'd angered, perhaps. Do you remember having a run-in a month or two ago with a knight of the road named Sid Diamond?"

Bayard's eyes widened. "Is that the highwayman's name? You think he had something to do with what happened to Toole?"

"It's possible. What about the Cambridge student you and your friends humiliated so brutally that same night?"

Bayard gave a loud, ringing laugh heavily tinged with scorn. "You can't seriously think *he* had anything to do with what happened, can you? The fellow's a namby-pamby nestle-cock."

Sebastian watched Bayard take another drink. "I understand Emmanuel Royston-Jones was with you the night you were picking on Felton."

Bayard frowned. "Was he? I can't remember for certain, but he might've been. Why? What difference does it make if he was there or not?"

"I'm wondering why he isn't your friend anymore."

"Who said he isn't? He basically lost interest in having fun when he was about to get leg shackled, and with the way he's been moping ever since the chit died, who'd want him around?" The sound of a carriage drawing up outside jerked Bayard's gaze to the window again. "Oh, lord, there they are, back already." He drained the rest of his brandy in one long pull. "Emmanuel doesn't know what a lucky break the Fates gave him."

There was no mistaking the younger man's meaning. Sebastian studied his nephew's plump, sweaty face. "What made you decide to get married, Bayard?"

"It was Mother's idea. To tell the truth, I don't know how she talked me into it. Battiest thing I ever did, listening to her." He slammed down his empty glass and headed for the stairs. "You will see yourself out, won't you, Devlin? I'm off."

Sebastian was in the entry hall, shrugging into his greatcoat, when Crowley opened the door for Amanda with a deep bow.

Some steps ahead of her daughter-in-law, the Dowager Lady Wilcox paused on the threshold, her jaw tightening at the sight of her half brother. "So it is you," she said in a bored voice, stepping into the hall. "I thought I recognized the baseborn urchin walking those grays around the square. I had assumed the affectation of employing a pickpocket as your tiger would pall over time, but in that I obviously gave you too much credit."

"Good afternoon, Amanda," said Sebastian, reaching for his hat.

She was his senior by twelve years, the first child born to the marriage of the Earl of Hendon and his beautiful, wayward countess, Sophia. Like their mother, Amanda was tall and gracefully formed, with guinea-gold hair little touched by gray even in her late forties. But her features were all Hendon's, and now that she was aging, the sour nature of her character had stamped itself plainly on her face. If she had been born a boy, all that Sebastian now stood to inherit—titles, estates, and wealth—would eventually have been hers. But because she was a girl, and because the truth of his parentage remained unknown, Sebastian was the heir to everything.

And she had never forgiven him for it.

"I take it you've come to see my son," she said, jerking off her fine kid gloves and going to work on the buttons of her black satin-trimmed gray wool pelisse.

"You heard another of his friends was murdered last night?"

"I heard."

"Who do you think is killing them?"

"I have no idea. And I must insist you refrain from discussing such a disturbing topic in the presence of my daughter-in-law," she hissed as the new Lady Wilcox reached the top step and hesitated, her anxious gaze going from Amanda to Sebastian.

Born Miss Francis Leadmont, she was a quiet, unassuming girl, neither pretty nor plain, with mousy blond hair and gray eyes. It was in many ways a brilliant match for the fifth daughter of Baron Leadmont. Her family might be noble and respectable, but they were neither wealthy nor well-connected. And with so many sisters and four brothers besides to be provided for, her dowry could only have been exceedingly modest. Yet Sebastian still couldn't help but wonder what kind of father would give an innocent seventeen-year-old girl in marriage to a man with Bayard's reputation. She struck him as young, unsure of herself, and frightened.

"Lady Wilcox," said Sebastian with a bow.

The girl colored noticeably as she sank into a deep schoolroom curtsy. "My lord."

"Lord Devlin was just leaving," said Amanda.

Sebastian glanced at his sister and said quietly, "If you know anything, you would do well to tell me, Amanda."

"Don't be absurd," she said, her nostrils flaring. "Good day, Devlin."

"Good day, Amanda," he said with a wry smile, touching one hand to the brim of his hat.

He was aware of his sister's malevolent gaze burning into his back as he walked away. Sister and brother had never been close, even as children, for she had hated him from the day of his birth. It had taken Sebastian many years to understand why, although the depths of her hatred still had the power to shock him. But Sebastian knew his sister well enough to know that what he saw in her face today was not only hatred; it was fear. For some reason, Amanda was afraid of him.

Afraid of what he might discover.

Chapter 18

That afternoon, Hero drove across the river to listen to Herr Friedrich Accum present a lecture at Blackfriars Rotunda on the harmful substances regularly added to British foods, drinks, beauty products, and medicines.

A large four-story brick building with a curved central portico, the Rotunda lay on the south bank of the Thames, near the approach to Blackfriars Bridge in that part of London known as Southwark. Dating back to the late 1780s, the building had originally housed the Leverian natural history collection before being adapted by the Surrey Institution for research and education in the fields of science, literature, and music. Its large round central room was frequently used for lectures that were open to the public.

Still wearing her sedate navy carriage gown and plain hat,

Hero took her place on one of the Rotunda's long benches, then listened in growing horror to the German chemist's presentation.

"There is death in our pots!" thundered Accum in his heavily accented but precise English. "Much of ze food ve eat no longer comes from farmers but from merchants, and far too many of those merchants use dangerous, newly discovered chemicals to 'improve' ze taste or appearance of their products. They use arsenic for everything from food coloring to vallpaper paste; there is alum in much of our bread; lead chromate is added to mustard to improve its color; there is even sulfate of copper in pickles! These merchants are *poisoning* us, and ve have no laws to stop them. Robbers and murderers are hanged for their crimes, but unscrupulous food producers take our money and kill us, then laugh all ze vay to ze bank. Something must be done!"

Afterward, Hero waited patiently to one side while Accum accepted the thanks of various members of his audience. But he soon made his way through the dispersing crowd to her.

"Lady Devlin!" he said with a deep, formal bow. Now in his early forties, he was a plump-faced man with an aquiline nose, full lips, and thick dark hair. Normally the German was cheerful and expansive, but today there was a nervous edge to his smile. "This is an honor—a great honor, indeed."

"Your lecture was both sobering and frightening," said Hero as they turned to walk together toward the front of the building.

"It *is* frightening. And ze men doing it von't stop unless they are forced to do so. If you can believe it, I have received death threats. Death threats, for trying to save people's lives! They vant me to shut up so they can keep on poisoning people for profit."

"Have you reported these threats to Bow Street?"

"I have. But far too many of ze men doing this are extraordinarily vealthy and powerful." He fixed her with a thoughtful, steady gaze and said, "But you did not come here today simply to listen to my lecture, did you, my lady? Do I take it you're here because of ze recent deaths of those three young gentlemen?"

"I won't deny it's a contributing factor. According to Lady Keebles, you recently sued her son and his friends for nearly burning down your house."

"Ya, I did—for all ze good it did me."

"When was this?"

"Ze explosion? Last September." They had reached the building's wide double doors, and he paused at the top of the curving steps, his gaze on the gray, sullen river spreading out before them. "They had made arrangements ahead of time for one of my private chemistry lessons, you see. But as soon as they arrived, I could tell they'd been drinking heavily. I gently suggested it might be better if ve vere to reschedule, but they vould have none of it. I vas afraid they'd become belligerent if I attempted to turn them avay, so I decided ze visest course vould be to simply go ahead vith things." He sighed. "A mistake, obviously. They refused to listen to my instructions and set about mixing chemicals together all higgledy-piggledy. That is the English expression, is it not? 'Higgledy-piggledy'?"

"It is, yes. And that caused an explosion?"

"It did. And started a fire. They thought it hilarious and became angry vith me for trying to interfere vith their 'fun' by putting it out. One of them—Keebles—vent so far as to physically restrain me vhile his friends set about throwing things on ze fire, chanting, 'Burn it down! Burn it down!' They even tore ze curtains from ze vindows and tossed them on ze fire. Fortunately, ze heavy cloth smothered ze flames."

"How did you get rid of them?"

Accum cleared his throat. "By that time, Keebles had relaxed his grip on me to ze point I vas able to free myself from his grasp. I then chased ze lot of them out ze house vith a poker. Vhen I first snatched it up and threatened them vith it, they laughed at me. So I set about svinging it. Gave one a good whack across ze back of ze shoulders and brought it down on another one's forearm vhen he tried to use one of my chairs to shift the curtains off ze fire. That's vhen they ran."

"Let me guess: When you tried to sue them for the damage they'd done to your house, they then sued you for assault?"

Accum nodded sadly. "In ze end, ze magistrate convinced both parties to drop our suits. Except those—those—" He muttered something, something she didn't quite catch, then sucked in a deep, steadying breath and said more calmly, "They vere left vith a few bruises, vhile I had over a thousand pounds' worth of damages. A thousand pounds!"

"I'm so sorry," said Hero.

"It's ze vay of our vorld." He paused, his forehead wrinkling with a nervous frown. "Do I need to vorry? Because they destroyed my house and now someone has killed three of them? Am I a suspect?"

"I don't think so," said Hero. "They seem to have done this sort of thing with alarming regularity."

Accum nodded again. "I've met their kind before, in Hanover. Vealthy, pampered young men raised with a dangerous belief in their own innate superiority and no regard for others. I probably shouldn't say it, but frankly, those men got vhat they deserved."

Hero met his troubled gaze. "That seems to be a common sentiment."

Chapter 19

"Herr Friedrich Accum doesn't strike me as a man who could easily sustain a thousand-pound loss," said Sebastian later, as he and Hero took advantage of a break in the rain to go for a walk with the boys in the park. But since the boys had to stop and stomp in every puddle, they were making little progress. He was thankful Guinevere had fallen asleep in her mother's arms; otherwise the little girl would have been howling to get down and join her brothers.

"I had the impression it hurt," said Hero, shifting the baby's weight. "And he obviously has something of a temper, given that he chased the lot of them out of his house with a poker—and managed to get in a few hits, too."

"Good for him."

Hero met his smiling eyes. "My feelings exactly."

His smile faded. "I wonder how much he knows about Celtic gods."

Hero shook her head. "I can see Accum being pushed to murder someone in a fit of rage. But to methodically pick them off, one by one, and then pose their bodies in ways that echo ancient human sacrifices? That suggests something more than simple anger over an unsuccessful suit, don't you think?"

Sebastian drew a deep, troubled breath. "It does, doesn't it?"

They walked along in silence for a time, watching Patrick and Simon race each other to the next puddle. Hero said, "I keep thinking about the awful things Bayard said to you about his marriage. If he felt that way, why did he agree to the wedding in the first place? It's one thing for him to say his mother talked him into it, but I can't begin to imagine how she managed to do so."

"Unless Fanny was already with child."

Hero looked over at him. "Do you think she was?"

"I don't know. She's little more than a child herself. But it would explain it."

"That poor girl."

"I wouldn't say she looks happy."

"I can't imagine being married to Bayard," said Hero, wincing as Simon stomped hard enough to send muddy water flying up into Patrick's face; Patrick laughed. She said, "You're certain Bayard recognized that wooden carving?"

Sebastian nodded. "He's seen it before, and the fact that I now have it worries him."

"Interesting. I wonder why."

"I have no idea," said Sebastian, reaching out to take Guinevere as the baby stirred. "But it obviously wasn't dropped on that hill by some neo-Druid celebrating Samhain. It's tied—*somehow*—to what happened up there to Marcus Toole. But I'll be damned if I can figure out how."

The brief winter daylight was beginning to fade from the cloudy sky by the time Sebastian ordered his curricle brought round and set out for Bow Street. It was only half past three, but the sun was already low on the horizon, dropping the temperature below freezing and filling the wet, miserable streets of the city with icy shadows. Leaving his horses in Tom's care, he was about to mount the public office's shallow front steps when he encountered Sir Samuel Toole in the company of a roughly dressed, short, squat man with a scarf wrapped across the lower part of his face. For an instant, the unknown man's watery blue gaze met Sebastian's. Then the man bowed jerkily to Toole and walked quickly away.

Unlike many men of his age, Sir Samuel had long ago abandoned the powdered wig, frock coat, and knee breeches that had been de rigueur in his youth. He wore fashionable knitted pantaloons and a fine black double-breasted tailcoat and had his hair cropped short. But his open greatcoat was slipping off his shoulders, his silk waistcoat had been buttoned askew, and it looked as if he'd cut his face while shaving. At the sight of Sebastian, he drew up abruptly, his fist clenching on his ivory-handled walking stick.

"Sir Samuel," said Sebastian with a bow, pausing beside him. "Please allow me to express my sincere condolences on the death of your son."

Marcus Toole's father stared at him with an undisguised hostility Sebastian couldn't begin to explain. "If you're thinking of meddling in this murder investigation the way you have in so many others, let me save you the bother by telling you straight out that your services are neither needed nor wanted. Bow Street and I have already ascertained precisely who killed my son and his friends, and I have every expectation of seeing the villain remanded into custody and hanged. And now, good day to you, sir," he said with a curt nod.

Then he pushed past Sebastian to where a footman held open the door of the Baronet's waiting black-bodied carriage. Breathing heavily, he stomped up the carriage steps, barked an order to his coachman, and drove off.

"So who does Sir Samuel think killed his son?" Sebastian asked Lovejoy a few minutes later as the two men settled at a table in a nearby coffeehouse. By now the last traces of light had leached from the day, leaving the richly paneled room lit only by lamplight and the crackling fire on the wide hearth.

The magistrate looked pained. "Damion Pitcairn."

Sebastian stared at him. *"Pitcairn?"* Born in Jamaica to a Scottish father and an enslaved African woman, Damion Pitcairn was a talented young violinist and composer attached to the opera. But he was also a brilliant, well-respected fencing master, and Sebastian had known him for some time. "Why?"

Lovejoy took a cautious sip of his hot chocolate. "It seems Marcus Toole and his friends had a run-in with Pitcairn down in Southwark several weeks before Keebles was killed."

"That's not good," said Sebastian after a moment.

"Indeed. You know he's a Spencean?" said Lovejoy. "Pitcairn, I mean."

Sebastian hesitated, then nodded. The Society of Spencean Philanthropists traced its origins to a passionate reformer named Thomas Spence. An advocate of such revolutionary notions as universal suffrage, the equality of the sexes, and society's responsibility to care for orphaned children, the aged, and those unable to work, Spence had been imprisoned multiple times for "seditious libel" and on charges of high treason. Thanks to the unhealthy conditions common in London's prisons, he'd been dead now for two years. But his movement lived on, closely watched by government spies and loathed by the likes of Lord Jarvis, the Prince Regent, and the Home Secretary, Lord Sidmouth. Recently, the Spenceans had held what they called a "mass public meeting" on the outskirts of London at a place called Spa Fields near Clerkenwell. The meeting had attracted over ten thousand people and produced a petition calling on the Prince Regent to do something to relieve the general distress caused by the ending of the French and American wars and the severe economic downturn that had followed. But the Regent had refused even to look at their petition because, he said, they weren't authorized to present one.

"Is that what Toole and his friends' confrontation with Pitcairn was about?" said Sebastian.

"It may have played into it. Personally, I consider it a ridiculous notion, but that doesn't mean people won't listen to Sir Samuel. Both the Palace and my colleagues at Bow Street are desperate to find someone to pin the killings on, and if they can blame someone tied to these Spa Fields meetings, so much the better. You know they've another one planned for next week? On Monday."

Mondays were always a good choice for this sort of thing, since artisans and craftsman had for centuries taken the day off:

"Saint Monday," it was traditionally called. Sebastian said, "I'd heard there was to be another but didn't realize it was so soon."

Lovejoy drew a grubby folded broadsheet from his pocket. "They appear to be quite . . . angry."

Sebastian unfolded the page and found himself staring at a cheap handbill.

ENGLAND

Expects every Man to do his Duty!!!

The Next Meeting in Spa Fields will Take Place on

Monday, December 2nd. 1816

to receive the answer of the PETITION to the

PRINCE REGENT, determined upon

at the last meeting held in the same place,

and for other important Considerations.

THE PRESENT STATE OF GREAT BRITAIN!

Four Million in Distress!!!

Four Million Embarrassed!!!

One and a half Million fear Distress!!!

Half a Million live in Splendid Luxury!!!

Death would now be a relief to Millions.

Arrogance, Folly, and Crimes

have brought affairs to this dread Crisis.

Only Firmness and Integrity can save the Country!!!

He looked up. "Prinny should have agreed to accept the petition they sent to him after the first meeting ten days ago. Even if he intended to completely disregard it, he could have given them the impression he was listening. That he cared."

"Yes, it would have been wiser," said the magistrate quietly. "Henry Hunt has agreed to speak again."

Sebastian wasn't surprised. A prosperous farmer turned political reformer, Henry "Orator" Hunt had become famous by using his prodigious talent for public speaking to champion the causes of what he called the "working classes." His speech at the November Spa Fields meeting, delivered from the second-floor window of a tavern called Merlin's Cave, had shocked many by attacking both the Whigs and the Tories, accusing the Whigs of cowardly complacency and dangerous complicity.

Lovejoy carefully refolded the tattered handbill. "Incidentally, we spoke to the proprietor of the White Horse in Piccadilly. It seems some half a dozen of their customers—as well as the cook and the proprietor himself—fell ill after eating a stew they served Friday night, although others who consumed the same meal were fine. So it doesn't sound likely that Upcott's illness was the result of a deliberate attempt to keep him and Bridgewood away from Chalk Farm."

"No, it doesn't, does it?"

Lovejoy frowned as he tucked the handbill back in his pocket. "Sir Lawrence Upcott is expected to arrive in London sometime tomorrow, but fortunately we were able to complete a thorough search of his son's rooms this morning."

"And?"

Lovejoy shook his head. "Nothing. I also asked Sir Samuel, once again, to authorize a search of his son's rooms, but he's still refusing. Seems the idea of such an invasion of Marcus's privacy is almost as revolting as the autopsy I ordered. So I contacted Lady

Keebles again, asking her to reconsider. Not only did she refuse our request, but several hours later we received a directive from the Home Office ordering us to stop 'harassing' the bereaved parents."

Sebastian met his friend's gaze. "Marcus Toole's father is a longtime friend of Lord Sidmouth, isn't he?"

"He is, yes," said Lovejoy.

Sebastian took a slow sip of his coffee, but it was cold. "None of this sounds good for Pitcairn."

Lovejoy met his gaze and nodded solemnly. "No. It's not."

Chapter 20

Damion Pitcairn, violin case in hand, was descending the cracked front steps of the aged building where he kept a room when Sebastian walked up to him. At the sight of Sebastian, he paused, the flickering light from the oil lamp mounted above the building's door flaring across his tense, fine-boned face.

Sebastian had known the swordsmith and musician since the previous summer. He was young, still in his early twenties, tall and slim, with tawny skin, thick dark hair, and eyes the color of a sun-washed meadow. Talented and brilliant, he was fiercely passionate about the sort of things that could get a man labeled a dangerous revolutionary—things like democracy, secret ballots, and the abolition of aristocratic rights and privileges. He was also the kind of man willing to take risks for the things he believed in, and that made him vulnerable.

"One of your friends from Bow Street just left," said Pitcairn, his face closed and unreadable. "A Constable McCarthy. He promised to arrange things with the hangman so that when they string me up outside Newgate I'll take at least thirty minutes to slowly strangle to death. Very slowly."

"I take it you don't need me to tell you that you've emerged as the prime suspect in Bow Street's investigation into the murders of Marcus Toole and his friends?"

Pitcairn shifted his grip on his violin case and turned to walk toward the King's Theatre in the Haymarket. "No."

Sebastian fell into step beside him. "It doesn't help that you're a known Spencean."

A muscle jumped along Pitcairn's clenched jaw. "There's no law against it."

"Not yet. But the public meetings at Spa Fields have thrown the Palace and the Home Office into something of a panic. They might not have been prepared for the popularity of the first one, but they're going to be ready next time."

Eyes narrowing, Pitcairn glanced over at Sebastian. "You know something?"

"No. But I know Jarvis and Sidmouth. And now we have Sir Samuel Toole telling Bow Street that you murdered his son and his son's friends because of some confrontation in Southwark. What the hell happened?"

Pitcairn looked away. For a moment, Sebastian didn't think he would answer. Then he said, "They went after a friend of mine who was distributing handbills near St. George the Martyr."

"What kind of handbills?"

"Advertising the first Spa Fields meeting. I . . . stopped them."

The area south of the Thames was a historically impoverished part of London. Sebastian said, "What were such fine sprigs of the ton doing in Southwark?"

"That I couldn't tell you."

"How many of them were there?"

"Five."

"Not six?"

Pitcairn shook his head. "Bridgewood, Toole, Upcott, Keebles, and—" He paused, then added, "Your nephew, Lord Wilcox."

"How do you happen to know them by name?"

The fencing master's lip curled. "I used to give Marcus Toole and Theo Bridgewood fencing lessons. The others would frequently hang around and watch."

"So you know Emmanuel Royston-Jones, too?"

"Yes." Pitcairn glanced over at him. "Why?"

"He wasn't with the others when they confronted your friend in Southwark?"

"No."

"When did the fencing lessons stop?"

"September."

"Any particular reason?"

"Sir Samuel learned of my association with certain individuals involved in what he called 'treasonous activities.'"

"And it was shortly afterward that Theo Bridgewood and the others confronted your friend in Southwark?"

Pitcairn nodded. "Bridgewood took a handbill, then laughed, crumpled it up, and threw it in my—my friend's face." The hesitation was slight but there. "I told them to stop it, so they turned on me. I remember Toole smiling and saying, 'Looks like you forgot to bring your sword, Sir Galahad. Too bad.'"

"Two against five aren't good odds."

"No," agreed Pitcairn. "I assume they were counting on that. But the parish had been doing some repairs on the church and had a stack of poles for scaffolding piled up nearby. I grabbed one and tossed another to my friend." Pitcairn's eyes creased with a hint of a smile. "Not proper shillelaghs, of course, but they worked."

"I didn't know you were familiar with Irish stick fighting."

Pitcairn shrugged. "Stick fighting uses many of the same skills and requires the same agility as fencing. Bridgewood and his friends . . . ran away."

"Men like that don't usually forgive or forget."

"I'd noticed."

"Did they come at you again?"

"Not yet."

"And now three of the five are dead."

"Not by my hand."

Sebastian studied the other man's half-averted profile. "Care to tell me the name of your handbill-dispensing friend?"

Pitcairn gave a slow smile. "I think not."

They had almost reached the King's Theatre. The usual assortment of young bucks had already gathered around the side entrance, ogling, groping, and shouting crude suggestions at the opera dancers trying to push their way through to the stage door. One of the dark-haired dancers, a tall, lean young woman with golden skin and familiar, delicate features, turned her head toward them. Sebastian watched as, for one telling moment, her gaze met Pitcairn's, and Sebastian knew where he had seen her before: dressed as a boy and fencing with Pitcairn.

"If I were you," said Sebastian "I would advise your 'friend' to avoid handing out Spencean broadsheets, at least for a while. And I'd stay away from next week's meeting at Spa Fields."

Pitcairn turned to look at him, his face hardened. "You have no idea what it's like to be me. Or my 'friend.'"

Sebastian drew up. "You're right; I don't. But I have a pretty good idea what Jarvis and his ilk are capable of."

"There are more important things than survival."

"I won't argue that. Just . . . be careful."

Sebastian was turning away when his gaze fell on a roughly dressed young man of perhaps thirty who was loitering near the arched entrance to the coaching yard of the George, a busy inn lying just across the street from the theater. He wore nondescript kerseymere breeches and a buttoned-up olive green coat and was quite ordinary-looking, with a snub nose and dark blond hair cut short. It was only by chance that Sebastian had noticed the man earlier, staring with apparent interest at the window display of a confectioner two doors down from Pitcairn's lodgings.

Settling his hat lower on his forehead, Sebastian began to stroll back toward where he had left Tom with the curricle. He thought it likely the man had been sent by Bow Street to keep an eye on Pitcairn. But then Olive Coat pulled a watch from his pocket and appeared to study it for a moment before turning to follow Sebastian.

Acutely aware of his shadow, Sebastian swung onto the first quiet lane that opened up beside him, then turned immediately left, into the more brightly lit Oxendon Street. The man stayed behind him, not gaining but not falling behind, either. Halfway up the street, Sebastian stopped to admire the window display of a plated-goods dealer. Olive Coat paused, too, his attention seemingly caught by a passing dowager's landau. But when Sebastian continued on, the man once more fell into step behind him.

At the next corner, Sebastian drew up abruptly and turned to stride back the way he had come. Caught off guard, Olive Coat swung away to gaze intently at the dusty window of an umbrella shop. Sebastian walked right up to him and said, "Why the devil are you following me?"

The man's eyes widened. Then he whirled and took off.

Sebastian tore after him.

They raced back down Oxendon Street, careened onto Panton. Erupting back into the surging, lamplit crowds of the Haymarket, Olive Coat darted in front of a heavily laden coal wagon that pulled up sharply, its team of six shaggy shires snorting and plunging, the irate driver shouting, "What the bleedin' 'ell?" as Sebastian raced past him.

A man in the scarlet frock coat, drab hat, and white trousers of a coachman spun around as Olive Coat slammed into him and then took off running again. Sebastian dodged the coachman, a blind man playing a flute, a middle-aged woman with a basket of hothouse flowers on her head, and a skinny black dog eating a discarded sausage beside the doorway of a shuttered cheesemonger.

But Olive Coat was deliberately leaving a trail of havoc in his wake. He flung up a hand to smack the handles of the soot-encrusted brushes held across the shoulders of a tired chimney sweep on his way home, sending the tools tumbling across the pavement, so that Sebastian had to leap over them as he ran on. Olive Coat tipped over the red-and-white-striped booth of a

Punch and Judy show at the corner of Little Suffolk Street, the audience howling as the portly, bald-headed professor tumbled out, his sock puppets still on his flailing hands. Then, after upsetting a man bent beneath a heavy trunk at the entrance to the Queen's Head, Olive Coat darted out into the street again. Nimbly hopping over a steaming pile of manure, he rammed a sedan chair, knocking over the lead porter and sending the white-haired, elderly passenger flying.

Aware of Olive Coat disappearing up the street, Sebastian stopped to help the trembling gentleman to his feet and offered to buy him a drink.

The old man accepted.

It was several hours later before Sebastian was able to tuck his elderly new friend into another sedan chair and send him on his way home. He returned to Brook Street, picked up a specialized set of skeleton keys popularly known as a picklock, and headed toward St. James's Street.

Running from Piccadilly down to the redbrick Tudor bulk of St. James's Palace, St. James's Street was the heart of London's fashionable male world. This was the site of White's, Brooks's, and various other exclusive gentlemen's clubs; of Berry Bros. and Rudd wine merchants; of Lock and Co. hatter; and numerous other famous establishments that catered exclusively to wealthy, privileged men. The rooms kept by Marcus Toole lay in a small gaslit court off St. James's Place. Typical of those in the area given over to fashionable young bachelors and the mountebanks and sycophants who fed off them, the buildings clustered around the court were respectable without being too expensive for a young man still subsisting on an allowance from his parent. As Sebastian let himself in the front door of the building on the left and climbed the darkened staircase to the second floor, he found himself wondering what it said about the relationship between Sir Samuel Toole and his only son and heir that Marcus had chosen to keep bachelor quarters here rather than remaining under the paternal roof.

The third skeleton key on Sebastian's picklock set tripped the old warded lock on the door to Toole's rooms. Quickly letting himself in, Sebastian eased the door closed behind him, then paused for a moment, his gaze drifting over the darkened front room. The space was lit only by the dim light cast by the gas lamps in the court below, but Sebastian's ability to see clearly at night had always been unusually acute.

The room was carelessly but fashionably furnished with a burgundy silk settee, a high-backed brocade armchair, a bulky Chippendale chest that looked as if it dated back to the eighteenth century, and a newer, classically styled mahogany table positioned below the front window. Between Lovejoy's request that Toole's valet avoid disturbing anything in the rooms and the valet's own shock and grief, the place appeared to still be essentially as Toole had left it Saturday evening. The table was littered with a pile of newspapers and a jumble of random objects that included racing guides, a riding crop, and a crumpled cravat; a boot lay discarded just inside the front door, with its mate halfway across the room. A couple of dirty crystal glasses stood near a half-empty carafe of brandy on a table beside the cold hearth; near it lay a portfolio that opened to reveal a collection of graphic satires making fun of everything from the deposed French emperor to henpecked husbands and pretentious cits. There was not a book in sight—at least, not if one discounted the *Debrett's Peerage* lying on the floor near one of the chairs.

Sebastian worked his way quickly around the room, then moved on to the small, shadowy bedroom beyond. Toole's neatly made bed was still turned down, its pillows plumped, just as his valet had left it in readiness for his master's return before retiring to his own bed in the attic on that fateful night.

Aware of a growing sense of futility, Sebastian set about methodically searching this room. He didn't know exactly what he was looking for, and so far he hadn't found anything unexpected. A drawer in a high chest near the door held an array of vowels and tradesmen's bills, but nothing exorbitant or shocking. A heavily scented billet-doux from an admirer of the fair sex lay discarded on the floor nearby; Sebastian noted the name, then moved on to where a tattered, decades-old copy of *Harris's List of Covent-Garden Ladies* lay open on the beside chest. Once sold as a risqué guide to the area's prostitutes, the books were now collected by some as humorously erotic. Picking it up, Sebastian read:

> Liz is truly worth the money; she knows it, and is prudent enough to realize that the harvest of pleasure cannot last long. The time will come when goldfinches will fly from her ground, and none but boobies, noddies, and old carrion crows will nestle in her bush . . .

He put the book back in place and moved on.

He was searching the pockets of a dark blue morning coat cast carelessly over the back of the chair drawn up to the room's dressing table when he came across a square of cheap, somewhat grubby paper. Carefully unfolding the crackling sheet, he found himself staring at a bold, crudely printed headline:

ENGLAND

Expects every Man to do his Duty!!!

The Next Meeting in Spa Fields will Take Place on

Monday, December 2nd 1816 . . .

A loud burst of male laughter from the courtyard outside jerked Sebastian's attention to the window. Tucking the broadsheet into his own pocket, he waited until he heard the men stagger up the stairs, still laughing and calling to each other as they shut the door to one of the sets of rooms on the third floor.

Then he slipped quietly from Toole's rooms and locked the door behind him.

Chapter 21

Tuesday, 26 November

"Thought you'd be interested to hear that I finally managed to speak to m' mother about Sid Diamond," said Calhoun the next morning as Sebastian was shaving.

Sebastian looked over at him. "And?"

"Seems he's been on the high toby for a little over a year, since a few months after he was shipped back from France. Hasn't killed anyone that she knows of—well, apart from when he was off at war, of course. Seems he's acquired something of a reputation for what I suppose you might call 'gallantry.' Says she's never heard anything to his discredit."

Sebastian reached for the towel Calhoun was holding out and dried his face. "Apart from the fact that he robs people at gunpoint."

Calhoun smiled. "Well, yes; except for that."

Half an hour later, Sebastian met Hendon for an early-morning ride in Hyde Park, as had become their habit when both men were in London. At this time of year the sun was still hovering below the horizon, coloring the sky a bright yellow and orange. It was cold enough that the exhalation of their breath hung around them like a mist as their horses cantered down the Row.

"Have you discovered anything? Anything at all?" Hendon asked when they reined in to a walk.

Choosing his words carefully, Sebastian looked over at the man who had raised him. "How much do you know about the activities of Bayard and his friends?"

Hendon was silent for a moment, his gaze fixed between his horse's ears, his jaw working back and forth in that way he had when he was thoughtful or troubled. "I've heard . . . murmurs. A few cryptic hints from old friends." He paused. "It's bad, is it?"

"If he and his friends were eighteen or nineteen, I know there are some who would be tempted to make excuses for them. But they're not eighteen, they're creeping up on thirty, and my concern is that what I've learned so far isn't the worst of it. I can see a group of spoiled, wealthy men with such a sense of entitlement and superiority crossing the line into the sort of behavior that is worse than ugly."

Hendon looked over at him. "What aren't you telling me?"

Sebastian shook his head. "If you've heard the rumors and hints, then you probably know as much as I do. Wanton destruction. Harassment that strays into the realm of cruelty and abuse. Beyond that I can only guess."

Hendon tightened his jaw. "I'd hoped marriage to Fanny would finally settle the lad."

"It might if he would stay home with his bride. I don't think he does."

"Damn," said Hendon softly. "I assume you know Sir Samuel Toole was in White's yesterday telling anyone who'd listen that the Radicals are behind his son's murder?"

"Did he say what this was based on?"

"Something to the effect that the Radicals know he and Lord Bridgewood are their enemies."

"And yet no one has gone after Bridgewood's son. And to my knowledge, Phineas Upcott's father has rarely left his estate in thirty years, while Gil Keebles's father is long dead." Sebastian paused, then said, "I could be wrong, but I suspect Toole's accusation comes from an article that recently appeared in one of the Radical journals, attacking the young men for their behavior."

"God help us. It's that bad? That a segment of the press has gone after them?"

"I'm afraid so."

"Do you think any of this is likely to come out at Toole's inquest?"

"No."

"When is it?"

"This afternoon. There's little doubt the jury will return a verdict of murder by party or parties unknown, and that will be it."

"The Palace will not be happy."

"No."

They rode on in silence for a time. Then Hendon said, "Did it strike you that there was something not quite right about the tale Bayard told us Saturday night?"

Sebastian hesitated, then said, "Perhaps."

Hendon swallowed, then said in a rush, "Is it possible *Bayard* is the killer?"

The question took Sebastian by surprise; he'd no idea Hendon shared his own fears. He chose his words carefully. "To be honest, I thought at first that he might be. I thought it was even possible he'd killed his friend, then passed out and not remembered doing it when he woke up. But now . . ." Sebastian shook his head. "I'm less inclined to think so. When I saw him yesterday, he struck me as genuinely frightened."

"You think he's truly in danger?"

Sebastian met Hendon's worried gaze. "I think he very well may be."

With several hours still before he needed to leave for the inquest, Sebastian went, again, in search of Erasmus Inkberry. This time he had more luck.

"Ah, Lord Devlin!" said the scholar, his craggy face breaking into a wide smile when his housekeeper showed Sebastian into the warm, overstuffed parlor. "Come in; come in and have a seat, please. I was hoping you'd return so that we might have a more extensive discussion on the question of human sacrifice in the ancient world. I fear I was not as frank as I might have been earlier." He cleared his throat. "As much as I admire Lady Devlin's formidable intellect, I still can't help but feel uncomfortable discussing such things as human sacrifice in front of the fair sex."

Diplomatically keeping his opinions on that subject to himself, Sebastian took one of the chairs offered and stretched his cold hands out to the fire. "You know there's been another murder? This one by hanging?"

Inkberry sank into the opposite chair and nodded gravely. "I saw it in the papers, yes. It's troubling."

"It's been pointed out to me that the three deaths—one by fire, one by drowning, and one by hanging—echo a certain passage in the surviving poem of the first-century Roman writer Lucan."

Inkberry leaned forward. "Someone else noticed that, too, did they? The thing about Lucan is that he's more believable than the others because he names three specific Celtic gods to whom human sacrifices were made: Esus, Teutates, and Taranis. Although most of the details actually come from later commentators on his work—one from the fourth century and another from the ninth."

"Details such as that the sacrifices to Taranis were burned in a wooden structure that sounds very similar to Caesar's wicker man?" said Sebastian.

"Like that, yes."

Sebastian studied the glowing red coals of the fire on the hearth before him. "When I was in the Peninsula, I remember hearing about a traditional festival in northern Portugal—the Caretos festival—that ends with the burning of a wooden or wicker human effigy. And I've been told something similar occurs in Catalonia during a festival held in May."

Inkberry nodded. "I'm not surprised. Wicker giants are also still burned in various parts of France on Midsummer's Eve. And before the Revolution, even Paris would burn a wickerwork warrior at a festival they held in July. The participants would sing 'Salve Regina' to the Virgin Mary."

"It's all very suggestive, isn't it?"

"Oh, yes, very. It's quite common to substitute effigies for what were once living sacrifices. We don't like to think that our ancestors did something so barbaric, but I fear the uncomfortable truth is that the Celts very likely did at one time practice human sacrifice. After all, is there an ancient society that did not? The Assyrians, Babylonians, Canaanites, Israelites—they all did it in the past. The vestiges of the practice in the Old Testament are almost too numerous to mention. Apart from the obvious example of the story of Abraham and Issac, there are several very specific passages in Leviticus prohibiting the sacrifice of children, which surely wouldn't be there unless it had once been the society's practice. Deuteronomy, Kings, Chronicles, Jeremiah, Ezekiel . . . a critical reading can be very eye-opening. Religious practices do tend to be conservative, so I suspect something like that was difficult to stamp out."

"'Shall I give my firstborn for my transgression, the fruit of my body for the sin of my soul?'" Sebastian quoted softly.

Inkberry nodded. "Micah. That's also a good example of the ancient idea of the 'sin offering.' A person—or sometimes even an entire community—guilty of a sin would lay their hands on a victim selected to be sacrificed, thus making him their representative; then the victim would be cursed and spat at before being killed. The idea was that when the victim died, the sin would be forgiven and the holy bond with the god reestablished. In later years a goat was substituted for the human victim, which is of course where we get the term 'scapegoat.' But the idea that something—or someone—could die for our sins lingered."

He leaned back in his chair, his hands steepled before him. "I fear even the ancient Greeks had the dark practice of human sacrifice hiding in their past. We tend to associate them with the finest flowerings of civilization—art, philosophy, poetry, statesmanship—but then we read the myth of Lycaon."

"Or Polyxena," said Sebastian thoughtfully. "And Iphigenia."

"Ah, yes; poor Iphigenia. Deceived into believing she was about to be wed to Achilles, only to be sacrificed by her father, Agamemnon, so that the Greek fleet could sail to Troy. In the later mythical version of the tale, the girl is rescued at the last instant by Artemis, who magically whisks her off to safety—much as in the story of Abraham, God stops the father's hand just as he is about to sacrifice his son. But did you know there are earlier versions of that tale where Isaac does not survive? The thing is, if you see human life as the most valuable of all lives, that inevitably makes human sacrifice the greatest gift one can give to the gods, doesn't it?" He paused. "Or at least, so it seems to our eyes. But that might not have been true two thousand years ago. One can imagine a society in which the life of a prized horse, for instance, would be valued far above that of a slave."

"Or a prisoner of war," said Sebastian.

Inkberry nodded. "Remember how Achilles sacrificed twelve Trojan prisoners on the funeral pyre of his friend Patroclus?"

Sebastian leaned forward. "So revenge could play a part in the selection of a victim for sacrifice?"

"Oh, yes. There were many different reasons for making a sacrifice to the gods. After a military victory, prisoners would be sacrificed as a way to give thanks to a war god such as Mars. Other sacrifices were made to appease the gods—as in the case of Iphigeneia. Various societies even used to practice what I suppose we could call 'foundational' sacrifices. Someone, often a child or a baby, would be sacrificed for the well-being of whatever was being built and then buried beneath it—things like ramparts, bridges, houses, even sanctuaries. That practice seems to have continued in Britain into Roman times and beyond."

"That late?"

"I'm afraid so. That's the thing that aggravates me about the Roman accounts of Celtic human sacrifice. In reading them, it's easy to come away with the impression that it was only the 'barbarians' who engaged in human sacrifice, but the ugly truth is that human sacrifice wasn't officially outlawed in Rome until 97 BC, and even then the Romans still allowed what they called 'ritual killings,' like the triumphal processions held for successful generals like Caesar upon their return to Rome."

"And the gladiatorial games," said Sebastian. "So tell me this: Why the different forms of sacrifice? Burning, drowning, hanging?"

"Well, think about this: If you're worshipping an earth deity, you would bury your offering, right? And if your god is a water god, you would want to drown your sacrifice. The Norse especially liked to throw their human and animal sacrifices off cliffs and into wells. But if your god is a sky god, how else are you going to get your gift to him besides burning it?"

"I'm glad Lucan only mentioned three gods," said Sebastian.

Inkberry scrubbed one big, blunt-fingered hand across his mouth and chin. "You think this killer is deliberately following what we know of the ancient Celtic customs?"

"It seems likely, wouldn't you say?"

The scholar nodded solemnly. "Unfortunately, the Celts were also very fond of cutting off heads. They believed the soul resided in a man's head, you see. So they'd hang the heads of those they killed in war from their saddles, and then nail them to the walls of their houses and display them on the ramparts of their hill forts until they rotted and fell into the ditch."

"Good God," whispered Sebastian, his throat feeling suddenly tight. "Hopefully this killer doesn't know about that."

"What do you think are the odds?"

Sebastian met the scholar's worried gaze. "Frankly? Not good."

Chapter 22

Small and shabbily dressed, with graying dark hair, untidy side-whiskers, and rounded shoulders, the man said his name was Ian Trent. One of many struggling shoemakers clustered between Fetter Lane and Shoe Lane, he agreed to talk to Hero in exchange for her buying a pair of his ready-made baby shoes.

"And will ye be writing the truth of what I tell ye?" he said, eyeing her warily as he wrapped up her purchase in brown paper. "Or will ye be prettying it up so's all the fine ladies in their grand, comfortable houses over there in Mayfair don't need to feel bad when they read about what life has become for the likes of us?"

Hero paused with her notebook halfway out of her reticule. "I am careful to avoid recording political opinions that might get those I interview—or the newspaper—in trouble with the authorities. But I can promise you I have no intention of coddling ignorance or shying away from the painful realities of our day."

His face lit up with reluctant admiration. "Right, then," he said with a quick nod. "What were ye wantin' to know?"

Hero opened her notebook. "How is business today compared to what it was three or four years ago?"

He laughed out loud. "How's business? I'll tell ye how business is. I used to earn three to four pounds a week. You wouldn't credit it to look at me now, would ye? But war is good for shoemakers. Soldiers on the march need a constant supply of boots, don't they? Problem is, all wars eventually end. And then what? It all comes crashing down, that's what. Between the weather and Liverpool's stinkin' Corn Laws, the price of bread keeps going up while wages keep going down. So who's gonna buy my shoes? Ye tell me that. Two years ago I had a proper shop. Now I can barely make a go of it here." He jerked his head toward the rough shed behind him, then looked away, his jaw set hard.

"I understand some shoemakers are trying to get into other occupations."

"Aye. Either that, or they leave town. If I were younger and single, I'd pack up my kit and go on the tramp myself. I know half a dozen or more who've done it. But from what I'm hearing, it's no easier making a go of it in places like Yorkshire or Cornwall."

"You're married?"

"I am. My Jenny does embroidery for a dressmaker over on Piccadilly. She didn't used to need to do that. But we've four little ones still at home."

"How many children do you have?"

"Well, there's five left alive, but my eldest, Liz, is in service. We had two older boys, once, but they took the King's shilling. Jack died at San Sebastian, while Graham, he disappeared in some place called Louisiana. Nobody knows what happened to him. My Jenny, she keeps hoping he'll come home someday, but me, I reckon he's dead, too."

"I'm sorry," said Hero.

The shoemaker blinked and looked away. "Time was, I considered myself a patriot. Thought everything England did was just and right—told myself my boys died fighting against tyranny and the ungodly." He gave a ragged laugh. "It's funny how, looking back, I realize I never gave a thought to so many things—things like how a government is structured, and who has a say in it. It was just something that . . . was. But hardship and fear change a man, ye know? Change him and make him think. And when ye think about it, ye realize how much just ain't right in our world. It's not right that there're millions of people out there who're working hard but still starving—starving and freezing to death, while at the same time there's a few thousand men who do next to nothing besides tell the rest of us what to do, and they've more money than anybody could ever need. How is that right? Ye tell me: How is it right?"

Hero closed her notebook. "Did you go to the public meeting up at Spa Fields a few weeks ago?"

"I didn't, no. But I'm plannin' on being at the next one. If we join together and make ourselves heard, eventually Liverpool and Sidmouth and the rest of that lot have gotta listen. Don't ye think?"

He looked at her with such hopeful expectancy that it made her heart ache, to realize how much he still believed in the system that was failing him and others like him so badly. "Surely," she said, because there was always a chance, maybe, that what he wanted to believe was true.

It was later, when Hero was going over her notes from her interviews beside her drawing room fire, that Jarvis came to see her.

"Good morning, Papa," she said, smiling as she rose to kiss his cheek. "This is a pleasant surprise. And how are Victoria and my little baby brother?"

"Both are well, thank you."

"Always good to hear. Shall I order us some tea?"

"Thank you, but no; I can't stay long," he said, going to stand with his back to the fire. "I've come to ask what your interest is in Kate Price."

Hero sank back into her chair, her head tilting to one side as she looked up at him. "Having her watched, are you? Or at least, I assume your men are watching her and not following me?"

"Of course she's being watched. The woman is an incorrigible Radical. If she had her way, we'd see guillotines set up at Charing Cross."

"Actually, I suspect she'd be content simply to see a wee bit more than three out of a hundred men having the right to vote."

"Perish the thought," said Jarvis.

Hero smiled.

He was silent for a moment, his features inscrutable as he studied her. "And the leather staymaker, Caleb Jackson? What have you to do with him?"

Hero no longer felt like smiling. "My, my, aren't your minions busy? Watching him as well, are we? As it happens, I interviewed him for an article I'm writing. Why?"

"The man is a troublemaker."

"Well, he's certainly articulate." She studied his grim, closed face. "What exactly are you planning?"

"The only thing I'm planning is to preserve this monarchy."

"To preserve it as it always has been?"

"To preserve it as it must be."

"What if you're wrong?"

His jaw tightened. "I'm not."

Chapter 23

The inquest into the death of Marcus Toole was held shortly after midday in the taproom of Chalk Farm Tavern.

By English law, any sudden, violent, or unexplained death required an inquest, open to the public and typically convened at the largest venue in the vicinity. Legal rather than medical in nature, inquests were the province of the local coroner, who impaneled a jury of between twelve and twenty-four "good and honest men" to view the body of the deceased, consider the evidence, listen to witnesses, and, if necessary, ask their own questions.

Sebastian reached Chalk Farm sometime after twelve to find the surrounding lanes thick with carriages from London and curious locals on foot converging on the tavern. Leaving his curricle in Tom's care, he was cutting through the yard toward the taproom door when Alison Cross stepped in front of him. She was wearing a high-waisted dark blue gown with a lace-trimmed scooped neckline and had her hair tucked up beneath a surprisingly prim cap.

"Well, look at you," said the tavern keeper, her eyes widening as she let her gaze travel over him in a way that underscored the change in his dress and appearance from the last time she had seen him. "I guess you weren't having me on when you said you're not with Bow Street. Who the bloody hell are you?"

"The name's Devlin."

She blinked. "Well. That does explain your interest in things."

Sebastian looked out over the crowd milling about the yard. "I don't see your friend Sid Diamond."

"Did you think you would?" She jerked her chin to where Lovejoy had paused just outside the tavern door, his head tilted to the side as he listened to a report from one of his constables. "With that lot here?"

"I suppose not."

She would have turned away then, but he put out a hand, stopping her. "I'm not your enemy in this."

She met his gaze, her jaw hardening. "Aren't you?" she said, and pulled away.

"Sir Samuel objected vociferously to the use of a tavern for his son's inquest," said Sir Henry Lovejoy as he and Sebastian pushed their way into the crowded taproom. The air smelled of the usual spilled beer, sawdust, male sweat, and tobacco mixed oddly with the stomach-churning stench of burnt flesh. "But apart from the nearest farmer's barn, there really wasn't anyplace else."

"At least the distance from London has reduced the number of gawkers," said Sebastian, then added, "somewhat," as they watched the motley assemblage push and shove their way closer to the table where Toole's blackened, grotesquely charred body lay. The viewing of the deceased's corpse was an important part of an inquest, so the victim was always on display for all to see.

Two sandy-haired, well-dressed gentlemen, one tall, skinny, and very young, his companion older and stouter, stood beside the victim's remains. Watching them, Lovejoy leaned over to whisper to Sebastian, "Who is that? Do you know?"

"That is Mr. Dudley Fenton, the youngest son of the Earl of Lisle, and his brother the Reverend Matthew Fenton. Toole and his friends humiliated the younger Fenton a month or two ago—here, at Chalk Farm."

The younger Cambridge man stood unmoving for a long moment, staring intently at what was left of his tormentor. Then, as they watched, a slow, nasty smile curled Fenton's lips.

Lovejoy said, "He seems quite pleased by the sight of Toole's burnt remains."

"Given what Toole did to him, I'm not sure I blame him."

"That bad, was it?"

"Yes."

The brothers turned away, their place taken by Theo Bridgewood and a beefy young buck Sebastian didn't recognize. Bridgewood stood beside his longtime friend's corpse for only a moment, stony faced; then he and his companion also moved on.

"They weren't very honorable young men, were they?" said Lovejoy thoughtfully.

"No."

A sense of being stared at caused Sebastian to look up. From across the room, Sir Samuel Toole's belligerent glare met his; then Lord Bridgewood leaned over to whisper something in the Baronet's ear, and both men turned to watch Emmanuel Royston-Jones slip quietly into the room.

It struck Sebastian as significant that not only was Royston-Jones alone, but he made no effort to work his way over to where Theo Bridgewood and his companion were now sitting beside Bayard. Instead, the shipping magnate's son shifted sideways to stand with his shoulders propped against a nearby wall, his arms folded at his chest as he stared with narrowed eyes out over the raucous crowd.

His curiosity aroused, Sebastian studied the younger man's expressionless face. There was something missing, he decided, in the various explanations he'd been given for the estrangement that had flared between Royston-Jones and his once tight circle of friends. And he found himself remembering what the man had said about his cousin, the young woman his friends had derided for her interest in the Druids. The seemingly undeniable links between the ancient Celtic methods of sacrifice and the three men's deaths suddenly made that information much more intriguing.

A flurry of activity near the taproom's front door jerked everyone's attention to the bustling arrival of the local coroner, a no-nonsense solicitor named Richard Callow. A graying, sparse man in his fifties, he took the chair reserved for him, positioned a pen, inkpot, and pad of papers just so on the table before him, then nodded briskly to the constable who'd entered in his wake.

The constable cleared his throat, sucked in a deep breath, and bellowed, "*Oyez, oyez, oyez!* Ye good men of this county are summoned to appear this day in the presence of Mr. Marcus Toole, lyin' dead here before you, to inquire for our Sovereign Lord the King when, how, and by what means he come to his death. . . ."

The jury was sworn in. Then, as the man who had discovered the victim, Bayard was called as the first witness to testify. He was dressed somberly, his face pale, his eyes bloodshot. He gave his evidence in subdued, halting tones, repeating essentially the same story he had told Sebastian: of the two friends leaving the tavern to climb Primrose Hill on a lark; of Toole setting about building up the bonfire while Bayard went off to relieve himself and then fell asleep. When he awoke, said Bayard, Toole was dead and in the fire.

"How the blazes do you sleep through a gunshot, man?" interrupted one of the jurors, a roughly dressed, heavily muscled blacksmith in his forties.

Bayard stared at him sullenly, then sniffed and said, "Easily, evidently, when you've been imbibing blue ruin half the night."

A titter of amusement drifted around the room, bringing a flush of angry color to the coroner's grim face. "Silence!" bellowed Callow, casting a furious glare at the crowd. "Enough of that noise." He nodded to Bayard. "Proceed."

But there was little more for Bayard to tell. Sebastian testified next, followed by Lovejoy and then Paul Gibson, who explained the nature of the victim's injuries. Marcus Toole's shamefaced, nervous groom was called, as were several men who'd been in the taproom the night of the murder. But none had anything useful to add.

The jury didn't need to leave the room to agree to return a verdict of homicide by party or parties unknown.

Sebastian was pushing his way through the crowd, headed toward Emmanuel Royston-Jones, when Theo Bridgewood stepped in front of him.

"Lord Devlin," said Theo as his beefy companion almost ran into the back of him. "I was hoping we might hear some explanation today of what the bloody hell happened to Toole, as well as to Keebles and Upcott. But from the sound of things, it's all still a muddle. Is Bow Street truly no closer to understanding any of this than they were before?"

"Not really, I'm afraid," said Sebastian, glancing toward the door. Royston-Jones had disappeared. He brought his attention back to the man before him. "You wouldn't happen to know the name of Emmanuel Royston-Jones's female cousin, would you? A young woman with an interest in Druidism?"

"Druidism?" Theo laughed. "I don't think so."

Theo's heavyset, earnest-looking companion nudged his friend in the ribs with one elbow. "Reckon he means Ciana O'Leary, don't you think?" he said, struggling with the name's Gaelic pronunciation, *Kee-ah-na.*

A shadow of annoyance passed over Theo's handsome features, then was gone. "Is that her name?" Theo shrugged. "I bow to my friend Abbott's superior memory. What on earth do you want with the woman?"

"I'm hoping she might help me better understand the significance of Primrose Hill," said Sebastian.

"You still think it's significant? Despite what also happened to Keebles and Upcott? Neither of them was killed here."

"I think it might be."

Theo shrugged again and pulled a face, as if to say Sebastian was entitled to his theories, however ridiculous they might be. But something flared in his hazel brown eyes.

Something he was careful to hide behind quickly lowered lashes.

Chapter 24

Giana O'Leary inhabited a world that was radically different from that occupied by her wealthy cousin.

A few simple inquiries brought Sebastian to a small shop in an eighteenth-century brick building in Little Windmill Street, off Piccadilly. Pushing open the shop door to a pleasant jingling of bells, he found himself in a narrow room crowded with a bizarre assortment of objects: Iron cauldrons of various sizes, baskets of acorns, polished stone ax heads, bells, runes, and hagstones jostled for space with reed pipes, drums, rattles, flowing hooded robes, bunches of herbs, several shelves of books, and clusters of quartz crystals. And everywhere he looked were various-sized carvings of animals rendered in stone or wood: horses, stags, boars, ravens, bears, snakes, and strange mythological beasts, all mixed up with images of men dressed in animal skins with horned or antlered headdresses. The air was heavy with the scent of incense and herbs and something else, something elusive Sebastian had smelled before but could not name.

"Interesting shop," he said to the raven-haired woman behind the counter. In her late twenties, she was slim, fine-boned, and striking. The resemblance to Emmanuel Royston-Jones was slight but inescapable.

"Thank you. I think." She rested her forearms on the counter and folded her hands together before her. "Or was that not intended as a compliment?"

Sebastian drew a calling card from his pocket and laid it on the counter beside her hands. "The name is Devlin."

"I know who you are." She didn't even glance at the card. "Why are you here?"

"I understand you're a cousin of Emmanuel Royston-Jones."

"And exactly what is it to you if I am?"

"He tells me you consider yourself a modern Druid."

She straightened abruptly. "So?"

"Have you noticed that his friends are being murdered in ways that precisely echo what are thought to be three of the ancient Celtic methods of human sacrifice?"

She stood stiffly before him, her arms now crossed at her chest, her face closed and hostile. "What precisely are you suggesting? Modern Druids do not practice human sacrifice any more than modern Greeks or Romans do."

"I'm not suggesting anything. I'm trying to understand who is killing these men, and why." He held out the carved wooden wolf. "Have you ever seen this?"

She stood as if frozen, the only movement the rapid rise and fall of her chest. Then she swallowed and shook her head. "No."

He cast a significant glance around the shop. "You've never had anything like it for sale?"

"Not like that, no."

He brought his gaze back to her face. "I was hoping you might be able to tell me what it was used for."

He was still holding the piece out to her, and after a moment she took it, turning it over in her hands. "Where did you find it?"

Not *Where did it come from?* he noticed, but *Where did you find it?* He said, "It was at the top of Primrose Hill, not far from where Marcus Toole was killed."

She handed the carving back to him as if it had suddenly begun to burn her fingers. "The Druids held a ceremony on Primrose Hill a few weeks ago for Samhain. Perhaps it was dropped then."

"Perhaps." He tucked the piece away. "So it is somehow related to Druidism?"

"It could be."

He nodded to a nearby shelf that held a number of different books, some new, some very old. "I see you carry works by Iolo Morganwg. Do you admire him?"

"I admire some of his work," she said, her voice guarded.

"But not all of it?"

She hesitated, as if choosing her words carefully. "We may not know exactly what the ancient Druids believed, but we can study the folktales, legends, traditions, and songs that have come down to us through the ages and perhaps find a wisdom that resonates with something within us. Or at least within some of us." She pressed a curled fist to her chest. "For me, a large part of that is a recognition of the divinity of nature and the need to revere the earth and seek to live in harmony with it. Respect it and protect it." She uncurled her hand to fling it out in the direction of the Thames. "All you need do is look at what's happening to the Thames. It's *dying*. Between the new coal gasworks and letting people empty their flush-down pedestals into the sewers, the river is turning into a cesspit. When I first came to London five years ago, we were eating salmon caught from the Thames. Are there any fish even left alive in it?"

"I wouldn't want to eat them if there are," said Sebastian. He let his gaze drift again around the strange assortment of objects she had for sale. "Do you know if Marcus Toole considered himself a Druid?"

She gave a quick, startled laugh. "You can't be serious. The only thing Marcus Toole worshipped was pleasure—and himself, of course."

"How well did you know him?"

She shrugged. "I met him a few times when I was with Emmanuel."

"Are you related to Royston-Jones through his mother or his father?"

A strange smile played about her lips. "My mother and Emmanuel's mother were sisters—Lady Elizabeth and Lady Jane Royston. Lady Elizabeth married a nasty but extraordinarily wealthy man and has lived a long life of comfort and luxury with someone she despises, while her sister, Lady Jane, fell in love with a dashing but poor Army captain, married him in defiance of her parents, and was blissfully happy until she died sixteen months later in childbirth." She paused, her gaze hard on his face. "Which of the two do you think made the wisest choice? Your answer will tell you a great deal about yourself."

"Your father was a Captain O'Leary?"

"No. Captain Sean O'Leary was my husband. He died at Almeida."

"I'm sorry."

She twitched one shoulder, blinked, and looked away.

He said, "Who do you think is killing these men—Keebles, Toole, and now Upcott?"

"I have no idea. How could I?"

"Why do you think the killer is styling his murders to look like Celtic sacrifices?"

She brought her gaze back to his face. "Perhaps he hopes to throw blame onto someone who considers himself a Druid. He could even hope to discredit the entire movement."

"Do you know someone like that? Someone with such hostility to modern Druidism that they would kill in an effort to destroy it?"

"No." She opened her mouth as if to say something else, then closed it and began again. "Those men—the ones who've been killed—were horrible people. They enjoyed hurting others; they thought it was *fun*. Because they were wealthy and came from old, 'good' families, they believed they could do anything they wanted, anything at all, and get away with it. And the sad truth is that they did—get away with it, I mean. All of it. Perhaps someone decided it was time they were stopped."

Sebastian studied her flashing eyes, the angry color staining her cheeks. "Who do you know that they hurt?"

"No one, personally. But Emmanuel used to talk to me about some of the things they did. It bothered him."

"Then why was he their friend in the first place?"

She huffed a soft, humorless laugh. "Have you ever met Zacharia Royston-Jones?"

"I don't think so, no."

"He's a harsh, ruthless, fiercely ambitious man. He wanted his son to be every bit as cold, insensitive, and callous as he is, except that wasn't Emmanuel. So when Emmanuel was a boy, his father tried to *make* him be that way, and in the process he almost destroyed Emmanuel. Then he sent him off to Eton, and Emmanuel . . ." She paused. "I think it all came close to killing him before he fell in with Bridgewood and Toole and the rest of them. They protected him and made him feel accepted, and even though some of the things they did troubled him, he found a way to live with it. But then he met Annie. She was good and kind and giving, and she saw and cherished those traits in Emmanuel. I don't think she ever came out and told him what she thought of his friends, but he knew. And he started distancing himself from them."

"How did she die?"

"She caught measles from one of her little sisters."

"How tragic."

"Yes. I'm not sure he's ever going to get over it." She hesitated, then said, "You think Emmanuel is in danger?"

"I don't know. I suppose it depends on who is killing his friends, and why."

He saw the leap of fear in her eyes and thought she might say something more.

But she didn't.

Chapter 25

Leaving Little Windmill Street, Sebastian drove north, to Clerkenwell.

Originally home to the monastic order of the Knights of St. John of Jerusalem, Clerkenwell was an ancient, once affluent parish dating back to medieval times. But those days were long gone. As London's wealthy inhabitants moved farther west, Clerkenwell had become a depressed area dominated by breweries, distilleries, watchmaking, cheap printing presses, and the infamous Cold Bath Fields prison. The barren, frost-encrusted open area known as Spa Fields began just at the end of Coppice Row and St. John Street. And as he reined in outside a dilapidated stone yard near the coffeehouse known as the Rising Sun, Sebastian found himself once again wondering what Keebles, Toole, Upcott, and their friends had been doing here, in a place like Clerkenwell.

The Rising Sun catered to what looked like a cross section of clientele ranging from butchers and blacksmiths to shoemakers, brewery workers, and clerks. Its owner, Sebastian had discovered, was a former militia officer named Adam York with a reputation for being something of a Radical.

As Sebastian paused across the street from the coffeehouse, watching, the door opened, and a familiar slim figure emerged wearing gray Wellington trousers, a slightly threadbare but well-tailored French-cut black coat, and a broad-brimmed hat. It was the same "youth" Sebastian had once watched fence with Damion Pitcairn in an abandoned courtyard off Swallow Street. And just last night Sebastian had seen her again, dressed as an opera dancer at the stage door of the King's Theatre.

"Bloody hell," he whispered, watching her walk away.

There was a thread that wove through much of what Sebastian had so far learned about Marcus Toole and his friends, a snaking cord that connected the Palace's obsession with the Spenceans and the Spa Fields meetings to the revolutionary ideas expressed by the likes of Damion Pitcairn and Kate Price's *Poor Man's Weekly*. But what the hell any of that had to do with an obscure first-century Roman poet and the disputed Celtic practice of human sacrifice was more than he could begin to understand.

Settling his hat lower on his forehead, Sebastian watched Damion Pitcairn's friend hail a hackney carriage and direct the jarvey to the Haymarket. Then he crossed the street to push open the door of the Rising Sun.

Filled with tobacco smoke and redolent with the scents of roasting coffee beans, hot chocolate, and freshly baked bread, the interior of the coffeehouse was starkly plain. But Sebastian could see the ghostly outlines of rectangles on the empty dark green plaster walls where he suspected mirrors and pictures had hung until smashed by Keebles, Toole, and friends. The tables and chairs also showed signs of recent repairs, with a few obviously having been broken so badly that they'd needed to be replaced and were new.

Perhaps a dozen men sat scattered around the room, some conversing quietly in groups, others by themselves, their heads bent over newspapers spread open on the tables before them. Coffeehouses always kept an extensive supply of newspapers, periodicals, and pamphlets, for the reading material formed one of their main attractions. At the cost of a few pennies, a man could drink coffee and read the kind of publications priced beyond his personal reach by the heavy government stamp tax.

The Rising Sun's patrons were, of course, strictly male, for coffeehouses were as much male preserves as the men's clubs of St. James's. A woman might work in one, but she would never be welcome as a patron. And while that might explain why Pitcairn's friend had chosen to visit the Rising Sun dressed as a man, it did nothing to explain why she had traveled all the way up to Clerkenwell in the first place.

The stout, middle-aged man behind the counter looked up as Sebastian walked toward him and said, "You're Adam York?"

The man frowned. "I am. Who're you?"

Sebastian set a calling card on the countertop between them. "The name's Devlin. We need to talk—in private, preferably."

York hesitated a moment. At just below average height, he had a plump face with full cheeks, graying fair hair, and watery light blue eyes. Obviously coming to some kind of decision, he nodded to the middle-aged woman washing cups nearby, then led Sebastian to a small office at the rear of the building, carefully shut the door behind them, and swung to face him. "What do you want from me?"

Sebastian let his gaze rove over the plain but comfortable room with its neat desk, an aged, shaggy dog curled up on a hand-hooked rug, and two worn armchairs drawn up before the hearth. "I need you to tell me why Marcus Toole and his friends trashed your coffeehouse a month or so ago."

York stared at him with hard, narrowed eyes. "I don't know what you're talking about."

"Yes, you do."

For a moment the coffeehouse owner held Sebastian's gaze. Then he sucked his lower lip in between his teeth and looked away. "You think I know why they did it? I mean, sure, I keep Radical newspapers and pamphlets for my customers. But so does every other coffeehouse around here. It's what men want to read." He jerked his head toward the coffee room and gave a harsh laugh. "How many you reckon'd be in here if all I stocked was the *Morning Chronicle* and the *Times*?"

"What were Toole and his friends even doing up in Clerkenwell?"

"Damned if I know. It was just my bad luck they decided to come in here to warm up. It was a bloody cold day."

"When was this?"

"Three, maybe four weeks ago. While I was fixing their coffee, one of 'em wanders over to look at my newspapers and goes, 'Hey, Bridgewood, come see the treasonous trash this bastard keeps in here.' Next thing I know, they're whooping and laughing like a bunch of idiots and ripping 'em all up. I told them to stop." He paused, then said, "I may've even told them it was that kinda shite that led to a guillotine being set up on the Place de la Révolution. That's when they picked up my chairs and started smashing my mirrors and pictures." He let out a pained sigh. "I had some real nice framed colored satires on my walls."

"What did you do?"

"I thought about fetching Constable Caldwell, but the truth is, he wouldn't have done a damned thing—not against that lot. So I got my blunderbuss and told them to cut it out. They laughed at me, of course. So I put a hole in the wall right above one of 'em's head. They left."

"Was that the end of it?"

"No. They came at me a few days later for attempted murder. So I sued them for destruction of property. Everybody around here knows I'm a good shot; if I missed, it was because I intended to. In the end, the magistrate got us both to drop our cases." He fell silent for a moment, his nostrils flaring with his agitated breathing. "It ain't right that they can do that to a man—wreck his business and then walk away without paying for it. But that's the way this bloody country works, isn't it? Two sets of laws, one for the likes of me, and one for the likes of . . . them."

Sebastian suspected he'd been about to say, *And one for the likes of you*. "Who do you think killed them?"

York stared at him. "I don't know and, frankly, I don't care. I'm just glad they're dead—or, at any rate, three of them are. They got away with everything a man can get away with except murder, and who's to say they didn't do that, too?"

"You know something," said Sebastian, studying the other man's hard, angry face. "What is it?"

York tightened his jaw and shook his head. "I'm not gonna say nothing might put a noose around some innocent's neck. I know what Bow Street is like."

"You think those men were killed in revenge?"

"Makes sense, doesn't it? To set fire to a man and cook him like a side of beef . . ." York shook his head. "That takes a powerful lot of hate, wouldn't you say?"

"Yes," said Sebastian, drawing the wolf carving from his pocket. "Have you ever seen this before?"

York stared at it. "No. What's it for?"

"I don't know. Do you know much about the Celts?"

The coffeehouse owner laughed. "The *Celts*? You can't be serious."

"I wish I weren't," said Sebastian, and tucked the strange carving away.

More troubled now than ever by the suggestive connections between the Spenceans and the three dead men, Sebastian went, again, in search of Damion Pitcairn.

He found the young musician and swordsmith enjoying a pint in a public house called the Cock, in Soho. Pitcairn's gaze met his across the crowded room. Then the musician said something to one of his companions and walked over to meet Sebastian.

"I take it you're here to see me."

Sebastian nodded. "You need to tell me about your friend the opera dancer."

Pitcairn kept his voice low. "What about her?"

"I know you teach her fencing, and this afternoon I saw her leaving the Rising Sun coffeehouse in St. John Street in Clerkenwell, which incidentally happens to be the same coffeehouse that Keebles, Toole, and their friends wrecked a month or so ago. Right before someone started killing them."

Pitcairn took a deep drink of his porter and said nothing.

"She's the friend who was handing out broadsheets in Southwark when Toole and his friends attacked you, isn't she?" said Sebastian.

Pitcairn hesitated a moment, then nodded. "Except she's not exactly my 'friend.'"

Sebastian waited for the musician to say, *She's my lover.* Instead, he said, "She's my sister."

A loud burst of laughter drew Sebastian's attention to a crowded table of bricklayers beside them. "Let's go for a walk, shall we?"

"Her name is Sasha," said Pitcairn as they walked toward Soho Square. This was an older, decaying part of London, with small two- and three-story houses and simple shops, its streets still lit by dim, flickering oil lamps. "Sasha Stone. Technically she's my half sister; we share the same mother but have different fathers."

"She's from Jamaica as well?"

Pitcairn nodded. "Our mother . . ." He paused as if reaching for words to express the inexpressible. "She was very beautiful, but she was also what slavers like to call 'willful.' A few years after I was born, the Scotsman who had planted me in her belly took me away from her and sold her to a plantation owner down the road."

Damion Pitcairn, Sebastian knew, had been well educated and set free by his Scottish father. "The man who bought your mother was Sasha's father?"

Pitcairn shook his head. "That slave owner preferred little boys. His brother fathered Sasha when he was visiting from England one time."

"And had his brother set her free?"

Pitcairn gave a bitter laugh. "Not hardly. The plantation owner—I guess you could call him Sasha's uncle—kept her enslaved until she was fourteen. That's when she blackmailed him into letting her go."

"By threatening to reveal his sexual practices?"

Pitcairn nodded.

"I'm surprised he didn't just kill her."

"I suspect he would have if she hadn't put safeguards in place."

"Clever."

Pitcairn smiled. "Oh, Sasha is very clever."

Sebastian studied the fencing master's hard, closed face. "There's something you're not telling me."

Pitcairn shrugged. "Perhaps."

"I'd like to talk to her. Where would I find her? Besides the theater, I mean."

Pitcairn thought about it, then shook his head. "I think she'd prefer to find you."

It was when Sebastian was walking back to where he'd left his curricle that he heard someone calling his name.

"Lord Devlin? I say, Lord Devlin!"

He turned to find one of Lovejoy's constables loping up the street toward him. "What is it?" said Sebastian.

The man drew up, his breath coming hard and fast as he put

up a hand to touch the brim of his round hat. "There's been another murder, sir!"

Sebastian felt his stomach clench. "Who?" he said hoarsely. *Not Bayard; please, not Bayard . . .* "Who is it?"

"The tavern keeper out at Chalk Farm, my lord. Alison Cross."

Chapter 26

By the time Sebastian reined in his steaming horses before Chalk Farm Tavern, the weak winter sun had long since disappeared below the horizon, leaving the night cold and tinged with the scent of woodsmoke. He found the old farmhouse ablaze with light, although it looked as if most of the taproom's regular patrons had fled. He could see the bobbing lanterns of Lovejoy's constables fanning out in what he suspected would be a futile search of the surrounding area.

"Don't make no sense," said Tom. "This killer offing her."

Sebastian handed the boy the reins. "No, it doesn't."

He found Sir Henry in a tumbledown old stone barn some two hundred feet up the lane. The magistrate stood just inside the door, his hands thrust deep into the pockets of his greatcoat, his head tipped back as he stared at the body of Alison Cross swaying gently at the end of a rope tied to the rafters above.

"What do you make of this, my lord?" he asked, turning as Sebastian paused in the barn's open doorway.

Sebastian took one look at the dead woman's distorted purple face and swallowed hard. "I can't even begin to explain it."

"It's possible, I suppose, that her murder has nothing to do with what happened to Marcus Toole up on Primrose Hill. But that seems . . ." The magistrate hesitated.

"Doubtful?" suggested Sebastian.

"Yes."

His heart weighing heavy in his chest, Sebastian went to stand beside the dead woman's limp body and forced himself to take a closer look. Her eyes were wide and staring, the features of her face dark and contorted with the terrified agony of her death. Her arms hung limply at her sides, her nails torn, her fingers bloody. She was dressed in the same simple gown of dark blue wool that she'd worn at that morning's inquest, although the prim cap was gone.

"Well, hell," he said softly, turning away to let his gaze travel around the shadowy, cobweb-draped interior of the old barn. The air smelled of moldy hay, mouse droppings, and dust; it didn't look as if the place had been used in decades. "What was she doing out here?"

"No one seems to know. We're told they realized she was missing several hours after the crowds attracted by the inquest had begun to disperse." Lovejoy dug his fists deeper into the pockets of his greatcoat, his head once again falling back as he stared up at the dead woman's distorted features. "I suppose it's possible that she could have killed herself."

"She didn't kill herself." Turning, Sebastian went to stand in the barn's open doorway and suck the cold, clean air of the countryside deep into his lungs. He watched the wind ruffle the dead grass of a nearby field, watched the bared branches of an ancient oak shift against the star-strewn sky. "She was in the taproom last Saturday when Toole and my nephew were there. And she was there the night Toole and his friends picked on Dudley Fenton. She's the one who stopped them."

"I can't see anything in that which would lead someone to kill her."

"Neither can I. Which makes me think she must have known something—something she didn't tell me. And whoever killed her did it to keep her from talking."

"Knew something about *what*?"

Sebastian turned to meet his friend's gaze. But all he could do was shake his head.

❧

Sebastian returned to Brook Street to find Sir Lawrence Upcott drinking a cup of tea with Hero beside the drawing room fire.

A thin, bow-legged man with a balding head and gaunt features, the Baronet was probably somewhere in his late fifties or early sixties, but he seemed older, with the grayish, parchment-like flesh and sunken eyes of someone who has been ill for a long time. "My lord," he said, rising shakily to his feet with the aid of a cane. "Lady Devlin has been kind enough to keep me company and provide me with sustenance while I imposed on her hospitality."

"My apologies for keeping you waiting, Sir Lawrence. Please, sit down, and allow me to express my sincere condolences for the loss of your son."

"Thank you," said the older man, blinking rapidly as he sank back into his overstuffed chair. "I'll admit I'm still finding it all difficult to grasp. It wasn't until I met with the magistrates at Bow Street that I realized two of my son's friends have recently suffered a similar fate. That can't be a coincidence."

"I don't think so, no," said Sebastian, pouring himself a cup of tea and going to stand by the fire. "When did you last see your son?"

"He came down to Berkshire at the beginning of the summer—early June, it must have been. Stayed for over a month, which was not typical of him." The Baronet made a wry a face. "Phineas was not fond of the country, I'm afraid."

"Did he seem nervous at that time? Anxious in any way?"

Sir Lawrence was silent for a moment, his thin, bony hands tightening on the arms of his chair. "As it happens, he did strike me as a bit . . . off, for lack of a better word. I even asked if something was wrong, but he laughed and said no, of course not. At the time I put his mood—and the unusual length of his stay—down to the hounding of impatient creditors. But the unfortunate truth is, Phineas typically had no difficulty at all ignoring tradesmen's bills. And while I kept expecting him to ask for an advance on his allowance, he never did—which was also unusual, now that I think about it. He wasn't exactly what you'd call thrifty, my firstborn son. I was always trying to coax him into spending more time down in Berkshire, interesting himself in the management of the estate, learning all the things he was going to need to know soon enough. But he'd just laugh, say he wasn't cut out to be a 'farmer.' It was my hope that maturity would bring with it wisdom and a deepening sense of what he owed his lineage. Perhaps it would have, in time." He paused, then said more quietly, "Perhaps."

"How well did you know Phineas's friends, Marcus Toole and Gilbert Keebles?"

Sir Lawrence shrugged. "I've seen them now and then over the years, but I can't say that I *knew* them. My estate lies in indifferent hunting country, so it's not as if there was anything to draw them down to Berkshire. And I don't think I've been up to London myself more than two or three times in the last dozen years. So if you're looking for me to help explain what is happening, I can't. It makes no sense to me. None at all."

"Do you know of anyone Phineas considered an enemy? Someone he quarreled with, perhaps?"

Sir Lawrence shook his head. "He never did talk to me about that sort of thing. At one time he might have mentioned it to his mother, but she's been gone these last eighteen months now."

"I'm sorry," said Sebastian, his gaze going to meet Hero's. "Might one of his siblings know something?"

"I don't think so, no. Can't say he ever got on well with either Mary or Emma, his two sisters, and they're both married and off on their own now. As for James—my younger son—he's still up at Oxford. With so many years between them, the brothers were barely acquainted with each other."

"Do you know if Phineas had any interest in the ancient Celts?"

Sir Lawrence stared at him. "The Celts? Not to my knowledge, no. He was never what you might call bookish, Phineas."

"Have you ever seen this?" asked Sebastian, holding out the small wolf carving.

Sir Lawrence took the piece and turned it over in his hands. "I haven't, no." He looked up. "What is it for?"

"I have no idea. It was found on Primrose Hill, near where Marcus Toole was killed Saturday night."

Sir Lawrence handed the piece back to him. "I'm told your nephew was there that night, too."

"He was, yes. Passed out drunk some distance away—which is probably why he's still alive."

"A fortunate young man."

"Yes. Do you have any idea what Phineas might have been doing out at Marylebone on Sunday night?"

"No. No idea at all."

"And you can't think of anything—however strange or unrelated it may seem—that might throw some light onto what happened to your son and his friends?"

"I can't, no. I'm sorry. I'm told the inquest is tomorrow morning, although nothing is expected to come of it. After that, I'll be taking Phineas home with me. Bury him with his mother and the three little brothers and two sisters who've gone before him. But now," said Sir Lawrence, heaving painfully to his feet, "it's late, and I've taken up far too much of your evening." He bowed politely to Hero. "Thank you for the tea, Lady Devlin."

"You're welcome," she said, rising with him. "I'm only sorry we had to meet under such sad circumstances."

"Thank you," he said again, swallowing hard as he turned away.

"I can't begin to tell you how sorry I am that this has happened to you," said Sebastian as he walked with the older man down the stairs to the front door.

Sir Lawrence nodded in silent acknowledgment, his fist tightening on the handle of his cane. It was a moment before he trusted himself to speak. "I won't deny I've always thought it a queer thing for an earl's son to do—interesting himself in murder investigations, I mean. But I must say, it gives me some consolation knowing you're intent on finding the truth behind this sad business. I've no faith in that new Chief Magistrate they have at Bow Street—Sir Nathaniel Conant, heaven preserve us!—to do what's right;

can't trust a man of his ilk at all. He'll do what the Palace tells him to do and whatever best serves Sir Nathaniel Conant himself." He paused at the door, then turned to say, "You'll let me know if you discover what it's all about? I don't care how unpleasant; I need to know the truth."

Sebastian met the older man's troubled gaze. "If that's what you want."

"It's what I want."

Sebastian stood for a moment, watching the Baronet carefully walk down the front steps toward his waiting carriage. Then he returned to the drawing room to find Hero standing beside the windows, the flickering light from the linkboys' torches below casting a dancing pattern of shadows across her face. She said, "I'm glad he has other children."

"Yes," he said.

She looked over at him. "Last June would have been around the time Emmanuel Royston-Jones and his friends parted ways."

Sebastian went to stand beside her as they watched the Baronet's carriage pull away from the kerb. "It would, wouldn't it?"

Chapter 27

Wednesday, 27 November

The inquest into the death of Phineas Upcott began at ten o'clock the next morning in a neat brick inn on Baker Street North.

It was as unproductive as everyone had expected.

The jarvey who'd discovered Upcott's body was still visibly rattled when he gave his halting testimony and knew nothing beyond the obvious. Because the area was so sparsely settled, no one in the few widely scattered houses around the construction site had seen or heard anything untoward, and no one seemed to know what the dead man might have been doing on the outskirts of London in the middle of the night. Upcott's valet, a nervous young man named Twigg, testified that his master had left his rooms shortly after seven without saying where he was going or at what time to expect his return. Throughout it all, Sebastian was painfully aware of Sir Lawrence Upcott sitting tense and straight-backed, his face ashen, his eyes haunted with a pain that was never going to go away. When the jury delivered the inevitable verdict of homicide by person or persons unknown, Sir Lawrence sank his head into his hands, and an ugly murmur spread through the assembled onlookers.

"People are frightened," said Lovejoy afterward as he and Sebastian walked along the empty, weed-choked building sites that lined the nearby Culloden Terrace.

"Understandably so," said Sebastian. "Although at least the nature of Upcott's death is ordinary enough that it hasn't provoked any more speculation about human sacrifices in the press." *At least, not yet,* he thought.

"Hanging is definitely less sensational than being burned alive." Lovejoy paused, then added, "Although certainly no less lethal."

"Have you heard the results of Alison Cross's autopsy yet?"

"Not yet," said Lovejoy. He stared across the dead fields toward the wind-whipped gray waters of the reservoir. "Sir Nathaniel Conant is convinced she helped someone murder Toole, then killed herself in a fit of remorse."

"She didn't kill herself," said Sebastian again.

Lovejoy nodded. "He's somewhat annoyed that we sent the body to Paul Gibson. Anyone else he might have been able to browbeat into giving the findings he desired."

"Not Gibson."

"No, not Gibson."

The Irish surgeon was in the stone outbuilding at the base of his garden, still washing the naked corpse laid out on his raised granite slab, when Sebastian arrived at Tower Hill a short time later.

"Can you tell me anything yet?" asked Sebastian, pausing in the doorway.

"Beyond the obvious observation that she was strangled, you mean?" said Gibson, carefully setting down Alison Cross's bloodstained hand and dropping his wet cloth into a nearby basin of water.

"She was strangled first, then hanged? Same as Upcott?"

"The same."

"Son of a bitch," whispered Sebastian. "What about her attacker? Anything at all?"

Gibson leaned back against the deep wooden shelf that ran across the rear wall of the building. "Well, it appears likely he looped the cord over her head from behind, so you're looking for someone who's taller than she was and fairly strong. But since she wasn't a particularly large woman, I suspect that won't narrow things down much." He pointed to a row of angry wheals on the dead woman's thin, pale neck. "She made those scratches herself, trying to loosen the garrote. It's why her hands are so bloody; she tore six of her fingernails trying to stop the bastard from squeezing the life out of her."

Swallowing another oath, Sebastian pushed away from the doorframe to go study a brown leather thong that lay curled up in a chipped basin on the shelves to the left of the entrance, beside the folded pile of Allison Cross's clothes. The cord had been fashioned of three lengths of leather braided together, the ends tied in simple knots. "Where did that come from?"

"One of the constables found it in the straw when they searched the barn again this morning."

"Think something similar was used to kill Phineas Upcott?"

"I'd say so, yes. It might even be the same garrote. I wonder why your killer left it this time."

"Maybe he dropped it and didn't want to take the time to search for it. Or he didn't realize he had dropped it," said Sebastian, his gaze drawn again to the distorted features of the dead woman on Gibson's slab.

Gibson pushed away from the shelf and reached for his wet cloth. "I haven't had time to do a thorough examination yet, but I can tell you one other thing that may or may not be related to her murder."

Sebastian looked up. "What's that."

"She was with child."

Sebastian felt a pain pull across his chest, his heart aching at the thought of what Allison Cross's last frantic moments must have been like if she'd known she was losing not only her own life, but the life of her unborn child, too. "How far along?"

"Four or five months, I'd say."

"So she definitely knew?"

"Oh, yes, she knew."

Sebastian returned to Brook Street to find a slim youth dressed in a slightly worn but fashionable navy blue coat, pale pantaloons, and boots hesitating at the base of the house's front steps, with one hand resting lightly on the railing.

"Stable them," Sebastian told Tom, handing the tiger his reins.

"Aye, gov'nor," said Tom as Sebastian hopped down to the pavement.

The "youth" turned at Sebastian's approach, her moss green eyes narrowed and wary. "Damion says you want to talk to me."

"I do, yes. Thank you for agreeing to see me. Would you like to come in?"

Sasha shook her head. "We can talk out here, while we walk."

"If you'd prefer," said Sebastian, turning their steps toward Bond Street. "I wanted to ask about your run-in with Marcus Toole and his friends in Southwark a month or so ago."

"Damion said he already told you about that."

"He did. But I thought you might be able to help me understand it better."

"Not sure there's much to understand. I was handing out broadsheets for the first Spa Fields meeting when they came at me like a bloody pack of wolves."

A pack of wolves. Wolves. *Wolves* . . . Sebastian felt his heart beat up against his ribs as the implications of that phrase dawned. But all he said was, "Had you ever seen the men before?"

She gave an offhand shrug that could have meant anything. "Their kind like to hang around the Round Room."

The Round Room was a mirror-lined circular chamber at the King's Theatre where the wealthy young bucks of the ton were encouraged to congregate, evaluate the season's crop of new opera dancers, and select their mistresses. "One of them approached you there?"

She drew up abruptly, raw anger flaring in her eyes. "Lots of men 'approach' me. Constantly. People think if you're an opera dancer, you're for sale. Well, I'm not."

He turned to face her. "I don't think you are, and it was not my intention to imply it."

A quiver passed over her features. She gave a quick, jerky nod, then turned to walk on.

He fell into step beside her again. "Did you have trouble with all of them, or just one in particular? At the theater, I mean."

She hesitated, then said, "Bridgewood. Theo Bridgewood. Men like him don't like to take no for an answer."

"How do you come to know Adam York?"

That question seemed to take her by surprise. She glanced over at him. "Why you asking about him?"

"You were seen leaving his coffeehouse yesterday."

"So?"

"I'm told Toole, Keebles, and the others wrecked the place a few weeks ago."

Her lip curled. "Does that surprise you? That they'd do something like that?"

"No. They seem to have made that sort of thing a habit. But I'm trying to understand why they would be hanging around areas as depressed as Southwark and Clerkenwell. Do you know why they were in Southwark the day they confronted you?"

"You think I asked?"

"I thought you might have noticed where they came from."

"No. I was just handing out broadsheets and talking to anyone interested in the meeting when suddenly they were . . . there."

"And Bridgewood took a broadsheet, crumpled it up, and threw it back at you?"

She nodded. "I don't think they'd noticed Damion sitting on a low stone wall nearby. Some workmen had taken copies of the broadsheets and were just walking away when Bridgewood and his friends came up."

"Were you dressed like this?"

She made a low scoffing sound, deep in her throat. "Of course I was. You think I wanted trouble?"

"So they didn't know who you were?"

"Oh, Bridgewood knew."

"How?"

She glanced over at Sebastian, her expression unreadable. "Perhaps he's unusually observant."

She was keeping something from him, he knew, but he was damned if he could figure out what it was or how to get at it. He tried a different tack. "How long have you been in London?"

"A couple of years. Why?"

"You came here from Jamaica?"

She nodded.

"You knew Damion was here?"

She nodded again. "He always found a way to keep in touch with us—me and our grandmama, even after Mr. Pitcairn sent him to Scotland."

"Damion tells me you have the same mother."

"That's right, but she died when I was eight." Sasha paused, her expression hardening. "You know how she died?"

Sebastian had a feeling he didn't want to know. "No."

"He whipped her to death. The man who 'owned' her, I mean. My uncle. After that, her mother—Damion and my's grandmama—raised me. I saw her whipped a couple of times, too. But she survived it."

"The man's name was Stone?"

"No, that's my name. Before I left Jamaica, I went to the slave cemetery where they'd buried my mama and piled her grave high with stones so I'd be able to find it if I ever came back. And then I took Stone as my name to remind me always of what those bastards did to her. You think I want to carry their name?" She drew up and turned to face him again. "What does any of this have to do with the death of those three men?"

"I'm just trying to understand why they decided to pick on you."

"Why? It's not all that hard to figure out, is it? To people like them, a woman like me—or a man like Damion—isn't quite human. We scare them, except not for the reasons they tell themselves. We scare them because just by being alive and looking different, we threaten their belief in who they are. As long as they keep us as slaves, then they can feel superior, convince themselves that we're lesser than them and deserve everything that happens to us. But when they see us walking down the street—maybe not as their equals, because how many are seen as the equals of that lot?—but when they see us free, our own masters, it forces them to maybe consider that we're human beings, just like they are. And that they're guilty of a grave sin for all the horrible things they've done to us and to people like us. And they can't bear that. It's an insult to everything they'd like to believe about the world and about themselves. So they hate us."

Sebastian was silent for a moment. It was a profoundly insightful analysis that applied not simply to Bridgewood and Toole, but to far, far too many others. He said, "Who do you think is killing those men?"

She stared up at him, her face hard. "I neither know nor care."

"That seems to be a common sentiment."

"Yeah? Well, that ought to tell you somethin', hmm?"

Sebastian drew the wooden carving from his pocket. "Have you ever seen this before?"

She glanced at it. "No. Why?"

"You described those men as a 'pack of wolves.'"

"So?"

"This was found on Primrose Hill, near where Marcus Toole was killed."

Some emotion he couldn't define flitted across her delicate

features, then was gone. Reaching out, she took the carving, then held it cradled in both hands. "'Now the hungry lion roars,'" she quoted softly, "'And the wolf behowls the moon.'"

For reasons he couldn't quite have explained, he felt a chill run down his spine. *"A Midsummer Night's Dream?"*

She nodded and held the carving out to him. "So maybe somebody else thought of them the same way I do—somebody who decided to give them their own back again. Although me, I'm thinking it's an insult to wolves."

"I have to agree with you on that," said Sebastian, tucking the piece away.

Someone else, he knew, had referred to Toole and his friends as a "pack." Not a wolf pack, though, so he hadn't made the connection with the carving. But the memory was ephemeral and slippery, there and then gone. And the harder he tried to retrieve it, the more it eluded him.

Chapter 28

Dudley Fenton was carefully oiling the wooden carvings on the pulpit in his brother's church when Sebastian came to lean against a nearby marble column, his arms crossed at his chest, his gaze on the recently expelled scholar. "I need you to tell me the significance of wolves in Celtic folklore."

The younger man looked up, his hand stilling at its task, his mouth falling open as he stared at Sebastian. "Wolves?"

"That's right; wolves."

Fenton dipped his rag in the pot of boiled linseed oil at his feet, then rubbed thoughtfully at the cross carved into the front of the pulpit. "Well, we can't really know for certain, obviously. But I get the impression they regarded wolves almost like the representatives of the moon here on earth. I mean, wolves seem to have stood for many of the attributes that people have typically associated with the moon for thousands of years, things like intuition, instinct . . . our ability to communicate with the gods. I've read that, in Iberia, they were seen as the embodiment of traits we like to associate with warriors—things like strength, courage, nobility, wisdom. Even as late as the Middle Ages, if you look at the Irish myths of that time, you see that wolves were generally portrayed as helpful guardians. They were protective."

"So they weren't seen as evil?"

"No. It was typically the later Christians who came to portray wolves as evil, as a symbol of darkness. It's why they were finally hunted to extinction here and in Ireland. But before then, wolves might have been portrayed as wild and fierce, but they were still admired, especially for the strength of the wolf family."

"The pack."

"Yes."

Sebastian drew the wolf carving from his pocket. "Remember this? I've now had three different people refer to Marcus Toole and his friends as a 'pack.' A young woman I recently spoke to compared them to a 'pack of wolves,' and while it took me a while, I finally remembered your saying they acted like a 'pack of wild dogs' when you encountered them at Chalk Farm Tavern."

Fenton let his rag plop back into the pot at his feet. "Well, they were acting like a pack—the way they circled me like they were predators; it was as if they were feeding off each other, egging each other on." Reaching out, he took the carving in his hands, his head bowed as he stared down at it. When he spoke, his voice was little more than a whisper. "You think that's why this was left up there on Primrose Hill, near where Toole was killed? Because those men reminded whoever is murdering them of a pack of wolves?"

"It's one explanation, isn't it?"

Fenton nodded.

Sebastian said, "What I don't understand is why it was dropped a hundred or so feet from his body."

Fenton looked up. "You think I can explain it? I can't."

"You heard that the innkeeper out at Chalk Farm Tavern was murdered last night?"

"I heard." Fenton's voice cracked. "Why would someone do that? Kill those three men and then kill her? She stood up for me—stopped them when no one else did. Why would someone who hated those men kill her, too? She was everything the Celts thought wolves stood for: strong, brave, and protective. So why kill her?"

"I'm still trying to figure that out."

He held up the carving. "You think *this* might explain it? Because three people who tangled with those men referred to them as a 'pack,' and someone dropped a carving of a wolf near where one of them was killed?"

"I suppose it depends on whom the wolf was meant to represent," said Sebastian, taking the carving back into his own hands. "The killer? Or his victim? And in which tradition? The wolf as a symbol of all that is good and noble? Or as a representative of the forces of darkness and evil?"

The sense that he must be overlooking something—something vital—drove Sebastian that afternoon to the sprawling Park Lane home of the Dowager Duchess of Claiborne.

Born Lady Henrietta St. Cyr, sister of the current Earl of Hendon, the dowager was one of the grandes dames of Society, with a well-deserved reputation for knowing—and remembering—every intricate relationship, every juicy tidbit, every scandal that had rocked the ton for the last sixty years. She was one of Sebastian's favorite people, and he still called her Aunt, although both now knew their relationship was considerably more distant.

She was crossing the town house's elegant marble-floored entry hall when her butler opened the door to Sebastian. Now in her mid-seventies, the Duchess had her brother's stout build, broad, fleshy face, and brilliant blue eyes. Always stylish, she wore a fashionable gown of lilac wool with an exquisite Kashmiri shawl draped over her shoulders, and drew up abruptly at the sight of him. A housemaid rushing behind her with a bucket and mop shrieked and nearly ran into her; a footman carrying an upholstered wing chair from one of the reception rooms quickly swerved to one side, while a fussy little man hectoring a waiter staggering under a heavy tray swerved to the other.

"Heaven preserve us," said the Duchess, one hand coming up to tighten around the quizzing glass that dangled from a gold chain around her neck. "Not now, Devlin! Have you forgotten I've a rout in a matter of hours?"

He stepped to one side as a workman carrying a potted palm tried to squeeze past him. "Is that tonight?"

"Yes, it is tonight. And you and Hero said you'd attend."

"I'll only take a few minutes of your time." He smiled. "I promise. Unless you'd prefer I come back tomorrow morning? *Early* tomorrow morning."

A spasm of pain crossed the Duchess's features. "You'd do it, too, wouldn't you, you unnatural child?" She sighed and turned to lead the way to the library. "Very well. But I warn you: You have five minutes. Not a second more."

The library was so stuffed with piles of chairs, tables, sofas, rolled-up rugs, lamps, and crates of breakables items removed from the reception rooms that there was no place to sit. Sebastian leaned his hip against an inlaid Italian table, crossed his arms at his chest, and said, "I'm interested in what you can tell me about Gilbert Keebles, Marcus Toole, and Phineas Upcott."

She looked thoughtful for a moment. "Nothing to their credit, I'm afraid. All three were—technically—eligible bachelors, destined to inherit tidy estates, with Toole and Upcott set to come into their fathers' titles as well. And yet you'll find few hostesses in town who would ever have considered inviting one of them to a party."

"Why?"

"Bad ton."

It was a damning insult, to call someone "bad ton." While "good ton" implied someone who was not only gently born but also stylish, socially at ease, fashionable, and popular, "bad ton" meant something far more damning than gauche or frumpy; it suggested an unsavory odor of scandal, poor manners, and dishonorable conduct.

"Why?" said Sebastian.

She shrugged. "I can't tell you anything that isn't common knowledge. They were arrogant, rude, and casually cruel. If I were to guess as to why they were killed, I'd say it's because they made the mistake of picking on the wrong person, but I've no idea who that might be." She paused, then said, "Do you think Bayard is in danger?"

"He certainly thinks he is, although he won't tell me why."

"Then more fool him." She glanced at the small gold watch she wore pinned to her bodice. "Now if—"

"What about the men's families or fathers? What can you tell me about them?"

She shrugged. "I know little of Sir Lawrence Upcott. He came into his title shortly after he returned from the American War, retired to the family's seat down in Berkshire, and has rarely been up to town since."

"He was in the Army?"

"He was, yes; cavalry, I believe. As for General Peyton Keebles, his exploits are well-known. He spent most of his time abroad but still managed to father an avalanche of girls on his brief sojourns home before he finally got his son. He was an arrogant, self-obsessed, mean little man, and I doubt anyone misses him—least of all his wife."

"What about Sir Samuel Toole? Did he serve in the American War as well?"

"He did, yes. He was a second son, you know, so he was making a career of it. Then his elder brother died, so he came home and sold out."

Sebastian pushed away from the table to gently rest his hands on the dowager's shoulders and kiss her cheek. "Thank you, Aunt; I'll let you get back to your rout preparations."

She stayed where she was, a troubled frown settling over her features. "You think their service in the American War is significant?"

"I have no idea. But it might be."

Sebastian went next to Westminster. The light was already fading rapidly from the cold, grim day, and he found Hendon just leaving

Downing Street. At the sight of Sebastian, the Earl paused at the kerb, and whatever he read in Sebastian's face led him to say, "You've discovered something, have you?"

"Possibly," said Sebastian as they turned onto Parliament Street. "I need you to tell me what you know about the military service of General Peyton Keebles, Sir Lawrence Upcott, and Sir Samuel Toole."

Hendon cast him a sideways glance. Sebastian thought he might ask why, but all he said was, "Well, let's see . . . If I remember correctly, Keebles shipped out to the colonies somewhere around 1774 or '5. He was part of Cornwallis's first, unsuccessful attempt to capture Charleston, then joined General Howe up in New York. He particularly distinguished himself at the Battle of Brandywine and was active in Pennsylvania, then went south again."

"He was with Sir Henry Clinton when we finally captured Charleston?"

"He was, yes." Hendon cleared his throat uncomfortably. "You're familiar with what happened at Waxhaw Creek?"

"I am, yes."

Hendon nodded. "Dreadful business, that. He was also at the Battle of Cowpens, before being wounded and captured at the Siege of Yorktown."

"That's when he returned to Britain? On parole?"

"Yes. Needless to say, he came home to great acclaim and was knighted. Although then some junior officer who was wounded and captured at Cowpens sent an anonymous letter to the *Morning Chronicle* harshly criticizing him. It was dismissed at the time as biased—the result of resentment and jealousy—and blame for the disasters settled on Cornwallis and Clinton."

"Any idea who wrote the letter?"

"As far as I know, it was never discovered. Keebles then stood for Parliament, won handily, and dedicated himself to opposing any attempt to abolish the slave trade. He was actually in the midst of giving a speech on the subject, calling it 'mistaken philanthropy,' when he had an apoplectic fit and died. Right there on the floor of the Commons."

"Fitting. What about Upcott?"

Hendon shook his head. "I don't actually know much about his service. I don't believe he was in long."

"But he was in the American War?"

"Oh, yes."

"And Sir Samuel Toole?"

"I believe he sailed for America sometime after Keebles. He was an aide-de-camp to General Clinton and saw action in both New York and the Carolinas, but his career wasn't particularly distinguished. It's best remembered for a letter he wrote home and had published. Basically, it criticized what he called the British tendency toward 'false humanity.' He thought the best way to restore our dominion over the colonies would be to lay waste to the land and 'extirpate the present rebellious race,' basically through the liberal use of plunder, pillage, rape, and slaughter. 'Let the wretches feel what a calamity war truly is,' as he put it."

"I've known men like that," said Sebastian. "They think the best way to convince an enemy to surrender is to violate their women and burn their houses, show the men they can't protect their families."

Hendon nodded. "It's the same philosophy Banastre Tarleton used against the southern colonies."

Sebastian looked over at him. "Keebles and Toole both served with Tarleton?"

"They did, yes. But . . . surely you can't think the fathers' activities in the American War have anything to do with what's happening now to their sons."

"You find that far-fetched?"

Hendon thought about it for a moment. "I'll admit it hadn't occurred to me, but . . ." He blew out a harsh breath. "Bridgewood was in the Carolinas as well, you know."

"He was?"

"Mmm. Not for long, but I know he was there. He was a second son, same as Toole. Didn't come into the title until '98 or '99."

"Did you ever hear of anything they did that might have inspired someone to seek revenge?"

"Something besides Waxhaw Creek, you mean?" Hendon thought about it a moment. "I can't think of anything. But knowing them . . . well, let's just say it's possible." Hendon paused again. "If you're right, I suppose we should be thankful that Martin Wilcox never served."

"You're certain he didn't?"

Hendon nodded. "Not a day. Although . . ."

"Although?" prompted Sebastian.

"He did have extensive investments in various shipping interests that played a part in the war."

"Were any of those interests involved in the slave trade?"

"I wouldn't be surprised. Why?"

"Just a thought," said Sebastian.

Leaving Whitehall, Sebastian went in search of Sir Lawrence Upcott. But Upcott had already left for home, taking his dead son's body with him. Sebastian then spent more time than he had to spare trying to run down Lord Bridgewood. He was leaving White's in St. James's Street when Sir Samuel Toole planted himself in front of Sebastian, stopping him. The Baronet's face was red and puffy, his starched shirt points sweat-stained and wilting, his breath reeking of brandy.

"What the bloody hell do you want with Bridgewood?" he demanded. "Bow Street knows exactly who's behind these killings, and the only thing you're doing by going around pretending like it's all some big mystery is to muck things up."

Sebastian wasn't going to argue with a grief-stricken father any more than he was going to badger the man about his military service. "Do you know where Bridgewood is?"

"Any idiot can see it's the Radicals behind it all!" sputtered Toole as if Sebastian hadn't spoken. "They want to burn this country down the way the Jacobins destroyed France, and these killings are the start of it."

"Why would Radicals want to kill a simple tavern keeper?" said Sebastian before he could stop himself.

"To shut her up, of course. She was working with them to get at my son."

Sebastian forced himself to swallow the obvious retort. "Would you happen to know where I might find Lord Bridgewood?"

Toole eyed him suspiciously. "He's dining with Jarvis and Sidmouth before going to some duchess's rout. Why? What the devil are you up to now?"

Chapter 29

"The first American War ended decades ago," said Hero as their carriage rolled through the dark, windswept, wet streets of Mayfair toward the Park Lane home of the Duchess of Claiborne. It was the first chance they'd had to speak in private, for Sebastian had arrived back at Brook Street with barely enough time to scramble into his evening clothes. "How could it possibly have anything to do with what's happening today?"

"It might not. But it is curious, don't you think? Of the five friends—six, if we count Emmanuel Royston-Jones—four of their fathers served in the American War. And the sons of three of those four men are now dead. I've sent a note to Lovejoy, asking him to look into the fathers' service records. But that will only tell us where they were and when; it won't necessarily tell us if there's something ugly in their pasts besides Waxhaw Creek. Something that might lead to murder."

"But it's been thirty-five years since Yorktown. Who would wait thirty-five years for revenge?"

"Someone who has only recently learned a painful truth about the events of those years, perhaps? Or . . ."

"Or?"

"Or someone who is only now in a position to exact their revenge."

"Such as someone who has been fighting in the French wars and recently returned home?" said Hero as their coachman reined in the horses to join the long line of carriages waiting to disgorge their passengers in Park Lane. "Or someone from America who has finally been able to reach Britain?"

"It makes a certain amount of sense, doesn't it?"

Hero met his gaze, her features solemn. "Yes. Yes, it does."

"Amazing," said the Dowager Duchess of Claiborne, greeting them at the door in a splendid gown of mauve silk, with three snow-white plumes nodding from her towering turban and the famous Claiborne diamonds glittering around her neck. "You came."

"Of course we came," said Hero, bending slightly to kiss the Duchess's rouged cheeks.

"Did you think we wouldn't?" said Sebastian.

"Yes," his aunt said baldly.

Sebastian laughed softly as he let his gaze rove over the hundreds of silk-and-jewel-bedecked aristocrats crowding Her Grace's reception rooms. A rout was something less than a ball but considerably grander than a mere card party, although there could be dancing later, and a room was often set aside for those who preferred cards to music and chatter. Basically it was a place to see and be seen, and the Duchess of Claiborne's routs were always so crowded as to be labeled a "crush" by those lucky enough to be invited. Many would be eagerly scanning the write-up in tomorrow's *Morning Chronicle* in the hopes of finding that their names had been mentioned.

"Heaven preserve us," said the Duchess, watching him. "I knew it. Who are you looking for?"

"Lord Bridgewood. Is he here yet?"

"As it happens, he is. He arrived perhaps twenty minutes ago with Sidmouth and Jarvis. And if you provoke a scene in the middle of my party, I swear I'll never forgive you. Do you hear me, Devlin?"

"I won't. I promise."

But the dowager simply huffed something under her breath and turned away to greet her next guest.

"It's interesting Aunt Henrietta thinks you might cause a scene in the middle of her rout," said Hero as they worked their way through the clumps of laughing, tipsy women in wispy silks and satins and sweating men in formal evening dress. "Have you provoked a brawl at one of her parties before?"

"Not that I recall," said Sebastian. He could see the Baron now, on the far side of the Duchess's vast front drawing room, deep in conversation with Lord Jarvis. Then Bridgewood turned and began to weave his way through the shimmering, candlelit crowd, toward the rear of the house.

"Is his lordship avoiding you, do you think?" said Hero, watching him.

"Perhaps," said Sebastian as Bridgewood disappeared into the room in which the Duchess had set out an array of drinks and delicacies to help sustain her guests until supper. "Or perhaps he's simply hungry."

Bridgewood was standing beside a table groaning beneath an array of everything from prawns and buttered crab to cakes, jellies, and ices, all artfully arranged on overflowing silver trays or in cut glass bowls that glittered and gleamed in the flickering light of three massive branches of beeswax candles. He had a half-filled plate in one hand and was stuffing a fat prawn into his mouth when Sebastian walked up to him.

"Lord Bridgewood," said Sebastian. "Do you have a moment?"

The older man swallowed. He was not smiling. "Toole warned me that you've been looking for me. What the blazes do you think you're about, bothering the man? He's just lost his only son, for God's sake."

"As it happens, Sir Samuel approached me," said Sebastian, aware of an obvious, pronounced shift from the Baron's earlier, pleasant manner toward him. "I was wondering if you were with General Keebles at the Battle of Cowpens."

Bridgewood's frown deepened. "I was not. Why?"

"What about Waxhaw Creek? You were there, weren't you? And at Yorktown. Were Toole and Upcott there as well?"

Bridgewood's face darkened. "Listen here, Devlin: If this is about the murder of my son's friends, I consider it in damnably poor taste for you to be haranguing me about it in the middle of a bloody rout."

Sebastian studied the older man's flushed, angry face and tightened jaw. "You think I'm haranguing you? By asking if you saw service with the fathers of the men killed?"

"I do, yes."

"So it has occurred to you that there might be a link between something that happened thirty-five years ago in the colonies and what's happening here in London now?"

"No, damn your eyes."

"Do you know who wrote that anonymous letter to the *Morning Chronicle* blaming Keebles for the disasters at Yorktown and Cowpens?"

"How the devil would I know that?"

"I thought you might . . . if you were there."

"I told you, I wasn't at Cowpens," said the Baron. "I know what you're doing. You think you can distract attention from the investigation of that damned Radical fencing master. Well, let me tell you right now, it's not going to work." He slammed his plate down on the table at his side and stalked off toward the entry hall.

A moment later, over the roar of aristocratic voices, Sebastian heard the Duchess say, "Leaving us already, Lord Bridgewood? What a pity."

It was when Sebastian was working his way back toward Hero that his father-in-law found him.

"What the devil do you think you're about?" demanded Jarvis without preamble, his voice low and icy. "Delving into events thirty-five and more years in the past!"

Sebastian studied the powerful man's narrowed eyes and hard face. "Well, that was fast. Know something about it, do you?"

But Jarvis simply shook his head, his face giving nothing away. "War is ugly. It always has been and always will be. In the heat of the moment, men get carried away by their passions. Things happen."

Sebastian snagged a glass of champagne from the tray of a passing waiter and forced himself to take a long, slow swallow before answering. "You think you need to tell me that, do you?"

"Given your own military service, one assumes it shouldn't be necessary."

"It isn't. But if the things Lord Bridgewood and his friends did thirty-five years ago are the reason their sons are dying today, then I'd say someone obviously doesn't agree with your opinion that war excuses any and all atrocities."

Jarvis pitched his voice even lower. "You're mad. You hear me? Gilbert Keebles, Marcus Toole, and Phineas Upcott are victims of the same Radicals who would tear our nation apart and kill us all if we let them. And if you weren't so blinded by your own prejudices, you'd see that."

"My prejudices?"

"That's right. Don't play stupid with me. I'm well aware of your friendship with a certain Jamaican swordsman. You've been seen meeting with him twice now."

"My, my, aren't your minions efficient? Watching Pitcairn as well as Kate Price and poverty-stricken staymakers, are we?"

"Of course we're watching them. They're *Spenceans*, in case you didn't know."

"Oh, I know," said Sebastian, taking another sip of his champagne.

Jarvis's normally iron composure was beginning to slip. "Consort with revolutionaries if you must," he hissed. "But you keep my daughter out of this. Do I make myself clear?"

Sebastian studied his father-in-law's angry, flushed face. "Up to something, are you?"

Rather than answer, Jarvis simply grunted and started to turn away.

"Tell me this," said Sebastian, stopping him. "Do you actually know something that might explain these murders?"

"As it happens, I do not. But anything that agitates the populace to this extent is a damnable nuisance. It's past time Bow Street found someone to hang."

"And if they hang the wrong man and the murders continue?"

"Then they'll simply need to find someone else to hang, won't they? Lord knows we've plenty of scoundrels in want of hanging—and that includes a certain seditious violinist of your acquaintance."

❧

"You think Papa knows what's behind these killings?" said Hero later as they settled in their carriage and headed for home.

"He claims he does not. But then, we both know Jarvis's attitude toward truth telling. And the fact that he felt moved to warn me to back off suggests that *something* happened in the colonies all those years ago. Something he'd rather keep buried."

"Do you think Lady Keebles would know?"

"She might, although I doubt it. And even if she does, I can't see her admitting to anything that might tarnish the General's famous legacy. But Keebles had a brother who made something of a name for himself as a barrister in the City, and from what I'm hearing, he and the General never got along. He might be willing to talk about it . . . assuming he's still alive."

Hero was silent for a moment, watching the flickering light

from the passing gas lamps catch the raindrops chasing each other down the windowpane beside her. "Think about this," she said. "Anyone old enough to have been a victim of General Keebles and company in the American War would need to be at least forty-five or fifty today, if not more. Do you think it's possible someone of that age has suddenly decided go on a killing spree—and somehow managed to single-handedly overpower three strong young men and a healthy young woman?"

"We don't know that whoever the fathers victimized is the same as the person now seeking revenge. What if the murderer is their victim's son? It could even be someone who wasn't born thirty-five years ago."

Hero turned her head to look at him. "You're thinking it's Pitcairn, aren't you?"

Sebastian met her gaze and nodded. "Or someone like him."

Chapter 30

Thursday, 28 November

Early the next morning, Sebastian went in search of the late General Sir Peyton Keebles's brother, Vernon, who turned out to be very much alive.

Now a widower, the retired barrister kept a house in Chancery Lane but was known for taking most of his meals in the various pubs and small hotels near the Inns of Court. "I don't like to eat alone," he would tell anyone who asked the reason for his peculiar practice.

Sebastian finally ran Mr. Vernon Keebles to ground eating beefsteak and potatoes in the low-ceilinged, oak-paneled dining room of an ancient inn near Temple Bar. The atmosphere was thick with the smell of roasting meat, strong ale, tobacco, and smoke from the fire that danced on the hearth. "I know who you are," said the barrister when Sebastian introduced himself and apologized for interrupting his meal. "Have a seat, please. Looking into what happened to my nevvy, are you?"

Sebastian nodded as he settled on the opposite bench. "He was friends with my sister's son."

"Ah, that's right; I was forgetting Martin Wilcox married Hendon's girl." Vernon Keebles reached for his tankard, took a deep drink, then wiped his lips. A thin, stoop-shouldered man with wispy white hair and deeply wrinkled, yellow-tinged skin, he was the General's junior by only a year. And given that Peyton Keebles had been over fifty when he sired Gilbert, Sebastian figured the barrister must be nearing eighty.

"Never cared for him, you know," the barrister was saying. "My nevvy, I mean. Peyton indulged him beyond all reason. Acted like the sun shone out the boy's backside, as they say. I can only be grateful my brother didn't live long enough to see what happened to his precious only son."

"Do you have any idea who might be doing this? Killing Gilbert and his friends, I mean."

Keebles pressed his shoulder blades against the high wooden back of his bench and let his hands rest idle on the tabletop. "No idea at all. And I won't deny I've spent some time pondering it."

"I understand your brother and Sir Samuel Toole both served in New York and the Carolinas in the American War. Were they together?"

"I know they were in the Carolinas together. Not sure about New York."

"What about Phineas's father, Sir Lawrence Upcott? He also spent time in the colonies. Was he in the Carolinas with them?"

"That I couldn't tell you." The old man's watery blue eyes blinked rapidly. "You think that's what's behind the murder of Gilbert and his friends? Payback for something my brother and the others did in the war?"

"I think it's possible, yes. I'm told that after Yorktown, when General Keebles was paroled and returned to England, someone sent an anonymous letter to the papers castigating him. Do you have any idea who wrote it?"

Keebles looked thoughtful for a moment, then shook his head. "I remember Peyton telling me he had a pretty good idea who was behind it. But if he named the fellow, I don't recall it." He stared at Sebastian for a long moment. "It's been thirty-five years since Yorktown. What makes you think you need to go back that far to find an explanation for what's happening today?"

"I don't have any actual evidence that points to the fathers' war service as an explanation, but I can't discount it as a possibility, either. At least, not yet."

Keebles brought up a hand to rub absently at his forehead. "As much as it pains me to say it, I suspect there's no need to go looking into what my brother or anyone else did in the war. Gilbert might've been my nephew, but that never blinded me to the fact that he was a disgusting little shite who thought he was better than everyone else. I always said it was a pity the lad didn't follow his father into the Army—put all those nasty impulses of his to work killing the French and Americans rather than making life miserable for whatever poor sod happened to have the misfortune to come across him in this country."

"But you can't think of who might have killed him?"

"Not really. The thing is, men like Gilbert and his kind are usually careful to pick on those who can't or won't fight back.

Why, the last time I saw him, he was laughing about how he and his friends went after some woman who publishes one of those Radical weeklies. A woman!"

Sebastian stared at him. "You mean, Kate Price?"

Keebles shrugged. "If he said her name, I don't recall it."

"When was this?"

"That I saw Gilbert?" Keebles pondered the question a moment. "Must've been a month or so ago, at least. I tried to avoid the lad as much as possible, you know. All I remember is that he was aggravated because just as they were set to destroy her place, someone came along and stopped them. Gilbert wasn't laughing about that."

"How does one man stop five or six?" said Sebastian.

"With a sword, apparently." The old man chuckled. "Don't know what he was doing walking around London with a cavalry saber, but from what Gil was telling me, the fellow has something of a reputation as a fencing master. He's Black, you know; from Jamaica. I don't follow such things myself, but you may've heard of him."

"Yes," said Sebastian. "I've heard of him."

Chapter 31

Dressed in a plain dark wool cloak with the hood pulled up against a miserable wind, Kate Price stood outside a print seller's shop in Fleet Street, her gaze on the colored satires arrayed in the shop's bow window. As Hero walked up, the journalist glanced over at her, then returned her gaze to the window display. "I take it you aren't here by chance." It wasn't a question.

"No," said Hero.

Kate nodded to one of the prints in the window. A satirical caricature by Rory Mackenzie, it portrayed two corpulent, over-dressed dandies mincing across the Strand, their heels comically high, a dozen or more gold fobs dangling from their watch chains, the buttons of their silk waistcoats strained by their bulbous bellies. Behind them loomed the facade of St. Paul's Cathedral; to one side slumped an exhausted, ragged little crossing sweeper; a stooped, aged woman held out a withered apple from a rusted tray, and at her feet lay the pallid corpse of a skeletal ex-soldier curled up in the gutter, his body frozen by rigor mortis in a grotesque pose. "I wish I could draw," she said. "I sometimes think just one of these images is more evocative than everything I've written taken all together."

"They can be very effective," said Hero, keeping her gaze on the delicately colored prints. "You didn't tell me Marcus Toole and his friends paid a visit to your press recently."

Kate Price stiffened. "It wasn't recent—not unless you call something that happened a month or more ago 'recent.' "

"But it did happen?"

"Oh, yes; it happened."

"Why were they there?"

She expelled a low huff that held no amusement. "Why do you think? They read my article."

"And decided to pay you back for it by smashing your press?"

"That was the idea."

"And Damion Pitcairn stopped them?" said Hero.

That jerked Kate's gaze back to Hero's face for one tense instant. She looked away again. "Who told you that?"

"Gilbert Keebles mentioned it to someone before he died."

When the other woman remained silent, Hero said, "Why was Damion Pitcairn there?"

"I sometimes print things for him."

"For the Spenceans?"

"You'd need to ask him that."

"And he just happened to have a cavalry saber with him when he dropped by to pick up his broadsheets?"

Kate Price shrugged. "He collects them, you know. Old swords, I mean. He's always on the lookout for them. He was coming from the secondhand stalls in Brick Lane when he stopped by to see if I had his broadsheets ready."

"And he found Keebles, Toole, and the others there?"

"Yes. It's one thing to destroy a printing press when the only thing standing between you and your fun is a small woman. But it's something else entirely to try it when confronted with a naked blade."

"Pitcairn drew steel on them?"

"You're suggesting it was wrong of him?"

"Not at all. And then they simply left?"

"Of course they left. When it comes right down to it, men like that are cowards. Oh, they tried to make out that it was all supposed to be a joke—that they wouldn't actually have done anything. But that was a lie."

Hero had no doubts about that. "Did they ever try to come back?"

The other woman was silent for so long that Hero didn't think she was going to answer. Then she shook her head. "Damion told them that if they did, he'd—" She broke off, her eyes widening as she sucked in a quick breath.

"That he'd—what? Kill them?"

But the journalist only tightened her jaw and refused to be drawn in any further.

"That doesn't sound good," said Devlin later when Hero told him of the conversation in Fleet Street. His own attempts to track down Damion Pitcairn had been less successful.

"No." She tossed her plumed hat onto a nearby chair and stared at it a moment before saying, "Do you think old Mr. Vernon Keebles has spoken to Bow Street?"

Devlin met her gaze. "For Pitcairn's sake, I sincerely hope not."

Chapter 32

The inquest into the death of Alison Cross was held later that morning out at Chalk Farm.

The murder of a simple country tavern keeper drew predictably few spectators from London. But a second killing in their normally peaceful neighborhood had understandably alarmed the local inhabitants, who braved the cold, damp wind to once again descend on the tavern.

"Think it's finally gonna snow?" said Tom as Sebastian turned his horses into the tavern's yard.

He squinted up at the heavy clouds pressing down on the surrounding hills. "Looks like it might, doesn't it? But hopefully not before we get out of here."

"I wouldn't count on it," said Tom, scrambling forward to take the reins.

Sebastian grunted as he hopped down to the cobbles, then

paused at the sight of a familiar, roughly dressed figure standing beside a distant outbuilding. Sid Diamond was deep in conversation with a dark-haired young woman clutching a knitted blue shawl over a white muslin gown. As Sebastian watched, she shook her head, fisted her free hand in her skirts, and ran toward the tavern without looking back. The highwayman lowered the brim of his hat and was turning away when he noticed Sebastian. For a moment Diamond hesitated, then altered his course to cross the yard.

Watching him, Sebastian found it hard to believe this was the same man he'd met just—what? Three? Four days ago? The rollicking insouciance, the devil-may-care jauntiness, the dashing aura of danger were all gone, leaving the man looking disheveled and defeated. Even his stride was stiff, as if simply walking took more focus and concentration than he could somehow muster.

"Who did this?" demanded the highwayman, his voice hoarse as he planted himself in front of Sebastian. "You know, don't you? Please tell me you know."

The former cavalryman was unshaven, his face gray and haggard as if he hadn't slept in days, his eyes bloodshot and glassy with the kind of grief that's like a silent, never-ending howl of despair.

Sebastian shook his head. "I wish I did, but I don't. Do you?"

"Me? You think if I did, I'd be here, rather than out doin' somethin' about it?"

"Was Alison Cross your lover?"

Diamond's head jerked back at the question. He hesitated a moment, then pressed his lips into a tight line and nodded.

Did you know? Sebastian wondered, watching the other man's throat work as he swallowed. *Did you know she was carrying your child?* But all he said was, "I take it she was also your informant?" It wasn't uncommon for rural tavern keepers, barmaids, and ostlers to pass word of a promising target to local highwaymen.

Diamond glared at him. "And if I said she wasn't, would you believe me?"

"It might help explain what happened to her."

"It doesn't. Apart from which, I ain't hit a carriage around here in months."

"No? And yet you claimed to have been working Saturday night."

"That was the plan. But the bastards had a bloody guard with a blunderbuss sittin' up next t' the driver. They'd no notion I was even there, watchin' 'em go by."

"So how many months are we talking about? Since you were last successful, I mean."

"Hell, I don't know. Sometime in late August, it musta been. What difference does it make? Don't you understand? This has nothing to do with me. It's all mixed up somehow with those nasty little sons of privilege who are being killed."

"Why would someone interested in killing the sons of a baron, a baronet, and a knight want to murder a simple rural tavern keeper?"

"I don't know!"

"She never said anything—anything at all—to you about something she might have overheard or seen? Something that might have put her in danger?"

"No."

"Would she have? Said something to you, I mean."

"Of course she—" Diamond started to say, then broke off, his chest lifting on a sharply indrawn breath.

"She wouldn't, would she?" said Sebastian, watching him. "Not if she thought you might try to do something about it—something that could end with you either dead or in prison, waiting to be hanged."

"Bloody hell," swore Diamond, swiping a trembling hand across his eyes, his voice a torn whisper. "Bloody, bloody hell."

The inquest was predictably anticlimactic.

Alison Cross had last been seen late in the afternoon on Tuesday. She'd been laughing with some drovers at one of the tables as if she hadn't a care in the world. Then she'd asked her young barmaid to take over while she stepped out for a moment.

She never came back.

The barmaid was the first to testify. A pretty young woman, she looked to be no more than sixteen or seventeen, with a heavy fall of dark hair, a creamy complexion, and winsome features. She wore a simple white muslin gown with a blue sash at its high waist and a modest scooped neckline, and even if he hadn't seen them together, such was her resemblance to the knight of the road that Sebastian had no difficulty identifying her as the highwayman's sister even before she gave her name as Jenna Diamond.

She was obviously badly frightened, and she cried silently throughout her testimony, the tears coursing down her cheeks so that she had to keep swiping them away with the flat of her palm. "It took me a while to realize just how long she'd been gone," said Jenna in a quiet, broken voice. "It wasn't till an hour or two went by that I realized something must be wrong."

"Do you know why she would go out to that disused barn?" asked the coroner.

"No, Your Honor. I've no notion at all. She never went there before that I knew of."

The ostler who had found the dead woman's body gave evidence next, followed by Lovejoy and Gibson. Then, after a quick whispered consultation, the jury returned a verdict of homicide by party or parties unknown, and that was that.

"The Palace is apoplectic," said Lovejoy afterward as they stood together on the tavern's wide front veranda and watched the first flakes of snow begin to fall on the wet, dreary countryside. "Sir Nathaniel Conant is determined to have someone remanded into custody by the beginning of next week."

"Have they selected their scapegoat yet?" asked Sebastian.

"They have, I'm afraid. I did suggest the arrest might be a bit premature, but . . ."

"But?"

"I was told the orders come directly from the Home Office, and that if I have any concerns, I should address them to Lord Sidmouth himself." Lovejoy tightened his jaw. "They're going after one of the Spenceans, of course—perhaps more than one. The idea is to portray these deaths as part of some vile revolutionary plot to bring down the monarchy and slaughter the aristocracy. The men will be charged not only with murder, but with sedition and treason. The Crown intends to seek the full ancient penalty."

Sebastian looked over at him. "You can't be serious."

"I wish I weren't. They're to be hanged, drawn, castrated, disemboweled, and beheaded."

Chapter 33

When Sebastian finally tracked down Damion Pitcairn, he was sitting on the worn stone stairs near Beaufort Wharfs, watching the snow fall gently into the river before him.

"You don't have anything better to do these days than look for me?" he said as Sebastian settled on the top step.

Sebastian stretched his legs out straight and crossed his ankles. "I'm told you like to collect swords—cavalry sabers in particular."

The fencing master stiffened, then returned his gaze to the Thames. "So? No one's had their head lopped off lately, have they?"

"Not to my knowledge. How much do you know about the Celts?"

"The whats?"

"The Celts: the tribes that lived in Britain and Ireland before the arrival of first the Romans, then the Germanic tribes."

A smile of amusement lit the younger man's eyes. "Sorry. Can't say I know anything about them. Why?"

"According to numerous Roman writers, the Celts used to practice human sacrifice. Their best-known ways of dispatching their victims—depending upon the intended godly recipient—were by drowning, burning, and hanging from trees—or wood, I suppose you could say."

Pitcairn's smile had disappeared. "Are you serious?"

"I am, yes."

"You think that's what's going on here? *Human sacrifices?*"

"I honestly don't know. Thankfully, the papers have been so fixated on Toole's burning on Primrose Hill that no one in Fleet Street has noticed it's part of a pattern. But I suspect it's only a matter of time."

Pitcairn was silent for a moment, his features a tense mask as he stared out over the gray surging river. The snow was coming down harder now, big wet flakes that melted almost as soon as they hit the old stone steps and nearby muddy bank. "Then I'd say Bow Street's finest should be looking for someone who spent his growing-up years reading Latin at Eton or Harrow, rather than sweating in the sugarcane fields of Jamaica."

"Maybe. But for some reason I can't understand, everything keeps circling back to you."

"And you expect me to explain it?" Pitcairn shook his head. "I can't."

Sebastian studied the younger man's solemn profile. "And yet you know more than you would have me believe."

Pitcairn twisted around to look at him again. "You think I owe you honesty? I don't owe you a damned thing."

"Not for my sake, no."

Pitcairn rested his elbows on his bent knees, his gaze once again on the river before them. After a moment, he said, "You ever been to Jamaica?"

"I have, yes. It's a breathtakingly beautiful place; clear blue skies, turquoise seas, and the lushest green hills I've ever seen. It was like a vision of paradise—if paradise came with slave auctions and the severed arms, legs, and heads of men and women dangling from the trees. I was told there'd recently been an uprising. It was put down . . . harshly."

"They always are. I was four the first time I saw a man whipped to death. I don't remember now what his crime was, if I was ever told, but I know I'll never forget the sound of his screams. Old man Pitcairn usually just sold off the slaves that gave him trouble; 'Why waste money by killing them?' was his philosophy. So whatever the fellow did must have seriously aggravated him."

Sebastian kept his gaze on the river. Impossible to think of this brilliant, accomplished young man as the son of a brutal slave owner. "Is he still alive? Your father, I mean."

"No. He was over fifty when I was born. He had three other children that I know of, older than me, and all from enslaved women. But they were girls. I was the only son."

"Did he free his daughters, too?"

Pitcairn stared down at the worn stone steps between his boots and shook his head. "Only me."

Sebastian found his chest hurt, just at the thought of it. How could any man—even one as debauched and amoral as a slave owner—father a child and then leave her to live and die enslaved? His own flesh and blood?

How?

Aloud, he said, "Because they were girls?"

"That might have been part of it. But it was only part." Pitcairn yanked off one of his gloves and held up his splayed hand, turning it this way and that in the cold light of the day. "He liked the way I came up pale. All his other children were dark." He dropped the hand to his lap but made no move to put on the glove again. "He took me away from my mother a week after we watched that man get whipped to death. My mother . . ." His voice trailed off, and he had to swallow before going on. "She didn't take it well. That's when the old man sold her down the road."

"Sasha told me your mother died when she was eight." The knowledge of the manner of the woman's death hung in the air between them, although neither of them mentioned it.

Pitcairn swiped his hands down over his mouth, then nodded. "I was gone by then. The old man sent me to Scotland when I was twelve. His intent was for me to become a solicitor or a surgeon."

"He sent you to his family?"

"Yes, in Fife. His brother William was a vicar in Dysart. It was my uncle's wife, Aunt Elaine, who taught me music."

"So who taught you to fence?"

"Ah, that was the old man himself. He saw something in me that suggested I had an aptitude, and it amused him to foster it. He died when I was seventeen. That's when Uncle William kicked me out of his house. And he didn't just kick me out; he also pocketed the money my father had sent for my apprenticeship. Funny enough, I hadn't realized all those years that the old man had been paying Uncle William to keep me. But when the money stopped—" He made an outward sweeping motion with his hands.

Sebastian watched as a quick succession of painful emotions flitted across the younger man's face—hurt, resentment, bafflement, and, inevitably, a ghostly shadow of reluctant, shattered love—

before Pitcairn's rigid self-control slammed back into place. "That's when you came to London?" said Sebastian.

"Yes."

"If your father was from Fife, you must be related somehow to Major John Pitcairn."

The other man's eyes narrowed. "He was my father's cousin. How do you know of him?"

"He was one of the first casualties of the American War—fought at Lexington and Concord before being killed at Bunker Hill."

Pitcairn's frown deepened. "That's significant?"

"Damned if I know."

"I don't understand."

"The fathers of Gilbert Keebles, Marcus Toole, and Phineas Upcott all fought in the first American War, as did Theo Bridgewood's father. It could be absolutely meaningless, or . . ." Sebastian shrugged.

Pitcairn was thoughtful for a moment, watching a barge working its way upriver. "He did, too, you know—old man Pitcairn, I mean. Before he set up as a planter in Jamaica, he was an ensign in the cavalry."

"Do you know where he saw action?"

"I think it was in the Carolinas, although I'll admit I didn't pay a whole lot of attention when he talked about it."

"Is that how your interest in collecting cavalry sabers began? Because of him?"

"Maybe. I don't know. I never thought much about it."

Sebastian watched the foam-flecked waves curl away from the barge's low sides. The snow was coming down so thick and fast now that he could barely see the opposite bank. "Which came first?" he asked. "The incident with Sasha in Southwark, or the confrontation with Keebles, Toole, and their friends in Kate Price's printing shop?"

It was a moment before Pitcairn responded. "Heard about that, did you?"

"Yes." When the younger man remained silent, Sebastian said again, "So which incident came first?"

"The printshop. Why?"

"I'm trying to figure out how you just happened to show up at precisely the right moment to protect first Kate Price, then Sasha Stone. That doesn't strike you as a bit . . . curious?"

"There's a word for that sort of thing, you know. It's called serendipity."

"Is that what we're talking about here? Pure chance?"

"What else could we be talking about?"

Sebastian shrugged and pushed to his feet. "You know the Home Office is having you watched?"

"I had noticed, yes."

"They're planning to arrest one of the Spenceans for this string of murders. What do you think the odds are it's you?"

Pitcairn looked up at him. "What exactly are you suggesting I do about it?"

"You could leave. Go someplace else. How's your French?"

"You think I'd be better off in Paris than here?"

"Possibly. They do seem slightly more accepting of people with darker skin. Look at Thomas-Alexandre Dumas. Joseph Serrant. The Chevalier de Saint-Georges."

"I'm not running away."

Sebastian shrugged and started to turn. "Just be careful, will you?"

"Why? What is it to you if your government should choose to hang me?"

Not only hang you, but have you castrated, disemboweled, chopped into four pieces, and beheaded, thought Sebastian. But all he said was, "'How can a people be free that has not learnt to be just?'"

Something flickered in the other man's eyes. "Sieyès, right?"

"You've read him?"

A smile of genuine amusement spread across the Jamaican's features. "Of course I've read him. He did play a rather significant role in France's revolt against monarchy and aristocracy, remember?"

Sebastian had to work to keep his reaction off his face. "So he did."

"Drawn and quartered?" said Hero in disbelief when Sebastian told her of his conversations with Lovejoy and Pitcairn. They had bundled the boys in coats, scarves, hats, and boots and were taking them for a walk in the snow.

"And castrated, disemboweled, and beheaded," said Sebastian. "We haven't moved on much from 1745, have we?"

"Are they serious?"

"Absolutely. It's what Edward Despard and his friends were sentenced to in 1803, remember? The only reason they weren't disemboweled and quartered is because Despard's wife and his good friend Horatio Nelson—Admiral Nelson, for God's sake!—successfully petitioned the King to reduce the sentences. So they were merely drawn, hanged, and beheaded."

She watched Simon plant his feet far apart, then throw back his head and squeeze his eyes shut as he opened his mouth to catch the wet snowflakes on his tongue. "They're frightened, aren't they?" she said quietly. "The government, I mean."

Sebastian nodded. "They're terrified—and with good reason. Prices keep rising while wages keep falling and jobs are disappearing. The weather has been worse all year than anyone can remember. Crops have failed, and livestock are dying. People are cold, starving, and deeply, justifiably angry. They sacrificed, bled, and died for over twenty years for the sake of the war against France, and for what? To put the Bourbons back on their throne and pay crushing taxes to keep the Hanovers fat and happy on theirs?"

She looped her hand through the crook of his arm and leaned into him. "If you're not careful, you're liable to be hauled into court on charges of sedition yourself." Her smile faded. "I never did believe Despard was guilty of treason."

"He wasn't. The evidence against him was a farce manufactured by government spies. I never understood how they managed to get a conviction."

They watched together as Patrick scooped a handful of wet snow off a nearby area's iron railing and laughed as it turned to mush in his fist.

Hero said, "I think it was because people didn't like the fact that an officer and a gentleman had taken a Black woman to wife. And now they're going after a man with a Black mother. Pitcairn is in serious danger, isn't he?"

"Yes."

She fell silent, her eyes narrowing as they came around the corner to find an opulent, gold-trimmed landau drawn up before their house, its beautifully matched team of creamy white horses stomping their hooves and shaking their heads in the snow as a liveried footman reached to open the carriage door. "Who is that?" she said quietly. "Do you know?"

"No."

As they drew closer, a stocky older man in an old-fashioned powdered wig emerged. At the sight of them, he drew up, then came down the carriage steps in a rush to stride quickly toward them.

"You're Lord Devlin, aren't you?" he said in a rough voice.

"I am." Sebastian exchanged a quick glance with Hero as she reached out to catch Simon by the hand. "May I help you?"

"I'm Royston-Jones—Zacharia Royston-Jones. I assume you've heard?"

Sebastian shook his head. "Heard what?"

"My son—Emmanuel—has disappeared."

Chapter 34

"Tell me what happened," said Sebastian, splashing brandy into two glasses.

He had brought Zacharia Royston-Jones into the library, where the older man now sat in one of the leather chairs drawn up before the fire, his elbows propped on his spread knees and his bowed head resting in his hands.

The merchant looked up as Sebastian held out one of the brandies. A medium-sized, thickset man with broad shoulders, a large nose, and prominent chin, the merchant was probably somewhere in his late sixties. Like many men of his generation, he wore the frock coat and old-fashioned breeches that had been the style in his youth. There was no mistaking their fine materials or exquisite tailoring. Yet there was a vaguely disheveled quality about him: His shoulders slumped, his powdered wig was askew, and his eyes looked pinched and hurting.

"There isn't much to tell, I'm afraid," he said, taking a deep gulp of his drink. "According to his servants, Emmanuel went out yesterday evening shortly before eight and never returned."

"Did he take his carriage?"

"He didn't, no. He set off walking—toward Bond Street, according to his butler."

"And he told no one where he was going?"

"No one."

"He's never done anything like this before?"

"No. Or at least, not in years."

"How was he dressed?"

"As one would when planning to spend the evening at one's club. Except no one at any of the clubs has seen him. I spoke to Theo Bridgewood and Wilcox, but both say they haven't seen him in weeks."

"Did you try asking his cousin where he might be?"

The merchant's nose wrinkled in distaste. "The crazy little Irish girl? What would she know?"

Sebastian let it pass. "But you have informed Bow Street?"

Royston-Jones nodded. "I've just come from there, for the third time." He brought up a shaky hand to rub his eyes with a splayed thumb and forefinger. "I don't know what else I can do, which I suppose is why I'm here. You don't know of anything—anything at all—that might explain what's happened to him?"

"No. I'm sorry," said Sebastian. "Have you spoken to his valet?"

Zacharia Royston-Jones nodded again. "I asked him if Emmanuel has seemed troubled or afraid in any way lately, and he just looked at me and said, 'Both.' "

"Did he elaborate?"

"He didn't exactly need to, did he? I mean, everyone knows

Emmanuel has been struggling ever since Annie took sick and died like that. And who wouldn't be afraid with some madman picking off his friends one by one?"

"The valet knew of nothing else? Nothing more recent or specific?"

"No." As if unable to sit still any longer, Zacharia Royston-Jones pushed to his feet and went to stand at the front windows, the brandy clutched in one hand, the other hand opening and closing at his side. "I'm told Bow Street thinks Radicals are behind these recent murders."

"So I've heard."

"You don't agree?"

Sebastian took a long, slow sip of his own brandy. "No. I think something else is going on here."

Royston-Jones turned to stare at him. "Something like—what?"

Sebastian studied the older man's craggy, worried face. "How much do you know about your son's friends?"

Royston-Jones snorted. "Havey-cavey bunch of blighters, if you ask me—not that anyone ever did, mind you. And with good reason, considering I'm the one who sent him off to that fancy school and told him to be damned sure and make the right sort of friends." He gave a harsh, mirthless laugh. "*The right sort.* Bloody hell. Oh, they're the right sort, all right. The get of sirs and lords, and bounders every last one of 'em. And there's no need to be telling me I've no one but myself to blame. Think I don't know it?"

When Sebastian remained silent, the merchant swiped a trembling hand across his face. "You reckon that's what this is all about? That lot have finally gone and done something nasty to the wrong man, and he's payin' them back for it—with interest?"

"I don't have any proof, but it seems distinctly possible, yes."

"Son of a bitch," he swore, starting to turn away. Then he swung back around to face Sebastian again. "What the hell did those stupid jackasses do that would drive someone to murder? Murder! Do you know?"

"I've heard of a half dozen things that might conceivably have inspired someone with a thirst for revenge, but I can only guess at what I haven't heard."

Royston-Jones nodded. "Last time I saw Emmanuel, he was telling me about how he ran into that lot a few weeks ago in St. James's Street and was standing there, talkin' to 'em, when some poor sod comes up swearing about how he was gonna see 'em all in hell for tearing his coffeehouse apart."

Adam York, thought Sebastian. But all he said was, "Do you remember any other similar incidents Emmanuel might have told you about?"

Royston-Jones shook his head. "I've never made a secret of what I think of that lot and their antics. Emmanuel usually knows better than to talk about them around me."

"I was under the impression he'd been keeping his distance from them lately."

"Has he? I didn't know that."

"He never said anything to you about it—about why he'd quit seeing much of them?"

"No. We've never been what you might call close. I know he's always thought I pushed him too hard when he was a lad, but . . ." He swallowed. "All I ever wanted was for him to have the chance to be what I can never be: a gentleman. A man respected for more than his wealth. A man who doesn't need to worry that people are snickering behind his back, calling him an uncouth mushroom, and laughing about the way he talks, about how he hasn't a notion of how to go on in polite society. Think I don't know what people say about me? I know. And I wanted somethin' more for Emmanuel. Is that so wrong?"

"He's a fine young man," said Sebastian. "A son any father would be proud of."

Royston-Jones raised his brandy to his lips and drained it in one long pull before saying bluntly, "You think he's dead, don't you?"

Sebastian shook his head, although it was a lie. Impossible not to remember that last Sunday Phineas Upcott had similarly left his rooms without saying where he was going. It was only by chance that his body had been discovered so quickly. But Sebastian wasn't about to say any of that to this frightened, grief-stricken father. "I wouldn't give up hope yet."

Royston-Jones set his empty glass aside, then glanced up, his bruised-looking eyes swimming with unshed tears. "He's my only son, you know—my only child. If he's gone, what's it all been for—all my hard work all these years? For my own vanity? God help me, but I'm a fool." He reached for the hat he'd tossed on one of the end tables and slammed it back on his head. "You'll let me know if you learn anything? Anything at all?"

"Of course."

Royston-Jones nodded and turned toward the door, his lips pressed tightly together as if he no longer trusted himself to speak.

"Zacharia Royston-Jones didn't fight in the American War," said Hero later, when Sebastian climbed the stairs to find her sitting cross-legged on the rug before the nursery's fireplace, building a tower of colored blocks with Miss Guinevere. "He was never even in the Army—or the Navy."

"No," Sebastian agreed, shifting a pile of nursery books so he could settle into the nearby overstuffed armchair. "Which means that if Emmanuel has indeed been murdered—and I seriously suspect he has—then all my speculation in that direction was a dead end." He paused. "Unless of course Emmanuel was killed for the same reason as Alison Cross—not because of something his father did, but because of something Emmanuel himself knew."

Hero watched Guinevere carefully wrap her small fist around another block, then looked up. "So where is the body?"

"Lucan mentions three of the Celtic gods to whom human sacrifices were made. The offerings to Teutates were drowned, those to Taranis were burned, and those to Esus were hanged from trees. But according to Erasmus Inkberry, the Celts had numerous other divinities, some of which were earth gods and goddesses. And in most ancient societies, sacrifices to earth gods were buried. Remember how the Romans used to bury the errant vestal virgins alive?"

Hero stared at him. "You think that's why Emmanuel hasn't been found? Because he's *buried* someplace?"

"It seems plausible, doesn't it?"

"That poor man," she whispered. "That poor, poor man."

Chapter 35

Sebastian arrived in Little Windmill Street a short time later to find Ciana O'Leary's shop shuttered.

The weak winter sun was already beginning to sink low in the sky, and he stood for a moment in the pool of light cast by a flickering oil lamp set high on a nearby wall, only vaguely aware of the snow falling gently around him. He realized he had no idea where the Irishwoman lived. And so he started going into first one shop, then the next—a chandler's, a button shop, a haberdasher's—until he finally found a stooped old fruit seller with a ragged brown shawl pulled up over her head, who eyed him appraisingly and said, "Ciana? And what would a fine gentleman such as yourself be wantin' with our Ciana?"

"I need to speak to her about her cousin."

The old woman nodded knowingly, then appeared to come to

a decision. "Reckon you'll be finding her in the chapel, prayin' for him." She crossed herself. "Wherever he may be, poor soul."

That took Sebastian by surprise. He said, "You mean the church of St. James's?"

"Ach, no." The woman's face crinkled with her amusement. "Not our Ciana. It's the chapel on Warwick Street you'll be wantin'."

The Catholic chapel in Warwick Street was less than thirty years old. There had been a time not so long ago when any Catholic priest or nun brave enough to venture onto English soil courted torture and a hideous death. But then came the French Revolution and the dire threat to monarchism and aristocratic privilege it represented, and the British Crown found itself allied with the Catholic royal family of its old enemy. The most oppressive prohibitions against Catholics were relaxed, and a Catholic bishop was allowed to establish his household in Golden Square. He then built a small chapel in his backyard, facing onto Warwick Street, for the benefit of the tens of thousands of Catholic refugees pouring into England.

As Sebastian slipped into the chapel, he could see Ciana O'Leary on her knees in the last row of pews, her head bowed, her face buried in her hands. The sound of the door being quietly eased shut brought her head up. Her eyes were dark and bruised-looking with worry, and the light from a nearby branch of candles shimmered over cheeks wet with tears.

"Do you know something?" she said in a hoarse whisper, settling back onto the pew. "Has Emmanuel been found?"

"No." His snow-caked hat held in one hand, Sebastian slid into the pew beside her. "I didn't realize you're a Catholic."

The faintest hint of a smile touched her lips. "I am and I'm not. I can find comfort and strength in the traditions of my childhood even if my own beliefs have . . . expanded. The Roystons have always been Catholics, you know, although of course they've had to keep it a deep, dark secret since the days of the Roundheads. It wasn't that long ago a Catholic couldn't buy land, own a horse worth more than five pounds, or even attend university."

"Things are better now."

"Better. But Catholics still aren't equal."

Sebastian wasn't going to argue with that. "And Emmanuel? Is he Catholic as well?"

She looked him straight in the eye and said, "I don't know."

"Or at any rate you won't admit to knowing?"

She shrugged.

He said, "But you've heard he's missing?"

Her gaze went to the crucifix that hung beside the altar. "Why do you think I'm here, praying?"

When he didn't answer, she said softly, "You think he's dead, don't you?"

"Why else would he disappear?"

She hesitated as if choosing her words carefully. "Emmanuel is . . . a very troubled soul. It troubles him that much of his family's wealth came from the wars and the slave trade, and it troubles him that he was friends for so many years with a group of men who can only be described as despicable."

Sebastian studied her candlelit profile. "I still don't understand why now—why would he sever his friendship with Keebles and the rest of them now, when he's known them since Eton?"

"I think the nasty things they did always bothered him at some level. But . . ." Again she paused. "Emmanuel is at heart a good, kind man, but he's weak. He tolerated the disturbing things his friends did because he needed them—needed what their friendship gave him. Acceptance, mainly, but also reassurance that he wasn't still that awkward, sensitive, ridiculed boy he was when his father first sent him to Eton."

"And so he turned a blind eye to the morally reprehensible things they did?"

"Aren't most of us like that? All too ready to find excuses for the nasty things our friends and allies—or we ourselves—do, even when we would harshly condemn those same actions if committed by someone else? We flatter ourselves that *our* army would never commit the kind of atrocities we blame the French and Americans for. And yet, somewhere deep down in the hollowness of our souls, we know the truth, don't we? What we did to Ireland . . . Scotland . . . the Peninsula . . ." She fixed him with a hard, level stare. "Or do you prefer to pretend those things don't happen?"

Sebastian shook his head. "I saw what happened on the retreat to Corunna. The truth is that most of us will accept far more reprehensible behavior from those we consider 'on our side' than we're willing to admit. But I can't help feeling that *something* must have happened—something truly horrific—that finally made Emmanuel decide after ten-plus years that his friends' behavior could no longer be borne. You're quite certain you don't know what it was?"

"No. If there was something, he never told me about it. I suppose he might have told Annie, but Annie's dead." She scrubbed the palm of one hand at the tears drying on her cheeks. "You think that's why his friends are being killed—because of something they did?"

"It's rapidly becoming the only viable explanation I can come up with. And you don't have any idea—any idea at all—what it could be?"

But she simply stared back at him with wide, hurting eyes.

Sebastian went next to St. John Street in Clerkenwell. The early winter darkness had fallen by the time he arrived outside the Rising Sun, but to his surprise he found the coffeehouse ablaze with light and ringing with loud voices and laughter that spilled out into the snowy night.

"Sounds like somethin's going on in there," said Tom, scrambling forward to take the reins.

Sebastian dropped lightly to the ground. "It does, doesn't it?"

He was aware of the soft kiss of falling flakes against his face, the snow crunching beneath the soles of his boots as he approached the coffeehouse. Someone inside shouted something in a heavy Geordie accent that was nearly unintelligible. The other men in the coffeehouse chorused, "*Hear, hear,*" and began to sing.

Why vainly do we waste our prime
Repeating our oppressions?
Come, rouse to arms, 'tis now the time
To punish past transgressions.
'Tis said that kings can do no wrong
Their murderous deeds deny it;
And since from us their power has sprung
We have the right to try it.
Each patriot Briton's song will be,
O give me death or liberty!

"Well, bloody hell," Sebastian said softly, recognizing the song. Its origins dated back to at least the 1790s, when a shoemaker named Thomas Hardy was arrested for treason. The words of the song—found amongst his papers—were read out at his trial as evidence of his guilt. As a result, the song was published in the official trial accounts and became hugely popular.

The men were starting on the second verse—"*The starving wretch who steals for bread / But seldom meets compassion*"—when Sebastian pushed open the coffeehouse door and walked in. First one voice, then another and another, faltered and fell silent as heads turned to stare at him.

"Don't mind me," said Sebastian into the sudden, taut stillness. He spread his arms wide. "Would I be dressed like this if I were a spy?"

Someone laughed nervously as Adam York, his face ashen, came bustling out from behind his counter. "It's all right," he told the men as he hurried to the door, the crowd parting before him. "It's all right." He kept a smile plastered on his face, but his voice was rough when he leaned in close to Sebastian to whisper, "What *now*?"

"We need to talk."

"Yes, of course, but outside, for God's sake," said York, jerking open the door again.

Sebastian waited until the door was closed behind them, then said, "Did you know Emmanuel Royston-Jones is missing?"

Face blank, the coffeehouse owner stared at him. "Who is he?"

"A friend of the men who wrecked your coffeehouse a month or so ago."

York looked puzzled. "But he wasn't with them?"

"No."

"So why are you here, asking me about him?"

"Because he was with his friends in St. James's Street a few weeks ago when you confronted them and threatened to—how did you put it? Ah, yes: 'see them in hell.'"

York stared at Sebastian as, inside the Rising Sun, one man, then another, picked up the song again.

And shall a Crown preserve a head
Of one who robs a nation . . .

The coffeehouse owner swallowed hard and brought up cupped hands to cover his nose and mouth. "God help me. I'd forgotten about that. I was drunk, of course."

"But it did happen?"

He nodded, his hands falling back to his sides. "I'm not proud of it. It was a stupid thing to do." He glanced toward the coffeehouse, where the men were singing, *"See Gallia's bright example . . ."* "But I swear to God, I didn't kill them, if that's what you're implying. I was just . . . spouting off. I never could handle my drink. Why do you think I run a coffeehouse instead of a tavern?"

Sebastian studied the other man's tense face. "I need you to tell me what you know."

York frowned. "What do you mean? I don't know anything. What could I know?"

"The last time I spoke to you, you all but came out and said that Marcus Toole and his friends had been allowed to get away with something—something considerably more serious than what they did to you. And you're not the only person I've heard imply something like that. What exactly were you talking about?"

York licked his lips and looked away. "It's a figure of speech, isn't it? Saying someone can get away with murder. It just means they're allowed to do things other people would be punished for."

"It can be a figure of speech, yes. But I'm not convinced that's all you meant in this instance."

York stared at him unblinkingly. "It was."

Sebastian was having to fight to keep a rein on his temper. "Three young men are dead, a fourth is missing, and a woman out at Chalk Farm had the life literally squeezed out of her. How many more people need to die before you have the balls to tell me what I need to know to stop this?"

"I'm sorry about the woman out at Chalk Farm; truly I am. But it's funny, I don't hear anyone talking about her. All the papers care about are those bloody young aristocrats." He flung his arm in a wide arc that took in the surrounding dilapidated houses and the snow-covered fields beyond. "There are people starving to death out there. Men, women, and children *starving to death*. Do the editors of the *Times* or the *Morning Chronicle* know about them? Of course they do! But they're not writing about them, are they? They don't matter." He jerked his head toward the crowded coffeehouse. "*We* don't matter. We're just here to obey all those bloody laws we've no hand in creating, work to make rich people richer, and die. That's it."

"The guillotine on peers shall wait," sang the men, their voices rising louder and louder. *"And knights we'll hang in garters . . ."*

Sebastian nodded to the coffeehouse beside them and said, "This isn't France, and the year isn't 1789. Prinny has a standing army of one hundred fifty thousand battle-hardened men at his command, and unlike Louis XVI he won't hesitate to use them against his own people. I don't know what you and your friends are planning, but you need to think long and hard before you try anything."

York's jaw tightened. "Are we finished here?"

"Sounds like it."

Sebastian stayed where he was, his thoughts in a bad place as the coffeehouse door opened and closed, and York disappeared inside. The song continued.

These despots long have trod us down
And judges are their engines
Such wretched minions of the Crown
Demand the people's vengeance.
Each patriot Briton's song will be,
O give me death or liberty!

As he watched, a man came out of the shadows of a nearby shuttered blacksmith's to walk rapidly toward the coffeehouse door. He kept his head bowed, his shoulders hunched as he glanced furtively around. He wore his hat pulled down on his forehead and had a scarf wrapped around his lower face, so that Sebastian could see little more than his eyes. But there was something familiar about the man's silhouette, about the way he moved.

Sebastian watched the man slip into the coffeehouse, watched him pat one of the other men on the back and laugh at something he said. The song was winding down now, the last phrases carried by the cold wind as Sebastian turned away.

And future years will prove the truth
That Man is good by nature:

Then let us drink with three times three
The reign of Peace and Liberty.

Tom had swung the curricle around up by Spa Fields and was walking the horses back toward him when Sebastian met up with him, the snow falling gently around them.

"There's a man in the Rising Sun," said Sebastian. "Probably somewhere around thirty or thirty-five, short and stocky, with light brown hair and a thick neck, wearing a gray greatcoat, buff breeches, and a slouch hat. I want you to follow him when he leaves the coffeehouse—see where he goes and what you can find out about him. I'll take the horses back to Brook Street and get Giles to stable them."

"Aye, gov'nor," said Tom with a grin as Sebastian hopped up to take the reins.

"Oh, and Tom?" said Sebastian when the tiger started to run off.

The boy paused to look back at him. "Aye, gov'nor?"

"Be careful. Unless I'm mistaken, the man's a spy for Bow Street and the Home Office."

Chapter 36

Friday, 29 November

Shortly after midnight, a warm wind blew in from the south, whistling through the eaves and turning the snow first to sleet, then to rain, so that by morning the white wonderworld of the previous day had turned into a slushy mess.

Shortly after breakfast, Sebastian was in the nursery, playing a rousing game of bilboquets with the boys, when a message arrived from Bow Street. The body of a young woman had been discovered floating in the duck pond out at Chalk Farm.

It was Jenna Diamond.

He found Sir Henry Lovejoy standing at the muddy banks of the old farm's pond, his hands shoved deep in the pockets of his greatcoat, the damp wind flapping his coat's hem as he stared out over the gray, sullen water.

The rain had melted most of yesterday's accumulated snow, but the day was still cold and damp, with a heavy leaden sky that seemed to bear down on the dreary, soggy countryside. The pond was small, probably no more than a hundred and fifty feet across, its shallows thick with the dead stalks of cattails and reeds. A stand of oaks rose on the far side of the water, their bare branches silhouetted against the gloomy sky. As Sebastian approached, he could see what was left of Jenna Diamond lying on her back at the edge of the pond's wind-ruffled waters. Her simple muslin gown was water-logged and muddy, but the features of her face looked surprisingly composed and calm, as if she were at peace.

He hoped she was.

"This is ugly," he said, drawing up beside the Bow Street magistrate.

Lovejoy sighed. "Indeed it is." He bowed his head, his gaze on the dead woman at their feet. "One of the ostlers says he saw her walking across the yard at around half past seven this morning, but no one else reports having seen her again until about an hour later when one of the cowherds spotted her floating face down amongst the reeds. He jumped in to drag her out and tried to revive her, but by then it was too late."

"Any strangers seen hanging around?"

Lovejoy shook his head. "We're still interviewing the staff and people from the surrounding farms, but so far without any luck." The magistrate fell silent, his eyes narrowing as he stared out over the wet winter landscape. "What if there is no logical explanation for how this killer selects his victims? What if whoever is doing this is simply mad?"

Sebastian was aware of the same rising fear, the panicky sense that they were never going to stop this killer because, despite the mirage of a hidden motivation, there was in fact no rational reason behind his selection of his victims. Nothing to tell them who he was or why he was doing this beyond happenstance and whatever sick, twisted pleasure he derived from killing.

When he remained silent, Lovejoy looked over at him and said, "Do you have any explanation? Have you discovered anything at all?"

Sebastian had to force himself to look again at the dead woman's pale, waxen face. She was so painfully, heart-wrenchingly young. And yet everything she might once have become had now vanished, leaving her eyes to dry and flatten and her body to shrink in death as they watched. "Not really," he said hoarsely. "Nothing that explains this. She was little more than a child. A *child*."

Lovejoy nodded, his features grim as he hunched his shoulders against a damp gust of wind. "Which Celtic god did you say liked its human sacrifices to be drowned?"

"Teutates."

"This can't be a coincidence."

Sebastian watched the strengthening wind flatten the nearby stand of dead reeds and whip up the gray surface of the silent pond into a choppy froth. "No. No, it can't."

Sebastian returned to Brook Street sometime later to find Hero out with the boys and Bayard awaiting him in the library.

He'd cleaned himself up since Sebastian had last seen him

three—no, four days ago now, Sebastian reminded himself. His nephew wore pale yellow pantaloons, a burgundy-and-white-striped silk waistcoat, and an extravagantly tailored blue coat with a nipped-in waist. He sat sprawled in one of the leather chairs beside the fire and had helped himself to a glass of brandy.

"Where the devil have you been?" he demanded when Sebastian walked in the door. "I've been bloody waiting forever."

"And it's not even one o'clock yet," said Sebastian, going to pour himself a glass of wine. "What's happened to rouse you from your slumbers at such a barbaric hour of the day?"

Bayard frowned. "Happened? Nothing's happened." He drained his glass, then set it aside and rose to his feet. "I've come to thank you for your efforts to sort out all this nonsense, and to apologize for having involved you in such a sordid affair in the first place. But now that Bow Street is handling things, you will give it up, won't you?"

Sebastian paused with his wineglass raised halfway to his lips. "I beg your pardon?"

"The business of chasing after this killer. It was damned stupid of me to have involved you in this whole sorry situation in the first place. Can't imagine why I did it, except I suppose I was too bosky to think straight. But there's really no need for you to continue meddling in things now, is there?"

Sebastian took a long, slow swallow of wine. "Did Amanda put you up to this?"

"Mother?" A faint flush touched the younger man's full cheeks. "No. It's just that, well, it's right what she's always said, you know. It's not seemly having such a close relative chasing after criminals like a bloody Bow Street Runner or something even more common. So I'm here to say thank you for your help, but you can leave off worrying about it."

Sebastian took another sip of wine as he studied his nephew's oddly sweaty face. "What are you afraid I might discover, Bayard?"

Bayard gave a hollow-sounding laugh. "What? What a ridiculous notion. What would I be afraid of?"

"I don't know yet. But whatever it is, I will discover it. You do know that, don't you? So you may as well come clean now and tell me what it is."

"I told you, there's nothing! You need to give up this nonsense and go back to overseeing the drainage of your fields, or breeding cows, or reading Plato, or whatever it is you normally do to pass the time. Just stop sticking your nose where it doesn't belong!"

Sebastian went to stand with his back to the fire, his gaze still on his nephew's face. "Did you know that another young woman was murdered out at Chalk Farm Tavern this morning?"

"No. Was she? How very odd."

"*Odd*. That's one word for it. You can't think of a reason why the same person who killed your three friends might also want to kill two of the women who worked at a tavern you liked to frequent?"

"I don't know that I'd say we 'frequented' it, exactly. I mean, we went there a few times; that's all. What makes you think these women's deaths have anything to do with what happened to Toole and Keebles?"

"And Upcott."

"Yes, yes; of course. Upcott, too. My point is, lots of rum characters hang around that tavern, you know. No reason to think this new woman's death has anything to do with us. I mean, only Toole was killed out there, remember?"

"Do you know Emmanuel Royston-Jones is missing?"

"Of course I know he's missing!"

"What do you think has happened to him?"

"How the bloody hell would I know?" said Bayard, his voice rising in pitch. "You think I can explain this? I can't!"

"You know something," said Sebastian, keeping his own voice even. "That's why you're here, now, trying to get me to back off. Because the thought of me discovering whatever is behind all this frightens you even more than the danger of being this killer's next victim."

A malevolent look came into Bayard's face, stretching the flesh taut over his cheekbones. "You're not bloody listening to me! You need to butt out of all of this. Do you understand? Forget I ever asked for your help. I don't want you pursuing this anymore!"

"Unfortunately for you, Bayard, I'm not a hireling. And that means you can't fire me."

Hot, angry color darkened the younger man's face. "You're just doing this because you don't like me. That's it, isn't it? You've never liked me, the same way you never liked my father. It's jealousy, I suppose. You might be the heir to an earldom while I'm simply a baron, but I'm a baron *now*, while all you have is a courtesy title. And it's all you will have as long as the old man is alive, and he doesn't show signs of going anywhere soon, does he? As long as he hangs on, all you've got to live on is what he gives you plus whatever paltry income you can scrape out of that wretched little estate of yours down in Hampshire, and it really burns your arse, doesn't it? Knowing how many tens of thousands of pounds my father's investments bring me every year."

Sebastian couldn't help himself; he laughed out loud.

"You think that's funny?" screamed Bayard, spittle flying from his mouth. "You think I'm still the 'nasty little boy' you've despised since I was ten? That's right; I heard you call me that one time when I was down from Eton for the holidays. Well, I stopped being a 'little boy' a long time ago. You think you can mess with me? Treat me like this? You don't know who you're dealing with." He snatched up his hat from where he'd tossed it and went to wrench open the door, pausing only to twist around and shout, "You hear me? You don't know!"

Sebastian stood where he was as his nephew stormed from the room, heard him swear at Morey as the majordomo moved to open the front door. Had he once said such a thing about Bayard as a boy? Sebastian wondered as he listened to his nephew stomp down the steps. He couldn't remember the incident, although it didn't surprise him. There had always been something worrisomely "off" about Bayard. But that didn't lessen the deep regret Sebastian felt for the pain he had obviously caused the child Bayard had once been—a pain that still festered deep within him as a man.

He was aware of the sound of the children's laughter coming from the street outside, of Hero's cheerful voice as she called out a greeting to Bayard.

Bayard ignored her.

"What's wrong with Bayard?" said Hero, coming to stand in the library doorway as the boys raced up the stairs with Claire. "He looks in a rage about something."

Sebastian walked over to pour himself another glass of wine. "He came to tell me that Bow Street has the search for his friends' murderer well in hand, so that my services are no longer required and I need to stop disgracing the family by acting like some lowly Runner."

"Functioning as Amanda's agent, is he?" said Hero, untying the ribbons of her hat and tossing it aside.

"That's what I thought at first."

She looked over at him. "But now?"

Sebastian shook his head. "I think he's afraid I might discover something—something he evidently sees as more of a danger than this killer."

"How is that even possible? Unless . . ." She paused.

"Unless?"

"Unless he now knows who the killer is and realizes the man's actually not a threat—not a threat to Bayard personally, I mean."

"That's an interesting theory," said Sebastian, taking a thoughtful sip of his wine. He was aware of quick footsteps on the pavement outside that turned to run up the front steps and rap the knocker. They heard Morey move to open the door again, heard a murmur of voices. Then Morey appeared at the entrance to the library with a folded note on a silver salver.

"From Paul Gibson, my lord," he said, holding it out.

Puzzled, Sebastian broke the message's seal and unfolded the single page as Morey bowed himself out.

"What now?" said Hero as Sebastian glanced through the brief note.

"It's not exactly from Gibson," he said, handing the note to her.

Lord Devlin,

I know something about the young girl whose body Bow Street just delivered here that you should be aware of. Something that might explain what's been happening.

A. Sauvage

Chapter 37

Sebastian had first encountered Alexandrie Sauvage years before, during the war in the Peninsula.

The daughter of a prominent Parisian physician, she'd grown up determined to become a doctor herself, despite the restrictions placed by society on those of her sex. Trained as a physician at Bologna in Italy, where such things were allowed, she'd been tending to the medical needs of a unit of French cavalry when they captured Sebastian in the mountains of Portugal. In the process of escaping, he'd killed her lover, and she'd vowed to kill Sebastian in revenge.

The complicated tangle of events that had brought Alexi to England had, in the end, helped save Gibson's life. But while Sebastian no longer questioned her devotion to his friend, a definite wariness persisted between Sebastian and the enigmatic Frenchwoman. He knew she had never entirely forgiven him for killing the man she'd once loved. And a part of Sebastian remained unconvinced that she'd completely given up her own lethal intentions.

Arriving at the ancient stone house in Tower Hill, Sebastian found Gibson sprawled in a chair drawn up beside the parlor's fire. He was in his shirtsleeves, his cravat askew, his face pale and unshaven. He had his head thrown back, his eyes closed, his mouth sagging open as his chest lifted rhythmically with his snores. Sebastian had seen his friend lost in an opium haze too many times not to know what he was looking at. And he felt a rush of raw fury, followed quickly by pity and helplessness and a sick sense of dread.

How long? he wondered as he turned away to cut through the kitchen and take the muddy garden path to the outbuilding by the back gate. How long could Gibson go on like this without killing himself?

How long?

Through the building's open door he could see Alexi Sauvage carefully laying out her surgeon's tools beside a woman's naked cadaver. Now somewhere in her thirties, Alexi was built small and almost unnaturally thin, with a riot of flaming red hair, milky white skin, and a dusting of cinnamon across her high-bridged nose. At Sebastian's approach, she looked up, her face expressionless as she watched him walk toward her.

"How much opium did he eat?" said Sebastian without preamble, his hands coming up to grasp the weathered frame at his sides as he paused in the doorway.

She crossed her arms at her chest and leaned back against the wooden shelf behind her. "I take it you saw Paul?"

"I saw him. How much did he take?"

"Enough to kill most men."

"Why?"

"Why?" she echoed, her eyebrows drawing together. "You should know why better than most." She flung out one splayed hand, then let it drop again. "The phantom pains from his missing leg might be gone, but I know of no magic box of mirrors that can take away all the other pains that war left him with—the memories of the men he's somehow convinced himself he might have saved if only—" Her voice cracked, and she looked away, blinking.

"I'm sorry," said Sebastian.

She nodded in silent acknowledgment, her throat working as she swallowed.

Sebastian forced himself to look at what was left of Jenna Diamond, lying on the slab between them. "What can you tell me about the way she died?"

Alexi Sauvage cleared her throat. "Judging from the bruising on her arms, around her mouth, and on the back of her neck, I'd say someone grabbed her, clamped his hand over her mouth so she couldn't scream while he dragged her to the pond, and then held her under until she quit struggling and died."

Sebastian studied the young girl's pale, even features, so deceptively serene in death. *"Damn,"* he swore under his breath, his arms dropping to his sides as he turned away. He stood for a moment, his gaze on the last vestiges of snow melting in the garden. Then he slapped one hand against the doorframe and said it again. "Damn, damn, damn."

Alexi said, "The reason I sent you the note is because this isn't the first time I've seen her—Jenna, I mean."

Sebastian turned to stare at her.

"I met her about a month ago, near the end of October," Alexi was saying. "She came to me because she'd been violated, and she'd heard I could give her a tea that would help bring on her menses." Alexi might have trained as a physician, but because England didn't allow women to be doctors, she served as a midwife instead.

"She was with child?" said Sebastian.

Alexi shook her head. "Not that she knew. But after what had happened to her, she wanted to make certain there would be no . . . consequences."

"Who did it? Did she say?"

"She did. Five men—five gentlemen."

My God, thought Sebastian, remembering the frightened young woman he'd watched testify at Alison Cross's inquest. "Did she recognize any of them?" he asked, although he knew only too well where this was going.

Alexi nodded. "She knew them from Chalk Farm. She could even remember three of their names from having heard them talk amongst themselves in the tavern: Bridgewood, Keebles, and Toole."

Sebastian was conscious of a rush of pure rage as he stared down at the dead girl's pale face.

"There's more," said Alexi.

He raised his gaze to meet hers.

She said, "A week or two before Jenna came to me, a different woman had asked for my help—not for herself, but for her young niece. The girl had also been violated by five gentlemen. She was only fifteen, and the poor child was so ashamed of what had been done to her that she'd tried to hide it from everyone—including her aunt." Alexi paused, her features hardening. "By the time I got to her, there wasn't anything I could do. She bled to death."

"It was the same five gentlemen?"

"The girl never named them—frankly, I don't think she even knew their names. But what are the odds?"

"Who was she?"

"I can't tell you."

He stared at her. "What do you mean, you can't tell me? Why not?"

"You know why. It's for the same reason that fifteen-year-old child hid what had happened for as long as she did: because she knew her world. She knew what her life would be like—knew the shame her family would feel—if the truth were to get out. She hadn't done anything wrong; she was the *victim*. But she couldn't bear the thought of anyone knowing what she'd been through, of people whispering about her, looking down on her family because of it. And that, combined with memories of what those men had said and done to her, was too much for her. She essentially killed herself because of it. And I'm not going to expose either that dead child or her family to what she died to prevent. I can't betray her trust."

"Even if it could help save lives? Someone has now murdered five people. *Five*. Do you think the killing is over? Because I don't."

Alexi shook her head. "The deaths of Jenna Diamond and Alison Cross are more than tragic, they're an outrage. But those other three—Keebles, Toole, and Upcott? As far as I'm concerned, they deserved everything that happened to them. They're murderers. I'm glad they're dead."

"Did Alison Cross come to you for the same reason?"

"No. I'd never seen or heard of her before she ended up on Paul's slab."

When Sebastian remained silent, Alexi said, "Does what I've told you help make any sense of what is happening?"

He nodded. "It might. It just might."

Chapter 38

The butcher's name was Silas McDougal, and Hero interviewed him that afternoon at a crude stall near Smithfield Market.

A big, brawny man with black hair and a wild, full beard, he told her a story that was already painfully familiar, of endless trips to the pawnbrokers until there was nothing left to sell, of a proper shop lost when he couldn't make the rent, of a wife and three children sent to live with family elsewhere. But then, as she was still scribbling his responses in her notebook, he surprised her by saying, "You ever read much Roman history?"

She looked up. "Some. Do you enjoy history?"

He nodded. "Been readin' it more and more. About men like Brutus, Cassius, Cato . . . how they fought back against Julius Caesar and what he was tryin' to do. Those men were real heroes, weren't they?"

"They certainly risked their lives for what they believed in," she said, choosing her words carefully.

He stared off down the ancient, crowded lane with its decrepit collection of tumbledown lodging houses, seedy pubs, and tiny, grime-smeared shops. "It's what they're afraid of, ain't it? Liverpool and Sidmouth and the rest of them, I mean. Did you know they hang more men, women, and children here in London than in any city in Europe? By far. And there's more private and public prisons here, too. Guess it takes a heap of work, keepin' John Bull under control. Just think about it: spies, constables, whips, sabers, shackles, gallows, gibbets, Botany Bay . . . All to keep us in our 'proper place.' But the day of reckoning has got to be coming soon." He brought his gaze back to her face. "Don't ye think?"

Hero closed her notebook. "These are indeed turbulent times."

Haunted by what she'd been hearing, Hero returned to Brook Street to find Devlin standing at the edge of the terrace, his head bare, the wind flapping the hem of his greatcoat, his outthrust hands braced against the stone banister before him as he gazed out over the dismal, wet garden.

"You saw Alexi?" she said, going to stand beside him.

He glanced over at her, his face solemn. "I did, yes."

She waited, and when he was ready, he told her what he had learned.

For a long time she simply stared unseeingly at the garden, her heart pounding with a sick combination of shock, anger, and outrage. She said, "For some reason, I didn't think those men could have done anything more despicable than what we'd already heard. But I was wrong."

"Yes."

She watched a robin come in to perch on a branch of holly, the wind ruffling his feathers as he seemed to stare back at her. "They tried to kill Diamond's horse to get back at him for spoiling their fun in Chalk Farm Tavern, but when that didn't work, they decided to violate his sister instead." She gave a disbelieving shake of her head. "Who would do something like that?" She glanced over at him. "You think they went after Alison Cross, too?"

"I wouldn't be surprised. She dared to stop them that night as well, remember?"

"And the fifteen-year-old girl Alexi told you about—the one who died? How does she fit into this?"

"It's hard to say without knowing who she was, but I suspect something similar was behind that, too."

"It's all about revenge, isn't it? Both what those men did to Jenna and what's being done to the men now." She paused. "What I don't understand is, why would whoever is killing the men start killing the women, too?"

Devlin pushed away from the banister and turned to face her. "I think we might be looking at two different killers. One—the first killer—has been going after Keebles, Toole, and their friends in revenge for something they did. He could be the brother, father, husband, or lover of a woman those men attacked, but he could also be someone else entirely, someone getting back at them for one of the many other nasty things we know they did. But for whatever reason the original killer started stalking those men, one of them is now afraid that an investigation into his friends' deaths is going to turn up the truth about what they did to those women.

So he's killing the women to make certain they never get the chance to talk about it."

"At this point, that can only mean either Bayard or Bridgewood," she said quietly. "If Emmanuel is dead—or had no part in what was done to those women—then they're the only two left alive."

"Or it could be both Bayard and Bridgewood, working together."

"But why stage the bodies to look like ancient Celtic sacrifices?"

"I don't know why the original killer was doing that, but I suspect the second killer adopted it as a strategy to make us think the murders are all the work of the same person."

A sudden gust of wind sent a whirl of dried leaves scuttling across the terrace. Hero let her head fall back, her eyes narrowing as she watched the heavy gray clouds bunching overhead. "It makes you wonder, doesn't it, how many times those men did that—went after some innocent woman as a way of getting their revenge on a man who had angered them. What a sick, perverted attitude toward women they must have, to do something like that."

"It happens all the time in war."

She looked over at him. "It's what Sir Samuel advocated, isn't it? In that letter he wrote to the *Morning Chronicle* about the American War?"

"It is, yes."

She fell silent, her gaze dropping to her clenched hands.

"What is it?" he asked, watching her.

She looked up. "How common is it? That attitude, I mean."

He met her gaze and held it. "More common than most people want to believe."

A short time later, they were turning back toward the house when they heard the clatter of hooves, the rattle of a carriage drawing up, and a woman's familiar, imperiously raised voice.

"That sounds like Amanda," said Hero.

Sebastian's hand tightened on the handle of the French door that led to the dining room. "It's Amanda."

Chapter 39

Amanda, Lady Wilcox, was calmly unbuttoning the fur collar of her gray wool pelisse when Sebastian reached the entry hall.

"Amanda," he said. "What is it? Has something happened to Bayard?"

She turned to look at him, showing him a tight, angry face. "Bayard is fine. But I would like a word with you, if you please. In private."

He went to throw open the door to the library. "Of course."

"This shouldn't take long," she said, jerking off her kid gloves as she went to stand before the fire. "I understand Bayard came to see you this morning."

"Put him up to it, did you?"

"I did not."

"Really?" Sebastian walked over to the small table that held a collection of carafes and crystal glasses. "May I offer you some wine?"

"Thank you, but no."

"I hope you don't mind if I have some," said Sebastian, pouring himself a generous measure.

She pulled down the corners of her mouth, but all she said was, "I didn't 'put him up to it,' as you so crudely phrased it. But I won't deny that I was hoping you'd listen to him."

Sebastian set the decanter aside and looked over at her. "Did you seriously think I would believe that Bayard—*Bayard,* of all people—is genuinely concerned about the damage my activities might wreak on the prestige and social standing of the family?"

Her fist tightened around the gloves she held in her hand. "And why, pray tell, do you find that so difficult to believe? Simply because you have no regard for our reputations, how dare you assume that the rest of us are equally lacking in a sense of what is owed the family!"

Sebastian took a deliberately slow swallow of his wine. "Well, in my experience, men who go around violating women aren't generally concerned about such niceties."

"Violating women?" She gave a low, harsh laugh. "Good heavens, what a ridiculous thing to say. Have you been talking to some silly chit who was more than eager to spread her legs for a fine lord, only to have second thoughts afterward and convince herself she was forced? Who is this shameless doxy? Give me her name and I'll have her taken up for slander. Six months in the Bridewell ought to teach her not to lie about her betters."

Sebastian was silent for a moment, his eyes narrowing as he studied his sister's smug, vaguely amused features. "You know, don't you?" he said incredulously. "You know what Bayard and his friends have been doing. That's why you're here: because you're afraid that if I keep digging into the deaths of his friends, it's all going to come out—every last sordid detail of their activities. And if you think my interest in solving murders is a stain on the family's honor, then what the hell are you going to do when it comes out that your son is a murderer?"

"A murderer?" This time her laughter was much less convincing. "Surely you aren't suggesting that Bayard killed Marcus Toole?"

"No. Not Toole."

"Then whom, pray tell?"

"A fifteen-year-old girl who bled to death after your son and his friends were finished with her."

"So she's dead? This young woman you're claiming my son forced?" A faint smile of satisfaction curled the corners of her lips. "Well, she won't exactly be testifying against him, then, will she?"

Sebastian stared at her, trying to comprehend how this self-obsessed, soulless monster could have been born of the flawed but gentle, loving woman who'd been their mother. And how a man as honorable as Hendon could have begat someone so utterly devoid of human feelings. He shook his head. "I'm not stopping, Amanda. Not for you, not for Bayard."

Hot, angry color flooded her face. "And Hendon? What about him? You might be his heir, but Bayard is his grandson—his own flesh and blood. Have you no consideration for what you would do to him?"

"You're not going to stop me, Amanda."

He watched the blood drain from her face, watched a venomous gleam kindle in the depths of the intensely blue eyes that were the hallmark of her family. "My God, how I hate you."

"I know."

She pressed her lips into a thin, tight line and swept from the room.

Sebastian stood for a moment, listening to his sister's angry voice in the street outside, giving orders to her coachman. Then he sent for Jules Calhoun.

"You wished to see me, my lord?" said the valet, looking vaguely puzzled.

Sebastian started to take another sip of his wine, then set the glass aside. "Three weeks ago, on the evening of Friday, the eighth of November, someone stabbed Gilbert Keebles on or near Westminster Bridge. Bow Street couldn't find anyone who would admit to having seen it happen. But it occurs to me that the kind of people likely to have been hanging around the bridge late at night might not be inclined to reveal their activities to Bow Street's constables."

A flare of amusement showed in the valet's eyes. "If anyone was around to see it, my lord, I'll find them."

Later that night, Sebastian stood beside his bedroom window, his gaze on the dark, angry clouds bunching over the frost-rimed rooftops and clustered chimneys of the city. He could hear the wind flapping a loose shutter somewhere, hear the rattle of distant carriage wheels and the soft patter of Hero's footsteps as she slid from the bed and came to him.

"It's worrying you, isn't it?" she whispered. "What Amanda said about the effect all this is likely to have on Hendon."

Reaching out, he took her in his arms, buried his face in the heavy fall of her hair, breathed in the warm, comforting scent of her. "Bayard is Hendon's grandson—his only true grandson. I've been standing here trying to imagine how I'd feel about someone who was responsible for betraying one of Guinevere or Simon's sons someday."

Hero was silent for a moment. Then she said, "I think if your grandson had done the things Bayard has done, you'd understand. You'd understand that anyone who brought them to justice was only doing what was right. What needed to be done."

"You think so? I'm not so certain."

She leaned back so she could look at him, her eyes searching his face in a way that made him wonder what she saw there. "What are you going to do?"

"Have a go at Bayard again in the morning."

"Think that will do any good?"

"No. But I need to try."

"Yes," she said, bringing up a hand to touch her fingertips softly to his lips.

Except that by the next morning, Bayard was dead.

Chapter 40

Saturday, 30 *November*

"When was he found?" said Sebastian, standing beside Sir Henry Lovejoy at the entrance to a noisome alley off Little Suffolk Street. The morning had dawned cold and cloudy, with a faint mist that smelled heavily of coal smoke, effluent, and the brine from the distant river. This was a depressed, disreputable section of the city that stretched to the north of Charing Cross, behind the aged, dilapidated assemblage of stables, barracks, and records storehouses that formed the King's Mews.

"An old woman collecting dog feces to sell to the tanneries stumbled upon him just after daybreak," said the magistrate, his features grim.

Sebastian drew a deep breath of the foul-scented air, let it out slowly, and forced himself to walk forward to where Bayard lay crumpled on his side some eight to ten feet inside the alley. His pale yellow pantaloons were smeared with muck, his fashionable high-crowned beaver hat rested upside down beside him, and the back of his extravagantly tailored fawn-colored greatcoat showed several ragged slashes soaked dark with his blood. Sebastian's eyes narrowed. "He's been stabbed?"

"So it appears," said Lovejoy. "His watch and purse are missing, but it's impossible to know if he was robbed by his killer or by someone who stumbled upon the body later. He's quite cold, so I suspect he's been here for hours."

His heart feeling painfully heavy in his chest, Sebastian crouched down beside his nephew. Bayard's one visible eye was open and staring and already beginning to flatten, his jaw sagged, and as Sebastian watched, a fly crawled out of his open mouth.

Before he could stop himself, Sebastian flinched and looked away.

Lovejoy coughed. "Sir Nathaniel is convinced that Lord Wilcox, like Keebles and the others, has fallen victim to the Radicals."

Sebastian glanced back at his friend. "And why does he think that—beyond political expedience?"

"No reason that I'm aware of."

Sebastian brought his gaze back to the body beside him. "He hasn't been posed to look like a Celtic sacrifice, although I suppose that could be because the killer was interrupted before he had a chance."

Lovejoy nodded. "The area is rarely deserted, even late at night. If we're lucky, we might find someone who saw something."

Sebastian let his gaze drift around the alley's soot-stained, ancient brick walls, the overflowing dustbins, the broken glass and muddy, urine-drenched cobbles. "Any idea where Wilcox was last night?"

"We haven't actually spoken to his lordship's household yet. Sir Nathaniel thought it would be best if Lord Wilcox's mother and wife were to hear the news from a family member."

Sebastian pushed to his feet and turned to face his friend. But all he said was, "Yes, of course. I'll go right away."

Bayard's long-suffering butler, Crowley, opened the door of the house in St. James's Square and frowned.

"Good morning, my lord," he said primly, holding the door open no more than a foot or two. "I regret to inform your lordship that Lord Wilcox is not presently at home."

"I know," said Sebastian, pushing the door open wider to brush past him. "Is her ladyship down yet?"

The butler's eyes widened with panic. "My lord—! Please! The younger Lady Wilcox has not as yet come down, while the dowager is currently at breakfast and is not receiving—"

"That's quite all right," said Sebastian, heading for the dining room. "I'll announce myself."

The butler closed the door with a decided *snap*.

Sebastian found his sister seated at one end of the long mahogany table she herself had chosen as a bride some thirty years before. A cup of tea rested at her elbow, and she had the *Morning Chronicle* spread open before her. "Good God," she said, looking up at his entrance. "What can Crowley be thinking, allowing you to have your run of the place like this? And at such an hour? I really must have Bayard give the man a—"

"I'm afraid I'm here as the bearer of bad news," Sebastian said as gently as he could. "And if there's an easy way to say this, I don't know what it is. I'm sorry, but Bayard is dead."

She stared at him in silence for a long moment, her expression utterly unreadable. She raked her lower lip between her front teeth, then said evenly, "I can't begin to imagine your purpose in coming to me with such an outrageous tale, but I wouldn't have believed even you could be so cruel as to—"

"It's not a tale, Amanda. I've just come from seeing the body myself. He was found stabbed in the back early this morning in an alley near the King's Mews."

She turned her head away, her expression oddly flat, her gaze seemingly fixed on the swirling mist outside the dining room windows. Whatever her thoughts, whatever her emotions, none of them showed on her face. "Why you?" she said at last. "Why were you sent to tell me this, rather than someone from Bow Street?"

"They thought it would be kinder."

"Indeed." She reached for her tea, took a sip, then carefully settled the cup in its saucer and looked at him. "Do they know who is responsible?"

"Not yet. But the area around the King's Mews is rarely deserted, even late at night. It's possible there may have been a witness."

Something flickered in those brilliant blue St. Cyr eyes before being hidden by carefully lowered lids. "They've linked his death to that of Keebles and the others?"

"It seems likely, although there are . . . differences."

Her features twisted into a sneer. "You're enjoying this, aren't you?" She flung one hand in the general direction of the King's Mews. "My only surviving son is lying out there, dead, with an assassin's dagger in his back, and you come here to gloat and play the expert?"

"I'm not gloating, Amanda."

"Aren't you?" She pushed up from her chair to stand with her curled knuckles resting on the table before her. "Get out. Do you hear me? With Bayard dead, the servants in this house are once again answerable to me, and I can assure you that I won't hesitate to summon every footman on the premises to throw you out."

"That will hardly be necessary," he said dryly, turning. "But if you need anything—anything at all—you have only to ask."

"Don't be ridiculous."

He had almost reached the door when her voice stopped him. "I take it you've told Hendon?"

He paused to look back at her. "Not yet. I'm on my way there now. My first thought was to tell you."

He saw the flare of surprise in her eyes. But other than that, her expression remained unaltered, and she simply turned her head away.

"I suppose it was inevitable, given the man he was," said Hendon later as he and Sebastian sat beside the fire in the library of the Earl's house in Grosvenor Square. "There's always been something not quite right about him, even as a boy." The Earl fell silent for a time, his face haggard, his gaze on the golden flames leaping on the hearth. "It's odd, isn't it, the way we can love someone even when we don't like them?"

"Yes," said Sebastian.

Holding his pipe cupped in one palm, Hendon reached for his tobacco pouch, then set about filling the bowl. "You've no idea who's doing this?"

"No. Although I'm told Sir Nathaniel has already placed the blame for Bayard's death on the Radicals."

Hendon looked over at him. "You don't agree?

"No."

Hendon nodded. "Nothing political about Bayard. Never has been." Leaning forward, he lit a taper, then held it to his pipe, his eyes narrowing against the smoke. He puffed in silence for a time, then said, "How is Amanda taking it?"

"Surprisingly well."

Hendon grunted. "Not so surprising, really. She never liked him, either. I always thought the way she treated him was half of what was wrong with the boy."

"Probably."

Hendon lapsed into silence again for some time, his thoughts obviously in a dark place. Then he roused himself and said, "Fancy a game of chess?"

Sebastian smiled. "Of course."

It was late afternoon by the time Sebastian left the grieving Earl and headed east, to Tower Hill. He found Paul Gibson in the old stone outbuilding at the base of the garden; the eviscerated body of Bayard lay on the slab before him, and the surgeon was washing his hands in a battered bowl of pink water.

"Don't say anything," he growled, looking up. His face was haggard, unshaven, and sallow, his eyes bloodshot and bruised-looking. Despite the cold, he wasn't wearing a coat, his shirt was crumpled and stained with sweat, his gray-laced dark hair rumpled and wild. "There isn't a damned thing you can say that I haven't already heard from Alexi a dozen times over."

Sebastian dropped his gaze to the pale, waxen corpse that had once been his nephew. "What can you tell me about him?"

Gibson reached for a ragged towel. "Nothing that you don't already know. He was stabbed in the back three times, presumably by someone who wanted to make damned certain he was dead."

"Doesn't sound like footpads," said Sebastian, his gaze on Bayard's face, its features now calm and peaceful in death. "They're usually more interested in incapacitating their target, robbing him, and getting away as fast as they can. Not sticking around to make certain their victim is dead."

"True. Although if Lord Wilcox here was screaming, and your footpad was trying to get him to shut up . . ."

"That's possible."

Gibson tossed the towel aside. "This killer of yours strikes me as unusually adaptable. He shoots, he stabs, he drowns, he throttles his victims. You sure you're dealing with only one murderer?"

"No. My guess is at least two, but it could be more."

Gibson nodded. "The papers are saying it's obviously the work of Radicals driven by a sick, twisted hatred of their betters. They're saying it's a whole gang of them, each with his own favorite way of killing."

"They're getting that from Sir Nathaniel and the Home Office. The Palace is probably even paying Fleet Street to run that nonsense. They do it all the time."

Gibson scraped the palm of one hand across the stubble on his chin. "They're worried about Monday's meeting up at Spa Fields, are they?"

"So it would seem." Sebastian forced himself to look again at what was left of Bayard. "You can't tell me anything about his killer? Anything at all?"

Gibson pressed his lips together and shook his head. "Not unless they had something to do with that nick that's missing out of his ear, although it's almost healed. From the look of things, I'd say he got it maybe a month or two ago."

That night, Sebastian lay with Hero in his arms and listened to a cold wind thrash the plane trees in the distant square.

"It's not your fault," she said quietly.

He didn't even try to pretend to misunderstand her. "You don't think so? Bayard came to me, afraid, because someone was killing his friends and he was terrified he might be next. He asked for my help, and my first thought was that he himself might be the killer. Now he's dead, along with three of his friends, with a fourth missing and likely lying buried out there somewhere. And with the possible exception of whatever has happened to Royston-Jones, I'm finding it hard to see any of those men's deaths as tragic. Alison Cross's and Jenna Diamond's deaths? Yes. Bayard's and his friends'? No."

"I suspect Theo Bridgewood isn't sleeping well tonight."

"Unless he himself is the killer."

She pushed up on her elbow so she could look down at him. "Do you seriously think he could be?"

Sebastian reached up to run his fingers through the heavy fall of her dark hair. "I don't know. But I don't see how I can ignore it as a possibility."

"Why would he do that? Kill his friends, I mean."

"To shut them up, perhaps? I suspect we don't know the half of what those men have done. Perhaps he was afraid they might start talking. He could actually be the one killing both his friends and the women."

She sat up completely, crossing her legs beneath her. "What about Emmanuel Royston-Jones? What if he's not dead? We know *something* caused him to become estranged from his friends, but no one seems to know—or at least be willing to say—what that was. What if the explanation that's always been given—the gentling influence of his beloved, now dead betrothed—isn't the true story? What if whatever caused the break between the men was so horrible that Royston-Jones is now bent on some mad mission of revenge?"

Sebastian watched her tuck a stray lock of hair behind her ear. "I wish I could say I haven't been thinking about that, too, but . . . as much as I genuinely liked the man, there's no denying he's weak. And weakness can sometimes drive a man to murder."

"If he is the killer . . ." Hero started to say, then hesitated before continuing. "Is he mad, do you think?"

"I suppose that would depend on what pushed him to kill. I can think of circumstances that would drive me to kill four men." He looked over at her. "Can't you?"

Something changed in her face, something that left her looking hard and fierce. "Yes. Yes, I can."

Chapter 41

Sunday, 1 December

Early the next morning, Sebastian sent for his tiger. "Any luck with the gray-coated man from the Rising Sun?" he asked the boy.

"Yes and no," said Tom. "Turns out 'e's a real piece o' work, that Castle. That's 'is name, ye know: John Castle. From what I'm hearing, 'e's a bigamist what was mixed up wit some brothel over in Soho before 'e and a friend started runnin' a nasty scheme where they'd pretend t' help French prisoners of war escape, only to then turn 'em in for the reward."

"Lovely," said Sebastian. "Any indication he might be working for the Home Office?"

"Well, I've found some coves who think he might be a spy, but I can't say for certain yet that 'e is. They've had enough of their mates sent t' prison an' worse because o' government spies that they're a suspicious lot—leastwise, the smart ones are." He paused. "Ye want I should keep workin' on it?"

Sebastian nodded. "See if you can find out more. But remember to be careful. This Castle sounds more dangerous than I'd realized."

"I assume you've heard the results of Lord Wilcox's autopsy?" said Sir Henry Lovejoy a short time later as he and Sebastian wandered the rows of stalls in Covent Garden Market.

"I have, yes," said Sebastian, looking over at him. "No surprises."

"No; none." Lovejoy fell silent, his gaze on the raucous, bustling crowd around them, his features troubled.

Sebastian said, "The Chief Magistrate is still determined to pin these killings on the Spenceans?"

Lovejoy nodded grimly. "He is, yes; now more than ever. And this is despite our having received new information to the effect that Toole and his friends were involved in an angry confrontation near the Rotunda down in Southwark just days before Keebles's death. There may be nothing to it, of course. But I would prefer to ascertain the particulars of the incident before we move against someone else."

"An angry confrontation with whom?" said Sebastian, more sharply than he'd intended.

"We don't know precisely. The costermonger who told us of the incident was inclined to believe the man involved was some sort of foreigner, but who knows? The truth is, anyone with a heavy Welsh or Lancashire accent is likely to sound like a foreigner to a Cockney."

"Have you asked Theo Bridgewood about it?"

"We have. He claims not to remember the incident. But to be honest, I'm not convinced we should believe him." He looked over at Sebastian. "You haven't heard of such an episode?"

"No," said Sebastian evenly. "No, I have not."

Sebastian found Herr Friedrich Accum at the Gas Light and Coke Company plant off Great Peter Street in Westminster. The German was deep in conversation with a tall, gangly engineer in an oil-smeared smock, with both men shouting to be heard over the clanging of the surrounding machinery. Then Accum nodded to his workman and walked over to where Sebastian stood watching the operation of the plant.

"My apologies for keeping you vaiting, my lord," said the German with a precise bow. "This is an honor; a great honor, indeed. Have you seen a gasvorks before?"

"I have not," said Sebastian, letting his gaze drift over the array of cylinders and pipes. "It's fascinating."

"Come, you must allow me to give you a brief tour."

They walked along rows of roaring furnaces with red-hot cast-iron cylinders and vats of lime while Accum talked of retorts and water traps and hydrogen gas. "Did you know that ze first pipes vere made from ze barrels of old muskets?" he said, smiling. "It's not exactly beating our swords into plowshares, but very similar, yes?"

"No, I didn't know. It's all quite extraordinary," said Sebastian.

Accum's smile widened. "Soon there vill be thousands of such plants all across Britain. Not only does gas produce brighter light than oil lamps or candles, but it does so at a quarter of ze cost. Ze theaters are planning to begin converting to gaslight soon. Someday, not only our streets and factories but even our houses vill be illuminated by gas. More people will be able to read at night, vhich is a good thing, yes? And ve vill be able to use it to cook and heat our homes as vell."

When Sebastian remained silent, Accum huffed a soft laugh and said, "You don't believe so?"

"Frankly, I don't know enough about it to have an informed opinion. But I must admit that the potential for deadly explosions gives me pause."

"Ze potential is real, yes. But you must remember that gas uses no vick, creates no smoke, and gives off no dangerous sparks, so in some vays it is safer. And ve vill get better at controlling it."

"Hopefully."

The German laughed. Then he shook his head, his amusement fading as they turned to walk along the river. "But I assume you did not come to see me today to discuss ze future of gas, did you, my lord? It is because of vhat has been happening to those nasty young men, yes?"

"I'm afraid it is, yes. I'm hearing you had another run-in with them. In Southwark, this time."

Accum made no attempt to deny it. "Yah, they came to one of my lectures at ze Rotunda. I suspect their aim vas to disrupt things, but fortunately I saw them vhile they were still outside and recognized them."

"What did you do?"

"I vent out and confronted them."

"Impressive," said Sebastian.

Accum looked at him in surprise. "You think so?"

"One against five? Yes."

Accum shrugged. "I told them I had instructed ze ushers not to admit them." He paused. "They did not take that vell."

"No, I wouldn't imagine they did."

"Ze most obnoxious one—Bridgewood—laughed, knocked off my hat, and informed me they did vhat they vanted, vhen they vanted."

"So what did you do?"

"I pulled my pistol on him."

Whatever Sebastian had been expecting, it wasn't that. "You what?"

Accum nodded. "It has long been my practice to carry a small flintlock pistol in my coat pocket, ever since I vas set upon by thieves one evening vhen I vas valking home from ze gasvorks. I pointed it at Bridgewood's face and told them they had exhausted my patience and it vas time for them to leave."

"And?"

"Bridgewood laughed again—less heartily this time—and said, 'You crazy old man, you vouldn't shoot me.'" Accum muttered something under his breath in German, then said, "So I pulled back ze hammer and said, 'I should perhaps vorn you that I vas considered something of a marksman back home in Hanover.'" Accum paused.

"And?" prompted Sebastian again.

"And then he said ze strangest thing. He vas no longer laughing, of course. And he says—he says, 'You know vhat ve used to do vit people like you two thousand years ago? Ve used them as offerings to our gods. Vould you prefer to be burned, drowned, or hung from a tree like a gutted buck? Because ve can arrange that.'"

Sebastian stared at him. "Theo Bridgewood said that?"

"He did, yes. I remember it because it struck me as such a strange thing to say. Don't you think so?"

"Have you ever read Lucan?"

The scientist looked puzzled. "The Roman poet? No. Vhy?"

Sebastian shook his head. "It doesn't matter. What happened after that?"

"They left."

"And when did this happen?"

"Some time ago now. Three or four veeks, perhaps?"

"Was it before or after the first meeting at Spa Fields?"

"It vas before. I remember because I had picked up a broadsheet about ze meeting that very afternoon from a pleasant young man handing them out near ze church of St. George ze Martyr vhen I vas on my way to ze Rotunda." Accum was silent for a moment, his frown drawing deep lines between his eyes. "Do I need to vorry? That Bow Street might come to think I'm ze man behind these murders? Because I once pulled a gun on those little shites?"

"I honestly don't know. Theo Bridgewood claims not to remember the incident, probably because it makes him look weak. But that's not to say he won't change his mind. Is there anything else—anything at all—about your various interactions with those men that you haven't told me about?"

"No, nothing! I swear it." Accum stared at Sebastian with wide, earnest eyes, then said it again. "I swear it."

"Do you believe him?" said Hero later.

"About there being nothing else?" Sebastian shook his head. "At this point, I don't know. But about the particulars of that incident? Probably."

"At least it explains what Toole and the others were doing in

Southwark the day they went after Sasha and Pitcairn. They were there to disrupt Accum's lecture, only he ruined their fun—and humiliated them on top of it. They must have been spoiling for a fight when they spotted Sasha, and decided to take out their frustrations on her."

"It does sound like it, doesn't it?" said Sebastian.

Hero looked over at him. "Do you think Accum is in danger—that Sir Nathaniel Conant might seize upon him as a likely scapegoat for hanging?"

"If he were some random immigrant, then I'd say yes, he might need to worry. But a lot of powerful, wealthy people have money invested in the gasworks, and Accum is too important to the success of their project. As long as nothing else turns up, I'd say he's safe."

"What a sad comment on our society."

"Yes," said Sebastian, his gaze on the fire beside them. "But the thing I find truly extraordinary is what Accum claims Theo Bridgewood said to him that day. If it's true—*if* it's true—then for someone who claims to know nothing about the ancient Celts, Theo sounds extraordinarily well-versed in their favorite methods of human sacrifice. And I find it difficult to believe it's simply a coincidence that he was talking about those methods just days before his first friend was killed."

"But . . . why would he do that? I mean, even if he did decide for some reason to kill his friends, why murder them in the most gruesome ways and then stage their deaths to look like ancient human sacrifices?"

"That I can't even begin to guess." He paused. "Although there is an alternative explanation."

"There is? What?"

"That Accum made up that part of the exchange in order to deliberately throw suspicion onto Bridgewood."

Hero frowned. "Have the papers made the connection between that verse in Lucan and the various ways the bodies have been staged?"

"Not yet."

"You can't think *Accum* is doing this!"

"Why not? Because he seems so earnest and erudite? Whoever's doing this is erudite."

"Or self-taught."

He looked over at her and nodded grimly. "Or self-taught."

Chapter 42

Theo Bridgewood was in Manton's shooting gallery in Davies Street when Sebastian came to stand with his arms crossed at his chest and his shoulders propped against a nearby wall. The younger man was stripped down to his breeches and shirtsleeves; his face was abnormally pale, his dark hair disordered, his eyes sunken and bloodshot. The attendant at his elbow was methodically reloading a fine set of dueling pistols, one after the other, as the lord's son cupped wafer after wafer. For an instant, Theo glanced over at Sebastian, then calmly sighted on the next wafer and pulled the trigger.

"Nice shot," said Sebastian as the crackling *boom* of the fiery explosion echoed around the open space and the air filled with the pungent scent of burnt powder. The thin round target had dissolved.

Theo handed the spent flintlock to the waiting attendant,

nodded the man's dismissal, then turned to Sebastian with an exaggerated bow. "Thank you, thank you." He straightened. "I take it you're here to see me? Has something else happened? I believe at last count, I'd run out of close friends to turn up dead."

Sebastian pushed away from the wall. "We need to talk."

Theo held up his hands, palms outward, and grimaced. "Let me clean up, and I'll get my coat."

Skirting the side of the square, the two men walked down Berkeley Street toward Piccadilly. The day was dull and overcast, with an icy wind blowing out of the north. "My father wants me to leave town," said Theo, his expression solemn as he kept his gaze on the line of plane trees at the base of the slope. "Rusticate for a while until Bow Street catches this killer and everything settles down."

"So why don't you?" said Sebastian.

Theo's jaw tightened. "I don't believe in running away."

"Sometimes retreat is . . . prudent."

"As in 'He who runs away may live to fight another day'?" Theo shook his head. "I'd rather stand my ground and fight now."

"Do you even know whom you're fighting?"

He huffed a low laugh. "No."

Sebastian studied the younger man's handsome, stony profile. "Of your original group of six friends from Eton, four are now dead and one is missing. You're the only one left."

Theo threw him a quick glance. "My mathematical skills might not be the best, but even I can subtract five from six."

"You think Royston-Jones is dead?"

"Don't you?"

"Probably."

Theo kept his gaze on the wind-tossed trees in the distance. "Sir Nathaniel Conant and my father think some group of crazy Radicals is behind it all."

"You don't agree?"

"In case you hadn't noticed, none of us has ever been what you might call interested in politics. Why would Radicals want to kill *us*, of all people? I can think of hundreds of more logical targets."

"Because of your fathers, perhaps?"

Theo frowned as if considering this. "I suppose I can see some Radical wanting to hit back at my father and Sir Samuel Toole, and maybe old Zacharia Royston-Jones, too, because of his wealth. But Gil Keebles's father has been dead since forever, and until this last week Sir Lawrence hadn't been near London in years. As for Bayard—well, you know as well as I do what Bayard was like. I mean, did he ever attend Parliament after coming into the title? Even once?"

"Not to my knowledge."

Theo nodded. "So no, I don't think we're talking about Radicals. But if you're looking to me to explain what's going on, I can't."

"Have you read Lucan?"

Theo looked puzzled. "What?"

"Lucan. The Roman poet."

An edge of annoyance crept into the younger man's voice. "I know who Lucan is. But what the devil has he to do with anything?"

"Have you read him?"

"Of course I've read him—years ago, at Eton. Why do you ask?"

"Because he identifies three of the ancient Celtic methods of human sacrifice. Thanks to Lucan, we know that offerings to the god Teutates were drowned, those to Taranis were burned, and sacrifices made to Esas were hanged from trees—although evidently a wooden bricklayer's scaffold or barn beam will do in a pinch."

Theo drew up and turned to face him. "You can't be serious."

"I wish I weren't."

Theo looked away to where some pigeons were pecking at a scattering of crumbs on the pavement, his gaze abstract as he chewed at the inside of one cheek. "Well, aren't you the clever one, seeing such a neat classical allusion in a random assortment of murders? The problem is, all the killings don't actually fit, do they? Bayard was simply stabbed, you know. In the back."

"And Keebles was stabbed in the side before being drowned, while Toole was shot in the chest before being burned, and Upcott and Alison Cross were both throttled before being hanged. Their bodies weren't so much sacrificed as staged to look like sacrifices. Bayard's killer could have been interrupted before he had time to stage that one."

Theo stared at him, his eyes going wide. "But . . . why would someone do something like that?"

"I was hoping perhaps you might be able to explain it."

"Me? I told you: I have no idea who's doing this!"

Sebastian said, "Three or four weeks ago, shortly before the first Spa Fields assembly, you were overheard somewhat gleefully attempting to intimidate a certain German chemist by describing in detail the various ways in which the Celts once performed their human sacrifices—by drowning, burning, and hanging—and then threatening to do the same to him."

Theo was silent for a long moment, his brows drawing together in a frown. "Told you that, did he?"

"No. As I said, you were overheard. That's what comes from letting your quarrels play out in the public streets." It wasn't strictly true, of course, but Sebastian had no intention of exposing Accum—again—to this man's wrath.

Something glittered in the younger man's hard eyes as he turned to walk on. "And did your informant also tell you the bloody little Hun drew a pistol on me? A pistol!"

"Yes," said Sebastian, falling into step beside him.

"So that's why you're rattling on about Celtic sacrifices? Because you think Accum is the killer?"

"I suppose that's one explanation."

"What other explanation is there?"

"From the sound of things, the reference to Lucan rolled rather easily off your tongue. I'm wondering if you've made a similar threat before. To someone else, perhaps?"

"Oh, bloody hell." Theo drew up at the corner of Piccadilly, his head falling back as if in stunned amazement as he started to turn away, then swung to face Sebastian again. "First of all, it was a joke, not a threat. A bit of a nasty joke, perhaps, but still a joke."

"Have you used that 'joke' with others?"

Theo hesitated, then huffed a low laugh. "As a matter of fact, I have—probably more times than I can count. It was a running gag we used all the time when we were lads at Eton. We'd pontificate about sacrificing the headmaster to Esas, or burning a particularly pedantic lecturer for Taranis, or tossing one of the more annoying younger lads into the Thames as a sacrifice to Teutates. We thought we were oh so clever and witty; you know how insufferably full of themselves schoolboys can be. I don't know why the hell I said it the other day to Accum, except the bloody Hun does seem to bring out the worst in me."

"So one of the others—Keebles, Toole, Upcott, Bayard, or even Royston-Jones—could have said something similar to someone else?" It was a discovery that had the potential to throw the entire investigation wide open again. If the men had been using that same nasty taunt since they were lads, the killer could be virtually anyone. Or at least anyone well-read enough to understand and remember the classical reference.

"I wouldn't be surprised."

The younger man's face had taken on a drawn, troubled look. Sebastian said, "Why didn't you go out to Chalk Farm with Toole and Bayard the night Toole was killed on Primrose Hill?"

"I was sick—sicker than a bloody dog. Upcott and I both were. Something we ate at a pub the night before must've been off. Why do you ask?"

Upcott himself had said the same, and the pub had confirmed the illness of some of their customers. It would be an easy claim to verify with Bridgewood's servants, which made Sebastian suspect it was probably true. Aloud, he said, "Who would have known that—that you and Upcott were sick, so that Toole and Bayard would be alone that night?"

"Who would have known? I've no idea. What precisely are you suggesting, Devlin? That someone we tangled with at some point has decided to use what was basically a schoolboys' conceit as a formula for murder? For murdering us all? Who would do something like that?"

"You can't think of anyone?"

"No! It's madness."

"You don't think this killer is mad?"

When Theo remained silent, Sebastian said, "If Royston-Jones isn't dead, where do you think he is?"

"Emmanuel? I've no idea. He's been acting strange for months, since even before that insipid chit of his died."

"Do you know why?"

"Why? 'Blood will out,' I suppose." Theo's lip curled. "One of his grandfathers was a lumper, you know, while the other was an impoverished Irish peer so down on his luck he was reduced to auctioning off his daughter to the highest bidder."

"And you've no idea why Emmanuel suddenly started 'acting strange'?"

"No. I always assumed it was because of the chit's influence. What was her name? Abigail? Agatha?"

"Annie," said Sebastian.

"That's right; Annie." Theo was silent for a moment. "You can't think that Emmanuel has been doing this? *Emmanuel?* You can't be serious."

Sebastian shook his head. "No, I'm not suggesting that—although I also don't think we can dismiss it as a possibility. Can you think of a reason why he would want to kill your friends?" *Something besides listening to the five of you sneer at his grandparents' humble origins for the past fifteen years?*

"Good lord, no. It's madness even to suggest it. Here the poor man's lying dead out there somewhere—that is, if he wasn't dumped in the Thames like Keebles and swept out to sea with the tide—and all you can do is accuse him of murder. Next thing we know, you'll be saying I must be the killer because I'm the last man standing."

"You have to admit it is rather suggestive."

"Oh, for the love of God!"

"You can't think of anyone with a powerful enough grudge against your friends to want to kill them? All five of them?"

"*No.*" Theo's voice rose in pitch, his eyes bulging with what looked very much like genuine fear. "Maybe Sir Nathaniel is right; maybe the Radicals are behind it. There's a coffeehouse out in Clerkenwell—the Rising Sun, it's called—where the Spencean who keeps it took a shot at us for objecting to the seditious literature he was supplying his customers. Maybe he's behind it all."

"Did you tell Bow Street about him?"

"I did, yes. And about that bloody violinist at the opera who fancies himself a fencing master."

"Anyone else?

"Isn't that enough? How many Radicals do you know?"

"Not many," Sebastian acknowledged. "How do you think the tavern keeper and barmaid out at Chalk Farm Tavern fit into this? Why would someone who's interested in killing your friends also target them?"

"What makes you think those women's deaths have anything to do with us?"

"Because one was hanged and the other drowned."

Theo shrugged. "Perhaps they killed themselves."

"They didn't."

"So certain?"

"The surgeon who performed their autopsies is."

Theo shrugged again.

"There's also the interesting fact that it's been just over a month since Jenna Diamond, the barmaid, told someone that you and your friends forced yourselves on her."

Theo stared at him for one intense moment, then threw back his head and laughed. "Is this some sort of jest?"

"No."

"She 'told someone,' did she? Do you know how ridiculous that sounds?"

"So you deny it?"

"Of course I deny it. Good God. Do you think it's so difficult for us to find a willing tumble that we've had to resort to taking the chits by force?" He laughed again. "Believe me, the world is full of women more than eager to spread their legs for wealth and the whiff of a title."

"We're talking about rape as a tool for revenge, not something done in a twisted quest for sexual release."

"Revenge?" Theo's lips quirked up in a strange, rollicking smile. "Revenge for what?"

"An ugly incident out at Chalk Farm Tavern involving two earnest young scholars recently sent down from Cambridge, the innkeeper Alison Cross, and a highwayman named Diamond—Jenna Diamond's brother. You were so annoyed with him that you stole his horse; remember?"

No longer amused, Theo met Sebastian's gaze and held it with a steadiness tinged with quiet menace. "I haven't the slightest idea what you're talking about."

"No?"

"No."

"If you think on it, I suspect you'll remember," said Sebastian. Then he turned and left Theo standing on the street corner, his fists clenched and his eyes narrowed to slits.

Returning to Brook Street, Sebastian sent a note to Lovejoy suggesting he look into Theo Bridgewood's whereabouts on the night of Toole's murder. After that, he sat for some time staring unseeingly out the library window. Then, standing up from his desk, he went to pull his copy of *Debrett's Peerage* from the shelf and looked up the Earl of Glenraven.

The entry was brief. Emmanuel's grandfather, James Alexander Royston, had been the First Earl of Glenraven. He had fathered three children—a son and two daughters. The current holder of the title, Emmanuel's cousin, was only the Second Earl, for he had inherited the earldom directly from his grandfather, the First Earl. Sebastian searched in vain for an explanation of what the First Earl had done to earn his elevation to the peerage; nor was the fate of the Second Earl's father—who would have been the First Earl's son and therefore uncle to both Emmanuel Royston-Jones and Ciana O'Leary—explained. His curiosity stirred, Sebastian was leafing through a volume on eighteenth-century Irish history when Jules Calhoun scratched at the door.

"My lord," said the valet, not even trying to hide his smile as he bowed. "I've located someone who was on Westminster Bridge the night Gilbert Keebles was attacked and killed."

Sebastian closed the heavy tome and tossed it aside. "And?"

Calhoun's smile widened. "I think you'll find what he has to say interesting. Very interesting, indeed, my lord."

Chapter 43

Dressed in broken-down shoes, a ragged, misshapen coat of brown homespun, and cut-down trousers held up by a rope cinch, the big-eyed, dark-haired, hollow-cheeked boy looked to be perhaps eight or ten. He said he was twelve.

"M' name's Joseph," he said, his thin, bony hands wrapped around one of the hot meat pasties Sebastian had bought for him. He took a large mouthful of the pasty, chewed quickly, then swallowed. "Joseph Tigger. But folks mostly just calls me Jigger."

They were in the burned-out ruins of an old house off Tothill Street in Westminster, where Calhoun had found the boy. Jigger was seated on the house's crumbling steps, with two more paper-wrapped pasties and a steaming mug of hot coffee resting on the worn stones beside him. "How long have you been living on the streets, Jigger?" said Sebastian, watching him take another bite.

The boy's throat worked as he swallowed. "Nearly a year, sir; ever since me da died of the ague last winter."

"You've been here in Westminster ever since?"

The boy nodded. "All 'cept this last September, when me an' some other lads went down t' Kent t' help with the hop harvest." A slow smile spread across his dirty, pinched face. "It was hard work—real hard work. But it was still ever so grand. That's what heaven must be like, don't ye think? Lots o' trees and grass, and blue skies, and air so clean ye can suck in as big a breath as ye want and still not fall to coughin' like you'd do here in London with all the smoke." His face fell again. "But the harvest only lasts a few weeks, ye know. Once it was over, they didn't want us hangin' around no more. Drove us off, they did, so all I could do was come back up here, to London."

Jigger looked away, his eyes blinking rapidly as if he were fighting back tears, and Sebastian felt his heart ache for the lad.

Calhoun said gently, "Tell his lordship about what happened that night a few weeks ago, when you were sleeping on the bridge."

"Yes, sir." A bleak, frightened look crept over the boy's features. "After I come back from Kent, I'd taken t' sleepin' in one of the alcoves of the bridge when it weren't raining. One o' the gaslights had broke, ye see, so if I curled up real small in the shadows, the watch wouldn't see me and make me move along the way they usually do. It can get right nippy out there over the water, but the air is so clean and fresh, it reminded me a bit o' bein' in Kent."

Jigger's gaze dropped to his pasty, and he bit his lip.

"Tell us what happened that night," said Sebastian. "You don't need to be afraid; we won't let anyone hurt you."

The boy shoved the last of the pasty into his mouth, swallowed, then nodded and said in a rush, "I was asleep, ye see?

Reckon it musta been maybe one or two o'clock in the mornin' when I hear this gentry cove come out onto the bridge, draggin' some doxy with him. Woke me up."

"He was coming from the Westminster side of the bridge?"

"Yes, sir."

"Did you recognize him?"

"No, sir."

"What about the woman? Did you recognize her?"

"No, sir. Ain't never seen her before or since. She weren't one o' the strumpets ye normally see workin' around there. And I can tell ye, she weren't happy about him takin' her out onto the bridge, neither. Said the watch was gonna tip 'em fer sure. But the swell cove, he just laughs and says, 'That's part of the fun.'"

The boy reached for his second pasty and took a big bite.

Sebastian said, "Was she working with a swaddler?" A swaddler was a thief who typically operated in cooperation with a prostitute and wasn't overly averse to murdering his victims.

The boy swallowed and shook his head again. "Don't think so; no, sir. Leastways, I didn't see one, and she didn't act like she was expectin' one t' come along."

"So what did happen?"

"Well, that swell cove, he takes her standin' up right there in the alcove next t' mine, directly under the gaslight for all the world t' see. Don't know why the watch didn't come after 'em, 'less maybe he was drunk or asleep. Truth be told, I think the swell cove was kinda disappointed the watch didn't come. But then, jist as 'e's really goin' at it—if ye know what I mean?—these three other coves come along."

"Three?"

"Yes, sir."

"Did you recognize any of them?"

"Not exactly. I mean, I'd noticed 'em hangin' around near the end of the bridge earlier, but I'd never seen any of 'em before then, if that's what yer askin'. I think maybe they was followin' the swell cove, because they showed up right after him, but then they jist sorta waited around in the shadows. At first, I reckoned they must be his friends because one of 'em says his name. But he says it low and kinda nasty, if ye know what I mean? I don't think the swell cove even heard him at first, on account of what the cove was doin' with the girl." The boy looked away, a tide of embarrassment staining his thin cheeks. He shoved the last of the second pasty in his mouth, chewed, and swallowed. "So then, all three of 'em says the swell cove's name, louder. And that time, he hears 'em. Whips around real quick-like to face 'em while workin' at buttonin' up his flap, and he's madder than the blazes at 'em, callin' 'em all sorts o' names."

"What did the girl do?"

"She musta thought he was workin' with them three, tryin' to cheat her, because she starts screaming at him and at them, sayin' as she wants her money and she wants it now, and not t' be thinkin' she's gonna fall fer any of their tricks. That's when one 'em—one of them three, I mean—says somethin' to her. He says it so low I can't hear it. But the girl, she gets this scared look on her face and takes t' backin' away. And as soon as she gets a little ways away from 'em, she turns around and runs."

"And where were you while all this was happening?"

"I was still in me alcove. It was dark where I was, like I said, on account of that gas lamp being out. So I jist stayed real low and as quiet as could be. None of 'em ever knew I was there."

Sebastian studied the boy's strained, frightened face. "What happened after the girl left?"

Jigger swiped the ragged cuff of his sleeve across his nose and mouth. "One o' the three, he says to the swell cove, 'Ye just tiffed yer last nell, Gilbert.' And the swell cove, he laughs and says, 'Not hardly.' He goes to brush past them, and then . . . and then . . ." The boy broke off, his breath now coming hard and fast.

"And then?" prompted Sebastian.

Jigger swallowed. When he spoke again, his voice was little more than a broken whisper. "And then one o' them three stabbed him."

"You saw it?"

Jigger nodded. "At first, I wasn't real sure what'd happened. I mean, I saw one of 'em lunge at the swell cove, and the swell cove, he staggers, swearin'. Then he takes off running back toward the Westminster side o' the bridge, with them other three chasin' after him. That's when I realized he was hurt—he was holdin' his hand to his side, and I could see the blood oozin' out between his fingers. He was kinda limpin' along, draggin' his left leg and not movin' very fast, so one o' them other three was able t' get in front of him real easy-like while another one, he comes up alongside him, so they've got him surrounded—penned up against the side of the bridge, if ye know what I mean? That's when he climbs up on the parapet. I don't know what he thought he was gonna do because he could hardly stand up and was weavin' all over the place. And then he lost his balance and pitched right off the side of the bridge, into the river." The boy paused. "He screamed as he fell. It was the most awful sound I think I ever heard."

Jigger was silent for a moment, his gaze on the hands he now held twisted together in his lap, the last pasty lying forgotten at his side. "That's when I heard the watchman's shout. Don't know where he'd been all that time, but he started out onto the bridge at a run, whirlin' his rattle over his head. Them three—the ones that'd done for the swell cove—they took off back the way they'd come, toward Westminster. Me, I crouched down in the shadows as small as I could. Like to have wet m'self, I did; I was that scared. I couldn't even look; jist squeezed me eyes shut, wishin' and hopin' as hard as I could that the watchman wouldn't see me."

"Did he?"

The boy shook his head. "No, sir. He was too busy chasin' after them three. So as soon as he was past me, I slipped out me alcove and high-tailed it t' the south bank. I ain't been near that bridge since. Had to go all the way down to Blackfriars to get back over here."

"Did the watchman see the 'swell cove' fall in the river?"

"I don't think so, no, sir. He was hollerin' about how no one was supposed to be climbin' on the parapets, but he didn't look down toward the river, which I reckon he'd have done, don't you think, if he'd seen the cove go over?"

"One would think so," said Sebastian. "Tell me about the three men who came up together. How were they dressed?"

Jigger shrugged. "They weren't turned out as fine as the first swell, but I wouldn't say they was shabby, neither."

"Tall? Thin? Short? Stout?"

"Not tall," said the boy without hesitation. "Not tall, at all. And built real slight, too. Tell the truth, I thought at first maybe they was boys. Their voices was kinda high, too, like maybe they weren't finished changing yet. They almost sounded like girls."

Sebastian was aware of a strange roaring in his ears as much of what he'd assumed up to that point suddenly shifted, realigning itself into an entirely new pattern. "You say at first you thought they were striplings. Did something happen to change your mind?"

Jigger shook his head. "Not exactly, sir. It was just that . . . well, the more I watched 'em and listened to 'em, they didn't seem all that young anymore. If ye know what I mean?"

"Yes," said Sebastian. "I think I do."

Chapter 44

Leaving his curricle at Chalk Farm Tavern, Sebastian climbed the winding path to the top of Primrose Hill and then turned, his hands thrust deep into the pockets of his greatcoat, his gaze narrowing as he studied the distant church spires of London, now nearly lost in the white swirl of a rising mist. He had stopped first in the tavern's taproom. And what he learned there from a brief but enlightening conversation with the middle-aged woman tending the bar had driven him here, to stand beside the blackened remnants of a bonfire that had been cold now for more than a week.

He supposed it was vaguely ironic that the modern descendants of those tribal Britons who, two thousand years ago, had ritually drowned, buried, hanged, and burned alive an endless stream of human sacrifices to their gods should now consider murder the ultimate sin. Today's Englishmen and -women typically reacted with a special kind of fear, horror, and revulsion to the deliberate taking of another human life. And yet Sebastian had long been of the opinion that, given the right circumstances, most—if not all—people were capable of murder. Oh, not the kind of casual, senseless killing committed out of a lust for cruelty or by those rare souls without conscience or scruples. But when in the grip of strong emotion—anger, fear, greed, jealousy, injured amour propre, shame, grief, or a burning thirst for revenge—ordinary people could find it surprisingly easy to kill.

He did not exclude himself from that calculation.

Most such murders were, nevertheless, roundly condemned by society. And yet not all killings were viewed with equal revulsion. Homicides committed in self-defense were generally considered excusable, although some might continue to look askance at the perpetrator. Wars could slaughter millions of innocents—*millions*—and still be seen by many as good and just, even holy. And many of the same Englishmen who would be appalled by the murder of a child typically saw no contradiction in nodding with righteous approval when a desperately hungry ten-year-old girl was hanged for stealing a card of lace.

Lace.

Such executions were, basically, a legally sanctioned system of revenge killing—that ancient, once widely accepted form of justice that the state had now abrogated solely for itself. But what happens when society refuses to enforce its own rules? When the rich and powerful are allowed to steal, rape, destroy, and kill with impunity, simply because they are rich and powerful?

What then?

Profoundly troubled by the drift of his thoughts, Sebastian found himself fingering the wooden carving of a howling wolf he still carried in his pocket. And he wondered, Was it fair to condemn those driven by the failures of their society to take the law into their own hands and exact their own revenge? And when they did, where did the true blame for their actions lie? With those who refused to accept the injustice and inequality of their society?

Or with the inescapable failures and blatant hypocrisy of the corrupt system itself?

The early winter darkness was already falling by the time Sebastian returned to the city. Finding the shop in Little Windmill Street once again closed and the Catholic chapel behind Golden Square deserted except for an elderly Frenchwoman, he stood for a moment in thought.

Then he turned his steps toward Fleet Street.

Running east from Temple Bar toward St. Paul's Cathedral, Fleet Street was famous as the home of the city's premier morning and evening newspapers—the *Morning Chronicle*, the *Times*, the *Post*, the *Morning Herald*, and so many others. But as the ancient thoroughfare that connected the City of London to Westminster, Fleet Street had long been much more than a street of ink. In addition to booksellers, this was an area known as the haunt of generations of reformers, heretics, freethinkers, and revolutionaries. Thomas Hardy, the boot maker whose trial for treason in 1794 had popularized the seditious song sung by the patrons of the Rising Sun coffeehouse, had lived here, as did men like Richard Carlisle and Oliver Goldsmith. The ancient labyrinth of narrow lanes, alleyways, and courts that stretched away toward Covent Garden to the north and the Thames to the south formed its own community. It didn't take Sebastian long to discover that Kate Price, her brother Barnabas, and his late wife Beth had all grown up here and were well-known. But as Sebastian trolled the area's coffeehouses, shops, and market stalls, he discovered that Beth had actually been Barnabas Price's second wife; his first wife had died giving birth to a daughter, Rosamund. A pretty, dark-haired girl with a quick mind and a ready laugh, Rosamund had worked part-time in the printshop still run by her father's sister, Kate. But, tragically, the girl had recently died at the tender age of fifteen.

The aged bookseller who told Sebastian the sad tale didn't know what Rosamund had died of. Whatever it was, he said, it had come on suddenly and carried the poor girl off in mere days.

Sebastian found Kate Price standing at a table positioned beneath the front window, her figure haloed by the wavering golden light cast by a brace of tallow candles at her elbow. She was setting type with quick, sure fingers, but looked up, faltering, when Sebastian pushed open the door to her small press. She hesitated, then set aside the half-filled wooden galley and turned to face him, her hands pressed flat against the leather apron that covered her simple black mourning gown.

"I know who you are," she said.

He closed the old wooden door behind him. "That's convenient."

Her chin lifted. "If you decided to come yourself rather than sending your wife this time, it must be serious."

Wordlessly, Sebastian drew the wolf carving from his pocket and laid it atop the half-filled galley.

She eyed it warily. "What is that?

"I'm told it's a copy—or perhaps, more accurately, an adaptation—of an ancient Celtic relief carving discovered some years ago at a site in Ireland known as Tara."

"And what has it to do with me?"

"You've never seen the carving before?"

"No."

"But you know an Irishwoman named Ciana O'Leary. She keeps a shop off Piccadilly selling books and various other objects of a kind that tend to appeal to neo-Druids. Things like drums, runes, and horns, but also various animals carved in stone or wood. Like this one. Very like this one."

Something flickered in her brown eyes, and he knew she was considering denying it. Then she shrugged and said, "And if I do?"

"How did you happen to meet her?"

"What concern is that of yours?"

He let his gaze drift around the small printing shop, now mostly lost in shadow: the silent, old-fashioned wooden press, the stacked bundles of paper, the ink-stained wooden cubbyholes of type stationed beside the table at which she had been working. The pungent scent of boiled linseed oil hung heavily in the air, mingling with the smell of hot tallow from the burning candles. "It was the seeming links to the Druids that confused me," he said, bringing his gaze back to her face. "Primrose Hill. The Celtic-styled wood carving. The bodies posed to look like the victims of human sacrifice. Taken all together, they suggested there was something ritualistic about the killings, something dark and mysterious. But I don't think there was—at least, not at first. And while I still don't understand all of it, it's starting to make a lot more sense."

"Is it?

"You were seen, you know. That night on Westminster Bridge. Three women, dressed to look like young men of the middling sort, following a foppish aristocrat who'd picked up a bit of muslin with the idea of taking her up against one of the new gas lamps on the bridge."

He saw the flare of surprise in her eyes, quickly hidden by lowered lids. "I don't know what you're talking about."

"Yes, you do. And because you were seen, we now know that Gil Keebles wasn't thrown into the Thames like a sacrifice to the god Teutates; he simply fell when he climbed up on the parapet to try to get away from his killers. You probably thought you were lucky, that the body would be swept out to sea; it was your bad luck it washed up at Rotherhithe instead. And while I could be wrong, I suspect you didn't throw Toole's body on that bonfire, either; I think he fell into it when he was shot. Taranis had nothing to do with it."

She stayed silent, but he could see the pulse in her pale, slim throat begin to beat fast and hard.

He said, "But it's what gave you the idea of posing the rest of them to look like sacrificial victims, isn't it? You even had me thinking the killer must be Theo Bridgewood. He's the only one of the original six friends left standing, and it seems he's rather fond of threatening people with a nasty schoolboys' taunt about human sacrifice. But I've just had a message from Bow Street, and they checked with his servants: Theo spent all of that fatal Saturday night a week ago casting up his accounts in a chamber pot. There is literally no doubt about that, which means he couldn't have killed Marcus Toole. And that's apart from the fact that I'd swear the man is genuinely terrified that he's about to become the next victim of his friends' killer."

"Is he?" she said, her voice low and harsh. "Good."

Sebastian paused, choosing his next words carefully. "I know about your niece, Rosamund."

She stiffened.

He said, "I take it that after Pitcairn stopped them from destroying your printing press that day, Keebles, Toole, and friends came back another time, looking for you. Except they found Rosamund instead."

"No," she said fiercely. "Rosamund died of a fever. Do you hear me? A fever!"

He shook his head. "What I don't understand is, why kill Alison Cross and Jenna Diamond?"

Her lips parted on a quickly indrawn breath. "But we d—" She broke off. "Why would I kill Alison and Jenna? You're wrong. Do you hear me? You're wrong!"

"Am I?"

Rather than answer, she turned abruptly away, one hand coming to her forehead as she drew up and swung to face him again. "What do you intend to do?" she asked, letting her hand fall. "Take this—this fantasy of yours to Bow Street?"

"No. I have no proof of any of it. But tell me this: What do you intend to do when Sir Nathaniel Conant arrests Damion Pitcairn for the murders? Will you let him hang for something you did?"

"Damion?"

"You didn't know?"

She stared at him. "Bow Street has arrested him?"

"Not yet. But Conant intends to. If you—" He broke off at the faint, telltale sound of a familiar click coming from the dark lane outside.

"Get down!" he shouted, throwing himself forward as the front window shattered in a cascade of splintering glass and a fiery, crackling *boom* flared in the darkness beyond.

Chapter 45

Sebastian saw Kate's eyes widen, saw the blood spill from her suddenly parted lips. He caught her as she crumpled.

"*Bloody hell,*" he swore, lowering her gently to the floor. He was aware of the patter of footsteps running away, toward Fleet Street. The urge to give chase was strong, but he tamped it down as Kate stared up at him with frightened, pain-filled eyes. He could feel her life's blood soaking through the cloth of her gown to run down his arm, see the light in her eyes already beginning to dim.

"You're wrong," she whispered hoarsely. "I didn't kill Alison and Jenna. Why would I?" A spasm of raw agony convulsed her features, and she sucked in a quick, shallow breath. "Keebles and Toole, yes. But not . . . not Upcott. Not Wilcox. Wanted to, only . . ." She coughed up a stream of bright red blood. "Someone beat us to them."

He lifted her head and shoulders higher, trying desperately to keep her from drowning in her own blood. "And Emmanuel Royston-Jones?"

Her head shifted from side to side in denial. "He never . . . never did us anything."

" 'Us' being the three of you? You, Jenna, and Alison?"

"Not Jenna. Alison . . ." Her breath wheezed. "Alison and I."

"Except there were three of you on that bridge. You, Alison, and who else? Ciana? Sasha? Tell me."

Her hand came up, the fingers clutching fiercely at the front of his greatcoat. "Promise me . . . promise me you'll get him. Bridgewood. Must be . . . must be him doing . . . doing it all." Her breath rattled in her throat. "Promise . . ."

"Whoever it is, I'll get them," he promised.

But by then, she was gone

"Poor woman," said Sir Henry Lovejoy, his features set in troubled lines as he stared down at Kate Price's crumpled form. The small printshop was now ablaze with lantern light; more lanterns flickered in the darkness outside as Lovejoy's constables searched the lane and knocked on doors in the hopes of finding someone who had seen . . . something. "I assume the shooter was aiming at you and hit her by mistake?"

Sebastian stood beside him, his throat painfully tight as he shook his head. "I think he killed the person he came to get."

Lovejoy looked up, his eyes narrowing in a frown as he studied the shattered window and the narrow lane beyond. "A rifle, I assume?"

"Actually, it sounded like a pistol."

"You're certain? Not an easy shot, surely, with a pistol?"

"Not easy, no, but possible. My guess is the killer came here intending to quietly kill Kate Price and pose her body like his other victims, but changed his mind and decided to shoot her when he saw her talking to me."

"But why? What has she to do with the other killings?"

Sebastian sighed. This wasn't going to be easy to explain.

"How much did you tell Sir Henry?" said Hero later as Sebastian set about washing Kate Price's blood from his hands and face.

He poured hot water from his dressing room pitcher into the basin, then leaned over and cupped his hands to splash his face. "I told him Kate confessed to killing Keebles and Toole but swore she had nothing to do with the other murders. But given that I couldn't betray Alexi's confidences about Rosamund Price, it doesn't make a lot of sense. I'll be surprised if either Sir Nathaniel Conant or Sidmouth believes any of it. Much easier to blame the Radicals and use it as an excuse to hang a few troublemakers."

Hero was silent for a moment, watching Sebastian lather his face and hands and rinse them carefully. Then she said, "Kate was dying; why would she deny killing Upcott and Wilcox unless it was true?"

He reached for a towel. "The convenient explanation would be to protect the unknown third killer, who could be Sasha, or Ciana, or someone else we don't even know about. But that doesn't really make sense. She freely admitted they'd murdered Keebles and Toole, so why deny killing the other two?" He tossed the towel aside. "And think about this: We know from Jigger that Keebles simply fell in the Thames, and Toole could easily have landed in that fire when he was shot. Yet, in every killing since then, the body has been deliberately staged to look like an ancient form of human sacrifice: Alison and Upcott were hanged from wood, while Jenna was drowned."

"Except Bayard wasn't posed; he was simply stabbed."

"Except Bayard," he agreed, reaching for a clean shirt. "In Bayard's case, the killer could have been interrupted. With Kate, I think he panicked when he saw me talking to her and decided to shut her up as quickly as possible. Who knows what contrived scenario he had planned? Fire, probably."

Hero watched Sebastian pull the shirt over his head. "It's Theo, isn't it? He killed everyone except Keebles and Upcott. He realized that any investigation into his friends' deaths had the potential to uncover their nasty way of getting back at anyone who angered them, and Rosamund Price's death means they could potentially be found guilty for murder. So he panicked. He killed Alison and Jenna—and Rosamund Price's aunt, Kate—so they won't be able to tell anyone what Theo and his friends had been up to. And he killed Phineas Upcott because the man was so nervous, Theo was afraid he might accidently betray them. Keebles's drowning and the bonfire that burned Toole gave him the idea to stage his own killings to look like Celtic sacrifices, so that way all the deaths would appear to be the work of the same murderer. And because Theo spent the night when Toole was killed clutching his chamber pot with his valet hovering at his elbow, he would seem to have an alibi."

"That works except for one thing: Why kill Bayard?"

"For the same reason as Upcott."

"Perhaps. Although the last time I saw him, Bayard seemed to have himself relatively under control." Sebastian reached for a clean cravat. "At least for Bayard. And Theo Bridgewood himself is obviously terrified that he's going to be the killer's next victim."

She frowned. "You're quite certain?"

"I suppose it could be an act, but I doubt it."

"So who does that leave? The unknown third woman from the bridge, who has now decided for some inexplicable reason to start killing everyone, including her friends?"

He looped the cravat around his neck. "Or Emmanuel Royston-Jones."

"Assuming he's still alive."

Sebastian met her gaze. "Assuming he's still alive."

Monday, 2 December

The next morning, Sebastian settled at the desk in the library, his hands pressed flat on the blotter. He sat for some time gazing at the big, long-haired black cat curled up asleep on one of the chairs by the fire. Then he pulled a sheet of paper before him, dipped his pen in the inkwell, and made a list of names down the left side of the page, in a column:

VICTIMS:

1. Gilbert Keebles, Marcus Toole
2. Alison Cross, Jenna Diamond, Kate Price
3. Phineas Upcott, Bayard
4. Emmanuel Royston-Jones???

On the other side of the page, he made a second column:

MURDERERS???

A. Adam York, Damion Pitcairn, Dudley Fenton, Friedrich Accum, Sid Diamond

B. Ciana O'Leary, Sasha Stone

C. Theo Bridgewood, Emmanuel Royston-Jones

He stared at the two columns for a long, long time. Then he added:

D. Lord Bridgewood, Sir Samuel Toole

He was drawing a circle around the last two names when he heard the front door fly open with a bang. Looking up, he heard Morey's hiss, then Tom catapulted into the room, his hat clutched in his hands and his breath coming in quick pants.

"Gov'nor! Wait till ye hear this! Ye was right about that sly-boots, Castle. Turns out 'e's been workin' with Bow Street all along. Sent more'n one poor flat up the steps t' the nubbing cheat, 'e 'as. Seems 'e and a friend was taken up fer forgery, but 'e agreed t' sing against 'is mate. So the mate was hanged, and our Castle, 'e now dances t' whatever tune Stafford and Conant decide t' play."

"You're certain?"

"No doubt about it at all. And listen t' this: 'E's got 'imself on the committee that's been plannin' these big meetings up at Spa Fields. Seems 'e's in real thick wit that feller Thistle or whatever 'is name is. But there's others on the committee as don't trust 'im at all, on account of 'ow 'e's always tryin' t' stir things up, gettin' men drunk and eggin' 'em on t' say things like they want a revolution or they think it's past time t' be puttin' heads on pikes."

Sebastian set aside his pen. "The second Spa Fields meeting is today?"

Tom nodded. "At noon. And get this: The government done already called out the Life Guards and the Ninth Dragoons, too. I hear tell they've closed all the gates at the Tower, pulled up the drawbridge, and loaded the cannons. They've even got soldiers stationed at Newgate and the bank, and Sir Nathaniel Conant an' that nasty Bow Street chief clerk of 'is what controls John Castle are already sittin' up there in Clerkenwell at Cold Bath Fields Prison, jist waitin' to bring treason charges against all the poor suckers they're planning t' haul in."

"Is Lovejoy there?"

"Don't know, sir. But a whole heap o' special constables 'as been sworn in. Hundreds of 'em!" Tom paused to draw breath. "This ain't gonna be good, is it?"

"No," said Sebastian, pushing up from his chair to head for the door. "No, it's not. Morey!"

"Yes, my lord?" said the majordomo with a bow.

"Do you know where Lady Devlin was planning to conduct her interviews this morning?"

"I heard Coachman John say something about Tothill Street, my lord."

"Thank God for that," said Sebastian. Lying just to the northwest of Westminster Abbey, the ancient byway was far, far away from any trouble that was likely to break out in Clerkenwell or the City.

He grabbed his hat. "Have Giles bring the curricle around. And, Tom, I want you to find Lady Devlin and warn her of what's likely to happen.

"Just in case."

Chapter 46

"I used to be a tailor," said a gaunt, one-armed man named Michael Thompson. Dressed in patched gray trousers and a threadbare black coat, he sat on a crumbling stone bench near Clerkenwell's ancient St. John's Gate, his one remaining hand resting in his lap. With his wispy gray hair, skeletal frame, and sunken, ashen features, he might have passed for a man in his seventies, but he said he was fifty-four.

"Even had my own shop not too long ago," he said in his soft voice. "But a man's life can turn in an instant, can't it? Especially if he's an artisan or small shopkeeper. He gets sick or hurt, or his shop burns down, and everything he's worked a lifetime to build up is suddenly . . . gone."

"Where was your shop?" asked Hero.

"Down in Southampton, my lady. Did a good trade, too, what with all the naval officers always in port. But then I fell and broke my arm must've been three—no, I guess it's been nearly four years ago now. They said it was broke so badly it would kill me if I didn't let them cut it off, so I did. But I shouldn't have. Whoever heard of a one-armed tailor? If I could've kept my shop, I might have been able to make a go of it with my apprentices. But I came down with an awful fever right afterward; thought I was gonna die, for sure. And even when it finally broke, I was so weak I wasn't good for anything for months. That's when I lost my shop, you see. I could still cut fabric, though, so I got along doing piecework for a couple of job tailors I knew who were working for the Navy. Only then the war ended and it ruined every last one of them."

He fell silent for a moment, his gaze on a trio of young women dressed in white who were walking toward Clerkenwell Green with a banner that read PEACE AND GOODWILL. It was because of the noontime meeting in nearby Spa Fields that Hero had changed her mind and decided to come to Clerkenwell today, although she was being careful to keep her distance from Spa Fields itself.

"Guess it would have ruined me, too," he was saying, "if my arm hadn't done it already. That's when I came up to London, thinking maybe I'd have more luck here." He shook his head, his lips pressing together in a thin line. "Guess it's bad everywhere, isn't it? Between the war ending and this cold, nasty wet weather we've been having all year, there's a heap of folks downright starving to death. Starving or freezing." He nodded toward another group of women, this time with a banner that read HAVE MERCY ON THE CHILDREN. "That's what the meeting here today is about, isn't it? Asking the Regent for relief for the people's suffering. If my wife and children hadn't already died long ago, I don't know what I'd do. I'd never be able to feed them or keep a roof over their heads. Half the time I can't even feed myself."

"I'm sorry," said Hero.

Thompson swallowed hard and looked down at the fist he now held clenched in his lap.

Hero waited a moment, then said gently, "Was your father a tailor?"

Thompson shook his head. "No, my lady. He was a sailmaker, down in Southampton. But I wanted to be a tailor, so he apprenticed me to a man named Evans. Only, Evans died four years into my apprenticeship. My father was dead by then, too, so I had no position and no money to buy a new one. I didn't know what else to do, so I took the King's shilling."

"You were in the Army?"

"Yes, ma'am, five years. Sent me to the colonies, they did, first to New York, then the Carolinas." A wistful, faraway look crept into the man's soft brown eyes, and he sighed. "I'd never seen anything like it—the Carolinas, I mean. The water there is so blue, you think it can't be real. They've got sandy beaches that stretch on for what seems like forever, and these great spreading trees draped with floating trails of long wispy stuff that looks like an old man's spun beard. It's so warm there, a man could sleep without a blanket most of the year, if he needed to. If I'd been smart, I'd have stayed there after Yorktown rather than letting them ship me back here." He watched a group of laughing men stroll past with white, green, and red cockades on their hats and a red banner inscribed LIBERTY OR DEATH, then said it again: "If I'd been smart."

Hero looked up from scribbling notes. "You were at Yorktown?"

"Aye. And at Cowpens and Waxhaw Creek before that."

"Were you with Lord Bridgewood and Sir Samuel Toole?"

Thompson turned his head and spat. "Yes, ma'am. Of course, they weren't no 'lord' and 'sir' then, just Lieutenants Bridgewood and Toole. Bridgewood had me flogged once, you know—a hundred and fifty lashes. That cat, it felt like a blizzard of razors, slashing and slashing at my back. I can still feel it when I breathe too deep. It's like there's something inside me hasn't been right ever since."

"Why did he have you flogged?"

Thompson gave her a long, steady look. "And if I tell you, will you be telling *him* what I said?"

Hero set down her pencil and closed her notebook. "No, of course not. You have my word as a gentlewoman."

He hesitated a moment. Then his jaw hardened and he said, "I knew what they'd been doing, you see. They were afraid I'd tell the Colonel, so Lieutenant Bridgewood, he accused me of stealing a watch. I hadn't done it, of course, but who was gonna take the word of a tailor over the son of a lord? Truth is, I saw him take it off a colonial farmer they'd killed when they chanced upon him plowing his field."

"Bridgewood murdered a man?"

Thompson nodded solemnly. "Him and Toole together. Wasn't the first time, neither—not by a long shot. They thought it served the colonials right, you see, for rebelling against the King." He paused, his eyes narrowing as he stared unseeingly at a laughing group of apprentices heading up the hill. "Until then, I don't think I'd realized there are men in this world who not only don't feel the pain of others but actually enjoy seeing other people in pain. They were like that, all three of them. They enjoyed hurting people they hated, and they hated the colonials."

"All three of them?"

"Toole and the two Bridgewoods."

"What two Bridgewoods?"

"Lionel—him as is Lord Bridgewood now—and his younger brother, Ensign Aiden Bridgewood. If they saw an isolated farmhouse, they'd push their way inside, kill the men if they tried to stop them, then rob the house and violate the women." Thompson paused, then added, "Well, Toole and Lieutenant Bridgewood would have their way with the women and girls. The Ensign had other tastes."

Hero felt a chill run down her spine. "What happened to Ensign Aiden Bridgewood? Do you know?"

"Last I heard, he took up a sugar plantation in Jamaica, right next to this other officer we had in the regiment. Pitcairn was his name. Ensign Pitcairn, from Fife."

Chapter 47

Sebastian made it as far as Gray's Inn before the throngs of people descending on Spa Fields forced him to abandon the curricle in Giles's care and proceed on foot.

The sky overhead was a dull grayish white, the air cool and damp and heavy with the scents of coal smoke and fermenting hops from the nearby brewery. But the streets rang with a cheerful, fair-like atmosphere, the laughing, shouting groups of children and women in their Sunday best mingling with throngs of apprentices off for "Saint Monday." And because it had been a hanging day, many of those who'd gathered at the Old Bailey to see four men "turned off"—two for the crime of stealing handkerchiefs—were now joining the crowds making their way up the hill toward Clerkenwell.

Even before he reached the top of Coppice Row, Sebastian could hear the haunting wail of a bagpipe and the steady beating of a drum, see the gaily colored pendants fluttering from rows of stalls selling everything from gingerbread and hot chestnuts to bottled ale and ginger beer. Keeping an eye out for Damion Pitcairn, Sebastian worked his way across the stretches of rolling, open fields now crowded with tens of thousands of tradesmen, small shopkeepers, market women, craftsmen, costermongers, and apprentices. Dozens of banners rippled in the breeze, proclaiming everything from PURITY OF ELECTIONS and RELIGIOUS LIBERTY to FEED THE HUNGRY. At the crest of the hill stood the early eighteenth-century, country-style tavern known as Merlin's Cave overlooking the millpond of the New River Head. It was from one of the public house's upper windows that the orator Henry Hunt had addressed the crowds at the first Spa Fields meeting in November, and it was where he was supposed to speak again today. But it was now well past the time when Hunt was scheduled to have arrived, and people were still milling around, waving their banners and waiting.

Damion Pitcairn was nowhere in sight.

Frustrated, Sebastian swung around, his attention drawn to a wagon parked partway down the hill. A simple high-wheeled farm wagon with a flat bed, it was hung with half a dozen tricolor flags, the blue, white, and red of revolutionary France replaced here by stripes of white, green, and red, representing England, Ireland, and Scotland. As Sebastian watched, a young man in a black coat and waistcoat, drab breeches, and long gaiters leapt up onto the wagon bed. Dark haired, with a pale face and slight frame, he couldn't have been more than nineteen or twenty and looked half-drunk, his words slurring slightly as he shouted, "Friends and countrymen! Lend me your ears!"

A portly shopkeeper to Sebastian's right recognized the borrowing from Shakespeare and smiled. But the nod to Marc Antony's famous speech eluded most of the men gathered in this part of the field, for these were the most desperate of the struggling poor: soldiers in tattered remnants of fading uniforms; gaunt laborers cast adrift by the recent ending of the great project to build the Regent's New Canal; clusters of ragged, unemployed sailors up from Wapping. Their faces earnest and intent, they now pressed forward to hear better.

"These are historically wretched times!" shouted the man on the wagon. "We live in a nation in which a few hundred thousand wallow in the lap of great luxury while millions face the threat of starvation. Starvation!"

An approving murmur of "Hear! Hear!" rippled through the crowd.

The orator continued, "Has there been a day since the time of the Norman conquest when the people of England were not oppressed by the descendants of those foreign invaders? They came here, made themselves our masters, stole our land, and claimed it as theirs. For eight hundred years they've kept their feet on our necks. They've denied us any say in our own governance. They've forced us to pay their ruinous taxes and tariffs. And for what? For what?"

The cries of *"Hear, hear!"* were louder this time.

"Wasn't expecting to see you today," said a familiar voice at Sebastian's elbow. "A bit out of place, aren't you?"

Turning, he found himself looking into the plump, serious face of coffeehouse keeper Adam York.

Sebastian let his gaze drift over the crowded hillside. "It looks peaceful."

"Why wouldn't it be?"

Sebastian nodded to the grim walls of Cold Bath Fields Prison rising on the western edge of the packed hillside. "You know Sir Nathaniel Conant and his nasty little chief clerk are already set up there, ready to bring charges of treason against anyone and everyone they can—particularly those involved in organizing today's meeting?"

"I don't see anyone rioting or causing trouble, do you?"

"Not yet," said Sebastian, his gaze going back to the man on the wagon. "Who is he?"

"Him? That's James Watson. He and his da are apothecaries—and more than half-mad, the both of them, if you ask me."

Sebastian nodded to a dumpy thirty-year-old man who had now appeared beside one of the wagon's massive rear wheels. It was John Castle. "You know him?"

"Castle? He and Watson are both on the organizing committee. Why?"

"Castle works for Bow Street."

York sucked in a quick breath that hissed through his teeth. "You're certain?"

"Yes. And I suspect he's not the only agent Bow Street has planted in this crowd." Sebastian let his gaze drift over the teeming fields. "The government has thousands of Hussars, Life Guards, and specially sworn-in constables stationed from here to the river. What do you think they're expecting to happen?"

On the wagon bed, the half-drunk, half-mad young apothecary was shouting, "A million pounds! A million pounds a year of our money he takes for his waistcoats and jewels, his palaces and women. And what has he ever done for us besides send us off to fight and die in a war that meant nothing to us? How much longer must this be endured?"

"Hear, hear," bellowed his audience.

"Hunt's finally arrived," said York quietly. "Thank God."

Twisting around to look back up the hill, Sebastian could see the famous, tall, elegantly dressed man standing on the front steps of Merlin's Cave, bowing and waving to the cheering crowds surging toward him. But the knot of ragged sailors, soldiers, and laborers gathered around the farm wagon were still focused on the young apothecary. As if aware of Hunt's arrival, John Castle seized one of the flags from the wagon and began waving it back and forth above his head.

"Are you ready to do something about it?" shouted Castle, his booming voice ringing out over the cheering coming from Merlin's Cave at the top of the hill. "It's time, isn't it? Will you follow me?"

"Yes!" roared the crowd.

"There they go," said Sebastian as the young apothecary seized another of the flags and leapt off the wagon to join his cheering audience.

"Bloody fools," muttered Adam York. "At least not many are following them. There must be thirty or forty thousand people here today, with only a few hundred following those two idiots."

"It doesn't matter," said Sebastian as they watched the cockade-waving band charge down the hill toward St. John Street. "It's that lot who'll be remembered—and used to justify whatever repressive policies the government is planning to impose." He brought his gaze back to the coffeehouse keeper beside him. "Were you on the planning committee?"

York nodded silently, his face troubled.

"And Damion Pitcairn? Was he?"

"Aye. Don't understand why he's not here. Haven't seen him or Sasha. It's odd, don't you think?"

"Yes," said Sebastian, aware of a hollowness that yawned deep in his gut. "It's odd."

Sebastian left Spa Fields soon after that, walking through empty, deceptively quiet streets as he followed the curve of Baynes Row down to Gray's Inn Lane. He had almost reached the intersection with King's Road when he spotted a familiar slender figure dressed in gray Wellington trousers and a black French-cut coat walking swiftly with her head down, her eyes darting cautiously this way and that as she crossed the lane toward Liquorpond Street.

His curiosity aroused, Sebastian trailed Pitcairn's sister along Liquorpond to an ancient, mean lane that wound back up toward Mount Pleasant. Still following at a discreet distance, he watched her duck into a narrow passage leading to a squalid, foul-smelling court.

The court was utterly deserted, its wet, muddy cobbles strewn with broken glass and rubbish and lined on three sides by boarded-up shops and dingy brick warehouses with barred windows. But marooned on the northern side of the court stood a small, wretched cottage, a relic of a vanished time before the spreading city had swallowed its pastureland and tilled fields. Once, the cottage had been whitewashed, with a blue-painted wooden door and cheerful yellow shutters. Now its walls were grimy and soot-stained, the paint on the old warped door faded and peeling, its shutters broken and hanging at drunken angles. The high brick wall of one of the warehouses butted up against the cottage on one side, looming over it and hemming it in. But an old fieldstone lean-to still survived on the other side, collapsing slowly into ruin.

Keeping his back pressed against the wall of the dark passage, Sebastian watched Sasha cross the court to knock on the cottage's warped wooden door.

There was no answer.

She knocked again, her features tense as she threw a quick, wary glance around the empty court.

A minute passed. Two. When there was still no answer, she reached out to press the latch, a shadow of surprise crossing her face as the door swung inward perhaps a foot and then stopped.

"Hullo?" she called.

Silence.

Throwing another quick look around, she hesitated, then pushed the door open wider and stepped inside.

"Damion?" Sebastian heard her call.

Then she closed the door behind her.

Chapter 48

More troubled than before, Sebastian waited a moment, then quickly crossed the court to the tumbledown shed that stood beside the cottage. Part of the shed's upper course of fieldstone had collapsed, and he used the fallen chunks of rock to scramble up onto what was left of the shed's crumbling roof. Careful to keep his weight on the stout beam that ran along the roof's high edge, he crab walked his way over to a small window that gaped open beneath the peak of the cottage's mossy slate roof.

The room beyond was no more than a low-pitched, dusty attic, empty except for the remnants of a mouse-eaten straw mattress against the far wall and what looked like a heap of old rags. There was no staircase leading down to the single room below, only a crude ladder, the worn, rounded ends of its rails poking up above the scuttle hole cut in the center of the floor.

Moving cautiously, he swung one leg over the rotten windowsill, then the other, easing himself inside. Wary of telltale creaks, he flattened himself on the filthy floorboards and slithered over to the opening to peer over the edge.

Sasha stood alone in the center of the small, dirt-floored room below, her elbows cupped in her palms to hug her crossed arms to her chest as she turned in a half circle, taking in the piles of wooden crates and barrels stacked against the surrounding walls. She looked uncertain and frightened, and he was still trying to figure out what the hell she was doing here when he heard two sets of footsteps crossing the cobbles of the court outside.

Then the latch lifted, and Sasha whirled to face the opening door.

"You're early," said Sir Samuel Toole, his brows drawing together in a frown as he drew up just inside the entrance. He was dressed more conservatively than was his habit, in a powdered wig, with a long plain duster buttoned up over his fashionable coat and breeches. "You were told to come between half past two and three."

Sasha stared at him, her nostrils flaring on a quickly indrawn breath, her voice scratchy and hoarse. "How do you know that?"

"Because we wrote the note," said Lord Bridgewood, following his friend into the cottage and closing the warped old door behind them with a screech of rusty hinges. "Or I suppose one might more accurately say we composed it. A certain convicted forger of my acquaintance was kind enough to transcribe it for me in a fair imitation of your brother's hand. The man's quite talented, wouldn't you say?"

She gave a faint shake of her head. "Why did you bring me here?"

Bridgewood and Toole exchanged glances. As Sebastian watched, the men separated, Lord Bridgewood staying where he was, his back to the door, while Sir Samuel Toole shifted to a position that put the young woman between the two men.

"What do you want?" she said, looking from one man to the other as the crackling boom of a rifle sounded somewhere in the distance, followed by another and then another.

"Ah," said Bridgewood with a faint smile. "It has begun. The streets are about to become decidedly unsafe, you know. Today's events will be written about in history books: theft, senseless destruction of private property, mayhem, riot, and murder—the usual panoply of civil disturbance."

Sasha's eyes narrowed. "The only way you can know that is if the government has arranged it."

"Of course they've arranged it. Did you seriously think these meetings would be allowed to continue, stirring up the people, filling them with a dangerous, mindless hatred for their betters? We've all seen where that leads." Reaching beneath the edge of his open greatcoat, he drew a sleek ebony-handled dueling pistol from an inner pocket and calmly thumbed back the hammer. "Order will be quickly restored, of course, but not before a few innocents have been killed. I fear London's opera lovers will be saddened to hear that one of the stage's beautiful young dancers is amongst the dead. But that dismay will turn to horror when it's discovered that not only was she found dressed as a man, but she had secreted on her person a letter from her brother—also kindly forged by my friend—implicating them both in the appalling string of recent murders."

No longer hugging her chest, Sasha had allowed her arms to fall to her sides. Now, as Sebastian watched, she tucked her hands into the pockets of her greatcoat as if she were cold. Neither Sir

Samuel nor Lord Bridgewood seemed aware of what she was doing. But Sebastian knew, for she made the move at exactly the same point as he slipped his own double-barreled flintlock pistol from his pocket.

Sasha said, "Do you seriously think anyone will believe that a sixteen-year-old opera dancer single-handedly killed—what? Five men and three women?"

"Not single-handedly," said Sir Samuel, smiling faintly as he drew a hunting knife from his pocket and removed its sheath. "You and your brother, working together."

"What have you done with Damion?"

"Nothing yet," said Bridgewood as another round of gunfire boomed in the distance. "He's proved unexpectedly difficult to locate today. But I've no doubt—"

He broke off at the sound of the latch lifting on the door behind him.

"Damion!" shouted Sasha. "Look out!"

His face sagging with shock, Bridgewood whirled and fired point-blank at the man coming through the door, the deafening explosion filling the small room with the stench of burning gunpowder. He was still turning when Sasha jerked a small ivory-handled flintlock from her pocket, thumbed back the hammer, and pulled the trigger.

Her bullet slammed into the side of Lord Bridgewood's head, splattering her with blood and shattered bits of bone and gore. He staggered, took one step, two, his eyes widening, his arms flinging out at his sides. Sebastian heard him gasp and say, "Theo!"; then the anguished cry was nearly drowned out by the crackling boom of Sebastian's own pistol when he pulled back the hammer and fired at Toole as the Baronet lunged toward Sasha.

The angle for the shot was awkward, the small flintlock wildly inaccurate at this distance. Sebastian's bullet caught Toole high in the throat. He reeled back, his mouth gaping open, the knife tumbling from his grasp as he brought up both hands to clutch at his neck. His gaze went from Bridgewood, to Sasha, to the shadowy opening above their heads. "Who?" he said, his voice gurgling.

The pistol still in his hand, Sebastian dropped through the scuttle. He landed in a low crouch in the room below, quickly thumbing back his flintlock's second hammer, ready to fire the other barrel. Then Toole's body convulsed, the blood spurting through his fingers as his eyes rolled back in his head and he collapsed.

His ears still ringing from the three deafening roars, Sebastian's gaze met Sasha's through the stinking, smoky haze of burnt powder. Wordlessly, she leapt to close the gaping open door while Sebastian went to check first Sir Samuel Toole, then Lord Bridgewood. Both men were still alive but wouldn't be for much longer. Then, his pistol still in his hand, he moved cautiously to the young man who had fallen just inside the doorway.

It was Theo Bridgewood.

Crouching beside him, Sebastian cast one swift glance at the bloody hole in the younger man's chest, then brought his gaze back to his face.

"It's bad, isn't it?" said Theo, looking up at him with pain-filled eyes.

"Yes."

Theo's shattered chest heaved and shuddered as he fought to suck in air. "I didn't know. Swear . . . I didn't. Not till . . . not till what you said about Lucan . . . about how the bodies were posed like Celtic sacrifices. That's when . . . figured it out. Confronted him." Theo brought up a shaky hand, his fingers convulsing as he clutched at the sleeve of Sebastian's greatcoat. "It was his jest, you know . . . not ours. Not sure . . . why I used it that day with Accum. Stupid thing to have done."

Sebastian kept his gaze on the younger man's increasingly pale, waxy face. "How did your father find out about the women?"

"Phineas . . ." Theo paused, his tongue leaving a bloody smear as it flicked out to wet his dry lips. "Phineas came to see me that evening, only . . . I wasn't there. So the bloody fool . . . poured it all out to my father . . . How he'd told you about Diamond, only now he was afraid that what we'd done to his sister and the other women might come out. The old man garroted him right then and there, in the library . . . Got Sir Samuel to help haul the body out to Marylebone and then kill . . . kill the women. Shut them up."

"He and Sir Samuel killed them all? Not Keebles and Toole, but all the others?"

Theo shook his head. "Just Phineas and . . . the women. He wasn't even ashamed of it. Said . . . said they deserved it. But he swore . . . swore he had nothing to do with what happened to Bayard or Emmanuel." A spasm of raw agony convulsed his features. "Oh, God, it hurts. I can't . . . can't believe he shot me."

"What were you doing here?"

"Following . . . him. Knew he was up to something." Theo blinked slowly, his gaze going to where Sasha stood with her back to the closed door, looking down at him. "I swear . . . swear I didn't know . . . He didn't tell me you . . . you're my sister. Not till . . . I confronted him. It's why . . . why he wanted to shut everyone up. If the truth had come out . . . the scandal . . . incest . . ." An expression of revulsion and horror contorted his features. "Wouldn't . . . would never have done that to you, if I'd known. He should have told me. Should have . . ."

Whatever he'd been about to say was lost in a fit of coughing. Sebastian could feel the tremors shuddering through the dying man's body as frothy pink blood bubbled up through his lips. Theo made a choking sound, his body heaving, his eyes rolling back in his head. And then the tremors stopped and it was over.

Swallowing hard, Sebastian eased the dead man's body down to the packed earthen floor. He knelt there for a time, resting back on his heels, his bloodstained hands pressed flat against his thighs. Then he looked over at Sasha.

She stared back at him, her breath coming so hard and ragged it jerked her chest.

He said, "Lord Bridgewood was your father?"

Her face was wooden. Unreadable. "Yes."

"Did he know? Before you came to London, I mean."

"He knew. His brother had told him years ago. He found it . . . amusing." Her gaze drifted to where Lord Bridgewood lay face down on the dirt floor, one leg half-bent, his arms flung out in an ungainly sprawl. "I'm glad I shot him." She looked back at Sebastian, her eyes huge and dark, her voice husky. "He's my father, and I'm glad I shot him. Does that make me an awful person?"

Sebastian did her the courtesy of considering the question before answering. "I can see how some might think so. But given that he raped your mother, deliberately left you to languish in slavery, and was planning to kill you and frame you and your brother for the murders he and his friend had committed, I'd say no."

She was silent for a time, her attention shifting to the sprawled, bloody remains of Sir Samuel. And then she gave voice to the question that was bedeviling Sebastian. "What are we going to do? I've just shot a peer of the realm, while you've killed a baronet, and I don't think anyone is going to believe Theo was accidently shot by his own father."

Sebastian pushed to his feet. "Where is Pitcairn?"

"He told me Bow Street was planning to arrest him after today's meeting and charge him with the murders. He said you wanted him to leave the country, but he was determined to stay and fight the charges. So I told him the truth—that Alison, Kate, and I had killed Keebles and Toole, and why. I said if he was arrested, I would turn myself in and confess." She paused. "That's when he packed up what he could from his room and brought it to me. Last I heard, he was going to Gravesend to try to arrange passage for both of us on a ship to France—leaving tomorrow, if possible. Then this came." She drew a folded note from her pocket and handed it to Sebastian. "It's a good forgery. Bridgewood must have had a sample of Damion's handwriting from when he was teaching Theo fencing."

Sebastian opened the single sheet and read.

Sasha,

Meet me at the cottage in Swine Court between half past two and three. Don't fail me.

Damion

"I was expecting to hear from him," she was saying. "So I wasn't surprised when a boy brought me that."

Rather than hand the note back to her, Sebastian went to

crouch down beside Lord Bridgewood. Rolling the Baron onto his back, he set about methodically searching the dead man's pockets. The forged incriminating letter was in an inner pocket of his lordship's expensively tailored dark blue coat. Sebastian glanced through it quickly, then slipped both the letter and the forged note into his own pocket. They would need to be burned and the forger—if he was still alive—found.

Sasha watched warily as Sebastian rose and went to search Toole's pockets as well, just in case. Blood still oozed from the wound in the unconscious man's neck, but it was slowing. He would be dead soon.

She said, "If you have a plan, I'd be interested in hearing it."

Sebastian wiped his bloody hands on his ruined greatcoat and looked over at her. "I'm working on it."

The winter sun was sinking low by the time Sebastian headed back to where he had left Giles. As he drew closer to the square, he found himself staring at a familiar yellow-bodied cabriolet and team of matched blacks drawn up at the kerb. A tall, well-dressed woman stood on the pavement beside his curricle, her head tipped back as she said something to his groom.

"Hero? What in the name of all that's holy are you doing here?" said Sebastian before he could stop himself.

She turned, her gaze going from the dirty smudges on his face to the blood-soaked greatcoat he'd taken off and was carrying thrown over one arm. "Looking for you. I've just found out that Lord Bridgewood is Sasha's father."

"I know," he said, his eyes narrowing as his gaze drifted back to the cabriolet. "And I need to borrow your carriage."

Chapter 49

Tuesday, 3 December

It was only a few hours till dawn by the time Sebastian's hackney drew up before the modest Bloomsbury home of Sir Henry Lovejoy.

The night was clear and cold, with a scattering of lingering stars that glittered out of the darkness like fractured ice. For one stolen moment, Sebastian leaned his head back against the hired carriage's worn squabs and closed his eyes. He was bone-tired, but the sense of urgency that had driven him now for over fourteen hours still thrummed through him.

Fleet Street was already calling yesterday's mass meeting in the open fields above Clerkenwell the "Spa Fields Riots." Tens of thousands of hardworking people had turned out to join together, wave banners, listen to inspiring speakers, and call on their government to do something about the widespread distress. But a few hundred hotheads led by a paid government agent provocateur had gone on a rampage, looting a gun shop and stealing food from a scattering of grocers and eating houses before turning up before the ramparts of the Tower of London. When they tried to persuade the Tower's guards to join them, the men on the ramparts laughed at them. By nightfall—which came before four o'clock these days—order had already been restored. The entire episode had lasted no more than three or four hours and caused little real damage.

But the peaceful assembly on Spa Fields was already being forgotten as the havoc wrought by the rioters was exaggerated and embellished. The repercussions, Sebastian suspected, would be swift and brutal. At least one of the meeting's organizers—the father of the young apothecary on the wagon—had already been arrested, and Bow Street had patrols out looking for the rest. Sebastian knew this because he had seen them on his way back to London from Gravesend.

Drawing a deep breath, he leaned forward to thrust open the carriage door. "Wait here," he told the jarvey, the ancient hackney swaying as Sebastian hopped down to run up the house's short flight of front steps and bang the door's knocker. Hard.

He was banging for the third time when the sash of an upper-story window flew up and a man's head peered out, his nightcap sliding sideways on his bald pate. "Have you no sense of—" The magistrate began, then broke off, his eyes widening as he leaned out farther. "Good heavens. Is that you, my lord? Whatever has happened?"

Tilting back his head to look up, Sebastian swiped a hand down over his beard-stubbled face and blew out a long, tired breath. "I'll explain in the hackney."

On the way to Swine Court, Sebastian gave Lovejoy a terse but largely complete explanation of what he knew, including the part played in yesterday's events by Sasha Stone and the deadly secret of her relationship to Bridgewood. He omitted only a few important details, mainly the actual timing of the shooting; what Alexi had told him about Rosamund Price; the fact that Sasha had joined Kate Price and Alison Cross in killing Keebles and Toole; and that Sebastian had just spent the better part of the night driving an admitted murderer and her brother to a French ship waiting at anchor off Gravesend, twenty-eight miles to the east of London.

They arrived in Clerkenwell to find the wretched, refuse-strewn court still deserted. For Lovejoy's sake, Sebastian had brought a lantern, and he paused outside the cottage to light the wick with a flint before pushing open the battered old door with a shriek of its rusty hinges.

"Merciful heavens," whispered Lovejoy, one hand cupped over his mouth and nose as a macabre interplay of wavering shadows and golden lantern light danced over the three bloody, hideously sprawled bodies within. Now cold and stiffening, their mouths agape, their widely staring eyes flat and dry, the three men lay exactly as Sebastian and Sasha had left them the afternoon before. The stench of their drying blood and relaxed bowels hung heavily in the air, overlying the smells of dust and old mouse droppings and the lingering hint of burnt gunpowder.

His features strained, his lips set in a tight, determined line, the magistrate walked solemnly from one man to the next. Beside each one, he paused, his head bowed, his shoulders hunched, his hands thrust deep into the pockets of his greatcoat. It was a long time before he spoke.

"Frightening, isn't it," he said, his head still bowed, "what men will do when they consider themselves above the law?"

"Yes."

He looked over at Sebastian, his voice strained with the effort of containing a tide of emotions he would never allow himself to reveal. "What I don't understand is, if Gilbert Keebles and Marcus Toole were killed by Alison Cross and Kate Price, and Lord Bridgewood and Sir Samuel then murdered the women and Phineas Upcott, who killed Emmanuel Royston-Jones?"

"You don't think it's possible he's still alive?" said Sebastian.

Lovejoy frowned as he considered this possibility. "But in hiding, you mean? Yes, I can see that." He paused, then said, "And Lord Wilcox?"

That question had been bothering Sebastian all night, and he didn't like the explanation he kept circling back to. But all he said was, "Footpads, perhaps?"

"I suppose footpads are, on occasion, truly responsible for the unexplained deaths we blame on them," said Lovejoy, although he didn't sound convinced that it was true in this case. Still looking thoughtful, he walked back to crouch beside Lord Bridgewood. "His lordship's use of a forger may help explain something that happened yesterday," he said, tilting his head first one way, then the other as he studied the ugly gaping wound to the side of Bridgewood's head. "The body of a well-known forger named Robin Easton was found garroted in a mean lodging house in Grub Street." Lovejoy looked up. "It seems reasonable to suspect he's the man Bridgewood employed."

"And then killed? It does sound likely. I can't see Bridgewood allowing the man to live, knowing what he did."

"No," agreed Lovejoy, stifling a grunt as he pushed to his feet.

The two men fell silent again, each lost in his own thoughts. Then Lovejoy said, "The Palace will never allow any of this to come out. It would be beyond explosive at the best of times, but now, after the events of yesterday . . ." His voice trailed off.

Sebastian said, "I won't watch an innocent man hang for this."

Lovejoy cleared his throat. "No, of course not. But it's going to be . . . delicate. Sir Nathaniel Conant will doubtless wish to speak to you at some point today, and I assume he'll have this opera dancer brought in right away for questioning. Stone, did you say her name is?"

"Yes," said Sebastian, somehow resisting the urge to look at his watch. The *Argonaute* wasn't set to weigh anchor until tomorrow morning, sailing with the tide at a quarter past four.

It was going to be a long twenty-four hours.

Shortly after seven o'clock that morning, Sebastian stood at one of the windows of his library, his outstretched hands braced against the sill, his gaze on a milkmaid struggling up the street, her body bent beneath the weight of the two heavy pails that dangled from the yoke she carried across her shoulders. He was acutely aware of the steady ticktock of the clock on the nearby mantel, slowly counting out the passing minutes.

"You need to eat something," said Hero, coming to slip her arms around his waist.

He turned to take her in his arms and hold her close. "I don't think I could," he said, glancing at the clock again before he could stop himself.

"Twenty-one more hours," she said, following his gaze.

He nodded. "A lot can happen in twenty-one hours."

"Have you seen the morning papers?"

"Not yet. Why?"

"Adam York is listed as one of men who've been arrested. They say he's to be arraigned for treason and committed to the Tower."

"The Tower? God save us." He rested his forehead against hers. "So the Home Office hires a bigamous brothel keeper and forger to foment a sham uprising and lure a few gullible idiots into joining him. Then Sidmouth and Liverpool throw up their hands in horror, act like they had nothing to do with any of it, pass all kinds of repressive laws, and start lopping off heads. Clever."

"It works."

"Oh, yes," he said. "It works."

She glanced again at the clock. "What do you think Bow Street will do when they realize Sasha and Pitcairn have both disappeared? Surely they won't think to start searching the ports right away?"

"They might. I wish that damned ship could have sailed this morning."

Her brows drew together in a frown as she searched his face, and he wondered what she saw there. "If you can't eat, you might try sleeping. There's absolutely nothing more you can do at this point, and you've barely slept in over a week."

He huffed a soft laugh. "You think I can sleep?"

"You could try."

He started to argue, then kissed her nose and said, "I'll try."

He didn't expect to sleep. But the past ten days had taken a brutal toll on him. He'd have sworn he'd barely stretched out on the daybed in his dressing room when he became aware of a voice calling him from far, far away. "Lord Devlin? I say, *Lord Devlin.*"

Sebastian opened one eye, saw the cheerful face of his valet leaning over him, and squeezed both eyes closed again. "What time is it?"

"Just past nine, my lord."

"Morning or evening?"

"Still morning, my lord."

"Unless someone is dead or the house is on fire, I don't want to know about it."

"It's Sir Henry Lovejoy, my lord," said Calhoun. "With Sir Nathaniel Conant and Lord Sidmouth. Morey has put them in the drawing room."

"Tell them to go away."

"Yes, my lord."

"Oh, hell." Sebastian groaned and sat up. "Tell them I'll come. But bring me some hot water first. They can bloody well wait while I shave."

It was half an hour later before Sebastian, washed, shaved, and dressed in fresh clothes, walked into his drawing room.

Two of the men who had come to see him stood together beside the fire. The Home Secretary, Lord Sidmouth, had one hand resting on the mantelpiece, his head bent as he listened to whatever Bow Street's unctuous Chief Magistrate, Sir Nathaniel Conant, was whispering in his ear. Lovejoy had taken up a position some distance from his companions. For a moment his gaze met Sebastian's, and the faintest hint of a wry smile glittered in his eyes before he looked pointedly away.

"Gentlemen," said Sebastian. "My apologies for keeping you waiting. May I offer you some tea? Ale? Wine?"

"Thank you, but nothing," said Sidmouth before either of the other two men could answer.

"You'll excuse me if I have some," said Sebastian, going to where an array of carafes and glasses stood on a side table.

"We've just come from the Haymarket," said Sir Nathaniel. "The opera dancer who was involved in last night's shooting has disappeared."

"Oh?"

"Neither her landlady nor the theater has any idea where she's gone. She cleaned out her room, leaving only this." His hand shook with rage as he held out a single sheet of paper crisscrossed with writing.

Sebastian glanced up from easing the stopper from one of the carafes but made no move to take the page being thrust out to him. He knew exactly what it said because he'd helped Sasha draft it. "What is it?" he asked, splashing a healthy measure of wine into one of the glasses.

"It's a statement that lays out the course of last night's events, essentially as relayed by you to Sir Henry. It's signed by this woman and witnessed by her landlady and Damion Pitcairn." The Chief Magistrate's lips twisted into a sneer. "Pitcairn, of all people!"

"Oh? It was generous of her to take the time to set the record straight."

"Generous of her? Generous! To scribble a terse explanation of this shocking series of events and then disappear before we have a chance to interrogate her?" He shook the offending page in disgust. "This woman freely admits to killing a peer of the realm. A peer of the realm! And as if that weren't bad enough, that damned violin player, Pitcairn, has also disappeared—presumably because he realized he was about to be arrested for organizing yesterday's riot."

"He didn't organize a riot," said Sebastian, replacing the carafe's stopper and picking up his glass. "He helped plan a public meeting."

"A meeting that turned into a riot! Did you know they broke some of the windows at Somerset House? And threw dung and mud at my carriage! Dung! We've already arrested several of the rascals, and it won't be long before we lay hands on the rest."

"And John Castle?" said Sebastian, taking a slow sip of his wine. "Have you arrested him? He's the one who actually started the riot, you know."

The Home Secretary and Sir Nathaniel Conant exchanged quick glances. Lord Sidmouth cleared his throat and said, "Mr. Castle will be serving as a witness for the prosecution."

"Of course." Sebastian looked from one man to the other. "You think he'll be effective, do you? When the jury finds out he was acting as both a spy and an agent provocateur?"

"He won't be our only witness," said Conant. "Several of the conspirators we've arrested have proved more than willing to cooperate and turn King's evidence. They're writing up their sworn statements as we speak."

"I see; they write what you tell them to, and you let them keep their heads. Is that the way it works?"

Sidmouth's face darkened. "Rather than sneering at those loyal subjects of the King who've seen the error of their ways, you should be grateful we have some of these rascals in custody. One or two of the most dangerous will be selected and charged later today with this entire string of ghastly murders—committed, of course, due to their rabid hatred of their betters."

"No," said Sebastian quietly.

Sir Nathaniel Conant stared at him. "What do you mean 'no'?"

"I won't let you pin these murders on a couple of naive, uneducated men whose only real crime is a passionate hatred of injustice combined with a dangerous dose of idealism and overblown romantism."

" 'Idealism'? 'Romantism'? If those men had had their way, they would have brought down the monarchy! You're quite cocky, aren't you, considering that you've freely admitted to having shot and killed Sir Samuel Toole. Are you so confident you won't be charged with murder yourself?"

The threat was anything but subtle. "You think I should have let Sir Samuel murder an innocent young woman, do you?" said Sebastian. "Stab her?" He suspected most people would argue that Sasha Stone's involvement in the deaths of Gilbert Keebles and Marcus Toole meant she was far from innocent, but that was a part of the story he was trying to leave out. He rolled his glass back and forth between his fingers, choosing his words carefully. "Let me put it to you this way: If you even think of charging me or any of the Spenceans arrested last night with murder, I will tell the world an ugly tale about how a peer of the realm went on a killing spree with his best friend to hide the fact that his son and heir had raped his own half sister. If you think the people of this city are stirred up now, what do you think will happen when they hear what their 'betters' have been up to? Rape. Murder. Incest. Miscegenation. Ritualized re-creations of heathen sacrifices. And if you're reassuring yourself that your captive press won't print any of it, let me remind you that there are dozens of small Radical presses scattered across this city that regularly churn out pamphlets and broadsheets with circulations the 'respectable' papers of Fleet Street can only dream of."

"You wouldn't do that," said Sir Nathaniel Conant, staring at him in horror.

Sebastian huffed a soft laugh and took another drink. "Of course I would. And in case you're thinking you can simply tear up the statement Sasha Stone was kind enough to provide, I should perhaps warn you that I have another copy—kept someplace safe."

"I don't believe it," said Sidmouth.

"Believe it."

Conant and Lord Sidmouth both glanced at Lovejoy, who simply pursed his lips and stared down at his feet.

"So what precisely are you suggesting we do?" said Conant, his voice rough with aggravation and barely controlled fury. "We have a peer of the realm, his son and heir, and a baronet shot dead in a wretched cottage in Clerkenwell! And that's in addition to the four murdered young men whose bodies were posed to look like heathen sacrifices—or at any rate, three of them were—and another still missing, besides."

"You left out the three dead women," said Sebastian.

"Yes, yes," said Conant, dismissing them with a careless wave of his hand.

Sebastian took another sip of his wine, feeling its warmth spread through his veins in a way that reminded him Hero was right: It had been a very long time since his last meal. He said, "A forger by the name of Robin Easton was found garroted in Grub Street yesterday. Blame the murders on him. Given that he was in all probability working for Bridgewood, I have confidence in your ability to come up with a plausible tale to explain it all. Blackmail, perhaps?" He paused. "Or would you rather I talk to the Radical press?"

Conant and Sidmouth exchanged fuming glances. "This is outrageous," sputtered the Chief Magistrate. "You talk of blackmail? I'll have you know that I consider this blackmail, sir. Blackmail!"

"Yes."

Lovejoy coughed, bringing up a fist to cover his mouth.

Sidmouth glanced over at him, then snapped, "Wait for me in the carriage below. Both of you. I'll be down in a moment."

The Chief Magistrate and Lovejoy were still on the stairs when Lord Sidmouth walked over to stand before Sebastian, his voice kept low and menacing. "The magistrates from Bow Street may not be familiar with Lady Devlin's yellow-bodied cabriolet and fine team of matched blacks, but I know them well. Not only were they seen in the Haymarket yesterday evening, but the turnpike keepers tell us they're now headed south, toward Hampshire." He paused, then added with emphasis, "And its ports."

"Oh?"

The Home Secretary's nostrils flared. "We will get them, you know."

"Get whom?"

"Pitcairn and the opera dancer!"

Sebastian raised his glass to his lips. "I don't have the slightest idea what you're talking about."

"You may be able to shield yourself—and them—from these murder charges. But you won't be able to protect those two from standing trial for treason." Sidmouth raised his chin and drew a pointed finger across his neck with a smile.

Sebastian took a long, slow swallow and said nothing.

"I don't understand you," growled Sidmouth. "The blood of the finest noble houses of England and Scotland runs through your veins, the blood of kings and queens! Pitcairn and his ilk would see your head on a pike if they could. You're a traitor to your own class." His lip curled. "To your class, and to God."

"To God? Really? To God?" Sebastian drained his wine and set aside the empty glass with a snap. "Do you seriously think that your God sent his only begotten son to die on a cross so that you and I could sit in smug judgment on the millions of men, women, and children out there who are languishing in wretched want?"

Sidmouth stared at him. "Heaven preserve us. You sound like a bloody Jacobin. You're mad. Do you hear me? Absolutely mad."

Sebastian smiled and looked over at the clock. It was nearly half past ten; the *Argonaute* sailed in seventeen hours. "Perhaps I am."

A short time later, Sebastian was holding a handkerchief to his nose as he followed a turnkey down the dark, tunnellike passage that led to Newgate's condemned cells. The men arrested last night and this morning hadn't been condemned yet, of course. But the Home Office wanted them kept isolated from ordinary prisoners, and yesterday's hangings had freed up four of the special cells.

"Ye got yerself a visitor," snapped the turnkey as he threw open the door to one of the frigid, stone-walled, windowless holes. "Ye mind yer manners, ye hear?"

Adam York looked up from where he sat cross-legged on the tiny cell's filthy straw mattress, trying to read a newspaper in the feeble light cast by a small lamp. At the sight of Sebastian, he pushed to his feet, his expression surprised and wary. "My lord?"

"Please, sit," said Sebastian, tucking the handkerchief away as he nodded dismissal to the turnkey. The coffeehouse keeper's clothes were torn, his bruised face crusted with dried blood, one eye swollen half-shut. "Looks like they roughed you up a bit."

"Just a bit," said York, wincing as he sank gratefully back down on the torn mattress. Mattresses were not free in Newgate, which meant that either York or his wife had paid for this foul-smelling, vermin-infested thing. Food also needed to be paid for; anyone unable to pay was forced to subsist on filthy water, a small allotment of moldy bread, and thin gruel. Men, women, and children had all been known to die of starvation in His Majesty's prisons. And the private prisons were even worse.

"I hear they're planning to move us to the Tower," said York, his head falling back as he stared up at Sebastian. "Is that true?"

"I understand they're talking about it, yes."

The coffeehouse owner gave a faint, disbelieving shake of his head. "Imagine that. Me, the son of a simple innkeeper, locked up in the bloody Tower of London like a disgraced earl or discarded queen. I guess that's the one measure of equality Liverpool and his lot are willing to give us—the right to have our guts pulled out and our heads chopped off like the Duke of Monmouth or something."

Sebastian studied the older man's bruised, tensely held face. "It might actually work in your favor. They're going to find it a lot harder to convict you of treason than a simple charge of aggravated riot."

"Maybe. But they don't castrate a man and burn his private parts in front of him for aggravated riot, do they?" York flexed his bruised shoulders and winced again. "And we call ourselves a civilized nation."

Sebastian said, "The treason charge also gives you the right to defense counsel, which means you'll get an actual trial. If the government is planning to rely on John Castle's testimony, it won't be difficult to prove he's been working as their spy. And there are dozens of men, including Henry Hunt, who can testify to the part Castle played in instigating the riot."

"If they don't charge Hunt with treason, too." York nodded to the newspaper he'd tossed on the mattress beside him. "My wife, Mary, brought me that this morning. It's all garbage, what they're saying. We weren't planning a reenactment of the taking of the bloody Bastille." He paused, then said, "Well, maybe the Watsons and Castle were. But not the rest of us. We already had another meeting set for February!"

"I know."

York was silent for a moment, his eyes narrowing as he chewed thoughtfully at his lower lip. "Mary also tells me people are saying Lord Bridgewood, his son, and Sir Samuel Toole were all killed last night—murdered—even though it ain't been in the papers yet. Is that true?"

"They were found dead, yes," said Sebastian.

York cocked his head to one side as if assessing the implications of Sebastian's careful phraseology.

Sebastian said, "You told me once that Gilbert Keebles, Marcus Toole, and their friends had been allowed to get away with murder in the past. Given that they're all dead now, if there's a reason to keep what happened quiet, I can't see it."

York hesitated a moment, as if thinking it over. Then he shook his head. "It's not my story to tell."

❧

Sebastian was seated at his desk, trying to pass the time by writing to his estate agent about finding a farm family willing to take in a likable orphan named Jigger, when Emmanuel Royston-Jones came to see him.

Looking haggard and drawn, with dark circles around his sunken eyes and a greenish tinge to his face, the younger man drew up just inside the entrance to the library, then waited while Morey bowed himself out before saying in a rush, "Ciana tells me I owe it to you to come and personally let you know I'm still alive." He hesitated, a faint flush lending a touch of healthier color to his cheeks. "Somehow it never occurred to me that people might think I was dead. I mean, it's not like I planned to be gone for long. I just . . . wanted to get away. Blot out the world for maybe one night. Except that one night somehow turned into two, and then three . . ." He swallowed. "I don't even know the girl's name. All I can remember is her holding my head up while I puked out my guts in her chamber pot."

Sebastian came out from behind his desk. "You're lucky you lived to tell the tale. Have you seen your father?"

"Not yet. I'm on my way there now." He paused, bringing up a hand to run his fingers through his dark hair. "The newsboys are out on every corner, you know, blowing their horns for the special editions Fleet Street's published on these new murders. They're saying some Grub Street forger killed them—killed them all. But that's not what really happened, is it?"

Sebastian met the younger man's gaze and shook his head. "No."

"I realize I probably don't deserve to hear it, but, well, I would like to know the truth."

Sebastian nodded. "Come sit by the fire."

He left some of the details out of his telling, but not many. Afterward, Emmanuel thrust up from his chair and went to stand at the windows overlooking the rainy street, his hands clenching and unclenching at his sides. Then he turned and looked back at Sebastian, his chest rising and falling with the agitation of his breathing. "You know how you asked what happened last summer that ended my friendship with Toole and the others?"

"Yes."

Emmanuel looked away again. "It's not something I'm proud of. We'd been out at Merlin's Cave one night and were leaving when Toole spotted a ragged old man sleeping on the banks of the reservoir. For some reason, it riled him up, and he started kicking the man, yelling at him to wake up and move on. I told him to cut it out, but, rather than back me up, the others just went over and joined in. The man was trying to get away from them, but the bank was muddy from a recent rain and he kept slipping and half falling down. Then he lost his footing completely and pitched into the water. He was drunk, and it was obvious he couldn't swim—he was splashing around, hollering for help, and his head kept going under. I can't swim, either, but Toole and the others could. I kept yelling at them to do something, please. But they just stood there laughing—laughing so hard they were having to hold each other up. I finally jumped in myself." He paused. "I honestly thought I was going to drown, too. I don't know how I managed to haul him into the shallows, but I'd waited too long. He was barely breathing. I remember kneeling there in the water, holding that dying man in my arms and begging my friends to help me."

"What did they do?"

"They told me to stop acting like a bloody plebeian. They said

I was embarrassing. Then they turned around and . . . left." His jaw hardened. "I had to run all the way to that coffeehouse in St. John Street before I could find someone to help me. The owner, he ran back up the hill with hot coffee and blankets and got some of his customers to help us carry the old man down and lay him by the fire. But by then it was too late."

He paused again, and this time it was a moment before he could continue. "They might not have deliberately killed that old man, but they did kill him. And I think what got to me more than anything else was that his death . . . it simply didn't matter to them. When I confronted them about it afterward, it was obvious they felt no guilt. No horror. No shame. They simply didn't care. It was a shattering realization, that I could be friends for so many years with men who were basically . . . soulless."

He turned, his gaze once more going to the street outside. He said, "Ciana told me about a fifteen-year-old girl who died because of what Keebles, Toole, and the others did to her. I keep thinking that maybe . . . maybe if I'd spoken up, told someone about what they'd done to that old man, the girl would still be alive today. That maybe none of this would have happened."

"Perhaps," said Sebastian, although he doubted it. He was silent for a moment, trying to fit what Emmanuel had told him into what he already knew. But something was still missing. He said, "How did Ciana know about the girl?"

Something flickered in the younger man's eyes, something he hid behind carefully lowered lids. "I don't know."

Standing up from beside the fire, Sebastian went to retrieve the Celtic wolf carving he'd left lying on his desk. "You'll see this gets back to her?" he said, holding the piece out to Emmanuel.

Emmanuel stared down at the wooden carving but made no

move to take it. "He liked to think of himself as a wolf, you know—Toole, I mean. He was always calling us a 'pack' or talking about 'going in for the kill' and throwing back his head and howling. He did it one time around Ciana, and she told him he was nothing like a wolf—that their most distinctive characteristics are loyalty, courage, and dedication to their families. She said they risk their lives to protect the vulnerable, they mate for life, and the female wolves are the real leaders of their packs. Needless to say, Toole . . . resented that." He swallowed hard. "I didn't know until today that he'd gone back to her shop with Keebles and Wilcox. That's when he took the carving. I still don't understand how it ended up on Primrose Hill, unless maybe he was dancing around with it that night, howling at the moon, and dropped it. You know he had to have been drunk."

Sebastian held out the wolf again. "Do you think she'll want it back?"

This time Emmanuel did take the carving, his nostrils flaring on a deeply indrawn breath as he swiped his thumb over the Celtic knot on the wolf's flank. He shook his head, a muscle jumping along his jaw as he walked over to rest the carving atop the glowing coals on the hearth. For a moment it lay there, a dark smoking shadow surrounded by shimmering red-hot embers.

Then the fire flared up hot and bright, and the wolf burst into flames.

Shortly before seven o'clock that evening, Sir Henry Lovejoy came to see Sebastian.

"I thought you'd like to know," said the magistrate as he settled beside the drawing room fire with a cup of tea, "that we've identified the ruffian who stabbed Lord Wilcox. He was seen at one point following his lordship up Cockspur Street, and then again by someone else a short time later as he left the alley behind the King's Mews."

Sebastian looked up from pouring his own tea. "You know who he is?"

"We do indeed. He's a blackguard from Tothill Fields named Reginald Dennings. The man has been implicated in so many murders he should by rights have been hanged long ago. But the truly interesting part is that he was found near the Serpentine about an hour ago, shot in the back."

"He's dead?"

"He is. We've spoken to his wife. She says someone paid him to kill your nephew, but she insists she has no idea who."

Sebastian came to stand beside the fire, his tea held forgotten in his hand. "Do you believe her?"

"Frankly? No. But the Chief Magistrate has discussed the information with Lord Sidmouth, and both agree Dennings must have been hired—and then killed—by either Lord Bridgewood or Sir Samuel Toole." Lovejoy paused.

"You disagree?" said Sebastian.

"I agree the suggested solution ties everything up neatly. And yet . . ."

"And yet?"

"I can't get past the impression that the woman knows more than she's willing to admit. Because with both Bridgewood and Sir Samuel dead, why is she still afraid?"

"When was Dennings last seen?"

"Around eight last night."

Sebastian raised his tea to his lips and took a slow swallow. By eight o'clock last night, Sir Samuel and Lord Bridgewood had both been dead for nearly five hours. But since Sebastian had fiddled the timing of the events in Swine Court to help account for the missing hours between the shootings and his own arrival at Lovejoy's house in Bloomsbury, there was no way he could say it.

He was careful to wait until later, when he was walking Lovejoy downstairs, before asking, "Are Sidmouth and Sir Nathaniel Conant still intent on finding Damion Pitcairn?"

"They are, yes," said Lovejoy, pausing at the base of the stairs. "Last I heard, they were sending Runners to the ports."

Sebastian looked over at him. "Dover?"

Lovejoy shook his head. "Southampton and Portsmouth. Personally, I find it unlikely a man with Pitcairn's background would be interested in a ship headed for either the West Indies or the United States, but Sidmouth is oddly obsessed with reports he's received of a yellow-bodied cabriolet seen first in the Haymarket, then headed toward Hampshire. Gravesend strikes me as a far more likely resort, but what do I know?" He settled his hat on his head. "I'll send word if I hear anything."

Sebastian watched the door close behind the magistrate. He was still standing in the entry hall, his arms crossed at his chest, his eyes narrowed as he stared unseeingly at the wooden panels, when Hero came to stand beside him.

"Short of hiding behind a boulder on the turnpike to Gravesend and shooting any Bow Street Runners headed east," she said, "there is absolutely nothing else you can do at this point."

He turned toward her. "You keep saying that."

She sighed. "Come eat dinner."

Shortly after nine that night, Sebastian ordered his carriage brought round and set off for Tothill Street. He took with him two stout footmen armed with blunderbusses.

He was in no mood for any nonsense.

Reginald Dennings had kept his wife and six children in a squalid basement room in a ramshackle seventeenth-century building off Child's Lane. Sebastian had to knock three times before the door was answered by a hard-faced, slatternly looking woman with a split lip, a purpling eye, and a hungry babe wailing in a basket on the floor behind her. If Reginald's widow was grieving the recent death of her husband, she hid it well. She tried lying to Sebastian, swearing at him, and weeping pitiful tears before giving in to a combination of subtle insinuations of a return of the constables from Bow Street and a nice bribe. What she told him took his breath, so that he had to squeeze his eyes shut for an instant, even though he'd been expecting it.

Even though he knew there was, really, no other explanation.

Wednesday, 4 December

At half past four the next morning, Sebastian stood at his bedroom window, his gaze on the dark wet rooftops and clustered chimneys that stretched away to the east. The light rain that had started up just after midnight was still falling; he could see the cold, silvery slashes caught in the light of the streetlamps below, hear the small, hard drops pattering on the wet pavement. But otherwise the night was dark and quiet.

"The ship should have sailed," said Hero, coming to stand beside him, her gaze, like his, on the sleeping city around them.

"Yes. The question is, Were Pitcairn and Sasha Stone on it?"

She met his gaze. He had left Tom at the port, supplied with funds, a swift horse, and instructions to ride for London as soon as the *Argonaute* sailed or if Bow Street showed up to make an arrest. But Gravesend was twenty-eight miles away, which meant it would still be hours before they knew anything.

One way or the other.

Dawn was just beginning to break when Sebastian drove to St. James's Square.

Leaving his curricle waiting beside the silvery waters of the square's wide central pool, he walked up the eastern range of elegant houses to where his sister's traveling carriage waited outside her door, along with a rented wagon piled high with baggage. As he drew nearer, he could see Amanda standing beside her carriage, a small leather case in her arms, her head tilted back as she said something to her abigail, who had already climbed up to arrange the pile of warm rugs and pillows on the carriage's velvet seats.

"Going someplace?" he said, walking up to his sister.

Amanda glanced over at him, then handed the case up to her woman and said briskly, "Fanny and I are leaving for Wilcox Hall. I've decided to bury Bayard in the chapel there."

She turned and was brushing past him toward the house when he said, "I know what you did."

She drew up abruptly, her features held tight with disdain as she swung slowly to face him. "I don't have the slightest idea what you're talking about."

He kept his voice low and even. "Where did you even get Dennings's name? From Bayard himself? Telling the man to meet you in Hyde Park for the balance of his payment was risky, you know. He might easily have killed you . . . although I suppose it never occurred to the poor sucker that you could kill him."

She threw a warning glance at the nearby servants. "What nonsense is this?"

"The veil was definitely effective; I don't see how anyone will ever be able to positively identify you. The thing is, try as I might, I can't think of a single tall, fair-haired, fashionably dressed woman besides you who might have an interest in hiring someone to stab your son in the back. Can you?"

She kept her lips pressed tightly together, her nostrils pinched as she stared back at him.

"I can understand why you did it," he said. "Not that I condone double murder, of course, but I do understand why you did it. Bayard was a loose cannon, and if the truth of his most recent activities were to become known, the scandal would have ruined not only you, but his wife and unborn child as well. But I'm curious, Amanda: Aren't you concerned the baby might be born a girl? It could be, you know. And then this house and Wilcox Hall will pass to that distant Wilcox cousin whose name I can never recall."

A slow smile curled her lips. "Fanny is carrying twins."

The implication was obvious. "Ah. How clever. This way you can essentially guarantee that at least one will be a boy. Who knows? You might even get an heir and a spare out of it. Have you already lined up a likely infant? Of course, given that you'll require a newborn, you'll need more than one pregnant woman standing by, just to be certain you get at least one male. How many do you reckon you'll need? Three? Four? I wonder: Are you planning to kill the mothers when you no longer need them, just to make certain they can never talk? Although I suppose a few well-aimed threats would probably suffice to keep them quiet."

"You are disgusting," she said, and turned toward the house again.

"I won't let you get away with this, Amanda," he said, raising his voice. "You know that, don't you?"

"And how precisely do you propose to accomplish that self-imposed task?" she said without even looking back at him.

"I don't know. But I won't stop trying."

At that, she drew up and turned to walk back to him, not stopping until she was right in front of him. "I did what I had to do," she said, her voice kept low. "And if you had any feeling for this family, you'd have done it yourself long ago. Bayard was mentally unwell, a disgrace to his family, and a danger to his society. You know that every bit as well as I do. Why do you care what happened to him? Would you rather Hendon have been forced to watch his grandson hang for murder? At least this way we've all been spared that. Or do you hate me so much that you'd actually have liked to see me thus humiliated?"

He shook his head. "I don't hate you, Amanda."

He saw the flare of disbelief in her eyes. "And now you really must excuse me, Devlin." She turned again toward the house. "We leave in a few minutes."

He let her go.

He was walking back to where he'd left Giles with the curricle when he heard a familiar voice calling him.

"Gov'nor! Oye there, gov'nor!"

Sebastian turned to find his tiger pelting across the square toward him, one elbow cocked skyward so he could hold on to his hat. He looked dusty, disheveled, and bone-tired.

"I like t' 'ave never found ye!" said Tom, skidding breathlessly to a halt beside him.

"And?" said Sebastian, his voice tight.

"The *Argonaute* sailed just after four."

"And Pitcairn and his sister? Were they on it?"

"They were on it, gov'nor." The boy's eyes danced as he flashed a toothy grin. "They got away!"

Historical Note

The economic hardships and resultant political turmoil against which this story plays out were real. The ending of the decades-long war with France, combined with the freakishly cold weather caused by the eruption of Mount Tambora in what is now Indonesia (which led to 1816 being called the Year Without a Summer), brought Britain closer to revolution than it had been in decades. Although the verbiage of the various interviews, speeches, banners, and chalked graffiti used here may sound modern to some ears, they are derived from early nineteenth-century original sources.

Chalk Farm Tavern was a real place and was indeed once a farmhouse. Interestingly, the soil of the area is actually London clay, not chalk; "Chalk" was in all likelihood a corruption of "Chaldecotes" or "Chalcotts," a former name of the farm. In the eighteenth and early nineteenth centuries, the area was famous as a resort for duels, and the tavern and its tea gardens continued to exist into the 1840s. By mid-century, both had disappeared as the region was engulfed by what is now northwest London, but the district is still called Chalk Farm, as is its Tube station.

Primrose Hill is likewise a real hill lying north of Regent's Park in London. It was indeed used as the site of neo-Druid ceremonies in the eighteenth and nineteenth centuries, when the romantic movement saw an increase in interest in the ancient Celts. Lacking any original written texts, a rigid dogma, or a centralized authority, the newly interpreted belief system was more a spiritual way of life than a religion and emphasized the importance of peace, justice, and living in harmony with nature.

Historians have long argued over whether or not the ancient Celts practiced human sacrifice. Recent archaeological discoveries have tended to tip the scale toward the affirmative, but there are holdouts. For the two sides to the debate, see Peter Berresford Ellis's *The Druids* and Miranda Aldhouse Green's *Dying for the Gods: Human Sacrifice in Iron Age & Roman Europe.*

The German chemist Friedrich Accum was an interesting historical figure. He did use his house as a school and lab, and sold portable laboratory kits for farmers and amateurs. Fascinated by gas lighting, he was instrumental in founding the first gasworks in London. But he was also concerned about the harmful effects of the resultant by-products, particularly the tar and sulfur compounds that were typically dumped in the river. He actually tried to get laws passed to prevent the discharge, but failed. In 1820 he published *A Treatise on Adulterations of Food, and Culinary Poisons, Exhibiting the Fraudulent Sophistications of Bread, Beer, Wine, Spiritous Liquors, Tea, Coffee, Cream, Confectionery, Vinegar, Mustard, Pepper, Cheese, Olive Oil, Pickles, and Other Articles Employed in Domestic Economy. And Methods of Detecting Them*, one of the first to address this growing (and continuing) problem. Eventually driven out of Britain by the wealthy merchants whose dangerous practices he exposed, he returned to Germany, where he continued to write, producing books on the scientific basis of cooking and bread. He also played an important part in the development of the process to produce sugar from beets in an effort to move away from America's slave-produced sugar.

Blackfriars Rotunda was used by the Surrey Institution for public lectures on everything from chemistry and mineralogy to natural philosophy and literature; Accum and Samuel Coleridge both presented lectures there.

Sir Peyton Keebles and Lord Bridgewood are my own inventions, but Sir Banastre Tarleton is not, and I have borrowed parts of Tarleton's history for Peyton Keebles, including the anonymous letter sent to the *Morning Chronicle* accusing him of misconduct at Cowpens and Yorkshire. The Waxhaws Massacre and the subsequent American murder of the Loyalists who surrendered after the Battle of Kings Mountain are both historical events. Likewise, Sir Samuel Toole's comments on the treatment of civilians are not my own invention but are taken from the letter written home by Francis Rawdon-Hastings, who served in the American War and later became the Earl of Moira and First Marquess of Hastings.

The atrocities committed by British soldiers against Portuguese and Spanish civilians during the Napoleonic Wars have recently received more attention from historians. Like the Irish, the Spanish were longtime enemies of Britain and, as Catholics, were typically portrayed as less than human. As we still see today, societies that dehumanize their enemies tend to commit the worst atrocities against them. See Alice Parker, "Incorrigible Rogues: The Brutalisation of British Soldiers in the Peninsular War, 1808–1814," in

British Journal for Military History 1, no. 3 (June 2015); Gavin Daly, "Plunder on the Peninsula: British Soldiers and Local Civilians During the Peninsular War, 1808–1813," in Erica Charters, Eve Rosenhaft, and Hannah Smith, eds., *Civilians and War in Europe, 1618–1815*; Charles Esdaile, *The Peninsular War: A New History*; and Charles Esdaile, *Women in the Peninsular War.*

Although we tend to associate the phrase "liberty or death" with Patrick Henry's famous 1775 speech before the Virginia Convention, the phrase is actually much older (the order of the nouns could be reversed to fit the needs of rhyme or cadence). A 1688 Irish token minted after the Londonderry siege is inscribed with the phrase "Death or Liberty," and Joseph Addison's famous 1712 play *Cato, a Tragedy* contains the lines "It is not now time to talk of aught / But chains or conquest, liberty or death." The play was enormously popular throughout the eighteenth century and is known to have been performed in the colonies many times before the Revolution. Handel's *Judas Maccabaeus* also contains the phrase, as did numerous ballads, including the one Sebastian hears sung at the Rising Sun to the well-known tune of "The Vicar of Bray." That song was indeed popularized after being printed in the official trial accounts of a reformer accused of treason, and can be found in Vic Gatrell's *Conspiracy on Cato Street: A Tale of Liberty and Revolution in Regency London.* (The reformer, Thomas Hardy, was defended by Thomas Erskine and acquitted.)

Cato and the other Roman tyrannicides were widely admired at the time.

Edward Despard was a historical figure whose brutal execution loomed large over this period. The son of a prosperous Irish Huguenot landowner, he served as a British officer during the American Revolution as well as in Jamaica and Central America, during the course of which he became good friends with Horatio Nelson. As superintendent in what is now Belize, he infuriated white settlers by insisting on treating everyone equally, no matter their race or sex, and by marrying a free Black woman from Jamaica. After his return to Britain, his belief in the need for equal rights for all landed him in prison several times, and when in 1803 the government moved to squash all calls for reform, he and six others were charged with plotting to kill the King and seize the Tower and mint. (The exact same charges were brought against the Spenceans thirteen years later, after the December Spa Fields assembly.) Most (but not all) of those who have looked at the evidence tend to conclude that Despard was framed by government spies. Admiral Nelson did speak on his friend's behalf at the trial, but to no avail. Despard was sentenced to the traditional traitor's death: to be drawn, hanged, castrated, disemboweled, beheaded, and quartered. His wife and Nelson successfully petitioned the King to reduce the sentence to drawing, hanging, and beheading. The crowds gathered to witness his execution applauded the speech he gave from the scaffold, doffed their hats in respect when he died, and then followed his coffin to its grave. Despard was the last man in England to be drawn.

Under the Home Secretary Lord Sidmouth, England had the most extensive spy network since the days of Elizabeth I. The Spa Fields meetings were real historical events, but virtually everything we know about what was said by the organizers of the meetings comes from the government spy John Castle, who was every bit as slimy as Tom describes him. Far too many historians have taken his "reports" at face value. It was indeed Castle who seized one of the flags from Watson's wagon and shouted for those listening to follow him. The orator Henry Hunt (also a historical figure) testified in court that Castle had deliberately delayed his arrival at the meeting. We likewise know little of what was actually said by the speakers at the December meeting. A journalist nicknamed Spectacle Dowling published what he claimed were verbatim transcripts of the speeches. But given that Dowling was on the Home Office's payroll, his paper (the *Observer*) was directly subsidized by the government, he took his articles to the Home Office to have them approved prior to publishing them, and others present that day reported that the supposed transcripts were falsifications, they should be taken with a giant heap of salt.

Adam York is my own invention, but five Spenceans were indeed committed to the Tower and tried at the Court of the King's Bench for treason, with the Crown seeking the full ancient penalty. When Castle's role in the "riot" became known at the first trial (of the apothecary James Watson Sr.), the jury ignored their instructions and voted to acquit. The government then gave up and released the remaining men, although Sidmouth continued to harass and persecute them, driving one of them insane (although that man, Thistlewood, wasn't exactly sane to begin with). It was just a few years later, in 1820, that Thistlewood and some of his friends would fall into another government trap when an agent provocateur tricked them into taking part in the farce known as the Cato Street Conspiracy. That time, the government learned from its earlier mistake and spirited its agent provocateur out of the country, preventing him from testifying. Five of the men convicted for that incident were hanged and beheaded. They were the last men beheaded in England, although several beheadings occurred later in Scotland.

At least two prominent Spenceans were the half-white descendants of enslaved African women from Jamaica. One, William Davidson, was beheaded after Cato Street. See Vic Gatrell's *Conspiracy on Cato Street: A Tale of Liberty and Revolution in Regency London.*

A few random facts: Judges in early nineteenth-century England regularly worked to get the parties in legal proceedings to settle their cases. Routs could include dancing and card rooms. I have seen some online Regency enthusiasts claim they did not; however, if you look at the primary sources, you'll see they frequently did. Those activities simply weren't the evening's main focus. We tend to think of the five-day workweek as a modern invention, but "Saint Monday" as an extra day of leisure was a centuries-old tradition that persisted into the Regency. It disappeared with the coming of the industrial revolution and the imposition of brutal working hours that accompanied the spread of steam-driven, gaslit factories. Victorian moralists saw the old tradition as "evil" because it gave the lower classes "too much free time."

And, finally, it had been illegal for many years to dump human waste into the sewers and from there into the Thames. But by 1816, changes in the law allowed toilets to be flushed into the sewers, and this combined with the chemical discharges from the new gasworks to kill most of the fish in the Thames. These changes eventually led to the infamous "big stink" of the Victorian era. Before that, the Thames (at least above the Rotherhithe tanneries) really wasn't that bad.